FATAL PARADISE

by T. C. Lawrence

Dark Matter Press
Honolulu, Hawaii

Sandwich Island Quintet
Book One

Dark Matter Press
3077 Ka'ohinani Drive
Honolulu, HI 96817

Published by arrangement with Griffith Publishing

Printed in the United States of America

Library of Congress Cataloging in Publication Data
Lawrence, T.C., 1942-
Fatal paradise / T. C. Lawrence. — 1st ed.
p. cm.— (Sandwich Island quintet; 1.Kauai)
Preassigned LCCN: 98-86165
ISBN 0-9663004-0-8

1. Hurricane Iniki, 1992—Fiction. 2. Kauai (Hawaii)—Fiction
I. Title. II. Title: Kauai
PS3562.A918F38 1998
813'.54
QBI98-826

**What keeps all Creation from flying asunder?
What saves Einstein's Constant from being a blunder?
What solves the cosmologist's densest conunder?
Dark matter!**

Dedication

This book is above all for the people of Kauai, especially those who survived Hurricane Iniki, suffered through its aftermath and helped restore the ineffable beauty of the Garden Island. I have taken some small liberties with your island's story, which I hope you will forgive. Kauai is, and hopefully always will remain, one of the earth's most glorious places.

September 7, 1992

"A tropical depression lying several hundred miles southeast of the Big Island may affect the weather in the state over the next several days. Right now, it is following the classic weather track for summer storms, drifting slowly westward well away from land. We'll keep an eye on it for you."

Morning weather report, KONG Radio

1

—Life is not a warrior's spear—

Andrew Chase stared at the words he had just written on his yellow pad. They were a good opening for the novel he was setting out to write, but in his semiconscious state he was having trouble figuring out what should follow them. Medium height, standard Caucasian features, not athletic but trim and good looking in his clothes, Andrew was in a distinct minority in his present environment, surrounded by ebony-haired, tawny-skinned people. He could feel them eyeing him guardedly from behind their shielded lids as he suffered through his private morning-after misery, laboring against fatigue, nausea and shame to present a picture of the self-contented, prominent American lawyer, in case someone who knew him walked into the lounge.

"Not a warrior's spear"? Sounds great, but what the hell does it mean? he asked himself. *Why did I...? Maybe....* The Mont Blanc began to move again, but not very far.

—said the hula master, whose course—

Okay. So we start out in Hawaii. But, "Whose course"? Strike that. Objection, Your Honor: grammatical error. His head ached, his eyes wanted to close. His brain, too exhausted to rebel against the urge to create so long as creation entailed no more than writing down the dreamlike phrases that came into his head, seemed equally prepared to shut itself down at any minute. It had been a bad night. A bad week, actually. And the new day was off to a rotten start.

A loud, rattling, rumble in the lounge drew Andrew's attention from his tenuous effort at authorship. The plate glass window separating the room from the elements was bowing in and out ominously in its steel frame, as rainwater sprayed against it in angry blasts. Stuck here for who knows how long, Janet counting on his being there when she arrived. He sighed and looked down at the ruled page again.

—the course of which—

Jesus, that's better grammar, but now it sounds like a goddam trust agreement. I can't—Oh, hell, just write, will you, and fix it up later if it's worth anything.

—Life is not a warrior's spear, said the hula master, the course of which, from the time it is loosed until the time the point buries itself in the target's dark belly, is determined at the instant of release—

There you go. Wait till Stella hears this. In his weakened state, Andrew indulged in the fantasy that his younger daughter would be persuaded by eloquent contradiction to abandon what he viewed as her radical spiritual beliefs.

—No, my children, life is a series of accidents, some fortunate, others unfortunate. Its ultimate path is not determined until the last breath of it is exhaled, which is why the words "determined" and "terminated" have the same root—

Nice touch, old man. How'd you dredge that up, firing on only one cylinder? No, wait a second, dammit. Those words probably don't have the same root in Hawaiian.

—You mean, Lokia asked doubtfully, that what we call "fate" is nothing but a series of happenstances that turn us this way or that?—

Andrew Chase stopped writing and capped his pen. The question he had just written made it clear to him which Muse had him in thrall. It was Guilt. His present circumstances, he realized, were a perfect example of the way the chaos that rules human existence can skewer the reckless. Today was September 8, 1992 in Hong Kong; September 7, 1992 across the dateline in Honolulu. Cathay Pacific flight 121, scheduled to depart that morning from the former city to the latter, was delayed because of weather, and that simple glitch foiled his plan to preside over a cheerful, well-organized family reunion in the Honolulu airport. It had been important for him to get this particular vacation off to a good start, a fact that had obviously been lost on Mother Nature, whose vagaries he had not anticipated.

Andrew looked confident and comfortable, a trick good lawyers learn early. Underneath that collected exterior, though, simmered a hopeless emotional mess. Memories of last night's debauch stalked the corridors of his mind: the naked Chinese teenager stepping from the stage on which she had just performed a full repertoire of sex acts with a variety of other "actors;" stepping down from that stage and coming unclothed to him, kneeling at his feet, and then caressing his knee, his leg, and more, as he drank with his client, Harry Wong; the reprobate

Harry Wong, who surely had arranged the sordid encounter without telling him. That and other disgraceful memories mingled with thoughts of his longer-term troubles: matters about which, at the moment he was too tired to do more than simply feel the weight of worry.

The weather at Kai Tak airport was beastly. A typhoon had blown in as Andrew returned to his hotel in the pre-daylight hours. Gale-force winds and driving rain had made air traffic impossible by the time he had checked out, and it appeared that the suspension would be in effect for a few more hours. Powerless to get his vacation back on track, Andrew had no alternative but to wait. As rain beat against the heaving windows of the Cathay Pacific first class lounge, and wind shrieked in through chinks in the outside walls, the normally sedate preflight rummery in which he sat had transformed into an overcrowded holding pen for surly voyagers. Andrew watched the room fill up with smoke, the Chinese inhaling reverentially as though drinking a magical elixir, and then blowing great grey puffs politely toward the ceiling.

The only silver lining in his situation, if there was one, was that he was too weary to be frustrated. Instead, he daydreamed about Kauai, which, even though this visit would be his first since adolescence, he distinctly remembered as a place of surpassing beauty, purity and gentleness.

A small disturbance at his feet distracted him. A boy of about two years, with spiky hair and an undeveloped sense of propriety, crawled over Andrew's shoes while his mother, separated in the crowd but apparently unconcerned either about her son's wandering or about Andrew's wing-tips, called to the child in high-pitched Cantonese. Her words, like the buzz of conversation around him, were all but incomprehensible to Andrew, who had taken private lessons in Mandarin in order to win a client in Beijing, but found it unnecessary to learn Cantonese, the dialect of Hong Kong, because Harry Wong considered it a mark of superiority to be able to speak to the foreign devil in its own tongue. As a result, the chatter in the lounge was to him just so much random noise, like the sound of the ocean. Little by little, it lulled him into a stupor, and in due course, he put away his pen and his note pad, and allowed his eyes to shut.

Moments later, he was jolted out of his slumber by an eruption of terrified screaming and the crashing of furniture. He opened his eyes to full-blown pandemonium. Everyone else in the lounge was either diving for the floor or lunging madly toward the rear of the room, where he was sitting. He turned toward the window in time to see blowing toward him on the storm a plywood panel behind which a barely fastened corrugated tin sheet gyrated wildly. The infant was again scrambling over Andrew's feet, greatly agitated by the sudden ruckus. There was just time to reached down, grabbed a miniature arm and swing the child to safety behind his chair.

With fatalistic detachment, Andrew watched the flying remnants of a utility shed roof shatter the half-inch glass plating. Crystalline shards sailed rapaciously into the lounge on a gush of rain and wind as he jerked his arms up in front of his face.

Cries of pain erupted around him, but he himself was not struck by the knife-like projectiles. Instead, it was the plywood panel that hurtled at him, trailing the corrugated sheeting. The high winds faltered inside the lounge, and gravity quickly dragged the panel downward. It struck the back of an armchair opposite Andrew and flipped over. With a sound like rolling thunder, the roofing tin came down on him abruptly, like a sprung trap. Its trailing edge slammed into his knees, letting out a gong-like ring, and the leading edge swung at his face. Still holding his arms up, he jerked his head back. The ribbed edge of the sheeting scraped the undersides of his jacketed forearms, thrusting them sharply back beside his head, and struck against his throat just above the knot of his silk necktie.

For a few seconds, Andrew Chase thought he had been decapitated. He felt no pain, but only an extreme pressure in his Adam's apple. Even though his life hadn't passed before his eyes, even though he hadn't had the presence of mind to say an unheard good-bye to his family, even though he hadn't seen the bright tunnel, and even though he believed that life is nothing more than a series of happenstances, he would not have been surprised if a Greater Force had just administered capital punishment for his dissolute behavior during the week just past.

Gradually, the shock subsided. Regular connections between his senses and his brain were reestablished. He wasn't dead, just temporarily frozen in place. Though he couldn't breathe, it was not because his head had taken leave of his body. With trembling hands, he reached up, pushed the executioner's blade away from his neck and took a rasping breath. His fingers slid over his throat and discovered that the skin, though raw, had not been broken. Suddenly conscious of the moaning, writhing bodies around him, acutely aware that something—a quirk of physics?—had spared his life by a fraction of an inch, he watched rain invade the lounge to mix with the blood of the injured, and heard the little Chinese boy crying for his mother. *Not a warrior's spear,* he said to himself, less convinced than he had been moments earlier.

The interior of the bungalow was painted white, inside and out. The front door—the only door—was also painted white, and black metal numerals nailed to the wood at eye level announced the unit's luckless number, 13. There came a knock. Inside, Adibi, a slender, swarthy, nervous man, crushed the joint he had been smoking and frowned. Though he was already wearing his business suit, the visitors he had been expecting weren't due for hours. The housekeeper again? He waited. Outside, he could hear traffic rolling by on the coast road, the surfers calling out to one another the conditions at this or that beach, the children playing in the sand on the other side of the road, the subdued whoosh of late summer waves swirling in the cove. Presently, the knock was repeated.

"Who is it?"

"It's me, Adibi. I have something for you."

A man's voice. He recognized it. Adibi's frown deepened as he cast his eyes around the room. Resignedly, he pushed himself out of the vinyl-cloaked armchair and walked over to open the door.

"Hello, my friend." The visitor was an unsmiling figure in a tee shirt and cutoff jeans, wearing a grimy backpack.

"What the hell are you doing here?" Adibi demanded, his r's rolling in the accent of his home country.

"Brought you a present," the visitor replied. "From the boss. Gratitude for all your hard work." He unslung his backpack and pulled out a bottle of cognac. Instead of handing it to Adibi, he held it in the air. "Let me in, Adibi. We'll have a toast."

Adibi stood in the doorway, looking at the man fearfully, as though he were the Red Death.

"For Christ's sake, let me in," the caller repeated with a frosty laugh, and pushed past the dark-skinned man.

"Just leave the bottle and go, please. I'm expecting company," Adibi said.

"Not for a while, you're not." The interloper sank into the vinyl armchair, picked up the stub of the reefer, made a little show of examining it and dropped it back into the white plate.

"Will you please just leave? You and I have no business today."

"Be more charitable, will you, Adibi? Look at the date on this bottle." He thrust it toward the frightened man. "Can you read that? Nineteen-twenty-seven. Sixty-five years old. When will I get another chance to taste something like this?" He picked at the lead coating at the top of the bottle until it separated, then pulled it off, exposing the old cork.

"I—I can give you money. I can disappear. Never come back."

The cadaverous man chuckled. "I don't want money. I don't want you to disappear. I just want glasses. Shall I get them myself?"

As Adibi retreated to his bedroom, the other man fished in his backpack for a corkscrew and a small vial. He opened the bottle quickly, poured the amber content of the vial into it, put his thumb over its mouth and shook it.

It was Janet Chase's first trip to Hawaii. She walked down the jet-way slowly, drained of energy by the long flight and more than a little apprehensive. What if Andrew wasn't waiting for her? The contingency plan was that she would round up her daughters as they arrived, and collect all the baggage, so that when he came in they could immediately take off for Kauai, where Andrew had rented a house for two weeks. It sounded simple enough, but she was completely unfamiliar with the airport and had been flying for more than half a day. *He had better be here.*

The gate lounge was already full of people waiting to return to the mainland, many wearing leis or hula shirts or shell necklaces, and most wearing glowing tans and smiles. Noticeably absent from their ranks, however, was Andrew. Janet stood in the middle of the crowd for a moment, not sure what to do. Her fellow passengers deplaned around her. Perhaps she should wait here for a while, since Liz's plane wasn't due for an hour, and Stella's not for an hour and a half. Or maybe she was supposed to meet Andrew somewhere else. Had she forgotten? After a while, she noticed an overweight couple in Bermudas and bulging tee shirts staring at her, and she realized that she looked confused, perhaps close to panic. With a grimace of self-reproach, she pulled herself together, stomped through the little shopping area, and headed down the open-air corridor toward the main terminal.

The afternoon was warm and humid, but the trade winds were blowing. Bathed in the lovely breeze, Janet felt relieved, energized, and once more in control at least of herself, if nothing else. Once in the terminal, she encountered a more elaborate shopping mall, which normally would have drawn her interest but at the moment did not. She was looking for a security guard, and when she found one, she asked him to direct her to the Cathay Pacific ticketing area.

"Can you tell me the arrival time of Flight 121?" she asked the agent at the counter, a middle-aged Oriental woman.

Without even looking at her computer screen, the woman answered, "That airplane is still on the ground in Hong Kong, ma'am. There was bad weather. A typhoon—you know, like a hurricane? They expect the flight to take off in about an hour."

"Oh, dear. And how long until it gets here?"

"We don't have an ETA yet, but I guess about six and a half hours after takeoff."

Janet looked around for a clock. There was a digital time readout on the board in the middle of the terminal that displayed departing flight information. "You mean nine o'clock this evening?"

The woman nodded. "Nine, nine-thirty, earliest."

"But—I'm supposed to wait for someone on that flight who's coming to Kauai with me."

"I don't think that flight will be at the gate in time for you to catch the last shuttle, ma'am. I'm sorry, but the weather—" The woman shrugged.

Two years into the divorce, Janet liked fending for herself instead of relying on and being subjugated to Andrew. Yet there were limits. Information is power, and Andrew hadn't told her where on Kauai their vacation house was, or how to find out. Now she was stuck in a strange airport half a world away from home, it was the middle of the night by her internal clock, and she faced the prospect of having to sit around the Honolulu airport for another seven hours. *It's my own fault,* she chided herself. *I know he's a control freak, yet I didn't ask for the address.*

Oh, she'd deal with it, all right, but this was not an auspicious beginning to what was supposed to be a mature reunion of two people who had grown irretrievably apart from each other and, as an unforeseen consequence, from their children as well.

Cathay Pacific Flight 121 surged upward toward cruising altitude through a low-hanging curtain of silvery cumulus clouds, the remnants of the morning's storm. Andrew was relatively unscathed by the departure lounge accident that had injured so many others, and to that extent, he was pleased with his good fortune. But he could still felt the bite of the corrugated panel against his throat. *Another fraction of an inch and I'd have been a dead man,* he thought. *You just never know.* There was a lesson in that brush with mortality, but he needed some distance from the event—and some rest—before he could work it out. He settled back against a burgundy leather seat that had been polished by the prior use of thousands of other privileged passengers. Sleep was out of the question until the nervous energy spawned by the accident had subsided, nor did he feel like wading through a newspaper or working on the novel he had recently decided to write. The only activity that seemed to fit his state of mind at the moment was worrying, something at which he excelled and which he had ample cause to do.

He was concerned, for example, about his largest client, the Asian multinational, Paracorp International. This week's meetings with its chairman, Harry Wong, had been less open and more discordant than usual, with no real explanation for the heightened dissonance. Wong was a difficult man under the best of circumstances. One expected a certain amount of yelling. One was prepared to be kept waiting, to be criticized, hectored, and otherwise treated like a serf. One suffered without objection the endless bouts with depravity in Hong Kong's seamy underbelly, seeing and doing things that, at the time and even more so on reflection, induced the urge to retch; things that, ironically, had cost him his marriage even though he had indulged his client's taste, he continually told himself, only to build the career that he thought was the foundation of his marriage.

What troubled Andrew Chase about the experience of the past few days was something different: an unusually hard edge to the discourse with Wong, a constant bickering and a seeming difficulty in keeping his client's attention. These things may have been warning signs. He could not afford to risk deterioration of the Paracorp relationship, because of another of his big problems: the precarious health of his law firm. Fowler & Greide, one of New York City's oldest law firms, had also been one of its most prestigious, in the days when prestige was a valuable commodity. Unfortunately, those days were over, and it was the profession's own fault. Andrew had seen it all coming. During the nineteen-eighties, when the business world went deal-crazy, merging, divesting, joint-venturing and cross-licensing on a scale not seen since the days of the robber-barons, law firms across the country turned themselves into merchants, seeking out profit centers within their operations and finding ways to charge clients separately for the activities of those centers. Did they provide the client with sweet rolls at that breakfast meeting? Charge for the food. Was that brief typed by the word-processing department rather than a partner's secretary? Charge for the typing. Did an associate use an electronic research service to check a point of law? Charge not only for the associate's time, but for the on-line service's time. And be sure the charges are marked up to include a profit.

The conversion of legal bills into bills for business services was regarded by most in the profession as a brilliant insight into the business of lawyering, and the practice of profit-center billing spread like wildfire. In the short term, it did in fact improve the profitability of the firms—but at a price. Over the long term, the practice shone a spotlight on a range of services provided by law firms that corporate clients either didn't want or could obtain more cheaply elsewhere or could do for themselves. Profit-center billing also made it easier to compare law firms against one another and tended to disrupt the good will between lawyer and client. As a result, the great patrician firms such as Fowler & Greide were forced to compete like bazaar traders for business, shaving their prices and reducing the hours they billed on client matters substantially below hours actually worked. The financial glow of the eighties turned into financial desperation in the early nineties. It happened so swiftly that by the time the lawyers figured out what was going on, it was too late to do anything about it. Firms that had been prominent in corporate practice faltered, shrivelled, and in some cases simply disbanded. In the case of the Fowler firm, partners' income shrank dramatically, leading to a profound and unhealthy discontent that threatened to sunder the institution.

In that environment, Andrew Chase could not afford to lose a large client like Paracorp. He had to find out what was eating Harry Wong. The company's general counsel was a friend, and as he sailed eastward over the Pacific, Andrew debated how best to raise the subject with him from Kauai.

Adibi sat in one of the straight-backed wooden chairs, his head bowed, while his visitor, across the little Formica dining table, poured cognac into two tumblers. "I don't know what's wrong with you, my friend," the visitor said, as he pushed one of the glasses across the table.

Adibi raised his head. "I want my life," he hissed through clenched teeth.

"Do you think a glass of vintage cognac will kill you?"

"Don't mock me." The dark-skinned man looked away, surveyed the cheap little bungalow, watched the leaves of the banana tree outside the window dance quietly in a gentle breeze. Whenever they parted, there was a flash of orange and blue: bird of paradise flowers, caught in a spray of sunlight. One of the small delights of daily life. He was not in the habit of paying attention to such things.

"Are you a religious man, Adibi?"

"More so than you, bastard."

"Oh, I'm not religious at all. But I've seen the light, I have."

Adibi didn't comprehend. "Will you really leave after we drink?" he asked, hoping but not believing.

"I'm a man of my word."

"Then let's drink." He picked up his glass. The other man did, too.

"A toast to Adibi, gambler extraordinaire, snatcher of opportunities! May you live in peace."

They held their drinks aloft and stared at each other. Adibi hesitated in that position. The visitor made a little encouraging motion, but Adibi did not bring the tumbler to his lips.

His unwanted guest laughed heartily. "Oh, ye of little faith." In a swift movement, he tossed down the cognac, caught it at the back of his throat, gargled gently and then swallowed. Holding his arms out like wings, he said. "Believe, Adibi. It is a libation of transporting savor."

Adibi looked at him quizzically. Then he swirled the fortified wine around in the tumbler, sniffed its bouquet, and drank it down. Its taste was exquisite, smooth yet potent, delicately piquant, with a slightly sweet aftertaste. It caused a little tightening in his throat. He sank back in his chair and looked out the window again.

It began almost immediately, as an involuntary cough. Then another, and then an uncontrollable fit of coughing. The tightening in his throat worsened, and his breathing became an audible rasp. He stood up and started for the bathroom. It was too great an effort. The dark-skinned man fell to his knees, gasping loudly, staring in wide-eyed horror at the smiling visitor. A moment later, the bird of paradise didn't matter any more, nor the banana leaves, nor the bungalow. The spear of Adibi's life was plunging headlong into the darkness.

Liz Chase arrived from New York at three o'clock. In her halter top, iridescent boxer shorts and glossy black running shoes, she looked like a raffish model. Janet watched the men's heads turn as her oldest daughter moved self-confidently through the arrival area. Feelings of disapproval, envy, and protectiveness all welled up in her at once, but were quickly overtaken by an expression of love as the two women came together in a hug.

"We should have been on the same flight," Liz groaned. "There was this Marine sitting next to me on the Dallas leg who kept asking me to marry him."

"What do you expect?" Janet answered with a wry smile, gesturing at Liz's attire.

"Mom, I wore a sweatsuit the whole way out. These were underneath."

Janet shrugged. "Anyway, we had to settle for what was available for frequent flyer tickets. Your father's firm is struggling again this year, I guess."

Forty minutes later, Stella disembarked from the Portland flight, grace and serenity flowing from the angular features of her face like a corona around a sun, her lissome figure hidden under a flowing tie-dyed caftan. Liz made a peace sign with her fingers and waved it vigorously to attract her sister's attention. They met in a three-way embrace.

"Oh, Stella!" Janet sighed, squeezing her daughter's shoulder. "You're so far away from us."

"I know, Mom, I know. But it makes the reunions more meaningful, no?"

"How was your flight, Stell?" Liz asked, stepping back. Close physical contact made her uncomfortable, except in the case of her boyfriend Harlan. Or other suitable males.

"Okay, although there was a sailor in the next seat who—"

Janet raised a hand. "Maybe you two should accept a marriage offer from one of these guys you meet in passing. Nothing definitive seems to be happening with the men you know best. Let's find a place where we can sit."

The three women strolled into the nearest snack bar, bought some mineral water and commandeered three stools around a tall, formica-topped cocktail table. "We have a problem," Janet announced when they were seated. "Your father's plane is late. He won't be here for another few hours, which means if we wait for him we miss the shuttle to Kauai."

"Hey, Waikiki Beach by night!" Liz made hula motions with her arms.

"No, I have a better idea," Janet said. She had been thinking about the problem while she waited for the girls. Staying at the airport was out, even though that's what Andrew would expect them to do. Going into Honolulu might be fun, but she hadn't packed an overnight bag and assumed Liz and Stella hadn't either, which meant they'd have to paw through their suitcases for a day's clothing. "I think we should go straight to Kauai. Right now. Leave a message for your father to take the first shuttle in the morning. That way, we don't have to drag our things back and forth to Waikiki, and we get to bed early instead of waiting up for Dad. Plus we'll have some time for just the three of us."

"Do you know where we're staying on Kauai?" Stella asked.

"No, not where the house is; but we can stay in a hotel."

"Which hotel?"

"Here, let's pick one." Janet reached into her satchel and brought out several guidebooks, which she plunked down on the table. They each took one and began leafing through the pages.

"Here, listen to this," Janet said after a moment, running her finger along the text as she read. "The 'Sheraton Kauai.' It's in Poipu, which I think is where our house is located. " 'Immediately adjacent to a beautiful crescent beach. Oceanfront rooms include Italian marble bath, separate dressing room.'...blah blah blah...'Three pools, including a keiki pool,' whatever that is, `jacuzzi, open air lobby, several shops on the property.' Sounds fine, doesn't it?"

Liz had a see-yours-and-raise-you-fifty look on her face. "Sounds ordinary, Mom. For one night, we should do something out of the ordinary." She began to read: " 'The Westin Kauai. Start by picturing a two-acre swimming pool surrounding seven charging marble horses and a sixty-foot geyser. Then imagine a twenty-six thousand square-foot swimming pool comprised of almost two million mosaic tiles, reminiscent of Hearst Castle and surrounded by five Grecian jacuzzi temples separated by cascading waterfalls.' Um, 'Five hundred acres,' 'carriages pulled by Clydesdales or Percherons.' 'Take one of eight mahogany launches or forty canopied outrigger canoes over the forty-acre lagoon.'"

"I don't think—" Stella began.

"No, wait; there's more. 'Facials, steam rooms, saunas, herbal body wraps.' 'Islands filled with zebras, kangaroos, wallabies, monkeys, flamingos, llamas—' And three shopping complexes, Mom. Three! One night of complete decadence before Dad arrives."

The sybarite stirred in Janet, but the mother in her knew that her younger daughter was temperamentally indisposed to decadence. She turned to Stella. "What do you think, Sweetheart?" A mirrored wall behind Stella threw Janet's image rudely back at her. It was not a pretty sight. Her hair lay matted against her head as a result of half a day spent in the desiccating air at cruising altitude. Her water-blue eyes were sunk back in their sockets, peeking out through half closed lids. On the positive side, she thought, grasping for something to cheer her, she was a good deal trimmer and fitter than she had been at the time of the divorce.

"It doesn't sound very Hawaiian, Mom," her younger daughter replied. "More like Versailles. Why don't we pick something with local color? We can always visit this Westin place later, if we want."

"Have you found one, Sweetie?"

For Stella's benefit, Janet had brought along a copy of the *Backpacker's Guide to Kauai*.

"The Pakala Inn," Stella replied with a hopeful smile. "It's in Poipu. 'Across the street from a good snorkeling beach,' it says. 'Tin-roofed bungalows with living rooms.' It sounds really quaint."

Liz rolled her eyes. "What kind of rating does it get?"

"This guide doesn't rate. It's for people who aren't interested in the number of stars. There's only a description."

Liz's eyebrow headed for her hairline. "And—"

"'A semi-gentrified shantytown. Rotten with character, and the proprietors are, too,'" Stella read enthusiastically. "Come on, guys. Let's have an adventure!"

Once the jumbo jet had reached cruising altitude, the first-class cabin crew began to serve their premium-fare passengers. A young Chinese woman of surpassing charm, who looked sixteen but was probably in her late twenties, Andrew guessed, brought him chilled Aloxe Corton. There were only five passengers in first class, which gave her the opportunity to practice her English. "You stay Hawaii," she began, "oah—" She made a flying motion with her hand.

"Continuing on? No," Andrew replied. "I'm meeting my family in Hawaii." Since the divorce, he was more open to bantering with flight attendants than he had historically been. Truth be told, he was more open to women in general, because the one he wanted continued to reject him.

"Oh. Big famiry, you— You have big famiry?"

"I have two daughters, and one ex-wife."

"Ex wife? That mean—?"

"My former wife. We're divorced."

"Ah. So, you, two daughtahs and one divoahced wife, alrh—togethah in Hawaii?"

"Yes, we're all vacationing together."

The woman nodded, her brows knit as if she weren't sure she had grasped the concept correctly, but her full lips turned up in a kind of grin. "I see. That vehlry—, vehlry—"

"Very progressive, perhaps? Or 'open-minded,' 'liberal,' 'tolerant;' you could use any of those. Or—" Andrew sighed, "—you could go in a completely different direction; for instance 'foolhardy,' 'hopeless' or 'unwise.'"

The attendant nodded uncertainly and moved on, but Andrew's thoughts continued to hover around his former wife and daughters. He pictured them sitting unescorted and impatient in the airport in Oahu. They would by now be experiencing the Pacific crossroads for the first time. Dazed travellers of every epidermal hue, religious persuasion and culinary preference would be wandering through the open-air corridors, ogling one another with race-based curiosity and suspicion. The Chase women would have to forego the last flight to Kauai in order to wait for him. Given the delay, it would not take Janet long to conclude that his plan for an airport rendezvous was grounded not in good sense but in his view that the vacation shouldn't start until he arrived—only because he knew Kauai and could see to it, he thought, that the two weeks would go smoothly. Instead, Andrew knew that as the girls dozed uncomfortably on the unyielding benches nearest his arrival gate, Janet would begin plotting some sort of retaliation.

The visitor rummaged in his backpack and retrieved a pair of latex gloves. He secured the deadbolt on the door. Grabbing Adibi's body from behind, under the shoulders, he dragged it into one of the two small bedrooms. The room was clean and the bed already made; the housekeeper had come and gone. Adibi's briefcase was on the bed, his hat resting on top of it. There was no other luggage. A closet protruded from the back wall.

The visitor maneuvered the dead man into the closet, knees up, arms resting at its sides. He turned the dead man's head toward the wall. Then he returned to the living room. In the backpack was a sealed plastic bag, and inside the bag, an ice pick with a decorated sandlewood handle. He brought the bag into the bedroom and knelt down. Adibi stared at him with sightless eyes as he slid the ice-pick out, pocketed the bag and rose up on his knees. With a push on Adibi's chin, he turned the head to one side. Then he gripped the handle of the pick with both hands, took a deep breath and plunged the instrument into Adibi's ear. There was no spurt of blood, just a welling inside the ear. He stood up and considered his handiwork. The blood brimmed, overflowed and began to trickle down Adibi's cheek. Drops fell onto the crisp white shirt. Eventually, a bright stain would spread across the fabric. The scene met the requirement set for it, but was lacking in panache. It needed a flourish, something to elevate its gruesomeness, to suggest callous cold-bloodedness. The visitor looked around the room, and then smiled to himself. With a gloved hand, he picked Adibi's hat off the bed and placed it on the corpse's head, cocked at a jaunty angle. A moment later, cognac bottle and drinking glasses safely in his backpack, the visitor was gone.

Janet, Liz and Stella collected their bags, made their way to the inter-island terminal and caught the next shuttle flight to Kauai. In the spirit of abandon that had overtaken them, they rented an open-cab jeep and headed for the town called Poipu and the lodging called The Pakala Inn.

As they drove toward the south shore, pillows of air, sweet, humid and still warm, buffeted them under a sky splashed with the peach, tangerine and mauve of advancing sunset. In the rear of the jeep, Stella pulled her long hair into a topknot to keep it from lashing her cheeks, then held her arms out as though she were soaring. "Doesn't the air feel wonderful here? So welcoming and restorative. We're going to have such fun!" she shouted. Janet turned on the radio. It was tuned to a station that called itself KONG. The music, a kind of surfer reggae, had them bouncing in their seats, in delight that a genre so perfect for three women at liberty in the tropics actually existed. When a syncopated cover version of a song from their youth burst from the loudspeakers,

Liz and Stella began to sing into the wind. "Island Girl," they shouted. "Island Gi-i-irl, Island Gi-i-i-irl!"

The Pakala Inn was at its best after dark. The main building looked downright charming in the spotlights. It was a large, two-story, wooden, quasi-Victorian structure, with an ample porch that fronted the ocean across a two-lane road. Behind the Inn, just visible through shadowy palms and hedge, simple bungalows on low stilts stood facing one another on either side of a generous lawn. The Inn benefited by comparison with the neighboring structures. Further along the road stood an unimaginative brick hotel that catered to vacationers on nine-day package tours of Honolulu plus three neighbor islands, airfare included. "Endless Beach," this glum structure was called. On the other side of the Inn, a simple fish restaurant, a dive shop and a "safari outfitter" occupied a modest commercial strip building immodestly named "Outrigger Mall." The Inn's large and well-lit porch hinted at tranquility and invited the traveler in, in contrast to the hotel next door, which was simply a hulking presence behind flaming tiki poles, and to the fish restaurant where patrons were enjoying themselves a little too loudly.

Subdued laughter ricocheted from the lobby walls as Janet opened the front door. Two people were sitting inside on aluminum beach chairs. There was no other furniture. The elder of the two, a woman, rose to meet them, still chuckling. She was in her middle years but clearly had done a lot of living in getting there. Her grey hair was cut short, quite mannish, and she hid whatever shape she had under a brightly-flowered muumuu. "Well, hello there," she said cheerily, in a voice like Lauren Bacall on meth. "You're the folks who called from the airport, I bet."

"Janet Chase," Janet said, and held out her hand. "My daughters, Stella and Liz."

"Carol Spencer. And this," the woman added, laughing again as her eyes met those of the stocky Filipino who was just getting out of his chair, "is Artemis." Janet estimated that the man was just on the carefree side of thirty. He wore a black tank top, a garish patterned swimsuit, a neat moustache and flip-flops. Although it showed some evidence of a combing, his jet-black hair clearly had a mind of its own. He wrapped his meaty hand around Janet's, then Stella's and Liz's.

"Right this way," Carol said, and led Janet to a folding card table that stood in a hallway at one side of the lobby. *Is this setup some peculiar affectation,* Janet wondered, *or is it a reflection of how little this woman really cares about appearances?*

"Rooms upstairs or a two-bedroom bungalow out back," the proprietor asked.

"Bungalow," Liz called out from behind.

An impression of Janet's credit card taken, Carol handed her two keys and pointed down the hallway to the rear of the house, behind which she would easily find the bungalow. "Do you need help with your bags?" Carol asked. Janet nodded, but Artemis, whom his mother had perhaps unwittingly named after a Greek goddess, had already gone out to the car with the younger Chase generation.

"I hope you're not superstitious," Carol yelled after her as Janet traced the back hall. "Fact is, the fellow who vacated number 13 today was sporting a wad of cash he said he won last night at the Flip cock fights."

Bungalow 13 was a large wooden hut, roofed in tin, that stood perhaps eighteen inches off the ground on cinder block footings. A narrow living room occupied the front half of the interior. There was no television, nor even a radio, and the sofa and chairs were low-budget and tired. The construction was single-wall slat and beam, with interior partitions but no ceilings below the vaulted tin roof except in the single bathroom. Doors near either end of the living room led down narrow hallways to the tiny bedrooms, and these connected through separate entrances to the bathroom. By the time Janet arrived, Artemis had dumped all the suitcases in the room the girls had selected for themselves. She joined the three of them there and identified her bags to the Filipino.

After Artemis deposited her luggage in the other bedroom, Janet tried to tip him. He held up a hand, rejecting the offer. "Service included," he said. She persisted, which forced him to explain.

"I know I look li' da bellboy, Ma'am, but da trut' is, I got one-half ownership o' dis place. Save yo' money for breakfiss. Carol, dere, she one good cook." With a toothy smile, he left her and waddled off on his boat-sized flip-flops.

Liz and Stella had just opened their suitcases when Janet called out to them from her bedroom, "Let's take a walk on the beach before we unpack!" The girls gave little cheers of approval, and moments later the three of them were barefoot on the sand. Stella looked heavenward and began to read and interpret the constellations aloud. Her sister, though perfectly happy to study her own horoscope in private, objected.

"Stella," she said, "let's not jump right into the New Age stuff, okay? It gets on my nerves."

"Okay, Liz," Stella replied brightly. "You sound a little strung out, big sister. Maybe I could give you a massage later. You'd be amazed—"

"—Don't start, all right?"

"Just a foot massage, then. It won't take very long, and you'll feel so relaxed. You know about reflexology, don't you?"

Janet stepped in to head off trouble between her flower child and her city kid. "I wouldn't mind a back rub later, Stell. That long plane ride has made me stiff as a board. A walk would help, too. C'mon." She put an arm around each daughter's shoulder and propelled them forward.

There was a three-quarter moon. In its glow the sand shone a pale, milky color. Wet underfoot, it felt good, and made the three of them feel good. They were liberated from their shoes, liberated from their workaday lives, in touch with the soft, mute goddess that is the earth as they strolled past the houses that commanded the beachfront, houses whose owners could not command the public away from the beaches, because access for all was mandated by law. Mother-daughter talk floated into the onshore breeze. Had Andrew been there, the conversation would have dazzled him with its extendedness, easiness and triviality.

Eventually, Liz raised the subject that weighed so heavily on the minds of the younger Chases.

"Mom," she murmured, "don't you miss living with Dad?"

Janet Chase laughed gently. "Not really, Sweetheart."

"You're not just saying that to—to—" Stella wasn't sure how to complete the thought.

"Mmmh-mmm. Divorce, child, was my salvation. Living with your father—toward the end, there, I mean—well, it was like living with an ice sculpture." A small dark cloud covered the moon briefly, and was for that instant outlined in silver radiance. The froth of an exhausted wave sighed between the women's toes. Liz felt New York leaving her lungs, Stella the transcontinental distance between her and the rest of her family shrinking and Janet her motherhood reviving.

"Are you dating yet?"

Janet squeezed her elder daughter's shoulder affectionately.

"I go out to dinner or to a show every so often, but I'm not looking for a relationship, Liz. I didn't liberate myself from your father in order to subjugate myself to another Fairfield County baronet."

"You must miss being close to someone, though," Stella mused, "after all those years."

"You mean sex?"

"Jeez, Mom," Liz protested.

"Oh, sorry, Dear. I didn't mean to offend your delicate sensibilities." Janet mugged. Her daughter, who was living with her boy friend in Manhattan, fell silent. "Andy and I weren't close in any emotional way at the end, and by then various sex workers in the Far East were at least as close to him physically as I was. No, what I miss most is the other kind of closeness, the kind we just didn't have during the last several years of wedlock: companionship." She exhaled audibly. "Can we talk about something less morbid, please? What do you girls want to do while we're here?"

"Oh, boy," Stella exclaimed. "I really need to get centered. I heard about a spa here that specializes in energy work."

Janet glanced at her daughter. Stella's face, pale by nature, looked positively ethereal in the moonglow. "What do you mean, 'centered,' Stell?"

Stella smiled wanly. "Got an hour, Mom? The short answer is that the energy flows in our bodies get out of balance because of the way we live, and they need to be re-centered once in a while."

Janet nodded. "I apprehend, but don't comprehend, as my eighth grade English teacher used to say. You can give me the long answer while we're beaching it one day. And what about you, Wonder Woman," she queried, turning to Liz. "Not parachute jumping, I hope!"

"No, Mom. I checked. They don't do that here," Liz responded.

"Parasailing, then?"

"Oh, please, Mother. Being dragged on a line behind a speedboat, like some kind of kite? I don't think so. A glider trip, maybe. What would really be fun would be to go over to Maui and hang-glide off the top of the volcano."

Janet slapped her hands against her thighs. "Oh, that would be great," she exclaimed sarcastically. "I'll never understand why you equate fun with mortal risk, Liz."

"You've said that once or twice before, as I recall. I don't equate fun with risk, Mom. I equate living with adventure. The feeling when you take that step out into thin air—it's all the fragility, wonder and exhilaration of life exploding inside you at once."

"Sounds like an addiction to me."

"Um—what do you want to do, Mom?" Stella asked, changing the subject. "The three S's?"

"Swim, snorkel and sun. Especially swim. I'm up to sixty laps in the pool now."

After half an hour the threesome walked back to their bungalow. Across the lawn on the steps of Number 12, Janet saw a seated couple embracing and murmuring, backlit by the open doorway behind them. He was wearing only a whisper of a bathing suit; she, an unbuttoned man's shirt over breasts encumbered by nothing other than the man's right hand reaching over her shoulder, and a bikini bottom unobtrusive almost to the point of invisibility. Between the fingers of their free hands, they each held half smoked cigarettes that gave off the unmistakable aroma of hemp. At once the old protective instincts bubbled up in Janet, even though they had been long-since rendered obsolete by her daughters' life experiences. She tried to focus the girls' attention on the birds-of-paradise, lobelias and orchids ornamenting the bungalows opposite the lovers. Her energetic nattering was futile, however, because when the women had achieved the steps of Number 13—

"Ello-o!"

"Bonsoir!"

Ah, French, Janet thought. The public display of ardor was suddenly explained, if not excused, in her mind.

"Bonsoir," Stella replied, turning and squinting in the direction of the greetings. Before Janet could say anything, her Francophile daughter was strolling across the commons to meet the neighbors. The other Chase women followed a few yards behind.

The young man's name was Luc, the woman's, Chantal. They were from Lyon, they said, but had been away from France for about a year, bumming around the Pacific. In a few weeks they would have to return and work for another year or so before setting off on their next low-budget, high-hedonism adventure.

"Well, Ay must say zat zis ees a vahst ahmprovemohn," Luc told the Chase women cheerily. "Ze lahst residahn' of *numero treize* was a beezinessmahn who dressed ze wole time een a sooht ahnd tie."

"What kind of business was he in?" Liz asked, not out of interest but just to make conversation. The French duo weren't her kind of people. Too openly libertine. Libertine was okay; she leaned in that direction herself. Openly libertine was coarse, and inconsiderate of the hang-ups of others.

"We dauhn't knouh," Chantal said with an innocent snigger, "except zat 'e sohlde us zhees." She held up the back of her right hand, with the custom-rolled cigarette protruding between her index and middle fingers.

"Just the two joints," Stella asked. Janet raised an eyebrow, but said nothing. In her college years, she had had her fill of cannabis. Unlike the current Democratic challenger to President Bush—if he could be believed—she had inhaled, and frequently. At the time, she felt that the liberating effects of cannabis was a healthy counter to the complex formalities that shaped the thinking of women raised in the Deep South, as she had been. At this stage in her life, she had come to the view that those formal complexities were not so bad, after all.

"Mais, non. Des kilos," Luc responded in French, with an echo of the surprise he had felt when the transaction was offered.

"Drole de business," Stella replied, using a dated colloquialism.

"Tu parles le Francais, alors. Genial! Est-ce que tu veut un coup?" Chantal's romantic ardor of a few moments earlier easily sublimated into a spirit of gregarious generosity.

"T'es tres gentille." Stella plopped herself down on the stoop next to Luc.

As Chantal stood up languorously to retrieve the stash, she asked, *"Et les autres?"*

Janet's command of French was not terrific, but she had got the drift of the conversation. "No, thank you," she said, with a polite smile. Then, to Liz, with a look that telegraphed the answer she expected, "Are you staying out for a while, too?"

Janet and Liz returned to their bungalow where they could discuss Stella in private. The Chase women played any available two-cushion carom with abandon. The daughters talked about Janet freely in her absence, and Janet readily gossiped with either of them about the other. It was, they all seemed to understand, a way of releasing family tension that might otherwise build to an unhappy flash point. "I don't know what goes through her head any more, Liz."

"What makes you think anything does, Mom? She's just floatin' on the current, man." Liz swung her arms in front of her, hands waggling.

"Floating. That's it exactly. She's floating through life."

For some reason, Stella-bashing didn't seem as much fun in person as it was over the phone. Liz yawned and said she felt like turning in. Janet kissed her good night and asked her to set her alarm clock so that they could be back in Lihue to meet the first flight in from Honolulu at seven. With that, mother and daughter retired to their respective chambers.

In Stella's absence, Liz felt free to choose the bed nearest the window. She moved her suitcase onto the thin white coverlet. A leather bag, it was much too heavy, but it had been to the ends of the globe with her. A clasp was bent as a result of a fall off a freighter onto a dock in Manaus. A smile cut into the skin on one side reminded Liz of the tall, blond Piedmontese who had rammed a ski into it at a hostel on an Italian Alp. She had immediately forgiven him, and after a week of skiing together they had spent a romantic weekend on the Italian Riviera near Sanremo. Every corner of the bag had been rendered to some extent concave by the abuses of airlines on five continents. Ungainly and unlovely, this suitcase was the story of Liz's fortune-spattered young adulthood, and she wouldn't think of replacing it.

As she opened her memory bag, the breeze at the window subsided, and she noticed a slightly repellant smell in the room. She resolved to check for its source as soon as she had found her toiletry kit. The sun dresses were on top of the jumble of contents of her bag, cloaked in dry-cleaner's plastic in a vain attempt to prevent wrinkling. They should be hung for the night, Liz felt, even though the plan was to vacate in the morning. She took them out, shook them out and carried them to the closet, thinking about whether she should try on her bathing suits again before she went to bed. The blue bikini made her bottom look fatter than did the zebra-striped one-piece, but it provided the maximum tanning surface one could have and still claim to be clothed. *Tough decision.*

For years after, Liz would revisit the disjointed steps that had led to the moment when she opened that door. Had her father's plane not been late; had her mother known the name of the rental agency; had they chosen the Sheraton Poipu instead of the "Pakalolo Plaza," as they came to call the Inn after their experiences there; had she not urged that they take one of the freestanding bungalows instead of adjoining rooms in the Inn proper—Had any of those things happened differently, she would have been spared the dubious honor of making the grisly discovery. "Yick! What's that!" Barefoot, she had stepped into a puddle of dark, viscous liquid just at the closet door.

"What's what?" Janet called from the adjoining bedroom.

"I don't know. Somebody spilled something in the closet, and it's leaking out onto—Aaaaaahh!" Liz's scream was loud enough to awaken the fire goddess Pele from her thousand-year slumber on Hawaii's oldest island. There, on the floor of the closet, its legs tucked up almost to its chin, was death itself.

Outside, Stella jumped to her feet. She thought that she had heard all of Liz's screams. The who-took-my-earrings scream. The who-ate-all-the-ice-cream scream. The hairdresser-ruined-my-hair scream. Even though they no longer lived together, Stella would have said that, even with a slight buzz on, she could identify Liz's problem by the timbre, pitch, intensity and length of her cry. But not this one. This one was pure, undifferentiated terror, a sensation neither she nor Liz had ever experienced before. In a single, swift movement, Stella Chase leapt from the porch of Number 12 and bolted across the lawn into Number 13. More quickly even than Janet could run in from the next room, she was at Liz's side, staring down numbly at the body.

It was a man of indeterminate age, in an inexpensive grey business suit. His shirt was white except for an ugly blood stain running from the collar all the way down his left side. His tie was dark, and unfashionably narrow. A snap-brim hat sat at a funny tilt on his head. Most significantly—and unfortunately—for him, an ice pick had been driven to the hilt into his left ear. "Dear God—" Janet breathed through the hand that was raised to her lips.

The French couple rushed in, and jumped onto the bed to see over the Chases' shoulders. "Eets 'eem!" Luc gasped.

Stella looked up. The young Frenchman was making ocherous footprints across the spread with his filthy feet. Chantal had dropped onto all fours next to him. The room was rapidly filling up with guests from the other bungalows and the main house. With the closet door open, the stench was oppressive. Suddenly the warm, humid atmosphere of the Garden Island in summer seemed less than a blessing.

With such presence of mind as she could muster, Stella grabbed her mother's arm and whispered, "Everyone has to get out of here." Janet nodded.

"S-someone—in the closet is—dead," she announced loudly, an uncertain warble in her voice. "I think we should all—"

"Let me through. Coming through." Carol Spencer had heard Liz's scream from the lobby, and was now elbowing her way into the tightly packed bedroom. "What the hell is going on?" Her maniacally husky voice silenced the others.

"The cleaning people didn't do a very good job in here today," Stella replied with a little snort. The absurdity of the situation had overcome its horror and sprung her pot-loosened mind. Here was a roomful of people, all of whom had come to Kauai to escape reality, jamming themselves around a closet to soak in at close range the grimmest of all realities. No one else laughed, though; not even Chantal and Luc, which surprised her.

She felt an elbow bump against her rib cage. "Shut up, Stella," Liz hissed, as Carol Spencer leaned over the bed and peered into the dark cubicle.

"Ye gods and little fishes," the proprietress exclaimed, and wheeled around to face her wide-eyed guests. "Yes, folks, anything can happen at the Pakala Inn. Now, please, everybody out. The police will want this room to be as undisturbed as possible. Come along." Like a sheepdog, she herded the other guests lawnward, calling over her shoulder, "You, too, Chases." The three Chase women shuffled after the receding, gabbling clot of neighbors. Liz, was still numb, not only because of the murder, but also because of the substance that was causing her foot to cling to the floor as she moved. Platelets were decomposing into formless goo. The ruby splash of life was browning against her skin. *Skin is an organ....* "I need to wash that guy's blood off," she said to Carol. In reaction to the woman's sudden, suspicious glare, she added, "I stepped in it when I opened the closet door."

"Do it outside," Carol replied brusquely. "There's a hose in the back."

The faucet was under the window of her bedroom. As she approached it, a large cloud darkened the moon and a gust of wind set nearby banana leaves and palm fronds clattering and clacking like an orchestra of dried bones. Standing there bathed in the unfamiliar sounds, Liz thought she heard movement inside the bungalow. *He couldn't be,* she thought, and not sufficiently unnerved to suppress her curiosity, she peeked in, half-expecting to see the corpse in motion. Instead, through the open blinds, reflected in the mirror on the opposite wall, she saw Luc. He was half into the closet, frantically pawing at the dead man's suit, searching for something, grunting and groaning under his breath. While Liz watched, the Frenchman straddled the body, slid both hands under it and, beginning to weep, grasped at the rear pants pockets. They were apparently empty, because a few seconds later he stood up again, shuddered and left the room, muttering a single word repeatedly to himself. "Merde!"

Liz waited until he was out of the house, then took a deep breath, put her foot on the faucet and climbed as quietly as she could into the room. A quick look was all she wanted, just to see if she could tell what Luc had been up to. Or was she propelled, she half-wondered, by a morbid interest in the remains of the former occupant of Bungalow 13?

The cadaver's expression hadn't changed, despite the recent mauling. Had she expected otherwise? *Death isn't that repulsive,* she thought as she stared into Adibi's eyes. *Just consummately vacuous.* She turned to go, the expressionless image seared into her consciousness. As is natural in the presence of death, she began reflecting on her own mortality. *A bad jump, or a bad landing, and my eyes would look just like that. Mom thinks I have a death wish. That's wrong; I'm in no hurry to end up like this guy. But then, why* do *I court the reaper?*

She felt her face knotted in a scowl, and realized that it wasn't because of the question she'd just asked herself, but because there was something wrong with the tableau that still hung before her mind's eye. Something missing—the hat! The corpse was no longer wearing its hat. Luc hadn't taken it; she had seen him leave. Maybe he'd knocked it off in his ungentle mauling of the body. But then—where?

Liz bent over to peer around the floor. There it was, under her bed. She lifted it out, thinking too late about fingerprints. There was no blood on it, but when she turned it over, she saw a folded piece of notepaper protruding from the inside band. Using a corner of the bedsheet as a glove, she slipped it out, intending to put it back after examining its contents. What she saw caused her hands to shake uncontrollably. Instead of returning the note to the hatband, she slid it into her pocket. Trembling with the uneasy lightness that wrongdoing evokes, she lifted the blinds and climbed back out the window.

"There you are!" Janet exclaimed when her eldest daughter reappeared at the front of the bungalow.

Luc was standing some distance away, whispering to Chantal. Liz saw his head turn in her direction. "Just retching in the bushes," she replied.

Carol Spencer laughed. "You and Frenchie, huh? That's what he said he was doing in the bathroom a minute ago."

"Um, yeah, I guess he set me off. I heard him through the window."

Coincidence or fate? Liz Chase was left questioning whether it was really fortuitous that she would be the one to discover the dead man in Bungalow 13 and then, having stepped barefoot into his blood, to spy Luc in her bedroom, which led to her finding a slip of paper that promised to turn the murder she had discovered into something much more than a brief, unpleasant encounter for her family. But at the same time that she was having that debate with herself, a stirring in the atmosphere far distant from Kauai was setting in play a chain of meteorological events that would soon lead the entire population of that island to believe—or at least to believe it possible—that a sentient force had willed great disaster upon them.

Several hundred miles to the southeast, a large atmospheric disturbance drifted toward the fiftieth state that night across warm Pacific waters, pushed on by gentle but persistent trade winds. It was making its way west from its birthplace, a placid stretch of ocean near the Baja peninsula. There, the temperature of the ocean had been in the neighborhood of eighty degrees or more to a depth of over two hundred feet. That enormous mass of heated water, undulating and splashing patiently off the coast of Mexico, was the world's largest humidifier, exhaling measureless quantities of vapor into the increasingly sultry air.

A stormy low pressure bubble floated into this superhumid zone. The bubble was an example of the phenomenon known in weather circles as a "tropical wave." It originated near the coast of North Africa, sailed across the Atlantic on the current of air that circles the globe from east to west north of the Equator, and then trekked across the narrows of Central America. Once free of land again, the tropical wave began to gather sustenance from evaporation rising from the steamy ocean; evaporation supercharged with energy in the form of heat.

When that hot, moisture-laden wave ballooned into the chilly upper atmosphere, the result was condensation on a grand scale. Rain fell in sheets back to the ocean, and the constant jostling of droplets—and, at stratospheric heights, ice crystals—created huge areas of electrical charge in the clouds. These eventually erupted in frenzied bouts of lightning and thunder. All the unleashed energy in turn increased the force of the winds blowing into the core of the disturbance, the Antaean inhalation of the tropical wave.

Gorging itself on the abundant mist given up by the sweltering ocean, the tropical wave pupated. Air pressure at its center dropped even further, sucking still greater volumes of vapor upward from the ocean's surface, and these simple changes caused a physical transformation of the disturbance. Over the course of the next couple of days as the unsettled system floated away from the Americas and northwesterly across the Pacific, the loose cluster of thunderstorms that defined its seething body began to circle, like a group of juvenile titanics playing ring-a-roses.

Coriolis forces, the same inertial magic said to make water swirl around in a draining bathtub north or south of the equator, had organized the storm cells into a slow cyclonic dance. That radial movement increased the chimney effect at the heart of the wave, and caused surface winds to spiral into its great, gulping, downward-facing maw with increasing vigor.

On the night the Chase women arrived in Poipu, the energetic disturbance was sufficiently organized, with sustained winds of between twenty-five and thirty miles an hour, to be upgraded to a "tropical depression." From the space shuttle, orbiting overhead that night, it looked like a massive, murky gathering of clouds lit up from within by silent scintillations of lightning. But underneath, the cloud cover, a growling beast was taking shape, building strength and biding its time.

When the 911 call came in to the Kauai County Police Department, Officer Manny Gabriel was sitting in a patrol car at his favorite speed trap. As Highway 58 approached the former sugar-mill town of Koloa on the road from the county seat of Lihue to the south shore resorts in Poipu, the speed limit dropped quickly from fifty miles per hour to twenty-five. The limits were posted, and during the day there were other cues that warned drivers to slow up: a baseball diamond on the left, signalling the end of the cane fields; a "T" intersection ahead; a glimpse of shops. Only the occasional stoned teenager would be likely to speed through the area in daylight.

Night time was a different story. The road was unlit for most of its length, lined on both sides with tenebrous domains of sugar cane that stretched away to the mountains. A driver turning south onto Route 58 from the main road travelled the gradual downhill in darkness, and saw nothing for miles, except the road under the glare of the headlights, until the lights of Koloa appeared at about the same time that the "25 mph." speed sign flashed into view. Permanent residents of this part of the south shore, having the rhythm of the route in their bones, instinctively slowed their vehicles in time. But the tourists—

Fuddled by the mid-ocean time zone, fogged by dinner and drink at distant restaurants, and unfamiliar with the road, tourists regularly missed the mark. And Manny Gabriel was there, on the dirt road just past the "25 mph" sign, to catch them. "No, it's not a speed trap," he told his Filipino drinking buddies who accused him of shooting fish in a barrel. "It's community policing."

They laughed, but Chief Nagato took a poll to see whether his force was serving the people of Kauai County as they wished to be served. What could the police do to improve the lives of the populace? he wanted to know. Surprisingly, investigation of robberies, arrest of rapists, quelling of disturbances, the meat and potatoes of police work, were not high on the list of citizen grievances. Rather, the list was headed by two persistent neighborhood problems: speeding and loose pets.

Speeding, at least, was something the police knew how to control, and although there was a tension between sating the desire of Kauai residents for safe streets and sating the desire of the tourists—on whom the island's economy depended—to zoom from place to place in search of the maximum number of tropical splendors in the least amount of time, the Chief was keenly aware that the tourists did not vote on Kauai.

The second shift dispatcher was a young Chinese woman named May Chin. Her voice came over the two-way radio high and nasal. "Base to Car 12."

"Yeah, May," the patrolman answered. "This is Manny."

"Hey, Manny. You lucky tonight. We got a murder down dere."

May giggled self-consciously for having made light of the macabre.

"Yeah, sure, May."

"Serious, Braddah. Look like one gangland killing."

"You're not jokin'? Where 'bouts, then?'

"Your cousin's place, Manny. Pakala Inn. The detectives are on deah way from Lihue now. Bettah you go and secu'e da area."

Manny Gabriel fired up his cruiser. The lazily turning red and blue lights on its roof silently strobed the bushes on either side of his stake-out. It was starting to rain. He flipped on the wipers and pulled out of his hiding place. Artemis Gabriel, the cousin to whom the dispatcher had referred, was the black sheep of his family. Manny half hoped that whatever had happened at the Pakala Inn would be Artemis' undoing. It was not easy for the policeman to ignore his cousin's adventures in marijuana cultivation. Pakalolo growers were among the most dangerous people on the island, and sooner or later Artemis was sure to become a problem that could not be covered up. *Maybe sooner,* the policeman thought. *Maybe tonight.*

Andrew had not been able to sleep much during the flight, even with the aid of the Aloxe-Corton, and was pleased to hear the captain announce that their jumbo jet was beginning its descent into Honolulu. He sighed to himself. In a little more than an hour he would meet up with his family, draped groggily around the nonergonomic circular benches in the main terminal. He would whisk them off to one of the hotels on Waikiki Beach for the day. The Surfrider, perhaps, with its plantation-style charm. Two rooms. Janet and Liz in one, probably, he and Stella in the other. Not that he was averse to sleeping with his ex-wife. To the contrary; one of the purposes of this trip was to gauge the prospects of the two of them getting back together. But that was a subject that could not be forced. *The Surfrider, if we can get in,* he decided. They would have a late, leisurely brunch overlooking Waikiki tomorrow morning, and then catch a flight to Kauai. He would make amends; everything would be all right. Andrew Chase enjoyed being the man of the family, even if it was a fractured family.

September 8, 1992

"You remember that tropical depression I told you about yesterday, folks? Well, the National Weather Service is now calling it a tropical storm. But not to worry. It isn't headed our way. It's a real monster system, though, so the fringes of the thing may cause some shower activity here over the next few days."

Morning weather report, KONG Radio

2

The actuality of Andrew Chase's arrival in Hawaii bore no relationship to his airborne expectations. Not only was there no one waiting to greet him at the airport, but his family wasn't even in Honolulu. According to Janet's terse message, they had gone off to Kauai already, something he couldn't do until the shuttle flights began at sunrise. Obviously, their departure did not augur well for his plan for rapprochement with his former wife.

He had several hours to kill. There was no point in going into town. He had seen enough night life with Harry Wong to last him quite a while. In the main terminal, a glorified flophouse offered transiting passengers a shower and bed in a tiny cubicle. It was not Andrew's kind of lodging at all, but it was only a few footsteps away, and proximity outweighed indignity for a man who hadn't slept the night before and was only able to doze intermittently on the plane. He fell into a deep slumber as soon as his head hit the latex pillow, and awoke at the sound of the alarm five hours later.

The sky was clear when the six-thirty Hawaiian Air flight took off from Honolulu, but Andrew Chase's head wasn't. The wine, the abbreviated sleep, the Paracorp problem, the Fowler & Greide situation, the anticipation of Janet's ire; all these factors worked in cruel ensemble to keep him in a muddle. He stared out the window, watching Oahu drift out of sight. The sprawl of Honolulu, the upsweeping, forested mountains, the irregular shoreline against which serpentine white stripes of breaking waves beat themselves, all came and went, after which there was only the ocean, the liquid surface of a huge orb shimmering in the sunlight. Whitecaps appeared and vanished far below, like daytime fireflies. Boats, moving points of artificial color, pushed along beneath the plane, trailing foamy, comet-tail wakes behind them. A bank of clouds loomed ahead, and Andrew felt the plane curving gently downward, the short flight all ascent and descent. Dense fog enveloped the craft momentarily. Andrew leaned his head back on the seat and closed his eyes. *When I get to Kauai,* he thought to himself, *I'll have time to work on all of my problems, the first being to patch things up with Janet.*

In fact, when he got to Kauai, the man of the Chase family ended up in jail for half a day, held on suspicion of conspiracy to commit murder.

The night before, Carol Spencer had given Janet and her daughters the suite adjoining hers in the main building. Small and sparsely appointed, mostly with plastic furniture and faded prints of palm trees and half-naked women, it offered little comfort, just three lumpy mattresses on metal frames. After the evening's discovery and the police interviews, all three Chase women would have passed a fitful night even in more comfortable accommodations. Janet had not fallen into a real slumber until shortly before the alarm woke her at five-thirty. She washed slowly in the phone-booth sized shower, without energy but purposefully, as if she could rub the emotional grime of the preceding evening out through her skin. Then, with uncharacteristic disregard for her appearance, she threw on the clothes that were at the top of her suitcase: boxer-style shorts and a Hawaiian-styled shirt with a muted tropical motif. In her mind, their Hawaiian idyll had ended when they found a corpse in their bungalow. As soon as Andrew appeared, they would make arrangements to restart their vacation on the mainland.

Lieutenant Akamai was waiting outside in the predawn darkness, as he had promised he would be. George Akamai was a tall, dark-skinned man with a broad face, doe-brown eyes and soft, prominent lips. His curly hair was slicked back, and he wore a royal blue short-sleeved shirt and slacks the same color. He also wore a service revolver at his right hip. "I don't usually carry this out in the open," he explained to Janet, who was staring at the gun uncertainly. "But a murder like last night's—real intentional, maybe preceded by torture—you don't take chances."

"You're expecting more trouble, Lieutenant?"

"No, Ma'am. Not at all. Just a precaution."

A warm rain was falling, droplets so small they were almost mist. Akamai climbed into the police cruiser, picked up the papers that had been sitting on the shotgun seat and shoved them into the glove compartment. Janet slid in beside him, and her daughters took their places in the rear. The car rolled onto the beach road. When they were underway, Akamai flicked on the flashing roof lights, but not the siren. Like the others, he was subdued.

In New Orleans when Janet was growing up, not to make conversation was tantamount to unmannerliness. Even the stressful circumstances of the night before could not excuse unmannerliness. "Are you a Kauai native?" she asked after a they had driven in silence for a few moments. Police officers are better at asking questions than answering.

"Maui," was all that Akamai said. It was the truth, as far as it went.

"Is it supposed to rain all day?"

"I don't think so. This time of year, there are always storm systems out in the Pacific, but they don't affect us much."

It sounded to Janet like a standard answer for tourists. She tried another subject. "I suppose this kind of thing is pretty rare on Kauai, isn't it?" she asked.

"Rain? Nah, we get more than our share."

"I meant murder, Lieutenant."

Akamai gave her another tourist answer. "Murder? Pretty rare. This is one peaceful island."

"It's very kind of you to do this, take us to the airport, with so much going on," Janet assayed. Maybe Akamai had got too little sleep to be sociable.

"Not at all," Akamai replied. "I'll feel better having seen you out there."

Feel better? The phrase flew at her like an angry bat swooping down the dark tunnel of overhanging trees through which they were riding on their way to the main road to Lihue. *So he's not just performing a kindness,* she thought. *Feel better!* "Why, Lieutenant? Are we in some kind of danger?"

"I didn't say that." Akamai flashed a mechanical smile. "I said I'd feel better, that's all."

Janet fell silent, her Southern sense of etiquette suddenly displaced by more serious concerns. Outside her window, low mountains rose, mounds of blackness against a sky still dark but mustering itself for dawn behind clouds glowing red from below. The impending beauty of the day did not impress her. She was not a woman well-disposed to danger. "But you think we should go back to the mainland too, don't you?"

Akamai glanced at her, then turned back. He took a deep breath. "Okay," he said relenting. "I don't want to confuse you, Ma'am. Here's what's going through my mind. The style of the killing says gang war. From the aesthetic of it, I'd say either mainland Chinese or

Vietnamese. We don't have gangs of either type on Kauai, which means the killer was probably from off island, maybe even from the Far East. Of course, these things aren't always what they seem. For instance, although there was a fair amount of blood on and around the body, I would have expected even more from a wound like that, right into the br—What I mean, Ma'am, is that until the coroner examines the body, we won't really know how the guy died."

"Call me Janet, please."

"I will, if you'll call me George. Looks like he was into drugs, marijuana at least," the police lieutenant continued, "so the safest assumption is, we're dealing with heavy criminals here, in which case it does make sense for you to worry about your family's safety. On the other hand, the deed was done a couple of hours before you got here. That means the killer is probably not thinking of you folks as witnesses. He doesn't have any reason to—um, to *deal* with you, you understand. From what we can tell so far, there wasn't anything left on the body that would lead us to him, which means he shouldn't want to make waves. A rational analysis would say there should be no problem for the Chases. But crimes like these happen fast, and afterwards the perpetrators sometimes get irrational and start wondering if they might have forgotten to take care of some detail. I guess the bottom line is, I'm escorting you this morning out of an excess of caution."

A sound was coming from the rear of the cruiser; a sound like water running in a distant room, or new leaves rustling in the wind. Janet twisted in her seat. "What are you girls whispering about?"

When Stella and Liz were little, she used to chastise them for whispering in the presence of company. "It's not polite," she would tell them, and they never understood, because it was almost always more polite to whisper what they had been saying about the company than to speak it aloud.

"Nothing, Mom. Sorry," Liz and Stella replied in unison, the formulaic answer from childhood. The knee-jerk simultaneity made the kids that were still inside the two young women giggle, despite the fact that their *sotto voce* conversation had been distinctly unfunny. "You have to give it to him," was the way Stella had started it, as soon as Akamai observed that nothing of concern to the killer had been left on the body.

"I can't," Liz hissed back.

"Liz, it's evidence. You're probably committing a crime."

"I can burn it. Then nobody could prove it ever existed."

"Oh, right. I think destruction of evidence only carries twice as long a jail term as withholding evidence. You picked it up, now you have to deal with it. It's your karma."

"Fine, Stell. Here. Now it's your karma. You deal with it." Liz shoved the note into her sister's hand, and with it the responsibility for the decision.

Stella unfolded the paper in her lap and read it again in the wan predawn light. She turned to Liz and shook her head. "You're right. Dad's got to decide."

What are you girls whispering about?"

"Nothing, Mom. Sorry."

Morning light was filtering through the overcast by the time they reached the Lihue airport. Great puffy slate-colored clouds pushed across the sky. Akamai brought the patrol car to the curb at the Hawaiian Air terminal, got out with his passengers and locked the doors. As they walked through the gentle rain shower—"pineapple dew," Akamai called it—into the open-fronted wooden structure, the foursome could hear the reverse thrusters screaming the early morning shuttle to a slow roll. A few minutes later, Andrew Chase strolled through the open portal at the back of the terminal, bleary-eyed, but vacation-ready in tangerine surfer shorts and a new Victoria Peak tee shirt. There were shouts and hugs and kisses. And then Janet took a good look at him.

"What happened to your neck?" she asked, reaching out a hand to touch the purple contusion, but then stopping herself just short of contact. "And your knee?"

"There was a cyclone in Hong Kong. A piece of sheet metal came right through the airport window and almost decapitated me."

The women stared at him, thunderstruck to a degree unwarranted by the extent of his injuries which were, after all, superficial.

"Oh, Andy," Janet muttered, as if coming out of a bad dream. "How awful." Akamai stepped forward. "Um, this is George Akamai. He drove us out here."

Andrew Chase shook Akamai's hand and, with a puzzled look at the patrol car, thanked him for driving his family to the airport. "I hadn't remembered the hospitality here to be quite so intensive," he said.

"I'm afraid the ladies had one hell of a scare last night, Andy," Akamai explained. Andrew Chase shot him a look both inquisitive and irritated. Only Janet called her ex-husband Andy. To the rest of the world, he was "Andrew," as befit his station. Or, even more appropriate here, "Mr. Chase."

"Yes, Daddy," Liz put in. "I found a body in my closet."

"There was an ice pick in his ear," Stella added, then stuck an extended index finger into her own ear, cocked her head and let her tongue loll out of her open mouth.

"And blood everywhere," Janet added, the injury to her psyche causing her to recall more goriness than the scene had presented.

Andrew Chase was used to the unexpected: a sudden shift in negotiations; a surprise call from the SEC about one of his clients; a hostile takeover bid by a corporate raider. None of these things flustered him. Surprises concerning his family, though, particularly surprises of an unpleasant nature, were a different story. In general, he handled them rather less well. Something in him froze up when his decision processes and emotional processes collided. Experience tended to give way to irrationality. It was a trait that would not serve him well during the next several days.

His first thought was that Janet had enlisted Akamai in an elaborate ruse as payback for his being late to get to Honolulu. "This isn't funny, guys," he said.

"Dad, it's not a joke," Liz cautioned.

"Don't get me wrong, I deserve it. I'm just not up to being made the goat this morning, is all. I arrived from Hong Kong at one a.m. and was up again at five-thirty. Didn't bother going to a real hotel, just lay down for a couple of hours in that knockdown at the airport. So congratulations on enlisting the Kauai P.D. in your very convincing prank here. But could we please cut the horseplay for now and just get going?"

Janet put a hand on his arm. "Andy, listen to me. Last night we stayed in a little hotel in Poipu. Liz opened a closet door and found a-a corpse inside. We all lost a night's sleep, too. Including Lieutenant Akamai."

"Not bad, Janet; quite convincing, actually. Now, if you'll excuse me, I'll go after the rental car."

"It's the truth," Stella said quietly. Her father stopped in his tracks and stared at her. Stella might be willing to stand mute during Janet's little pretense, but if she spoke, it would be to tell the truth.

"Wh-what? It really happened? But you—you're all okay, aren't you? I mean—officer, there's no problem, is there?"

George Akamai shook his head. "Not that I know of, Andy. But I'm glad you're here to tend to your family."

Andrew held out his hand. "Well, thank you, officer. I appreciate your thoughtfulness, driving out here so early in the morning." He emphasized his expression of gratitude with an emphatic nod. "Beyond the call. Um, that's it for us, is it, then? No further involvement? I mean, you have all the information you need from them, right?"

"Andy," Janet exclaimed.

Akamai held up a hand. "I never like to say 'never,' Andy, but I don't guess Janet and your daughters have anything more to tell us—"

Andy. Janet. Where is this guy's sense of etiquette? Andrew wondered.

"—unless they know where the French couple has gone." Akamai shot Stella a questioning look. In return, she gave him a shrug of her shoulders.

"What French couple?" Andrew demanded.

"Two other guests at the hotel. They skipped out last night. An ill-advised action." Akamai kept glancing back at Stella. "If they stay on Kauai, we'll find them eventually. And if they try to board a plane or boat off this island, we'll get them as well. When we've apprehended them, the fact that they ran out on me will definitely not be a point in their favor. Up to then, they were only witnesses, as far as the police were concerned—purchasers of a small quantity of *pakalolo*, a crime easily overlooked in exchange for sworn statements describing their involvement with the victim. Now? Now, they're suspects."

"I see. Well, I'm sure you'd like to get on with the case, Lieutenant," Andrew suggested, "and I'd like to collect my bags, rent a car and get the family down to Poipu."

"We have a jeep down at the Inn," Janet put in.

"A jeep!" Andrew echoed, incredulous. "Is that all they had left when you arrived? Why didn't you take a cab? No matter. We'll pick up the convertible I reserved, and turn in the jeep—"

"Maybe we should keep two cars, Dad," Liz suggested. "In case, you know, Stella and I want to go off on our own once in a while."

"Liz, the idea of this vacation is to be together."

Janet gave a sardonic laugh. "Well, we've got off to a great start in that regard, haven't we? Andy, I think we should decide whether we are going to stay here or not before we rent a second car."

"Stay here or not?" Andrew was not tuned to his former wife's wavelength, a common circumstance during the quarter century of their marriage. It had made his life with her eternally surprising, if not uniformly pleasant. "Like the officer said, the murderer doesn't have any reason to be interested in us. We have no connection to the victim, other than the accident of Liz's having discovered him. Plus, I doubt that hit men hang around after a murder to see whether the police figure out who done it. Besides, the house is paid for. I'll get the car."

Akamai had been watching the Chase daughters as their father spoke. When Stella moved to follow Andrew down to the rental car counter, he called out, "How about riding back down to Poipu in the squad car with me, Stella? Everyone can probably use a little breakfast. I'll introduce you all to this little place in Koloa town that has real good muffins and industrial strength Kauai coffee."

Stella hesitated, her hands clasped together. "I'd better go with him, Dad," she said softly. "He wants to ask me about Chantal and Luc, I'm sure. Might as well get it out of the way now." To Akamai, she responded, "Okay, George. Let me just walk my Dad over to get the car. We haven't seen each other in months."

The rental agents were setting up for the morning in the open-air sheds across from the wooden terminal building. Small lines of Andrew's fellow passengers had already formed in front of each counter. As Andrew and his daughter crossed the road to take their place in one of the queues, Stella slipped the note out of the pocket of her flowing tie-dyed skirt. "Take this, Dad," she whispered.

"What is it, Stell?" Andrew said aloud, and began to unfold the paper.

Stella grabbed his hand.

"Don't open it," she whispered urgently. "Lieutenant Akamai has eyes like a hawk. You can look at it after you get into the rental car."

"But what is it, Stella?" They were standing in line behind a Minnesota couple, whose idle conversation in the vowel-bending accents of the upper Middle West was like a musical duet.

Stella put a finger to her lips. "Shh. On the way to breakfast, ask Liz. She found it in the room—Dad! Don't open it right here!"

Andrew Chase was not all business. He drove convertibles, and anyone who drives convertibles is not all business. Or so he told himself, ignoring the possibility that he favored convertibles not because he enjoyed the roar of the wind in his ears or the heat of the sun on his balding head or the attention of passersby as he cruised the streets with his radio blaring—now Mozart, now Marsalis, now Morrison—but rather because people who saw him driving one would *conclude* that he was not all business. The car he had reserved was a small American convertible, the cheapest one available from the rental agency. It had a manual top, not the best choice in light of the intermittent rains that are characteristic of the Garden Island, but Andrew was learning to economize.

He left the top up for the time being, given that it was still drizzling. After settling into the driver's seat, he drew his sunglasses from his shorts and slid them on. *Not all business,* he thought as checked his casualness quotient in the rear-view mirror, but then, because it was still not light enough to drive comfortably with shades on, he removed them and set them on the dashboard. Stella had walked back to rejoin the others, and Akamai was out of view, so before starting off Andrew fished out the paper Stella had given to him so melodramatically a few moments ago, and unfolded it against the steering wheel.

On it was a list, printed in rough block lettering, as if by someone trained only late in life to write in English. There were six company names on the list, and, next to three of these, the names of individuals. Two of the entries sent a shiver up Andrew's back: "Paracorp," the fourth line read, and next to the corporate name appeared "A. Chase." He stared at his own name, uncomprehending. His mind felt like an engine racing in neutral. What could it mean? Looking at the list produced no immediate explanation as to why his name—his name!—and that of his client should be found on the body of a murdered man. Was there a clue hidden in the other names?

France-Orient—Bouchard/Minot,
Nihon Investments,
Chung Bank,
Singapore/Vision,
ROC Overseas—X. Song.

The individuals' names meant nothing to him, but the firm names were familiar. All of them were large finance companies operating in the Far East. Like Paracorp, they were not manufacturing firms, but rather companies active in funding land development projects around the world. They were his client's competitors in the world of construction financing.

The lawyer's face knotted in an troubled scowl. That Liz had found this list in the hotel room was quite disturbing. The Paracorp matter he had come to Kauai to handle was highly confidential. He hadn't even told Janet about it. How could the murdered man have known? Were France-Orient and the other finance companies going to be competing with Paracorp here on Kauai? More importantly, could there have been a connection between Paracorp and the killing itself? Concerned and confused, he slipped the note back into his pocket, started the car and drove around to the passenger pickup area.

"Okay, let's go!" he called to his family through the passenger window. "Liz, toss my bag into the trunk, please," he added, pulling the release lever under the dashboard.

"Just follow us down to Koloa," George Akamai shouted back and motioned Stella to join him.

Buttery early-morning light bathed the police vehicle, which still glistened with the sheen of predawn rain. Stella, walking slightly behind George, eyed him closely—his hair, brown and wavy, his features, squarish, Polynesian and altogether appealing, his barrel chest and lean but powerful arms. *Jogging, universal machines and swimming,* she thought. Coupled with his stressful occupation, these made him a prime candidate for a massage regimen. *Which, from the looks of those muscles,* Stella concluded, *he is not pursuing.* Stella Chase deeply believed that in manipulation of the soft tissues of the body lay the salvation of humankind.

They drove south toward Poipu, making what Stella thought to be small talk about their respective backgrounds. Akamai was twenty-eight, a graduate of Dartmouth, and single. She was twenty-four, a graduate of Barnard, and single. He had majored in computer science but was a policeman because there was not yet much need for computer scientists on Kauai. She had majored in comparative literature but was a waitress because there was not much need for comparative lit majors anywhere, and also because before she graduated she had decided to pursue a non-materialist path, which meant no wealth-oriented career path.

He had majored in computer science with the thought of leaving Hawaii for the mainland, but after four years in New Hampshire at college, with visits to Manhattan, Chicago, San Francisco and Silicon Valley, he concluded that the mainland had little of a positive sort to offer him. She had lived in a hippie community in southern Arizona for a while, but after being mugged there (something that had never happened to her during four years of college in Manhattan), she had moved to Portland, which people had told her was a good place for spiritualists. He liked being a policeman because it made him feel as though he was a guardian of the island's well-being. She liked being a waitress because it left her days free to study alternative modes of healing and pursue her spiritual journey. He disliked being a policeman because he was enforcing a mainland-type legal system disproportionately against native Hawaiians, who were overrepresented in the island's lower class. She disliked being a waitress because it was a night job.

"Where did you learn to speak French—in college?" Akamai asked.

"No, in Paris. My father's firm has a Paris office—or had; I think it's closed now. We lived there for a few years when I was in grade school. I also went back for a semester during college."

"So you had no trouble understanding Luc and Chantal when they conversed in French?"

Ah, thought Stella. *We're getting right down to business.* "You want to know what we talked about?"

"Yes."

"We talked about their travels. Where they had been, what they did when they weren't travelling, how they managed."

"Where had they been?"

"On this trip? Turkey, India, Indonesia, China—and Thailand, I think. Yes, Thailand."

"And what do they do when they're not travelling?"

"Chantal is a commercial artist. Luc is a folk singer. And he waits tables, like me. How did they manage?"

"Right." Akamai liked Stella. She was smart, but open and unguarded like people who were not smart. It was an unusual and disarming combination.

"Well, they work for a year or so and save as much money as they can. Which isn't a lot, maybe a few thousand dollars between them. Then they go off in search of adventure. Cheap adventure. They camp out until they can't stand it any more, then sleep in hostels or inexpensive hotels. Luc sings for money on the street—" She broke off, not wanting to incriminate her French friends, but then decided that catching the ice-pick murderer was more important. "And they sell marijuana to other tourists."

"*Pakalolo*, we call it here. Crazy smoke. Did you buy some?" Stella laughed nervously. George was very appealing, but he was, after all, a policeman. "Do I need to consult my lawyer before answering that question?"

"No, we have a fairly relaxed attitude toward casual use. I was just curious, that's all."

"Well, I didn't buy any, George."

"But you smoked a little with them?"

"Lieutenant—!"

"That's what they told me. You know, the aroma was so strong in their bungalow, they couldn't really deny using the stuff, so they were pretty open." Akamai glanced sidelong at his passenger. "Do you think they were telling the truth about their backgrounds?"

The question caught Stella by surprise. "I-I don't know, but why would they lie? They didn't kill that man, George."

"Maybe not. But why did they run away?"

Stella stared through the windshield. In the morning light the tunnel of trees that had seemed a brooding presence the night before had become a beautiful construction of arching boughs and broad leaves. "They were afraid."

"Of what?"

"Of the murderer, I imagine. When Chantal saw that body, the fear in her eyes was—well, I've never seen anyone more frightened."

"Did you talk to them about it afterward?"

"No. I did overhear them talking to one another, though."

"—And?"

"Well, it wasn't about the dead man. It had something to do with property. An estate. That's all I remember."

"What kind of estate?" Akamai shot back, stiffening.

"I really don't know."

Stella had been watching the detective as they talked. His lips moving, his jaw muscles flexing, the blink of his long-lashed eyelids. "George," she asked, "what sign are you?"

"Sign, did you say?"

"You know, astrological sign."

Akamai chuckled and shook his head. "I'm not sure. Why?"

"When is your birthday?"

"January fifth."

Stella clapped her hands together and exclaimed, "Capricorn! I knew it."

Capricorn. Sympathetic, broad-minded, generous, perceptive. Perhaps a little pessimistic, but basically philosophical and idealistic. Best of all, a water person. Stella, a Cancer, was a water person, too. Water people were mystics, the ones who connected the rest of humanity with its spiritual roots. And two people of the same element, if they fell into a relationship, tended to live in harmony and stability. *What would the sound of it be?* she asked herself just for fun, and then tested it out in her mind. *Stella Akamai. A-ka-mai. Wild!*

Sitting in the back seat of the convertible, Liz Chase was feeling miserable. She should have burned the note, she told herself. Leaning forward into the open space between her parents, she yelled, "I should have burned it!"

"Don't be silly!" Andrew shouted back at her over the rushing wind. He had lowered the top at a stoplight when it was clear that the rain had passed. "I'll straighten this out with the officer."

"Straighten what out with the officer?" Janet demanded. "You have no idea what that list signifies. And as of now, George Akamai doesn't even know it exists. What can you possibly straighten out by giving him that scrap of paper?" Janet saw very clearly the proper course of action for her family. It did not involve sharing incriminating evidence with Lieutenant Akamai. It involved having a pleasant breakfast with the policeman, then packing up and flying back to New York, all four of them. The French couple had the right idea. "A drug pusher gets killed by a triad enforcer, and you want to insert yourself into the issue? For God's sake, wake up and smell the coffee, Sweetheart."

"Does this mean you still care, dearest?" Andrew returned with a hopeful smile.

"It's the alimony, Andy. I care about your continued existence because I care about the payments."

Andrew glanced at his former spouse, and saw no amusement in her eyes. "Okay, let's just try to calm down about this, can we? If you're so worried about alimony, then you should keep in mind that I'm a member of the bar. Suppression of evidence could have disastrous effects on my livelihood, not to mention my liberty. Maybe the risk of discovery is low, but the risk of disbarment is so high that it makes no sense to take the chance. No, we'll give the list to the police."

At that, Liz slumped back into the wind. Though she didn't agree with her mother about cutting their vacation short, the fact that her father was opting for form over substance filled her with dread. "I should have burned it," she said again, but the wind kept the repeated remark from reaching the front seat.

The delivery of the note took place over a round marble table outdoors under a bougainvillea arbor. The two men were waiting for the Chase women to bring back coffee, juice and muffins. Andrew Chase explained that his eldest daughter had found the scrap of paper under her bed and, seeing her father's name on it, had thought it was a business note.

"And it's not?" The look of sincere curiosity on Akamai's face told Andrew that, despite the fact that his story made no sense, the officer was willing to accept the note without questioning Liz further, at least for now. Andrew allowed himself the trace of a smile, partially out of relief, partially out of self-satisfaction. At the same time, he shook his head so that the smile looked like the accoutrement of an honest admission.

"No," he replied softly. "It's not. I've never seen it before."

"Why would she think it was a business note?"

"Because of the reference to Paracorp," the lawyer replied with what he hoped was the right degree of earnestness. "That's a client of mine. A Hong Kong company."

"Uh-huh." Akamai stared at the paper. "What about these other names?" he asked, waving a hand over the list.

"They're big Asian multinationals, too. I don't work for any of the others."

Akamai nodded, stuffed the note into his shirt pocket, leaned back in his chair and folded his arms. "I'd like you to come down to the station with me, Andy." He made it sound like an invitation to dinner.

"Wh-what for, Lieutenant?" Andrew had anticipated that, at some point during the family's vacation, he'd be called in to talk about the list. He'd assumed that the police would want to look into the other names, try to determine what commonality—if any—existed among them, and then interview him. George Akamai was suggesting a greater immediacy. Maybe greater suspicion?

"Questioning."

Janet, Liz and Stella arrived at that moment, carrying trays laden with breakfast. Janet looked at her husband and saw the glumness. She turned to the Hawaiian policeman beseechingly.

"May we have our breakfast first? Please, George," she asked.

3

"Oh, my God! It's—arresting."

"Very funny, Liz."

"Oops, wrong word, I guess," Liz Chase teased. "Well, at least you're out of the big house now, Dad."

Andrew Chase and his daughters had just rounded a turn on a steeply ascending trail, and were greeted with an expansive view of the cliffs that form the Na Pali coast. Ranks of razor-ridged mountains, carpeted in greenery, marched in receding perspective down to the sea. In its enthusiastic, endless caressing of these volcanic formations, the sea had chewed the ends of the plunging ridgelines into sheer-faced precipices. Standing one behind the other, the dragon-toothed mountains seemed painted from a cool palette, changing from vermilion to pale violet until the farthest of them faded from view in the salt haze that whitened the horizon.

"It *is* an arresting view, though." Andrew Chase laughed. Father-daughter bonding. After the morning's embarrassment, it was needed. Being taken into police custody, however politely, was a blow to the lawyer's self-image and, he had no doubt, to his image as viewed by his daughters. Their image of him was, he knew, diminished a great deal already because of the divorce. Not about to participate in restoring her ex to his former lofty pedestal in the eyes of their children, but badgered into letting Liz and Stella join their father on what he claimed was one of the most beautiful hikes in the world, Janet had stayed in the rented house to call the travel agent and arrange a flight back to the mainland.

At liberty on the Kalalau Trail, Andrew knew that he had not seen the last of the Kauai County police. The dead man's list was of much greater significance than Andrew had let on to Akamai. Andrew's guess was that each of the enterprises named on it was doing just what Paracorp was doing: preparing a bid for the purchase of a substantial slice of the island that had quietly been put up for sale by its owner, the proprietor of the Makai Sugar Company. The sugar planter and processor was reportedly trying to cut his losses in the face of the cheap competition from corn syrup and third world cane sugar that was slowly strangling the Hawaiian sugar business.

If it became generally known that the Makai Ranch was up for sale, anxiety would ripple across not just Kauai, but the other islands as well. The state's leaders would face a torrent of public opposition. There was already widespread concern that the decline of the sugar business was changing the face of Hawaii irretrievably. The sale of a large portion of Kauai's south coast would give those concerns a concrete focus. Of course, some people already suspected as much. One of them, Andrew had discovered that morning, was Akamai's sister, who worked in the assessor's office. She had told Akamai of the sudden interest by off-island parties in the valuation for tax purposes of the pie-shaped parcel. "The murder your daughter discovered could be the first step in the rape of Kauai," he had told Andrew before releasing him.

"Do I look like a rapist, George?" Andrew demanded, a bit self-righteously.

"No, not a rapist. An accomplice, maybe. Or an innocent dupe."

"Thanks for your confidence, officer. Listen, maybe that poor bastard in the closet was a competitor of mine, I don't know. But he was also dealing drugs, from what Stella says, and from everything I know, murder is a lot more closely associated with the drug trade than with real estate development." *Besides,* Andrew thought to himself, *my leaving the island now would be an irreparable loss of face in the eyes of Harry Wong.*

"Yes, that's still the working hypothesis, but we can't be sure. I'm beginning to agree with your wife about you guys leaving here."

"You think I might end up with a sharp object stuck in my ear?"

"Hey, I don't know what Paracorp is paying you. Maybe it's worth the risk."

As he and his daughters negotiated the now slippery windblown trail, Andrew was in reasonably good spirits in spite of Akamai's warning. He had not disclosed to the police any client confidences, or anything that Akamai did not already know or couldn't easily find out. He had been treated with the respect he felt was his due. Though he had to wait over an hour before being called for questioning in a little interrogation room that was cluttered, like all the hallways of the single-story concrete block building, with filing cabinets and cardboard document boxes, at least he had been waiting alone in a holding cell, which allowed him to stretch out on the bench and nap a bit. It wasn't until his last few minutes in the tank that he had to share the quarters with another person. His temporary cell mate was a young man, mid-twenties probably, with short hair and long, powerful muscles. A surfer, Andrew judged.

"So-o. Whatcha here for, Andrew?" he asked the lawyer.

"Suspicion of murder," Andrew replied, in the full and glorious knowledge that—in the county lockup—the capital charge carried the ultimate worthiness. "What about you?"

"Dumpster diving." It sounded salacious enough to Andrew until he learned that it was just grub work. "They caught me in the dumpster at the Hyatt, going through the trash."

"Looking for recyclables?" Andrew said tentatively.

"No, dude," the young man chuckled. "I was readin' the mail. You know, the office files that get thrown away, the notes that guests toss out. That kinda stuff. So—didja do it, Unc?"

"No." The diver's clarification triggered a recollection. Many years earlier, there had been a story about a fellow who was sorting through Bob Dylan's garbage up in Woodstock, New York. He claimed to be a sociologist. This blond Adonis didn't look like a sociologist. "Did you?"

"Hell, yeah. It's my job."

"Your job?"

"I'm a private eye."

"Really? Really! A private eye. Wh-what were you looking for?"

The young man chuckled. "Sorry. I can't disclose client confidences."

Andrew and his daughters followed the Kalalau Trail downward toward the Hanakapi'ai Beach, a secluded crescent of sand bounded on both sides by lava cliffs and split by a stream rushing down the declivity between the cliffs to the sea. Stella was leading, walking quickly in order to be alone, and lost in her own thoughts. She was worried that Luc and Chantal might be the "Bouchard/Minot" mentioned in the dead man's note. If true, it meant they had used false surnames with her, and perhaps told her untruths about their backgrounds. It also meant that, in not recognizing the deception, she had failed to read the true colors of their auras, and that was what really worried her.

Behind Stella, Liz and Andrew moved at a more leisurely pace, together, talking. Liz wore her blue bikini and her hiking boots. Slathered with Hawaiian tan enhancer, she smelled more or less like a pina colada. She was more than a little miffed at Stella for leaving her on her own to suffer cross-examination by her father. It was always risky for the girls to engage in one-on-one conversation with Andrew because sooner or later the discussion would turn to their “situations.” Liz had taken a degree in botany, a subject that satisfied her ecological leanings and therefore interested her until it came time to turn studies into a career. Junior botanists didn’t make much money and—in Manhattan, anyway—could spend their time clipping dead tips off the leaves of rented plants in office buildings. Lacking any other direction, she had spent the four years since graduation bouncing around the record business in Manhattan, and was currently a contract album-cover artist at Polygram.

“Stella,” she called out. “Wait for us!” Her sister, near the edge of a cliff one ridge ahead of them, her ears filled with the sound of the wind, didn’t hear. “Dad, we should all be staying together, shouldn’t we?”

Andrew nodded and cupped his hands. “Stella! Wait for us!” he bellowed. Stella turned, waved to them and sat down on a rock by the side of the trail.

“So—how’s the job?” Andrew inquired as he and Liz passed a small clump of succulent-petaled red flowers growing on low stalks out of leafy beds.

Liz bent over the plants. “Know what this is?” Her fingers squeezed the crimson pod, releasing a stream of slick, transparent liquid onto her hand. She stood up and held the sample under her father’s nose. The smell was pleasantly familiar to him, but he couldn’t place it. She grabbed his wrist and smeared a little of the juice onto his thumb. He rubbed his thumb against his forefinger. The substance had the feel of soapy water.

“It’s *awapuhi*,” Liz explained. “They use it in shampoo. You can wash your hands with it on the trail.”

“Hmm. Interesting. So—how’s the job?” Andrew asked again, smiling and throwing his arm around his daughter to set her back in motion.

“I love it!” Liz replied, knowing that it was not exactly the answer her father wanted.

“You love drawing covers for compact disks?”

“Dad, it’s creative work. I invent, I use my imagination, I make something out of nothing. People think my work is great. Millions of folks all over the country see it, have it in their homes. What’s not to like?”

“Millions of people have corn flakes in their homes, too, Liz. That doesn’t mean they are fascinated by the box art. Whatever happened to botany, to environmentalism?" Liz could tell that her father was trying not to sound argumentative. He was trying to project an air of genuine curiosity about the abrupt shift in the direction of her career plans. The trouble was, they'd had this same conversation in different forms dozens of times since graduation. There could be no doubt that Andrew was more negatively disposed to her current occupation than he was genuinely curious about it.

"Dad, I wasn't interested in paying the dues. Tending to potted plants or marching through wetlands collecting samples of dirty water and dying pond weed isn't my idea of how to save the environment."

"And helping sell nonbiodegradable CDs and jewel boxes is?" It was a classic Andrew Chase retort, leaving no leeway for response.

They were walking single file downhill on a narrow stretch of rocky trail. Ahead of them at a switchback and several hundred feet below, the ocean sparkled, a mesh of diamond flashes moving on its surface. Underneath, its colors were indigo, cobalt, aquamarine, pea green, violet and, where reefs approached the surface, sable. To one side of the path, the land dropped away into lushness: a deep valley, almost a ravine, rich in verdant leafiness, here and there a pinprick of crimson or yellow where flowering trees or bushes stood. To the other side, the volcanic land rose up sharply, rock the color of strong coffee, the texture of petrified sponge, infiltrated by green botanical invaders insisting on their rights to live wherever they wished. *The setting's not conducive to argumentation, anyway,* Liz thought.

"Is this gorgeous or what?" she said as they rounded the switchback and, putting the ocean to their back, headed down into a little vale at the meeting of two ridges.

"It's as beautiful as any place I've ever been," Andrew remarked, giving up the father-daughter debate for the moment.

Further down, the trail was shrouded in trees. Liz looked up at Stella, whose position was now higher than theirs. She put her hands on her hips in a sign of frustration, and Stella put her own hands over her ears and rocked her head from side to side, just before she was hidden from view as Liz passed under some tall *ohio* trees, their tufted red flowers looking like tiny pom-poms. Daughter and father descended and came to the point at which the two ridges met. There a gentle rivulet cascaded over a bed of black stone, ran under the path through a culvert, and fell down toward the sea. It was a charming spot that, four days later, would no longer exist. As they stood looking at it, a figure emerged from the shadowy bower that covered the valley trail ahead of them—a tall, well proportioned blond fellow, walking uphill with a bounce in his step. Andrew started at the sight of him.

"Hello again, Unc!" the figure shouted as he approached.

"Well, what a coincidence!" Andrew shot back, his voice betraying wariness of further coincidences on the island. "Out on bail?"

"Nah," the young man called. "They dropped the charges."

As his former cell mate reached them on the narrow path, Andrew turned to his daughter and said, "Liz, this is Race Kendall. He and I met in jail this morning."

Liz held out her hand. "Liz Chase," she said. "Chase and Race. Sounds too frenetic for such an idyllic spot." The hand she held in hers was large and smooth. *Good grip,* she thought. *Firm but not overpowering. Good shake.* The way a man shook hands with a woman was, in Liz's experience, a window deeper into his character than most men realized.

"I dunno," the young man replied. "Sounds like a partnership to me. This your first visit to Kauai?"

Liz nodded. "My dad's been here before, but it's the first time for my sister and me."

"I'd be happy to escort you around some, if you like. Been livin' here a while, so you'd find me a pretty good guide."

"That's really nice of you," Liz answered, at the same time that Andrew, his fatherly warning antennae vibrating, was saying, "Actually, we came here to spend time together as a family."

The three of them laughed awkwardly. Liz backpedaled. "I guess I should ask what you were charged with before I accept your kind offer."

"Well, they were going to charge me with trespassing," Race answered, "but it's really hard to trespass in a hotel parking lot, so in the end, they didn't charge me with anything." He gave the same cryptic description of the dumpster escapade that he had given Andrew earlier. "I've got a pristine record, I promise you. So, what do you think? Dinner tonight?"

No wonder they call this guy "Race," Andrew thought.

"Could you join us at the house we rented?" Liz asked. "We're having a cookout, and then we may be flying back to the mainland."

"Uh, um—Didn't you just get here?"

"The murder I told you about," Andrew explained. "It's put my wife—I mean, my former wife—in a real emotional state."

"Well, uh—"

"We're the white house with French doors across the front," Liz injected, "just up from the Whaler's Cove condos. Around six?"

"Um, yeah—Yeah. Perfect."

"Race, are you coming up from the beach?" Andrew inquired doubtfully.

"Uh-huh. You're wondering how I got down there and back so fast? Not on foot, Andrew. One of the tour pilots is a buddy of mine. Rode in his chopper down to the beach. Had agreed to meet a client who was camping there, and because of the cops that was the only way I could get there in time."

"I see," Andrew said, neither believing nor disbelieving. "Well, in any case you must have passed Liz's sister a minute ago. She's just ahead of us on the trail."

Race returned a clouded look. "I don't think so," he said. "I didn't pass any other good-lookin' babes on the way up from the beach."

"Sitting on a rock," Liz insisted, "just at the next turn in the trail. Hair's lighter than mine, kind of angular face."

The young man shook his head. "She wasn't there when I came by."

That was how Andrew Chase learned that his daughter Stella had disappeared.

George Akamai sat across the desk from his boss, Captain Barry Saga, in the little room that passed for the office of the chief of detectives. The concrete block walls were painted a pale institutional green, the lone window was too high to give a view of anything but sky, and the room was crowded with furniture: cabinets, Saga's desk, a clerk's desk—complete with clerk—and a computer table. Cramped and uncomfortable, it was at any rate an office, as opposed to the disorganized bullpen where Akamai and the other junior officers did their deskwork. Akamai was keenly aware, sitting there, that Saga was of Japanese extraction, as was Chief Nagato. Both of them were descendants of cane workers, peasants who had come to Hawaii to work their way out of debt. Meanwhile, George Akamai, descendent of the *ali'i,* the kings who once ruled the island, would need a miracle to attain the rank of police chief given the politics of the island. The prospect rankled him, though he knew that neither he, nor Barry, nor the Chief—all professionals without any racist animosities—could do anything about it. Native Hawaiians could hold many political offices, but the job of top cop went to someone of a race more closely associated with institutional discipline.

"How did this guy Chase strike you?" Saga asked.

Akamai shrugged. "I doubt he had anything to do with the killing itself. But I think this was more than just a rubout. The poor stiff that took it in the ear was a grunt in a bigger game."

"Yeah? But what kind of game?"

The clerk was a middle-aged Caucasian woman, pudgy and haughty. She stopped typing and pretended to search for something among the papers on her desk.

"Do you have an answer, Katherine?" Akamai asked without turning his head.

"Who, me? I'm just an administrative assistant," Katherine Robinson demurred.

Saga looked at her expectantly. For a second, she stared back, confused. She had said all she intended to say. Then she got the hint, grabbed some papers and stood up. "Excuse me," she muttered in a vaguely supercilious tone. "I have to take these over to the Chief's office."

"So—" Saga said when his clerk had disappeared.

"Either drugs or land," Akamai speculated.

"Land?"

"Tens of thousands of acres. Cane fields that reach the ocean in one direction and the mountains in the other. If the list that Chase guy gave me is, you know, the real thing and not a red herring, that's what it says to me. The Makai Ranch could be up for sale, and there may be a thug or two among the potential buyers. What scares me as much as the murders, Barry, there could be a lot more at stake than just the Makai Ranch. I mean, Makai Sugar is in serious financial trouble, but so are the other growers. I'm worried that Web Chamberlain has started something here that will affect the whole island."

"Chamberlain's a shrewd operator, George. Christ, he owns a tenth of Kauai, more or less, doesn't he? That sale should generate one hell of a retirement fund for him. At his age, why not cash out?"

"Shrewd as he is, he's not up to dealing with someone who would snuff out a life because of a real estate deal."

"And who would that be?"

"I don't have any idea. The corpse was discovered only last night."

"In other words," Saga said, "you want to talk to Chamberlain, then?"

"Yeah," Akamai conceded, "I'd like to talk to him." As teenagers, George Akamai and Nate Chamberlain, youngest son of sugar magnate Webster Chamberlain, had surfed Kauai's north shore, the Pipeline on Oahu, and Hawaii's other great surfing venues together. They were as close as brothers during that period, even though they lived on different islands, and Web Chamberlain was like a second father to Akamai, a father connected with the highest levels of financial and political power in the islands. The elder Chamberlain had been open and generous with his son's friend, an impoverished Hawaiian kid trying to figure out his place in Hawaii's polyglot society. The sugar king had encouraged Akamai to expand his horizons beyond the shores of the fiftieth state and had paid for his Dartmouth education. Although homesickness had driven him back to Hawaii, Akamai remained deeply grateful to his aging mentor.

Saga pursed his lips. What he was about to say was going to hurt his lieutenant. "I don't think you should talk to the guy, George. Not as a cop, I mean. You're too close to him."

"Too close? Why does that matter?"

Saga laid his hands open on the desktop. "See, George, that question just illustrates the problem. You're thinking about Chamberlain's safety, maybe about asking some questions, getting some leads."

"Right. So?"

"I'm thinking he might be a suspect."

Akamai sank back in his chair, deflated. The possibility that Web Chamberlain might be a suspect in the murder at the Pakala Inn rather than a potential target of the same murderer, had not occurred to him. "Wow," he sighed. "But Barry, you do it, please don't send anyone else. And get out there right away, will you?"

Saga's reply was interrupted by the sudden return of his clerk. "Captain," the woman said urgently, "the Chase woman is on the phone. She's screaming!"

Barry Saga pushed the speaker button. "This is Captain Saga," he announced in a tone he thought might be soothing to an hysterical woman.

Janet Chase was beyond being soothed. Alone in the Poipu house, oblivious to the graceful fluttering of palm, banana and papaya trees out the open glass doors and the splashes of tropical flowers brightening the margin of the back yard, she could barely hold the telephone. "My daughter Stella has been k-kidnapped! She's gone! Oh, God. Do something, captain. Dear God! I-I—"

"Janet, this is George Akamai." Though she heard his voice, Janet could not stop crying. "We're going to help you. Janet. Calm down!" Her words continued to tumble out, impelled by forces stronger than reason. "Calm down and talk to us, please," the policeman shouted. "Okay? Take a deep breath, will you? *Now, Janet!*"

Janet Chase subsided, but could not stop trembling. "Oh, George," she rasped, "what kind of a place is this? God help my poor Stella?"

"Mrs. Chase, this is a beautiful island, a friendly island," Barry Saga said firmly, "and we are going to help you find your daughter. Just tell us what happened, please."

"Well, c-captain," Janet replied in a quavering voice, "Stella and her sister and my husb—former husband, Andrew—uh, George has met him—went around to the other side of the island or wherever to do the cliff walk."

"You mean the Kalalau Trail? Na Pali coast?"

"Na Pali, yes, that's it. Um, they were well along, I guess, and—and Stella got a little ahead of the other two. A-and, well, she—she disappeared. Oh, gee—Jesus."

As she struggled to keep control of herself, she heard Saga tell Akamai to get some patrol cars, a chopper and an ambulance up to the trailhead. A chair scraped across the floor and Akamai's voice came hollow across the line. "I'm on my way up there, Janet."

"Mrs. Chase," Saga called out to Janet, whose breath was coming in little gasps. "Mrs. Chase, how do you know this has happened?"

"M-my husband—I mean, Andrew—called from somewhere, a restaurant, I think." It had in fact been the worst phone call of Janet's life, and doubtless of Andrew's as well. At some later time, they would both apologize profusely to one another for what they had said in their mutual hysteria.

"Your husband told you that your daughter had been kidnapped?"

"No, I guess I—he said that Stella had disappeared on the trail, and as we talked, we began to think—"

"I see. All right," Saga continued. "Is your husband reachable?"

"Y-yes. He's waiting by a pay phone." Janet's body was shivering with fright and distress. She felt small, vulnerable and empty.

"Good. I want you to call him back right now. I want you to tell him to return to the head of the Kalalau Trail."

"Kalau—?"

"Ka-la-lau Trail. Tell him to wait on the road, not to go up the trail. The police are on their way. Will you do that for me?"

"Y-yes, I'll call him right now."

"Okay. Now, listen to me, Mrs. Chase. I'm coming to pick you up, so after you talk to your husband, don't leave the house. I'm going to get you up north to where your family is. It will take me fifteen minutes to get there, all right? There's no place for a helicopter to land near your house, but I have a brief stop to make after I pick you up, and the chopper will meet us there."

"All right, captain. Thank you. Thank you." Janet began to compose herself. Andrew had panicked her. Facing the unknown, he and

Janet had worked themselves into a frightful, debilitating lather. Captain Saga was calm, authoritative, reassuring.

"Oh, captain, we're at 265 P-Puo—"

"I know where you are staying Mrs. Chase. I'll get there as fast as I can. And, ma'am?"

"Yes?"

"This is an island. A fairly small island. Kidnapping makes little sense here. Your daughter is more likely to have fallen into a gully and broken her leg than she is to have been kidnapped."

A few moments later Andrew Chase was standing dutifully at the trailhead. He was alone; Liz and Race had remained on the trail to search for Stella. As if in confirmation of his dark thoughts, the first official vehicle to reach him was an ambulance from the firehouse in Hanelei. The driver was Vietnamese. One paramedic was a dark Tongan man, the other a doe-eyed Hawaiian woman with skin the color of milk chocolate. All three looked to be in their twenties. Andrew wanted to know why they had come.

"Does this mean that she's been found?" he asked. "That she's hurt?"

"No, sir," the young woman said soothingly. "We're just here to stand by in case we're needed."

A police helicopter veered into view overhead and then disappeared around the steep hillside that marked the start of the cliff trail.

"Was the trail still wet?" the Tongan asked.

"In some places," Andrew said. "The sun had dried it out for the most part, but in the shady spots—Why? You think she may have slipped, don't you?"

The big fellow shrugged. "It happens, sir."

"Kona, don't scare the gentleman," the woman chided. She put a hand on Andrew Chase's forearm. It was a warm and energizing touch. "It's okay, sir. We'll find her. She's probably sitting on a rock above the trail somewhere, sunbathing."

The long-haired Hawaiian was comely, and her voice was light and liquid, but Andrew's mind was elsewhere. The prospect that Stella might have fallen down the mountain gave a new dimension to his fears. When he, Liz and Race had arrived at Hanakapi'ai Beach, the Chases' intended destination for the afternoon, and confirmed that Stella was nowhere on the broad, sandy crescent, nor in any of the caves that punctuated the lava cliffs beyond, Andrew had jumped to the natural conclusion that Stella's vanishing was connected with the murder the night before. Talking to Janet had only reinforced that assumption—the two of them frightening each other, Janet envisioning a dark conspiracy that would swallow up their family one at a time. If Stella had been swept off not by a kidnapper but by a misstep on the trail, the problem was entirely different, but the consequences could be just as dire.

Andrew Chase, confidante to CEOs, denizen of the corridors of power, deal maker extraordinaire, stepped away from the three people of color in whose hands his daughter's life might lie and stood helplessly waiting for a fourth, George Akamai.

At that moment, the lieutenant was a thousand feet above the surface of the Pacific in the jump seat of a police helicopter. Behind him sat a forest ranger named Cal Simpson.

"I have a theory," Akamai said into the microphone that extended from the headset he was wearing.

"Speak," Simpson said into his own microphone.

"I think she met somebody."

"Rape?"

"Rape, on the Kalalau Trail? At midday? Get real, Simpson. No, I think she met somebody she knew and took an unplanned detour."

"Where did this theory come from?"

Akamai shrugged. "Sixth sense."

"A detour, huh? Well, there's only one detour between the trailhead and Hanakapi'ai Beach."

"Right," Akamai responded. "Got that, Paolo?"

The Portuguese-American pilot snapped a nod at Akamai, and banked the craft toward the shoreline. Above the beach, the Hanakapi'ai Valley rose steeply, a sharp notch in the side of the ancient, quieted volcano that was the defining feature of the island. The detour that Akamai had in mind was a trail that followed the valley upward, ending after a mile or so of difficult climbing at a beautiful waterfall.

On the ground, Stella Chase heard the thrumming sound of the chopper's engine and blades. A shout from the nearby hillside rang in her ears. "Come, Stella!" Overhead, long, spiky leaves of pandanus trees rustled in the downdraft. There was a moment of uncertainty, a moment in which Stella held her breath, trying to hear the voice of God within her, impelling her one way or the other. The noise of the engine and rotors invaded her being, but still she didn't move, couldn't hear the inner voice. Then, over the roar from above, came a loud report, followed by another, and up the hill, a scream: "Guns!" Were they gunshots? There was so much noise from the helicopter—Stella couldn't be sure they weren't. It was so difficult to hear—

Finally, the voice came to her: *Go, Stella.* Bending down quickly, she pushed her finger into the soft, red mud at her feet, scooped up a daub of the pigmented clay and in two rapid strokes drew the stylized outline of a swan on a flat rock. She tossed the rock down onto the trail, then scrambled after the slender figure who was climbing furiously out of sight along the wild pig run.

The house at 265 Puuholo Street was a single-story white affair with board-and-batten siding and double sets of french doors at the front and back of the cavernous great room. It sat close to the road, partly obscured by a tall hedge. The modest front yard consisted mostly of flowers. Alone in the living room, Janet Chase slid off the sofa and onto the floor in tears, thinking about how, just three hours earlier, she had sat at the circular glass table in the same room with Andrew, Liz and Stella, debating what to do about their vacation.

"What did the police say, Andy, about our situation?" Janet had asked him.

"All they know at the moment, sweetheart, is that the dead man is apparently an Iranian Greek named Adibi."

"I don't care about the corpse's situation, Andy. What did they say about our situation?"

"Well, you see, Janet, I-I'm supposed to handle a client matter while I'm here. I-I didn't tell you before because—"

"—Because I'd think you were a cheapskate, piggybacking your family vacation on a business trip. Is your client paying for the rental house, Andy?"

"I didn't tell you because it's a highly confidential matter. It, uh, it involves real estate. Property that Paracorp wants me to bid on for them."

"Paracorp, Dad?" Liz echoed. Janet's eyes widened.

"Yes, honey. A-and the other companies listed on the paper the dead man was carrying could logically be bidders for the same property. So Paracorp could conceivably—and I emphasize the remoteness of the possibility—could be a target of whoever killed the man with the list."

"And you might be," Janet returned heatedly. "And Luc and Chantal might be, but they had the good sense to disappear. This clinches it. What did the police say, Andy, or do I have to call them myself?"

"Well, Lieutenant Akamai would agree with you about leaving, I suppose. But what do you expect? If we leave, we're four fewer *haoles* for him to worry about, whether we're really at risk or not. Now, as I told him, we don't know that the killing had anything to do with the land deal. I think the possibility is really, really remote. It looks more like a drug killing."

"You keep using that word, Andy. 'Remote.' I like the sound of it. 'Remote.' That's what I think we should be, remote from this island. I want us out of here today, on our way back to Connecticut, where we can spend the rest of our two weeks together in the family house with the dogs, the central station alarm system and an environment that we know."

Janet glanced at Liz and Stella, and saw that they were exchanging glances sufficient to communicate mutual ambivalence over her suggestion.

"I can't leave yet, even if I wanted to," Andrew insisted. "I have a negotiation to do."

"Dad," Liz interrupted, sensing a parental fight in the offing. "Tell us about the property. Maybe it will help us decide what to do."

Andrew Chase stared at his daughter. Her question had unintentionally struck at the one thing that was bothering him most about the Paracorp matter. "Well," he answered slowly, "normally I couldn't answer that question because of attorney-client privilege—"

"Oh come off it, Andy!" Janet exploded. "We're talking about life and death here, not professional niceties."

"Let me finish, please, Janet." Andrew was trying to maintain an even tone. "What I'm trying to say is that normally I couldn't tell you what I know for attorney-client reasons, but in this case I don't know anything. There's a large piece of land for sale on this part of the island, Paracorp is interested in buying it, and I'm supposed to meet with the seller, learn what his terms are and make an offer. That's it."

"Who is the seller, Dad?" Stella asked.

Andrew shrugged. "A guy who owns a sugar plantation. From what I gather, an upstanding member of the community here."

Janet turned to her daughters. "Are you girls as concerned as I am?"

Liz nodded. "We're uncomfortable, too, Mom. How could we not be? The memory of Adibi's blood sticking to my foot is still giving me goose bumps. Yet Kauai looks like such a beautiful place," she said, motioning toward the palm trees that stood at the boundary of the small yard, "and besides, we're in the middle of a mystery. Who killed Adibi? What happened to Chantal and Luc? I'd really like to stick around and find out."

A look of exasperation spread across Janet's face. "Why am I asking the family daredevil for advice?"

Stella weighed in. "Look out the window, Mom. Rolling mountains, puffy clouds floating by, a soft breeze. Listen to the birds, the sound of the ocean. Liz and I don't want some thug to deprive us of our two weeks here. On the other hand, now we're all painfully aware that even paradise can be fatal. It's not up to Liz and me to balance those things out. Whatever you guys decide is fine with us. I'd just like to say—well, that if we do stay, I-I don't think we should lull ourselves into believing that our encounter with Adibi is the end of the story for us."

"What do you mean by that, Stell?" Andrew demanded.

"I just have a feeling, I guess, that we'll be drawn further into the murder investigation, Dad."

"Why? We've given the police all the information we have."

Stella raised her arms in a sign of helplessness. "I can't explain it, Daddy. It's just one of those messages that I get, you know."

"From the Big Guy?" Andrew pointed toward the ceiling.

"Don't start with the sarcasm, Andy," Janet snapped.

"The Big Gal, Dad. Or the Big Emptiness. Whatever." Stella sighed.

"You don't need a guru to figure that out, Dad." Liz ventured. "The list—"

Andrew Chase drew himself up in his chair. In his eyes, resignation played against resolution. And won. "Okay, I'll tell you what. There's a flight back to New York tonight from Honolulu. To make it, you have to be on the eight-thirty from here. That gives us all afternoon to explore Kauai, and time enough for an early barbecue on the patio this evening. I have to stay for a few days, but I think you should all go back to Connecticut, or wherever else you want, and I'll join you there over the weekend."

Janet gave her ex-husband a long look. She recognized that he had been eagerly looking forward to this vacation, whether or not it was an appendage to his business trip, and that he was very disappointed to have to give it up. *It's not just that he's spent the money already,* she thought. *He really wanted us to be reunited for just a little while. Maybe he's beginning to realize what he's lost.* "Thank you, Andy. I—I'm sorry. I know this trip meant a lot to you. It just didn't turn out the way any of us expected, did it?" She touched his arm. He turned to her, unsure what the gesture meant, and saw her fingers curling over her palm as she drew her hand back against her chest. "It's okay, Janet. We can't unspoil the milk. Look, for this afternoon, I'm thinking about a hike along the north coast. Spectacular scenery, sunshine—guaranteed to make you feel better."

Janet demurred. "I don't think so, Andy. We just don't know what's waiting for us out there."

"Oh, caution is the watchword, I agree with that. But if there were anyone 'out there,' he'd be more likely to find us right here in the house than on some random trek. I think the hike would be safe, and it would give you all a chance to get a feel for Kauai." Janet glanced at her daughters. It was obvious that Andrew's proposal seemed reasonable to them.

"No, you three go," she said. "I'll shop for the barbecue and make reservations for our return. I wouldn't be very good company out there, I'm afraid." She sighed. "You know, if we leave you here tonight, we'll all be worried sick until you join us."

As Barry Saga ran the stoplights along Rice Street in Lihue and then swooped down the hill past the old sugar mill at the edge of town on his way to pick up Janet Chase, a gentlemanly looking figure stopped to admire the garden at 265 Puuholo Street. He was Cornelius Freeman, "C. B." to most who knew him on the island. Of moderate stature, Freeman had silvery hair and craggy features that echoed the great handsomeness he had enjoyed during youth. He was wearing a blue boxer-style bathing suit, a lime green polo shirt with the collar haphazardly raised in back, and sandals that looked like racing flip-flops. The publisher of the Kauai *Progressive*, a copy of which he had just pulled out of his delivery box on the way out the driveway, Freeman had recently bought a beachfront house nearby, and was ambling through the new neighborhood. While contemplating the decorative plantings, he heard a woman sobbing inside the open French doors. Stepping around the hedge, he saw a figure kneeling on chalkboard-grey floor tiles, head bowed, shoulders heaving. He knocked on the wall. The woman looked up. "Can I help you?" he called out.

"Who are you?" the woman said.

"My name is Freeman. I publish a newspaper on the island. See?" He unrolled the newspaper, turned to the editorial page and held up his thumbnail-sized likeness. "I live around the corner."

The woman rose.

"What's the trouble, ma'am?"

Janet Chase looked into a pair of grey-blue eyes. The face was tanned and wrinkled, chiselled as if by a sculptor wanting to express the idea of manhood persevering into old age. She did not like the fact that a newspaperman was seeing her at her wit's end, but on the other hand, kneeling on the floor and crying accomplished nothing, whereas telling her story to someone who knew the island might help her understand what could have happened to Stella.

"Why don't we sit down, Mr. Freeman?" she sighed, adding out of habit, "Would you like something to drink?"

Freeman shook his head, and they took their places at opposite ends of one of the pale, overstuffed sofas that faced each other across a white wicker coffee table. He listened attentively as Janet spun out her tale. When she was done, he sat silent for a moment, thinking.

"One of my reporters talked to you and others at the Pakala Inn briefly last night," he said. "She told me the next day that she thought there might be a bigger story here than met the eye. Sounds as though she was right." Janet stared at him coolly. This was not the time to be digging for a scoop.

"Forgive me," Freeman said, when he realized what was bothering her. "It's in my blood. I promise not to ask any questions. Let me give you my reaction to what you just said. In terms of your daughter, Mrs. Chase, I would agree with the police. The Na Pali coast trail, in particular, would be a surprising place for a kidnapping. Great place to hide someone after snatching her, for sure, but how would the kidnapper know when to expect the victim to wander by, or whether she would be alone? It's not a place where one goes every day like clockwork. The other thing is that the early part of the trail, where your family was, is pretty popular. People are hiking along in both directions most of the day."

Janet was unconvinced. "I hear what you're saying," she sighed, "and I'm grateful for that perspective, but my daughter is missing. We came here for a family reunion, and now my daughter is—"

She couldn't hold it together. Her shoulders began to heave again. "Oh, dear," she blurted out, angry at herself. "I'm sorry—"

Freeman slid across the cushions and put his arm around her, preparing to say something soothing.

Just then a presence moved through the open doorway. Dark jacket, revolver at the hip, a tall, trim and fit silhouette. Freeman removed his arm and sat back. "Hello, Captain," he said.

"Mr. Freeman." The chief of detectives nodded. "Will you excuse us, please?" As in many places, the relationship between the police and the press on Kauai—particularly *The Progressive*—was civil bordering on antagonistic. The newspaperman got to his feet as Saga stepped into the room.

"Thank you, sir," Saga said. He waited until the publisher was out of earshot before he addressed Janet. When he spoke, it was in a businesslike tone. "Mrs. Chase, I'm Barry Saga. I'd like you to get an article of your daughter's clothing, recently worn please, and come with me. One of my lieutenants will meet us with a helicopter, and take us up to the trailhead in Haena, where you will join your husband and your other daughter—"

"Former husband."

"Yes. You can wait with them up there until—well, until your daughter Stella comes walking back down the Kalalau Trail."

"The clothing is—for the dogs?"

"The dog. Singular. We have one sniffer dog, but he's very good at his job."

"Oh, captain. I'm so afraid for my daughter. After that murder, I just can't stop thinking—"

"I understand, Mrs. Chase. It's only natural. I can't tell you not to worry. But I can tell you we are doing everything within our power to find your daughter, and to find her quickly."

Janet smiled behind her tears. "Well, that's a substantial improvement over the time her older sister ran away from home. We were living in Paris at the time, and when we reported to the police that she hadn't come home from school, they said they wouldn't consider her missing until forty-eight hours had passed. So they did nothing for two days, and Andrew found her himself within that time by interrogating her friends."

"An effective cost-cutting strategy on the part of the French police, perhaps, but here we emphasize service and results. Please, fetch that shirt or whatever, and let's get you on your way."

When Janet returned from the back room, she was kneading a tie-dyed tee shirt in her hands nervously. Her legs wobbled, her breath caught. "Stella's kind of a—a hippie." She was losing it again. As Janet fell away from him, Saga shot his arms out, wrapped them around her lower back and clamped his right hand over his left wrist. Pushing up gently, he kept her on her feet. Her hands were squeezed against his chest. She felt the strength there, the power in the biceps and forearms that encircled her, the sureness in his bearing. *So different from Andy*, she thought. Andy, completely useless, as lost as she was, hadn't even called the police before calling her, had worried her not only about Stella's disappearance, but about his lack of ability to do anything about it. Barry Saga exuded confidence, strength, character, reliability. That was what Stella needed, what she herself needed at this moment.

"Ma'am, are you with me? Shall I sit you down for a moment?"

"No, no. I mean, I-I'm okay. Forgive me."

He loosed his arms and Janet stepped back, combing her mid-length hair back into place with her fingers.

"Then let's be on our way." The policeman slipped his hand around her waist, lest her legs buckle again. "Do you mind, ma'am?"

"No, captain. Not at all. Thank you."

4

Webster Chamberlain sat on the front porch of his up-country plantation house, surveying his demesne—sensuous hills and valleys as far as he could see, most of it carpeted with spiky, green-leafed sugar cane. The land rolled down from the central mount until it terminated in ten miles of undeveloped Hawaiian oceanfront.

In the distance below him, a cane fire that had been set by one of his crews before dawn was now a plume of dense smoke. A lone tractor worked the rubble, pushing it into heaps. Along the earthen roads that cut through the fields, large yellow trucks covered with the red grit that was the island's soil kicked up great clouds of dust as they hustled back and forth on their cane runs just beyond the range of his hearing. The drivers, Chamberlain knew, were bouncing hard against sprung seat cushions, permanently damaging their backs in the cause of the Makai Sugar Company. He couldn't afford to refit the cabs. He couldn't really afford the drivers, either. Land rich but cash poor, for the first time in his long tenure at the helm of Makai Sugar, Webster Chamberlain did not know how he was going to meet the payroll.

Two figures approached him along a walkway lined with low, flowering hedge. The man was a senior police officer. *Big guy, for a Jap,* he said to himself. The man had attended the luau he had held for police officers and their families at one of the plantation's beaches a few weeks ago. That evening, Chamberlain had been concentrating on the chief, from whom he needed a favor, and he hadn't paid much attention to anyone else. He couldn't recall this fellow's name, and was slightly annoyed at the fact that the man had appeared without asking for leave in advance. The ranch was not in need of police assistance today.

Behind the policeman, a woman walked unsteadily, seemingly in a state of complete dejection. He had never seen her before. He stood up, feeling the ancient works that moved his body groan under the weight of the good life. Near the edge of the porch he stopped, and watched the police captain mount the last step.

"Good afternoon, sir. I'm Barry Saga."

"Yes, um, Captain Saga, isn't it? And you are—?"

"Janet Chase," the woman answered softly. She seemed very ill at ease.

"Hmm. Chase, is it?"

"Mrs. Chase and her family are visiting Kauai from the mainland, sir. One of her daughters found that corpse at the Pakala Inn last night—I'm sure you heard about it. And we've just learned that her other daughter has gone missing up on the Kalalau Trail."

Chamberlain didn't move, didn't invite the visitors to sit down. He had no idea why these people had come, and wanted to be rid of them as quickly as possible. "I'm so sorry, my dear," he intoned. "But you know, the Kauai police are quite good at finding lost tourists. Lots of experience in that department, eh, Captain? I'm sure they'll solve the problem in short order."

"I took the liberty of bringing Mrs. Chase here so a police helicopter could meet us and take us up to Haena," Saga explained. "I'm sorry for showing up unannounced, but I wanted to talk to you and was afraid that if I called first you'd tell me to make an appointment with the office—you have that reputation, you know—and it's a matter of your personal safety that I need to discuss with you."

"I appreciate your solicitude, Captain. You're right, I'm not receptive to unscheduled visits, from law enforcement or anyone else. Over the years, I've found that they usually have some unpleasant import."

"Believe me, Mr. Chamberlain, I'm not here to bring bad news, or even ask for a contribution for the PBA. I'm only concerned about your welfare. What is that, sir?"

There had been a noise in the house, and Chamberlain had jerked his head around. "Nothing, Captain, nothing. Perhaps we should go somewhere where we can discuss this in private." Chamberlain motioned Saga and Janet back down the stairs.

"This comes out of our investigation of that murder at the Pakala Inn, Mr. Chamberlain," Saga said as he descended.

The screen door opened behind them. "Not now, please," Chamberlain said loudly without looking back, as if speaking to a servant. He gripped Saga's arm and led him onward. Saga glanced over his shoulder anyway, in time to see a figure turning back toward the entrance hall. "That's your son Nate, isn't it?" he asked. "I hadn't heard that he was back on the island." George Akamai hadn't said anything to Saga about Nate having returned, and in normal circumstances, the younger Chamberlain would have phoned Akamai well before leaving Oregon to come home.

"Nate," Chamberlain said with a laugh. "Naw, Captain. That was one of my household staff. I thought it better that we not discuss what sounded as though it might be a delicate matter back there where the walls have ears." He led Saga and Janet along a path that traversed the side porches of the manor. Peacocks, some pure white and some in shimmering blues and greens, pecked their way quietly across the lawn. The planter waved a hand in their direction.

"Funny. I hated the goddamn things while my wife was alive," he confided. "Now that she's dead, I love them as much as she did."

Saga nodded. "It's not easy to lose a spouse, is it, sir?"

"Not the ones you like, no. I've had three of 'em, liked the last one best. She was thirty-five when we were married, and I was just on the downhill side of forty, so both of us had kind of grown up by then. It was a real nice relationship. Ah, well." The sugar planter glanced at the police officer. "'He who binds to himself a joy,'" he pronounced, "'doth the winged life destroy; but he who kisses the joy as it flies lives in Eternity's sunrise.' Blake, Captain. You married?"

"I was. My wife died last year."

"Sudden?"

"Cancer."

"Damn shame. Kids?"

"Yes, sir. Two boys."

"Mmm. Why don't you cut the formalities, Captain, and call me Web. And your first name again?"

"Barry."

They had stopped in front of a large reflecting pool. A sculpture of a nude *wahine* stood at the far end, her long hair flowing over her left shoulder and down between her breasts. From an outsized, upended lobelia flower held in her arms, water fell into the black-tiled pool. "Who takes care of your kids while you're down at Umi Street, Barry?"

Umi Street was the address of the mustard-colored headquarters of the Kauai County police department. Was Chamberlain really interested, or was he just jockeying for some kind of psychological advantage? Saga looked at Janet to see how she was taking the conversation, but she seemed lost in her own thoughts. He gave Chamberlain a straight answer. "Either my parents, or my wife's—my late wife's parents. Why?"

The older man put a hand on Saga's shoulder as they walked. "Oh, you know, our life was this plantation and the mill, Nate's mother's and mine, from early morning to well after dark, for years and years. Our kid was brought up by other people, even though we were only down there at the office most days. I found that very hard, and, I'm sure you're aware, not particularly successful. Well, enough small talk, Barry," Chamberlain announced, as though he had been monitoring an internal civility meter. "What do you want to say to me?"

"Sir—Web, the Pakala Inn victim had a list on his person when he died. A list of companies we believe are interested in buying the Makai Ranch." Saga stopped walking and turned to face Chamberlain, who, hand still on the policeman's shoulder, was almost nose to nose with him, and stony-faced as the granite *wahine* they had just passed.

"Oh my, Barry!" Chamberlain murmured, glancing warily at Janet. "I hope you are not going to spread this around."

"Spread it around?"

"I mean, I know certain people down at the county building have encountered foreign—um, representatives of foreign interests researching the Ranch; but I wouldn't want it being kicked around the island that I was selling out, or even interested in doing so. You understand, Barry."

"I have no reason to broadcast this, Web."

"Mrs. Chase?"

Janet raised her arms helplessly.

"Thank you both. There'd be such agitation." Chamberlain made small gesticulations with both hands. "But what—"

The sugar king stopped in mid-sentence. A car was coming up the long driveway at high speed, throwing an umbra of red dust up behind it.

"Are you expecting anyone, Web?" Saga asked. Chamberlain, squinting at the careening vehicle, shook his head.

Without warning, Saga tackled the old man and Janet, knocking them both into a low irrigation trench and falling on top of them. As they hit the mud, they heard automatic pistol fire from the driveway. The policeman's service revolver was quickly in his hand and, without raising his head above the trench, he began shooting back in the direction of the noise. From the sound of it, the car did not even stop, but rather spun around the reception circle and sped away again, weapons firing harmlessly into the sugar cane.

Barry Saga lifted himself off the shaken land baron and the terrified woman and helped them to their feet. Muck the color of sunburnt skin clung to their clothing.

"A 'beautiful—friendly—island,' you said, captain," Janet Chase quavered as she tried vainly to brush the mud off her chest.

"Well, I—uh—" Chamberlain stammered. "I thank you, captain—uh, Barry. How, um—how did you know that—?" Again, the little gesticulations, his hands quivering like Janet's.

"I didn't know, Web, sir. But I came to warn you that there might be some violence up here." It served Saga's purpose to suggest that Chamberlain was the shooters' target, but he wondered for which of the three of them the show of force was intended.

"But why would anyone want to kill me?"

"Actually, considering what those *lolos* just did, racing in here, shooting the place up and racing out again, I think it's likely they wanted to scare you, rather than kill you. Can we sit and talk about this for a couple of minutes?"

Chamberlain motioned to a nearby gazebo furnished with padded lawn chairs.

"Are you okay, Mrs. Chase?" Saga asked before taking a step. She stared at him.

"I haven't been shot, if that's what you mean. But I've never been this frightened before in my life, between—"

Saga put his arm around her shoulder. As they walked toward the gazebo, a current of air came up from the ocean across the plantation. They could see it drawing a path through the cane, like the finger of God, the stalks bending, rustling madly and then straightening as it passed. It wafted over them, tousling their hair, fussing at their garments. All along the horizon, well out on the ocean, an endless bank of clouds moved slowly from east to west. Underneath it, a strip of darkness lay on the water. *Rain.*

"When I look around me here, Barry and—" Chamberlain glanced at Janet, the confusion in his eyes indicating that he could not remember if he had been told her given name.

"Janet," she said with a wan smile.

"Barry and Janet. When I look around me, do you know what I see?"

"A big business, Web. Huge."

"I see a millstone the size of Manhattan Island, that's what I see. I feel it around my neck, pulling me down, down, inexorably down. Those cowboys back there would have been doing me a favor by shooting me."

Saga gave the old planter a long look. "How can that be? After all these years, the business pretty much runs itself, doesn't it?"

"Yeah. Into the ground. There's no money in sugar any more, Barry. Not on this island, anyway. The world market is awash in the stuff. Prices are so low it's laughable. Corn syrup is even cheaper. And production costs! Forget it. Forget it!" He waved his hands, then slapped them against his knees. "I used to grow a lot of pineapple. The Philippines took that business away years ago. Now I just keep a little plot for the tourists. Cane is going the same way."

"I see you're experimenting with coffee down below."

"Coffee, macadamia. So far, it's cost me more to try out new crops than I ever see getting back."

"So you're in trouble."

"Big trouble. People think of me as a wealthy man, and of course they're right in a way. I do own a fair chunk of this rock. But as a business, Makai Sugar is going broke."

Saga blushed at a thought. "I should have said earlier, Web. Mrs. Chase's former husband is representing one of the companies interested in bidding—"

"Yes, yes. I'm meeting him tomorrow, Barry. Don't worry. I'm sure he's done his homework and knows even more about my situation than I've told you and Janet."

Saga looked out to sea. The storm was moving closer.

"Why don't you do what everybody else does? Develop it?"

"I tried that, down between Highway 50 and the ocean. It taught me two things. First, one needs up-front money to do it in a big way, which I haven't got without selling land; and that I won't to do just to be a builder. Second, I'm not a developer. It kills me to tear out the growing things—'the force that through the green fuse drives the flower,' you know—and erect dead edifices."

"You're selling out altogether, then?"

Chamberlain covered his face with both hands for a moment, breathed deeply, then put his hands back in his lap. "There are half a dozen companies interested in buying the whole thing," he answered flatly.

"Is that why Nate's back?"

The two men stared at one another. The question brought Janet out of her funk. Hadn't Chamberlain already denied that his son was here? She looked at the two men. Saga's eyes displayed unwavering determination, a penetrating inquisitiveness, the single-mindedness of a man driven to excel in his work by forces he didn't bother analyzing. In Chamberlain's eyes, defeat struggled to cloak itself in past attainment and failed.

"Nate's in Oregon, Barry. We don't speak any more."

"Mmm. The problems between the two of you are legendary, Web. What can you tell me about the potential buyers for the Ranch?"

Chamberlain shrugged. “I don’t know anything yet. I’m meeting representatives of a couple of them this week.”

“Andrew Chase, of course. And Mr. Song of ROC Overseas, I think.”

Chamberlain leaned back in his seat and folded his arms. “Captain, you amaze me.”

Saga smiled and shook his head. “Just doing my job, Web.”

“Yes. Chase followed by Song. But other than those meetings, everything’s being handled by a realtor in Oahu.”

“Named—?”

“Low. Li-Ann Low. Paradise and Commerce Realty in Honolulu. I’ve never met her. She works with my lawyer. You want his name? Carter Robinson of Robinson, Chung, Kitashiro and Guerrero, also in Honolulu.”

“Do you have any idea what’s going on? The murder. The shoot-’em-up out here. Mrs. Chase’s daughter. Can you help us?”

Chamberlain looked straight at Saga and shook his head. “I’m at a complete and utter loss, Barry.”

Saga stared out at the line of clouds closing in on the south shore. He could see the surface of the ocean roiling in the pelting rain that fell from them. The search for the Chase girl would become a messy exercise once the showers began in earnest. “I doubt your lawyer would tell us any more than you have, Web, but we’ll talk to Ms. Low.”

A blue police helicopter appeared over the ridge to the east, flooding the yard with its sound. He stood up. “I’m afraid we have to be going. If you’d like to give us any more information, or if you feel the need for greater security, give me a call.”

“Why do I sense that you think I’ve been less than forthcoming, Barry?”

“Because that is what I think. No offense, Web. It’s natural, with such a sensitive matter, to try to keep the details hidden. I didn’t come out here to give you the third degree. Not yet, anyway. But that charade with the automatic weapons just now should have told you something. We’re at the front end of a murder investigation here, and your property and even your person seem to be implicated. If you are an innocent bystander, the police are your best friends right now, because we’re going to turn over every stone on this island until we find the killer. Just think about what you can tell us, okay?”

An hour and a half later, Janet Chase sat with her husband and eldest daughter at a table in Charo’s restaurant on the north shore.

Rain thrummed on the roof and plunged into the sand and sea outside the open window.

"This is supposed to go on until late tonight," Andrew said resignedly. "Which means the search is over until tomorrow morning."

"I can't stand it," Janet said through her teeth. "Not knowing, not being in charge. It's just horrible."

"She disappeared so quickly," Liz puzzled. "Between the time that we stopped to look at the *awapuhi* plants and the time that we met Race on the trail couldn't have been more than ten minutes."

Janet shuddered involuntarily. "In less than a day, Liz finds a corpse in her bedroom, Stella vanishes and I'm thrown into a ditch to protect me from being shot. Even you can see that bad things are happening to this family, Andy. We need to find Stella and get out of here."

Andrew rubbed the back of his fingers against her arm, which she promptly pulled away. "Okay, let's think where Stella could be," he suggested after a pause. "Put to one side the worst possibilities. Let's say she didn't fall off the trail. She wasn't pushed off. She wasn't kidnapped. I mean, if any of those things happened—well, things would be out of our hands."

Janet shook her head furiously. "Wrong, Andy. You said it yourself. We have to take control of our family's situation, goddammit." Her eyes flashed with conviction.

"Okay, okay. I didn't mean otherwise. Let's just suppose that none of those things happened, all right? What else would explain Stella's disappearance?"

The three of them stared at one another blankly for a moment. "Well, she could have achieved Nirvana and turned into pure energy," Liz offered at length.

Andrew Chase looked at his daughter. "I can't believe you said that. This is neither the time nor the place for jokes."

"As I told you earlier, Dad, I don't think Stell's a victim of foul play at all. I think she's hiding."

Janet's gaze met her eldest daughter's. "We'd all love to believe that, Liz, but do you have any evidence? Maybe you're just in denial."

"I—" Liz hesitated. She had seen something on the trail, something she hadn't seen for fifteen years, but she was not sure whether she should tell her parents about it or not.

At that instant, George Akamai walked in the door, wearing a slicker with rainwater sliding off of it onto Charo's planked floor. He was carrying a transparent plastic bag containing what appeared to be a single, heavy item. Liz sighed, partly in relief, partly in distress. The policeman was about to save her the trouble of deciding how to answer her mother's question, which was a relief; but he was also about to press her, she realized, to explain something that Stella wanted kept secret.

"Where are we, Lieutenant?" Andrew demanded as Akamai walked over to the table.

"Nowhere yet, Andy. We can't do anything substantial in the pouring rain."

"You mean poor Stella has to stay out in this deluge all night?" Janet asked.

"Ma'am, with a little effort, she can find places to keep just as dry out on the pali as we are in here. I'm sure she'll be fine."

"I'm so glad that others have got such great insights into Stella's welfare, even though they have no idea where she is, or what shape she's in," Janet said with a reproving glance, which she shot at Liz as well.

Akamai sat down. "Let me show you what I found on the trail," he said. He held up the plastic bag. Inside it was a dome-shaped red rock about six inches in diameter. He turned the bag until the flattish side of the rock was facing them. On its surface was the simple line drawing that Liz had spotted before it started raining, when she was showing Akamai where she and her father had lost sight of Stella. Though she thought she had kicked the stone into the underbrush so that Akamai would not see the glyph, he'd found it anyway. Had he seen her trying to hide it?

"This was sitting near the place where Stella was last seen. Does the artwork mean anything to anyone?"

It was a simple combination of curved and angular lines. "It looks like a bird," Janet offered. "That's all it means to me."

"Anyone else?"

Andrew Chase shook his head sadly. "Are you reduced to grasping at straws already?" he inquired, disheartened.

"Maybe I should put this in perspective for you, Andy." Akamai wet the tip of his finger on his slicker and drew a damp line on the table-top. "This is the Kalalau Trail. Eleven miles of hills and switchbacks along the Na Pali coast. Here," he drew a vertical line about a quarter of the way down the trail, "is the trail going up from the beach where you looked for Stella today to Hanakapi'ai Falls. Stella disappeared a little ahead of this intersection, maybe a couple of minutes walking time, right, Liz?" He traced another line about the same distance from the other end of the trail. "Here is the next place where Stella could have turned off the main trail, at Hanakoa, two and a half hours further along. Now, this rock here was sitting near the first intersection. It could be that Stella dropped it there and kept on walking toward Hanakoa. Or it could be that she left it as a signal that she was going inland at that point. Or maybe this wasn't done by Stella at all. That's why I asked whether it means anything to you. What about you, Liz? Take a good look."

She did. It was a swan. Its head, neck and chest were made by deforming the letter "S", and its wing and upper back were made by rotating the letter "Z". Stella and Liz. A coded symbol that the younger Chase girl had developed at age six, for signalling to her sister that a secret needed to be shared. Maybe Akamai had deconstructed the symbol already; maybe he hadn't.

Liz shrugged. "It's a bird."

Akamai gave her a hard look. "Right. Did Stella draw it?"

"It's possible."

"Mmm-hmm. Well, if Stella did draw this, and let's say she left it for someone to find—maybe you, Liz—what would it mean?" Liz shook her head slowly.

"I can't really say, George," she replied with finality.

Akamai stared at her. "Okay," he sighed at last. "A dry hole, I guess." He stood up. "The weather should clear tonight. If it does we'll be out here before sunrise with a full-scale search. Meantime, we'll need to get a sketch posted around the island and with the authorities on the other islands. Who can help us with that."

"Liz is the artist in the family."

"Fine. Come with me, please."

"We'll all come," Andrew decided for the others. "Then we'll go back to the house. That way you can reach us easily if something comes up this evening." He and Liz stood up. Janet remained seated. "Janet? Let's go." Janet hugged her body tightly with her arms. "I'm not going anywhere. My daughter is up here, and this is where I'm staying until we find her."

"But where will you sleep, sweetheart?"

"Don't 'sweetheart' me, Andy. You want to get back to the house because that's where your partners and your clients can reach you. That's fine, go ahead. As for sleep, I couldn't do that no matter where I was. If the police are leaving the trailhead for the day, then that's where I'm going to take up vigil until they return."

"Janet, she could come out at the other end of the trail. Couldn't she, lieutenant?"

"Not really, Andy. The trail just sort of ends at Kalalau Beach. If she gets that far, which would be next to impossible under current conditions, we'll find her there tomorrow and take her out either by boat or by chopper."

Andrew tried again. "Listen, Janet, if Stella has in fact been kidnapped, you should definitely not stay up here alone."

Akamai put a hand to his badge. "We're not all leaving, Andy. There will be a patrol car stationed near the trailhead all night."

The lawyer shot him an exasperated look. "Give us a minute, will you?"

"That's fine. I've got Captain Saga in the car. We'll be waiting."

"Look, Janet," Andrew said after Akamai was gone. "What's the point of—"

"—There is no point, Andy. It's completely irrational, okay? I'm just not leaving Stella up here alone. Period."

"Mom," Liz interjected, and then hesitated, biting her lip while she struggled with herself. "That rock. The picture was made by Stella, okay? I've seen the swan sign a thousand times before. She's all right."

"What?" Andrew roared. "Liz, what is this penchant for suppressing evidence? Why didn't you tell the cop?"

"Because Stella's fine, and I think she wants to be left alone for now."

"How do you know she's all right, Liz?" Janet demanded.

"Because if there were any kind of problem, the swan would be shedding tears. That was the code."

Janet rocked back in her chair and folded her arms around herself again. "I'm not persuaded. Maybe she didn't have time to draw tears on the stupid rock."

"I can't tell you not to worry, Mom. But I'm sure that, at least when she drew that swan, Stella was telling me that she was cutting out for a while, but that there was no problem."

Andrew and Liz walked out to the police cruiser and went back to Lihue with George Akamai, leaving Andrew's car behind for Janet. Barry Saga, who lived on the beach in Haena not far from the trailhead, came into the restaurant.

"I'll stay with you, ma'am" he said. "Here's what I propose. We go back to Hanalei and pick up some food. My kids are with my parents, and I'll call and arrange for them to stay overnight. Then we'll go down to the trailhead and wait. Pizza okay?"

"I'm not hungry, thanks."

"Pizza, then. Let's go."

5

The north shore road ended at Ke'e Beach. On sunny days, Ke'e is a lovely crescent of tawny sand crouched below an upsweeping ridge line. A reef creates a safe swimming area in summer, providing a haven for sea creatures and a place of constant diversion for snorkelers. The sea within the arms of the reef captures the color of the sky and warps it toward pale green. In the rain, though, Ke'e Beach is less than lovely. The sky and water turn gray, the sand darkens, the trees become somber; nothing in nature draws the eye, and one notices instead the little blockhouse restrooms and the flooded ruts in the parking lot.

The scene fit Janet's mood. Consumed by Stella's disappearance, she had declined to drive Barry Saga back to Hanalei, and instead dropped him at his house in Haena on her way to the trailhead. When she reached the end of the road, she sat in the rented convertible on the road outside the parking area, listening to raindrops pop frenetically against the vinyl roof of the convertible and staring through the windshield at the yellow sign that marked the start of the Kalalau Trail. As water streamed down the windshield, the sign seemed to contort, split and reassemble itself. The forested hill behind it danced grotesquely, as did the patrol car tucked into the recesses of the parking lot. Though the storm had cooled the air a little, the temperature remained close to eighty, and with the humidity, the atmosphere in the car was oppressive. She cracked both front windows slightly to create some circulation, but with the circulation came rain, and both she and the cloth-covered seats of the convertible were getting wet.

Alone with her torments, she tried to banish them by playing Andy's game—assuming that Liz was right, that Stella had in effect run away, and then trying to figure out what might have caused her usually considerate daughter to do such a thing. For a while, nothing at all occurred to her. As best she knew, Stella loved her family and would not intentionally do anything to hurt the rest of them. The murder must have been as unsettling to Stella as it had been to Janet herself, and to Liz, but Stella had always been a paragon of emotional stability, not one to be set adrift by the demise of a stranger, gruesome though the sight of it was.

Then again, Janet couldn't put herself in Stella's shoes anymore. Her younger daughter marched to the beat of a drum no one else could hear. Maybe when he drove her down to Koloa Town, Lieutenant Akamai had said something that propelled her into hiding. She did, after all, smoke a joint with those French kids—but no, surely George would not make an issue of that when he had a homicide on his hands. Maybe it was Andy. Maybe he had offended her somehow when they went off to get the rental car, or on the trail. It was certainly possible. Andy had turned into a real grouch since the divorce, not just with herself but with the kids, too. Janet sighed. The trouble was that, compared to the ominous scenarios crowding her mind, the benign scenarios evoked by the swan sign lacked compulsion.

"George thinks it's the French couple."

Saga's voice startled her. He was standing outside her window, holding an umbrella. "Let's sit in my car," he added, glancing down at Janet's rain-spotted sundress. "It has cowls over the windows so we can open them without getting wet. It's got a police radio, too."

And it had a large cheese pie from Pizza Hanalei that filled the interior of the Land Rover with the smell of Italianate earthiness. The trinity: garlic, cheese and tomato. A whiff of fresh-baked crust. Even one too frightened to be hungry might be induced to have just one slice.

"You said George thinks Stella's being—what?—held captive by those French kids?" Janet asked after she had swallowed the first bite.

"Not held captive. Just that she's with them."

"Where did he get that idea?"

Saga shrugged. "You and I would call it a hunch, that's all. It's not illogical, in the sense that she'd met them, she liked them, they probably need help right now and the longer—" Saga paused.

"The longer what, Barry?"

"Well, the more time that passes without a ransom call, the less likely it is that your daughter's been abducted. So it's not illogical. But George puts it more strongly. He says it's probable that Stella's with Luc and Chantal. He—well, ma'am, there are many pure blood Hawaiians who see these islands and everything on them through very special eyes. Not being one of them, I'm not sure I can describe it well, but there is, to these folks, a connectedness among all things here—a spirit world that moves through our world and gives meaning to events and material things that seem unexplainable to the rest of us. George is connected to that other world."

"A *kahuna*, isn't that the word?"

"Yes, George Akamai is a *kahuna.* And actually, it makes him a damn good cop."

"No—but Barry! The murder, her father's name on that infernal list, Luc and Chantal missing. We were so on edge. Stella wouldn't just drop out of sight on us, for God's sake."

Saga folded a slice of pizza lengthwise with one hand and bit the end off it. He looked out the driver's window as he chewed. After a moment, he pulled a bottle of mineral water out of the Pizza Hanalei bag, twisted the top off and took a drink. Then he looked at Janet again. "You know her, and I don't," he said at last, "but I've got to tell you that 'on edge' doesn't sound like the young woman George Akamai described to me today. He said she was as calm as a summer lake at sunrise."

"Well, yes, she—she has acquired an inner peace somehow. God knows how, since neither of her parents have it. But even so—"

"I said it was just George's gut feeling. We're not going to change the search because of it, don't worry. I just thought I'd tell you, because it might ease your mind a little."

Janet nodded, her hands pressed over her heart, her gaze drilling deep into Saga's. "Okay," she sighed. "Then you'd better tell me more."

"Akamai thinks that the French kids went up to the Na Pali to hide out. That area has been a refuge for outlaws and renegades for centuries because the terrain makes searching so difficult. Luc and Chantal could have found themselves a hideout overlooking the trail so they could see who was coming and going. Cops, people they'd met here, whatever. This afternoon—bingo! Stella appears. Whoever was on sentry duty scrambles down and calls her into the bush. Stella then—for some reason— decides to go with them." Janet Chase shook her head.

"Without telling her father? I don't think so. I mean, Andrew was right there, just a few minutes behind her."

Saga cocked his head toward Janet. "Your daughter's not a child anymore. She lives three thousand miles away from you. She comes and goes every day without reporting to her parents." Janet put her hands over her eyes, feeling another crying spell coming on. She fought off the emotional wave, moved her hands over her temples and drew her hair back with her fingers.

"We were going to leave tonight," she said darkly. Saga blew a breath out through half-pursed lips.

"Back to the mainland?"

"Mmm-hmm. Andrew thought—Well, to be fair, in the end we all agreed, I guess, that it would be okay to show the girls a bit of the island before we left. Assuming that Stella—" Her voice broke, but she caught herself again. "—Assuming that Stella shows up in the morning, the girls and I will be gone tomorrow."

"And Andrew's staying behind because of Paracorp? Well, I can't say it's a bad idea for you to leave."

Janet Chase laughed nervously. "Can you say it's a good idea?"

Saga smiled. "I guess I can't say for sure one way or the other, yet. Under the circumstances, I think you all have to do what feels right to you. Tell me about Stella, would you? Give me her whole life history," he urged. "It's going to be a long night."

Janet nodded, and started in. She didn't know whether Saga had made the suggestion for therapeutic or investigative reasons, but no matter, it felt good to talk. They talked about the youngest Chase until the subject exhausted itself; then about Saga's boys, and then about Saga's wife, Riko. "Short for Noriko. She was a sculptor. A very good one. Her works could seem so real and at the same time so fanciful."

"She was a professional artist, then."

"Yes, very much so. Her work was shown all over the world. Not so much here; it wasn't tourist stuff. Present company excluded, of course; I'm sure you'd appreciate it."

"Do you still have any pieces?"

Saga passed a hand over his forehead before answering. "Yes. There are some pieces that I'll never part with. Pieces that, when I look at them, I can remember her hands moving over their surfaces, her arms swinging her tools so confidently, so—lovingly, really." Hearing the faintest shudder in his voice, Janet looked at him apologetically.

"I—I shouldn't be asking—" she murmured.

"It's okay. In fact, I like to talk about her. Keeps her alive in a way, you know?"

Oh, God, Janet thought. *This man is so real. If Andy had the same mix of presence and authenticity, we'd probably still be married.* "Maybe you'd let my daughters and me see her work one day this week? Once Stella is—"

"I'll be amazed if she doesn't turn up by tomorrow afternoon, Jan. Is it Jan, or Janet?"

"Jan," Janet replied matter-of-factly, not certain why she had done so. She had been "Janet" all her life.

"So you can all come over any evening after that." He looked at her thoughtfully in the waning grey light. "I guess in a way you lost a spouse, too, Jan."

"Oh, but that was so different, Barry. I was trying to lose him."

Suddenly, the sun, now low in the sky in front of them, burst through the heavy clouds as rain continued to pour over the vehicle. Saga looked into the rear-view mirror. "Look at that," he said, pointing behind him as he turned on the rear wiper blade. Janet swivelled in her seat. In the distance down the road behind them, a double rainbow had formed; one brilliant, the other a faint echo above it. Beneath the arcs, the landscape was a revel of leaves tinted yellow-green in the instant of evening light. She had just enough time to take in the spectacle and say, "Oh, how beautiful!" before the clouds swallowed the sun again.

"May I ask why?"

"Why the rainbows were beautiful?"

Saga laughed. "No, why you divorced your husband."

"Oh." Janet smiled weakly. She looked down at her hands. "Well, Andy loves his work. He loves his station in life. He loves his house and his sports car. In a funny way, he loves his kids, I guess, though I'm not sure they can tell. And I certainly couldn't tell if he loved me. We had a fairly distant relationship toward the end. I mean, w-we went through the motions of being married, but—"

"—Was there another woman?

"There were other women. Not affairs, Andy's probably incapable of that; just a series of one-night stands on his trips to the Far East. He justified them in his own mind as being done to maintain client goodwill with this lascivious guy who's the head of Paracorp. Not something he was doing out of lust at all. Can you imagine? When I think about it, I get so—" Janet slammed her hands against the dashboard, and caught her breath. Saga sat motionless, silent, letting her control the moment. "But that wasn't the real problem. We probably could have gotten over that, because I was such a spineless wonder at the time. The real problem with our marriage was that he had just stopped trying and, you know, you can't sustain a marriage without trying."

"So it was really an irreparable situation?"

"Irreparable. Um, I'm not sure that's the—well, here's the way I'd say it. It was like when your old TV set stops working. You could repair it, perhaps, but at a certain point, it's really not worth what it would cost to fix it."

Wild pigs can climb mountains. Not only can they climb up, but they can then climb down the other side. When they do this, they care little for preserving the underbrush through which they snuffle, scrape and charge, and so, as one pig blazes a trail, and later pigs follow the path of least resistance, they create a run wide enough, though perhaps less than comfortably tall, for larger beings—such as humans—to use. The feral pig, descendant of domesticated ancestors brought to Hawaii by the Polynesians, its bloodline heavily corrupted by liaisons with escaped porcines imported by immigrants from other parts of the world, had made a happy home for itself on Kauai. And so it was that, although the trail to Hanakapi'ai Falls dead-ended at that spectacular chute of water, forcing the climber eventually to return to the Kalalau Trail, the same cannot be said for the pig run up which, and then down the other side of which, Luc, Chantal and Stella had clambered that morning.

It was muddy, steep and slippery most of the way, and downright dangerous at times, but after three hours, the climbers had abandoned the sweeping ocean view that had been at their backs, skittered their way down the other side of the ridge and were well along in the valley called Limahuli, downstream of the eight-hundred foot falls also called Limahuli, and following the stream bed that led from the falls northward toward the tortuous two-lane road known as Highway 560.

Along the little-used valley trail, the Limahuli Stream flowed past them in spiritless summer languor toward Ha'ena and the sea. The overgrown trace shadowed the creek, sometimes close to the bank, sometimes at a distance. Rain forest loomed above them on either side. Clouds soon moved in overhead, bringing welcome relief from the heat. Birds twittered and chirped through the leafy valley, their high-pitched happiness floating above the steady, mellow gurgling of the watercourse. The three spoke French, just a native tongue to Chantal and Luc, but a luxurious treat for Stella. The conversation was truly Gallic. They were talking about bullets and metaphysics.

"But you don't know whether what we heard was gunfire," Stella was saying, "and if it was, whether someone was shooting at you or at a wild boar."

"True, no one knows," Luc replied. "But we took precautions, nonetheless."

"Someone knows," Chantal interjected.

"Who, the shootist?"

"God," Stella offered.

Chantal nodded. "Yes, the universal mind that is all and therefore knows all."

"But then, in your conception, is this cosmic consciousness that knows whether someone was shooting at us the sum of all human intelligence, including the shootist?" Luc asked, "or is it the consciousness of a superior being?"

"Yes," Stella answered.

"You see, Luc, those are not separate concepts," Chantal concurred. "It is known that a colony of ants has a collective intelligence greater than the intelligence of all the individual ants. In the same way, the cosmic consciousness may be a superior consciousness that is the collective sum of the consciousness of all humanity."

"Well," Stella said. "I think of it more along the following lines: human consciousness is a part of the cosmic consciousness, but not all of it."

"Frankly, I think it's obvious that the collective consciousness of the human race is inferior to individual consciousness, not superior. But tell me, Stella, what's the rest of the cosmic consciousness made up of, in your conception?" Luc wondered.

"The rest of what makes the cosmic consciousness is God."

Chantal shook her head in disagreement. "I think not."

"But either way," the young man persisted, "when I pray that whoever shot at us has fallen into the sea, am I praying to you and Chantal and everyone else on earth, or am I praying to God?"

"What's it matter?" Stella said, "as long as it works. Which it apparently has."

"For now," Luc retorted. "And not because of praying—which I never do—but because no one who was not in mortal fear like we were would attempt the climb we just made."

They were perspiring, filthy and sore, so when the rain began, it was welcome. There was no clearing in view except for the stream bed. With one mind, they slid down the bank into the water and stood with their faces turned skyward, mouths open and arms outstretched. The mud began to run off their skin. Their shirts and shorts were quickly soaked, and the freshening breeze cooled them. After a few moments of bliss, the rain began in earnest and the three ran for the cover of the forest again. "So did you pray for rain, then, Stella?" The earth under Luc's feet was turning to slime, starting to suck at his shoes.

"No, not really."

"I did," Chantal exulted.

"And I prayed we would be down from the ridge before nightfall, which we are," Stella added.

"But this proves nothing," Luc protested. "It rains in the north of Kauai all the time. And it took us as little time as it did to cross the ridge because we slid on our asses all the way into the valley."

"So, Luc, you think it was an accident that my father brought us out to Na Pali this morning, and that I passed by the place where you were hiding, and that I was alone so you weren't afraid to call out to me?"

"It was fate, of course," Chantal affirmed.

"If everything were determined by fate, there'd be no such thing as luck," Luc objected, "and no point in going to the casino. Listen, Stella, are you sure about this policeman, Akamai?"

"Pretty sure. Why?" Stella, in the lead now, was having trouble following the trail in the rain. As best she could tell, it was directing them down to the stream again.

"Why? Those bullets, of course."

"Oh, please, Luc. You think the police were trying to kill us?"

"Kill us? No. Pin us down? Why not? In France, you see, one doesn't really trust the cops. I think it is true here, too, no? Not that they are all corrupt. Maybe they are in some cases, but mostly not, I believe. Still, they have their agenda. A 'law enforcement' agenda."

"What's that?" Stella asked.

"You see, a crime is committed. After that everyone is either a suspect, a potential witness or a nonentity. And a clock is ticking. They must have a suspect, an arrest before too long. Especially in a murder case."

Chantal elaborated. "You understand, Stella, the police think we ran away from them. That is their mentality. So we are suspects. But we do not need to be suspects, Stella. We need to be protected."

As soon as she had heard of their disappearance, Stella had known that the French couple fled the Pakala Inn out of fear, though she did not then know what it was that they frightened them. On the afternoon of the murder, Chantal explained, she and Luc had been sitting in their bungalow, sampling the marijuana bought from the strange businessman across the way, when they heard voices coming from Bungalow 13. The businessman had checked out, and Chantal had seen the cleaning people leaving the cabin shortly before, so she assumed that someone else was moving in. They stepped out onto their postage-stamp porch to see who the new guests were, and saw two figures emerged from number 13 in a state of considerable agitation. One was a Caucasian man, tall, well-formed and dressed in a shirt, tie and slacks. The other was a striking Chinese woman in a tight miniskirt and silk blouse. The man saw them and began to run toward them, but the woman chased him and grabbed his sleeve. She said something, and the two of them turned and ran out through the brush at the rear of the property. Curious as to what the man and woman had been doing in the vacated bungalow, she and Luc had walked across the yard and tried the door. It was locked. They thereupon lost interest, and returned to their afternoon smokes. Only that night, when they saw the body, did they realize the danger they were in.

Chantal thought the woman's exclamation had sounded like "nah naw." "'Not now,'" she told Stella, her eyes wide. "Which means, 'later.' Which is why Luc and I fled after seeing what happened to Adibi."

"And what is it that explains," Stella asked, once Chantal had subsided, "why your names were on that list?"

"What list?" Luc responded quickly.

Stella turned around and walked backward for a moment while she regarded the Frenchman. "My sister saw you mauling the corpse after everyone left our bathroom last night. The list I'm talking about is the list you were looking for, Mr. Bouchard."

Luc stopped walking, and so did Chantal. The two of them stared at Stella wordlessly for a few heartbeats. Then Chantal took a deep breath and said, "I'm Bouchard. He's Minot. We gave Adibi the names on the list. It's all the companies we knew of that were interested in buying the Makai Ranch, and, if we knew who their agents were, those names, too."

"Don't stop there," Stella prodded. "Why did you give him the names?"

"Because he asked us to," Luc replied, with an excess of detachment, but then adding, "and because he offered us a dozen kilos of Maui Wowie in exchange."

"Keep going. Why was Adibi interested in the names?" Stella demanded, feeling like her father cross-examining his daughters.

"We don't know," Chantal replied. "He said he was a real estate broker, interested in trying to get even a little piece of the Makai Ranch deal. We couldn't tell what he had in mind."

"But could you at least tell whether he was being honest with you?"

Chantal blew a puff of air sharply out between her lips. "We were more interested in the *pakalolo*," she said. "Do you know how much twelve kilos of high-grade marijuana is worth?"

"What were you going to do, my dears, sell it on the streets of Lihue?"

"Of course not," Luc put in. "We sold eleven kilos to Artemis Gabriel for a good price, and kept one for ourselves."

"Artemis?"

"Oh, yes," Chantal affirmed. "He's quite the trader in *pakalolo*."

They resumed walking. After ten minutes, the trail crossed the stream. Stella stood at the water's edge, looking up and down the opposite bank. Though the flow had increased rather quickly in the rain, they could still ford easily at this point, if that was what they were supposed to do.

"Are you sure this is right?" Luc asked.

"Not entirely. Can you see anything on the other—Yes— there! Can you make out the trail rising up the bank a little downstream, then bending left, then—See—?" she made a curving motion with her hand, "—coming around again in the other direction."

"I see it. Okay, let's go."

They waded in. The current pressed itself against their ankles, their calves, their knees. Smooth and slippery, the rocky stream bed provided only tenuous footholds. Moving slowly, the three travellers picked their way across the insistent current.

Stella was just stepping out onto the opposite bank when the flash flood thundered down the valley. She heard its sound first, the ominous cacophony of surging, roiling water, clattering rocks and snapping branches. She turned her head to look upstream and saw what looked like a giant, voracious serpent surfing the streambed, racing down on them. She shouted to the others as she scrambled up the incline. The path underfoot was slick in the rain, and her legs slipped out from under her, pitching her prostrate into the mud.

Clawing and crawling upward with only seconds to save herself, Stella felt for the first time what it was like to have one's life in the balance. All of her energy was focused on surviving. The roar in her ears drowned out all other sound. She saw nothing but the path ahead of her and, in the corner of her vision, the demon. Fifty yards away. Twenty. In a heartbeat, it was on her! She leapt for the trunk of a mango tree that had grown almost horizontally out of the hill before angling upward, and flung her arms around it just as the flood caught hold of her legs. It chewed at them, tossed them against the earth, pulled them out into the stream, struck at them with flotsam. She fought back. The more the torrent sought to dislodge her, the more tightly she clung to salvation. Even though she believed that she had lived many lives before, and had many yet to live, Stella Chase was not ready to part with this one just yet.

Froth and foam smacked at her face, obscuring her vision. Mayhem surrounded her. The earth shook and the mango tree bent low in the wind created by the cataract. Now she was entirely underwater, now out. And then the crest of the flood engulfed her, and she could not breathe. *Don't let go*. She fought, not only against the turbulent current, but against her own instinct, which told her to loosen her grip and rise to the surface or die by drowning.

Nothing stretches time more than not being able to take a breath. The sightless, airless tumult lasted only a few seconds, but not knowing how long it would continue made the experience seem much longer and more harrowing. Eventually, her face cleared the surface, and she gasped air into her burning lungs. She could see again, and though the current was still thrashing her around, she could tell that it was subsiding. The surface of the water was littered with debris: leaves, branches, stalks, torn from their mooring-places and sent tumbling toward the vaster waters encircling Kauai. As the monster's grip on her body eased, Stella sagged against the bank, its grasses flattened into a soggy mat. And then she saw fate descending on her. The broken trunk of a sapling fig, uprooted and somersaulting as it hit obstacles at the margin of the flood, was swinging straight toward the crook of the mango tree. Had she escaped death by inundation only to be killed by an afterthought?

Oh, no! she thought, too exhausted to climb out of the way. *Cosmic unconsciousness!*

"I'll get it, Dad." Andrew Chase was on the phone in the bedroom. *Some family vacation*, Liz thought as she walked to the door. If George Akamai's hunch was right, Stella was smoking dope tonight with the Gauls in a cave. Her mom would be sitting in a car all night with Captain Saga, struggling to keep a conversation going with half her mind while she worried with the other half. Her father seemed intent on talking on the phone all evening, first with his partners in New York and then with his client in the Far East. She was bored. And it was raining. She looked through the double-lensed peephole. It was Race Kendall.

"Hi," she said as she opened the door.

"Is the, uh, barbecue rained out?"

"What are you talking about?"

"Dinner. Don't tell me you forgot."

"Forgot! Hey, Earth to Race: there's been a little crisis here. Twenty-five percent of my family is missing. We're not going to have a barbecue, for Christ's sake!"

The young man shrugged. "Well, uh, then maybe you and I can go out for a bite."

Liz crossed her arms. "I don't believe you, Kendall."

"Give yourself a break, Liz. Your dad's been on the phone all evening, right? I know someone has, 'cause I've been trying to call. From what I hear, your Mom's staying up north for the night. Stella's—

well, wherever she is, we're not likely to hear from her tonight, either. So what're you doing here? Sitting on your thumbs, right?"

"Waiting for something to happen."

"Hey, it's happening. Here I am. Look, I've got a beeper. Give your father the number; if 'something' happens, you'll know right away and be back up in Ha'ena before he is."

Liz shook her head. "I don't think so. He'd worry," she said, jerking her thumb in the direction of the bedroom.

"Jesus, you'll be safer with me than you are with him. I'm a professional bodyguard."

"I thought you were a dick."

"Oh that's nice. Dick, huh? Yeah, I'm a private investigator, but I'm also a bodyguard. The occupations kinda go together, y' know?"

Liz stared at him for a moment. They clearly were on different wavelengths, but the cocky surfer dude was not unperceptive. He had made a valid if fairly soulless point. Sitting around waiting for her father to get off the phone wasn't productive; and given his state of mind this evening, things might be even less productive once he was off the phone.

"Where would we go?"

"Duke's. It's about a twenty-minute ride from here."

"What's 'Duke's?' she asked. It sounded crude.

"Duke's Canoe Club. It's a great restaurant in the most bizarre resort on the island. You'll love it."

"You mean, the Westin?"

"That's it."

"And I don't have to dress up," Liz guessed, eying Race's white tee shirt, linen pants and sandals.

When his daughter appeared in the bedroom doorway, Race Kendall moving behind her like a shadow, Andrew said, "Hold on a second, Galen," into the receiver. Then, to Race: "I've had you checked out, Dumpster Boy. Come in here."

"Sir," Race queried, stepping up next to Liz.

"My firm's security people. When you appeared on the trail, so soon after Stella had—"

"Sure, I don't blame you, Andrew. I'd have done the same thing if I were in your shoes. So, am I clean or what?"

"I don't know about clean. Let's say, more respectable than I had expected. Cal Tech, double major in computer science and management. Stanford Business School. Direct descendant of Phineas and Charity Kendall, who brought Christ to the Big Island. Your father was Quentin Kendall, CEO of United Hawaiian Bank and developer of the

Kendall Estate lands on the Big Island. When he—Well, why don't you—"

Surprised by her father's description and seeing her would-be escort in a new light, Liz turned to Race with an expectant smile. His mouth was half open and there was sadness in his eyes. Her smile faded.

"We had been dropped on top of a remote mountain in the Canadian Rockies," he said quietly, "to do some extreme skiing. It was late in the season. There was an avalanche, and my dad was killed. I was working in a Silicon Valley venture capital firm at the time, but never went back to the office after the accident. Instead, I came here."

"I'm so sorry," Liz murmured.

Andrew picked up the slack. "I don't know how you got into the investigation business; there's probably another story there. Anyway, you seem to be more or less legitimate. I'm told that in addition to investigating, you also provide personal guard services to a number of well-known personalities in the music business when they are visiting the islands. Only women, as far as my people can tell."

Race resumed his self-assured persona. "Yeah, they seem to be a better source of repeat business for me. Actually, I'd like to provide guard service for your daughter tonight, Andrew."

"That's not appropriate—"

"Daddy, you haven't exactly been great company."

Andrew glanced at the receiver, and pictured the Paracorp general counsel holding on at the other end of the line.

"I'm talking just dinner, Andrew," Race promised. "Bring her back early. No funny stuff." He made a little cross over his heart with his index finger.

Andrew considered briefly. He needed to get back on the line with Khoo. Race was apparently a bona fide security guard. "You want to go, Liz? All right. But stay together, the two of you," he admonished. "And be back by nine-thirty."

Race scribbled his beeper number and the restaurant phone number on a supermarket receipt fished from his pocket, and he and Liz left Andrew Chase sitting on the bed, once again deep in conversation with Hong Kong.

The car was an abused MG that leaked rainwater around the windows. It made a little too much noise to permit casual conversation. Race turned on the radio. "—kinda wet," the announcer was saying. "That tropical storm southeast of the island of Hawaii"—he pronounced it "Huh-Vuh-ee"—"will affect our weather pattern for the next several days. The weather service estimates that the winds in this baby have increased over the course of the day from thirty-five to fifty miles an hour. On present course and speed, it will pass a couple hundred miles south of Kauai by the end of the week. The cloud structure is so large that we can expect rain on and off until after that. Oh, and as usual, the storm chasers have given it a name. *Iniki*."

"Seems like we picked a real bad week to visit this island," Liz said loudly, her dreams of relaxation and suntan now under attack by the weather as well as by Stella's unusual behavior.

"There's no bad time to be on Kauai," Race answered. "Here, even the rain feels good."

"Oh, sure. So, you just sorta dropped out after your father died, hmm?"

"I wouldn't call it 'dropping out.' My whole life had been devoted to proving myself to my dad, and once he wasn't around any more, I realized that I could live for myself. Do what's important to me."

"And what's that?"

"Surf. Date beautiful women—like you." Race winked at Liz, who grimaced. The compliment was not objectionable, but the notion that Race considered her one in a long line of conquests definitely was. "And be a private eye, which I've wanted to do since I was a kid."

In fifteen minutes they were on the grounds of the Westin Kauai Resort, the formerly pedestrian hotel that had been re-imagined by someone who had to have been the reincarnation of Louis Quattorze's decorator, from what Liz had read in the Honolulu airport. Her expectations for the place were exceeded, which was not necessarily a good thing. It was as if the Palais de Versailles had somehow coupled with Caesar's Palace to produce a garishly splendiferous offspring that had stopped in Kauai on its way to Tokyo and decided to stay. The storm gave an air of operatic melodrama to the courtyard, with its two-acre reflecting pond dominated by seven sculpted, rampant horses, its huge tiled swimming pool overlooked by five pseudo-Grecian jacuzzis, and its electrified waterfalls. The oversized oriental sculptures and paintings in the lobby and along the open walkways around the pools were also both pretentious and imposing. Taken all together, it was a splendid tribute to the spirit of material indulgence, and totally out of place on Kauai.

Duke's, which occupied a small but choice portion of the resort property, was a welcome contrast, more comfortable, more Hawaiian. Entrance was onto the second floor, where a thirty-foot waterfall plunged past the catwalk over which patrons strolled into the restaurant. The open interior was done in contrasting woods, and dedicated to the memory of Duke Kahanamoku. Duke was revered in aquatic memory outside Hawaii as a great Olympic swimmer of the early third of the century, who single-handedly caused the flutter kick to replace the scissors kick in freestyle swimming; and revered in Hawaii as the man who turned surfing into an international sport. Accordingly, the walls were adorned with vintage surfboards, outrigger paddles, surfing memorabilia and photos of Duke and his longboard being admired by various celebrities of his time. A see-through wooden staircase angled its way down to the first floor. From that level patrons could walk out onto Kalapaki Beach, a sizable cove next to the deep water harbor where the cruise boats docked. The upper deck, too, was open to the Kalapaki view, and would have been Liz's choice for seating had the weather been better.

Race gave the hostess a kiss on the cheek. "Niki, this is Liz. Liz, Niki. She just had a tropical storm named after her."

Niki looked confused.

"Tropical Storm Iniki. We heard it on the radio coming over here."

"Oh, my! I wonder what that signifies." Niki was a dark- skinned Hawaiian with penetrating eyes and long hair that fell in undulating rivulets over her naked shoulders and down her back. Under her floral-patterned wrap, the lines of her body were statuesque. Liz was instantly jealous. The women shook hands. "Does the name 'Iniki' have a meaning?" Liz asked.

Iniki Makana smiled. "A few, actually. It can mean a sharp, piercing wind, which is appropriate for this storm, I guess. Or, a pinch." She squeezed a thumb and index finger together and twisted them in the air. "Or, the pangs of love," she added, with a glance at Kendall.

The young man winked. "How'd we do on a table, Niki?" he asked.

"I got you as close as I could. They bought the tables immediately around theirs, so you're at a little distance. Follow me, please." The latter, directed at Liz, was delivered with commercial politesse, rather than the easy informality that Niki used with Race.

The table was on the lower level. A few feet away, rain poured itself onto the tropical plantings that separated Duke's from the beach, filling the air with marvelous hissing and burbling sounds. Niki stood behind one of the chairs and motioned for Liz to seat herself. "You get the view of the stars," she breathed in Liz's ear.

"That's so sweet of you," Liz replied courteously, but when the hostess was gone, she gave her escort an acerbic look. "Stars? On a night like this?"

Race laughed. "Over my left shoulder. See the table there," he said, without turning around. "Five people seated, and a buffer of unoccupied tables all around them. The guy with the beard, the one facing you, is Spielberg."

"Spielberg?"

"The director, knucklehead. And the one with his back to the rain? That's Sam Neil. Across from him, his co-star, Laura Dern. They're filming here on Kauai. 'Jurassic Park.' I believe the whole crew is staying at the Westin."

"Cool! Have you met them? Omigod! Don't turn around, but I think Laura Dern is checking us out."

"She's probably curious to see what kind of girl would go out with a lowlife like Race Kendall. I met her the other day in the hall at the hotel."

"Are you a lowlife?"

"Well, I'm sure she thinks so. I was going through the trash from her room while my friend Aurora was cleaning the room next to it."

"Jeez! I agree with her. Maybe you'd like to elaborate, before my impression of you regresses."

"In investigative work, you have to take some liberties, Liz. It's for a good cause. I'm doing a pro bono case for the Kamehameha Society."

"Kamehameha? Wasn't he a Hawaiian king or something?"

Race nodded. "He was several Hawaiian kings. Kamehameha the First was the dude that united the Hawaiian Islands. The Kamehameha Society is an organization devoted to achieving sovereignty for the Islands."

Liz's unrequited social consciousness stirred. "Take back the islands, you mean? Now that could give a sense of nobility to pawing around in Laura Dern's garbage."

"Noble, yeah. Fruitless, maybe, but noble."

"And this sovereignty group asked you to look at the Jurassic trash? It doesn't make sense yet, Holmes."

"That's okay, I don't expect you to think like a private eye. See, I'm completely uninterested in Laura Dern's discards, okay? The guy I'm interested in was staying at the other end of the floor. But since I don't want Aurora to know who I'm investigating, I look at all the trash she collects on her shift. Every five rooms or so, I pick it up, take it to a quiet place, look through it, and bring it back."

"Uchh. And you touched me earlier?"

"I wear rubber gloves on the job. Can we talk about something else for a while?"

Liz wasn't about to let go of the subject. She questioned Race about his relationship with the Kamehamehas. He was, he said, under contract with the group to investigate the rumored sale of a very large piece of the island. Not that the Kamehamehas would want to buy it;

they had no call on funds of that magnitude. But the Hawaiians were worried that if someone bought such a dominant parcel of land and changed its use from agriculture to, say, residential development, it would start a stampede by other growers on Kauai and elsewhere in the islands to sell out to interests that would increase the *haole* population and *haole* institutions to such a degree that the sovereignty movement would collapse.

"So, is the buyer going to change the usage of the land?" Liz asked.

"Right now, there's no buyer, only interested bidders. I haven't been able to find out what the individual bidders have in mind for the property, but they're all companies that generally work with large-scale developers."

"Then your clients want—what? To prevent the sale?"

"No, no. Go too far down that road and you'll have the Hawaiians killing bidders with ice picks."

"That's exactly where I was going."

Race shook his head. "The Kamehamehas are nice people—the officers, anyway; like every political group, they have some extremists. Niki, there, is the head of the Kauai branch. All she and the other officers want is for the public to know what's going on as early as possible. That way, the county government can be pressured to block any major change in use."

It wasn't until the meal was over and the movie people had left that Race Kendall dropped the bombshell. They were sipping their Kona coffees and watching the falling rain. They could see it in the spotlights' beams, making the leaves of nearby trees dance crazily and streaking toward gravity in vertical flashes just beyond their reach. The air was warm and steamy. Liz could feel the microscopic coat of water vapor on every pore of her skin.

"You are aware," Race assayed, clearly expecting the opposite to be true, "that your dad represents one of the parties who's interested in bidding on the property I've been talking about—"

Liz stared at him, mouth slightly ajar. "What?"

"Your father represents a Hong Kong company called Paracorp."

"Right."

"Well, Paracorp has had its scouts snooping around this prop—oh, hell, I guess I can tell you. It's called the Makai Ranch. It's a huge sugar plantation—covers most of the arable territory on the southeast side of Kauai. The Paracorp advance team's driven around the property, done soil tests and other stuff, scrubbed the title. And the day after tomorrow, your dad is meeting with the owner and his negotiators."

"I don't believe it. I mean, my dad mentioned a real estate transaction, but it didn't sound anywhere near as big as the one you're talking about. Plus, he belongs to more environmental groups than I do."

"Helps keep his conscience clear, maybe."

"Hey, lay off," Liz protested. "You have no right to disparage my Dad." Even though her relationship with her father wasn't overflowing with unreserved affection, she was not prepared to hear Andrew maligned by a wise-ass who hardly knew him. "Blood's thicker than Chardonnay, Kendall."

Race leaned toward her across the table. "I'm sorry, Liz. But think about it this way: if you don't like the idea that your dad's helping a Hong Kong multinational to desecrate this beautiful place, maybe you've, like, found out about it early enough to help him see the light. And if you do, than you'll have something to thank me for. Maybe forgive me for."

Liz sat back. Race took her hand in his. Under the circumstances, the gesture struck her as presumptuous at best, and she withdrew. "I don't know about that," she replied. Once again, Race's technique had been inelegant, though his point had been valid. "But I guess I can reserve judgment for now." She looked out over the railing. "I'd like to have walked on the beach."

"Who says we can't?"

"What? The rain—"

"It's warm, like taking a shower. Come on."

He pulled her up and led her at a trot toward the downpour.

"My shoes!" she protested.

"Throw them in the corner there."

Shrieking, laughing, pushing the streaming hair out of her eyes, Liz followed her muscular blond escort, a strange, egotistical fellow whose only appealing characteristic seemed to be wildness. It was a trait that resonated with her despite the fact that the rest of his act didn't. The storm poured itself over them as they ran onto the beach, where the gentle contours of the sandy shoreline were dimly visible in the glow of Nawiliwili Harbor.

6

Could Andrew Chase really be blamed for having become increasingly grouchy over the years?

A decade ago, he was a midlevel partner in one of the oldest, largest and most prestigious law firms in Manhattan. His share of firm profits exceeded $600,000 per year, and a few years later was pushing a million. Now he was a senior partner in the same firm—a firm that was crumbling before his eyes in the increasingly competitive market for legal services. His share of partnership profits last year was $350,000, and next year it would likely be much lower.

A decade ago, he was forty. This year, he had turned fifty.

A decade ago, he was the head of a family unit, or at least thought that he was. Today, his family was not a unit, and it had no head. Yet, he was still paying for a family, or at least a family home, and, due to the decline in his professional fortunes, had to keep dipping into his capital reserves to do so.

A decade ago, clients listened to their lawyers, followed their advice and were loyal to law firms that were loyal to them. Today, clients shopped for lawyers the way people shop for toothpaste, and in order to sustain revenues his firm had to take on clients less familiar with the American legal system, and often less respectful of American law. Like Paracorp.

Paracorp was an investment vehicle for a group of fabulously wealthy individuals from around the Far East. Based in Hong Kong, the company was basically a funnel for money, moving billions of dollars of profit each year from Singapore, Taiwan, Hong Kong and Korea into real estate, bonds and stocks in the Group of Seven countries, particularly the United States. Paracorp was governed by a board of directors who trusted one another's business acumen but not one another's word. Consequently, control of its day-to-day operations fell to the company's CEO, Harry Wong, a Hong Kong Chinese also known as the "sweat shop mandarin" for his pre-Paracorp success in providing Western corporations with outsourced labor at rates on the order of a dollar or two per day.

The company could best be thought of as a shark in international financial waters, an opportunistic predator feeding on the weaknesses of others. It gobbled up firms that were on the verge of collapse, allowing grateful management and shareholders to walk away with some semblance of their dignity, then took the companies into bankruptcy, shedding debt, wresting favorable discounts from suppliers, and securing wage concessions to transfer wealth from labor to corporate capital. When the firms were brought out of bankruptcy, it was with a new management team that had been given a three-year mandate to manufacture growth and profit sufficient to support a large secondary stock offering. If the mandate was achieved—and it almost always was, whether by honest industriousness or by less honest means—a minority share would be offered to the public, leaving control of the subsidiary in the hands of Paracorp. If the subsidiary proved incapable of generating cash flow that met Paracorp's objectives, however, the entirety of the holding would be sold off, but only after artificially inflating the financial statements to attract investor interest.

Together with techniques more commonly accepted outside the G7 countries, such as bribery and extortion—techniques about which Andrew could legitimately claim ignorance, as they were used after the acquisitions he arranged had been completed—this management formula produced spectacular results for the two dozen owners of Paracorp and generated substantial legal fees for Andrew's firm.

The Makai Ranch deal didn't fit Paracorp's predatory formula. The Ranch was on a seemingly hopeless downward spiral. No amount of accounting chicanery could hide the basic economic fact that Hawaiian sugar was a fading business, with little hope of resuscitation. In one of the meetings that so worried him, Andrew had asked Harry Wong what the point was of pursuing this particular investment. They were sitting in Wong's office, an entire floor at the pinnacle of Paracorp Tower, with views in all directions. It was nine p.m. Across the harbor on the mainland, Kowloon glowed with multicolored illumination: neon, fluorescent, incandescent and vapor lights painting the surfaces of the city of nine dragons in mystical colors. Bobbing dots of light moved on the water between Kowloon and the Island, aquatic commerce continuing well after dark. The office towers that marched away from Paracorp Tower up and down the Central District were still lit from top to bottom, testifying to the industry of the colony's workers. Overlooking all sat Victoria Peak, a dark presence above the man-made luminance, the lights of the homes and businesses that had invaded its heights growing increasingly indistinct in the gathering fog.

Wong had smiled at Andrew's question. He looked over at his general counsel, Galen Khoo. The three men were sitting in armchairs covered with baby-soft leather that whispered when Khoo leaned forward. "Our interests regarding the land in Hawaii are somewhat different from those that drive our normal business model, Andrew. For reasons that you will understand in due course, we cannot share those with you at the moment."

"You should tell me only what you feel comfortable in telling me, Galen," Andrew responded, burying his deep discomfort beneath a cordial smile. "Obviously, the more I know about Paracorp's interests, the better the job I can do."

Harry Wong set his teacup down on the glass coffee table that separated him from the American. "This negotiation will not be conducted like the past deals you've done for us, Andrew. Much more tightly controlled from Hong Kong. In fact, we're only asking you to front this one because we believe that the gentleman who owns the property is a racist. I don't mind that. I'm a racist, too, as you know well." Wong's smiled broadened, and the American shifted in his seat. "We're sending you without any helpers from Paracorp so the poor fellow won't have to suffer the insult of pleading with a bunch of chinks for a fair price for his heritage." The Chinese billionaire laughed heartily. "This is something the other bidders will never think of. Their egos are too big, I guarantee you."

"You'll have no authority, really, Andrew," Khoo added apologetically.

"None?"

"I'm afraid not. You'll be expected to make sure that the terms of our offer are clearly understood, and that the terms of any counterproposals are sufficiently articulated for us to consider them seriously. We want you to report in at each turn in the road and, most importantly, to give the impression that you are a tough negotiator without actually being able to negotiate anything on your own."

"But—well, you gentlemen don't need me for this kind of work. I can supply you with somebody who can do this admirably at a much lower hourly rate."

"You're quite mistaken, Andrew," Harry Wong answered quietly. "We want Mr. Chamberlain to appreciate that we have sent one of the most expensive corporate lawyers in America. It will signal to him that we have a high regard for him and his negotiating team, and at the same time that we are not going to be taken in by any country-boy trickery." He stood up. "And now, if we have finished our tea, shall we go out on the town? I have in mind starting at the Bottoms Up on Kowloon side, and seeing what develops from there."

The rest of that evening was a blur of bare-breasted bar girls, sex shows, dirty dancing and a lot of drinking, but no further guidance on how to conduct the negotiations for the Makai Ranch. As Andy sat now in the Poipu house, less than a day away from meeting with the Makai Ranch people, he had little in the way of a negotiating pitch, other than a cash price that he regarded as far too low and a proposed schedule for transferring ownership. To make matters worse, there were now more critical things on his mind. Stella's disappearance was eating away at his very being. If it was in any way connected with the Makai Ranch deal, then he was at fault. It was a burden he could not bear. He knew that, and so was clinging to the small ray of hope offered by the painted rock. As if this potential family tragedy were not enough, he had just learned that he was facing a professional cataclysm back in New York.

Earlier in the evening, he had spoken with Charles Barton, managing partner of Fowler & Greide, who reported that a third of the firm's litigation department was defecting. Not a random third, naturally, but the best midlevel litigators and their associates, who were going to set up their own law firm and, no doubt, take valuable clients with them.

"This is the beginning of the end, Charles," Andrew had predicted. "Without those people, the litigation department is nothing, and without the litigation department, the firm is nothing."

"That's why we need to replace the defectors right away with some high-profile, star-quality trial lawyers."

"Good idea, Barton. Only one problem: we can't afford it. The senior partners have already given up vast amounts of income to the rest of the firm, and the midlevel partners won't give up a cent."

There was an extended silence on the other end of the line, and then Barton asked, "What has happened to the practice of law, Andrew? What these litigators are doing is completely unprofessional."

"Oh, Charlie, the law isn't a profession any more, for Christ's sake. It's a business. In fact, I don't think there are any professions any more. You go to the doctor's office, or the dentist's, and you're part of an assembly line. The big accounting firms are in so many businesses other than accounting that they've lost their identities. Our energetic young defectors don't see the law as we do, as a learned calling. They're bottom-line guys. They've assessed their street value and decided that it's higher than the value of their partnership shares. So off they go. The idea of a partnership as a long-term commitment to common purpose, collegiality, service to clients and to the law—hell, that idea probably never entered their minds from the time they joined Fowler & Greide until today."

"Goddamit, Andrew! What's wrong with them?"

"With them? That's not the question. The question is, what did our generation do wrong? This is all our fault, Charles."

They continued to talk for over an hour, but no solution to the problem came to either of them. After hanging up, Andy stretched out prone on the bed. *I'm fading away,* he thought. *Fading, fading, fading.* The things that had defined Andrew Chase were disappearing one by one. First, his marriage. A quarter century of living with the same woman had made her a part of his identity, and him a part of hers. Two years after the split, he still felt less than complete without Janet. For that reason, he had simply dropped out of the social circles they had enjoyed as a couple, and that action had further shrunk the meaning of his life.

Next, his law firm. If F&G cratered, what would be left of his career? He had poured his life into the firm and its clients, and in return had gained powerful professional credentials, and teams of hard-charging associates and paralegals to carry out his every directive and make every one of his projects successful. Take the firm credentials and the support structure away, and who would he be, professionally? In an earlier time, his clients would have followed him if he left, making it easy for him to land at another first-tier firm. But those days were over, and so was the certainty of Andrew Chase's future.

Finally, his children. A father is defined by his children, something the kids themselves never appreciate. They are the projection of his essence into a time beyond his life. A magnet drawing unconditional love from him where he would once have said there was no such thing as unconditional love. He had only two kids, and if one of them—

He couldn't bring himself to finish the thought. For a long time, he lay immobile, staring at the white slats of the peaked wooden ceiling. Eventually, he roused himself. Inaction was not helping. The only problem he could work on at the moment was the question of his own street value. Was he really a nobody without Fowler & Greide? He ticked through his personal client list on his fingers, and realized that the only large client likely to continue giving him substantial business if Fowler & Greide dissolved was Paracorp. Galen Khoo was a law school classmate and fellow law review editor. He had been an associate at the Fowler firm before being bought by Harry Wong fifteen years ago. He would help. Although Andrew could not make a significant contribution to another firm out of Paracorp work alone, the notion of being Harry Wong's kept

Caucasian consigliore suddenly didn't seem so awful, except for one terrible fact: keeping the irascible Wong happy meant he had to acquit himself well in the Makai Ranch negotiation, which might well pit his professional interests against the interests of his safety, and his family's.

He picked up the phone again and called his old friend in Hong Kong. "Something's gone very wrong here on Kauai, Galen," he began, and went on to recount the events of the past twenty-four hours. It was during that narration that Liz and Race walked in on him. "I still believe the murder was drug-related," he told Khoo after they had left for Duke's, "but the police have a broader view, and of course so does Janet, after all she's been through. I wanted you to know everything, so that you—uh, you can take appropriate action with regard to Mr. Wong's security."

"Harry Wong's security?" Galen Khoo laughed. "Jesus, Andrew. It would be easier to kill President Bush than it would be to kill Harry Wong."

"I—Look, I know there are things you don't want to tell me about this situation, Galen, but you would say, wouldn't you, if you knew of any risk to me or my family in connection with this deal?"

"You know I would, my friend. I can't conceive of anything. You must be right and the police wrong. Andrew?"

"Yes."

"I think you should call me back on a scrambled line." Andrew Chase hung up. Frayed nerves caused his hands to fumble as he retrieved a black box from his suitcase and inserted the device between the phone and the wall plug. Then he looked up Khoo's secure phone number in his pocket organizer and dialed it. "What is it, Galen?" he asked when they were reconnected.

"We've had people on Kauai off and on for some weeks now, Andrew." Unscrambled, Khoo's voice sounded hollow, artificial.

"Oh, really?" Andrew paused. A significant fact that Paracorp had neglected to share with him previously. "Doing what?"

"Uh—Doing feasibility studies. Collecting information about the property, and about the owner. Arranging for soil tests. That sort of thing."

"Yes. And—?"

"Well, for one thing, we discovered that others were beating the bushes, too. You know, the names on the list your daughter found.

"Mmm-hmm—"

"And for another—well, a couple of our reps there were beaten up pretty badly one night as they walked back to their hotel in Poipu. We thought at the time that it was a racial thing. They'd been drinking in a local bar, talking up some white girls. But in light of what you and your family have experienced, hell, I don't know."

"So what are you saying, Galen? Do you know of anything—"

"I swear, I can't think of any reason—" Khoo's voice broke. He inhaled and exhaled deeply on the other end of the line. "You know I would feel terrible if anything's happened to Stella, Andrew."

"Of course I know. I—know." The sudden shift from the professional to the personal, the heart of Andrew's internal conflict, caught him up short. Outside, the rain slid off the asphalt-tiled roof and hissed through the border of marble chips around the house. Banana trees and palms clattered in the wind. He was aware of being alone in the family hideaway, and all at once felt very lonely. "Thanks, Galen. Um, tell me: the beatings. Were there any arrests in connection with them?"

"Yes. Now you mention it, I got a report that one fellow was arrested, but I'm afraid I had pulled our people back from Kauai by then, and when the cops found out that there was no one around to make the ID, they let him go."

"What would you think about sending your people back to finger the guy? That would sure help from my point of view."

"Why, I guess we could do that."

"Could? Galen?"

"No, no, we'll do it, Andrew. We'll do it for sure. I just need to find out where those folks are and what they're doing, that's—"

"Jesus! What was that?" Andrew croaked. There had been a footstep in the crushed marble outside the bedroom window, then a yell, and then what sounded like a gunshot. "Galen, I have to go."

He leapt for the light switch, doused it, and then dived for a dark corner. Light filtered down the hall from the great room, and as his eyes acclimated he realized that the corner was not dark enough for his comfort. Frightened, he thought about how the intruder might get into the house. *Are the doors locked or not?* he wondered. With his heart palpitating in the wake of the gunshot, Andrew Chase was becoming incapacitated. The assessment he had given Janet earlier in the day was proving deadly accurate: the Poipu house was the easiest place for potential malefactors to find the Chase family, if that's what they wanted to do. Barely thinking, he crawled along the edge of the bed to an open closet, eased himself in and swung the door shut, latching it as quietly as he could.

Now he was in the dark, but it quickly occurred to him that anyone outside the closet would not be in the dark. It also occurred to him that, seated in this cramped little receptacle, he was in roughly the same position as the corpse his daughter had discovered in another closet. That perception panicked him, and his normally facile mind, the source of his livelihood, froze up. He could think of nothing to do but wait.

The phone rang. A stimulus. Would the organism respond? Would it? *No.* Although the organism's sensory machinery was functioning, its brain was in no condition to process the stimulus. Eventually, the ringing stopped.

Presently, there was a knocking at the front door. Another stimulus. Would the organism respond? Andrew Chase stirred. He forced himself back into focus. More knocking. He stood up. A third series of knocks, louder, more insistent. By now, the lawyer, although trembling uncontrollably, was able to think again. Either Liz had locked the door on her way out to dinner, or the person standing outside was unwilling to enter without an invitation. Finding out who was at the door, he concluded without excessive confidence, was a reasonable risk.

He walked down the hall to the great room and, standing at a distance and an angle to the door, shouted, "Who is it?"

"Police. Officer Gabriel. Let me in, will you?"

Andrew could see from where he was that the door was unlocked. That meant it was more likely than not that the speaker was indeed Officer Gabriel, and if the cop was the one who had fired the shot outside the house...

He approached the door silently and squinted through the peephole. The caller was in uniform. He moved to the front wall, near the hinged edge of the door, and took a breath. "Come in, officer."

Manny Gabriel stepped across the threshold into the entry area. He saw no one, heard nothing save the storm outside and the water dripping from his slicker onto the tiles. He peeked behind the door, and found an intelligent looking fellow standing there, staring warily back at him. He held out his hand and introduced himself. "Manny Gabriel."

"Andrew Chase. What are you doing here, officer?"

"Guarding the house. Didn't Captain Saga call to tell you?"

"I've been on the phone most of the evening—"

"Mr. Chase, there was someone pussyfooting around your house here. I chased him, fired a warning shot." He cocked his head slightly toward the door. "Caught him."

"Wh-where?"

"He's cuffed and in the cruiser, sir."

"Who is he? Do you know?"

"Yeah, I know. He's my cousin, Mr. Chase. He's my goddam cousin."

Manny Gabriel seated himself across the white formica table from his inglorious relative. Artemis Gabriel, still wearing a rainsoaked windbreaker over his bare chest, held up his hand, now sporting a bandage from the police cruiser's first aid kit.

"Dis is what you call one warning shot, Brah? You need go target practice."

"You moved after I said 'Stop.' How'd I know you were gonna do that?"

Andrew Chase brought a pot of coffee over from the stove, three cups dangling from his crooked finger.

"Black okay for everybody?" He sat between the two Filipino-Americans, and leaned toward the disreputable one. "Here's the situation, Mr. Gabriel."

"Artemis."

"Artemis. I have no interest in having you arrested. All my attention at the moment is focused up north, where I hope and pray my daughter is passing the night in safety. The only thing I want from you is an explanation. Why you were prowling around outside my window?"

The detainee's gaze dropped to the table. He said nothing.

"Hey, cuz," his uniformed kinsman said. "It'd be my pleasure—believe me—to haul your chubby ass up to Lihue for booking. If you weren't family, that's where you'd be right now. The three of us are just tryin' to work out—"

"—Don't give me dat 'family' shit, Manny. Nobody in da family see you anymore. You move in different circles from da res' of us. You Da Man, now, Braddah, enforcer for da powah structshah on this island. Far dat we concerned, you might's well be da Gestapo."

"And you're the *pakalolo* farmer, poaching on plantation land to plant your crops and expecting your cousin to turn a blind eye."

Andrew broke in. "Look. Look, Artemis. If we get bogged down in familial disputes, we're not going to come to closure here."

"He da one wen' start it—"

"Let's stay on the point, shall we?" Andrew demanded, "so we can get you out of here as quickly as possible. What the hell were you doing out there, anyway?"

"Oh, man," Artemis mumbled, looking down again. "It's embarrassing, sir. I don' wanna—"

"—Jesus," Manny Gabriel exclaimed. "Now he's gonna claim that he was tryin' to peep in on your daughters."

The co-owner of the Pakala Inn stared at his cousin, stony-eyed. "I' li' t'ank you for dat heartfelt 'sistance, Manny."

"Oh, bullshit, Artie. Bullshit! You wanna see nude pussy, you can go up Donkey Beach way any time."

"There's mostly men on Donkey, man. More yo' kine place, maybe."

The MG pulled up to the Puuholo Street house. Race glanced at the police car parked across the street, and groaned. "Manny Gabriel's here."

"Maybe there's some news about my sister."

"No. Manny's the local patrol cop on the night shift. He wouldn't have anything to do with Stella's case. This is a different problem. Oh, well."

"Oh well, what?"

"There goes my big chance for some good night kissy-face."

Liz collapsed against the passenger door. "I've never met anyone so self-centered. You ask me to spy on my own father—"

"Which you agreed to do."

"I did no such thing! What I agreed was to give you a little help with your work for the Kamehamehas, that's all. You ask me to spy on my own father, you take me around in this leaky, rolling matchbox, force me to trudge up and down a soggy beach in the pouring rain, and then expect me to submit to foreplay before we say good night!"

"Well, that's only because in this car, foreplay is about all I can reasonably expect. On the first date, anyhow."

"Oh, please! Let's go in."

As Liz opened the front door, Andrew Chase was saying, "If what your telling me is that you're a peeping tom, then I'm inclined to press charges. That kind of behavior is quite repugnant to me. So to the extent that might affect your story—" He stopped. The three men in the kitchen area stared at the new arrivals across the tiled floor that stretched from where they were sitting through the open living space to the entrance hall. With their matted hair and clinging apparel, Liz and Race were unexpected comic relief.

"Liz!" Andrew exclaimed. "Welcome back! Has the younger generation lost the ability to open umbrellas? Why don't you—Why don't you change into some dry clothes, and then join us? Race, nice to see you again." He waggled his hand and smiled. "Good night."

"Well, actually—" the young man began, moving a step forward.

"Good night, Race. See you soon."

The young investigator stood there briefly, then shrugged and let himself out. Through the open windows, the three men heard a car door slam, an engine cough into life and tires crunch across the loose stone of the driveway. Andrew turned to say something to Artemis, but before he could speak, he felt Manny Gabriel's hand on his shoulder.

"Not yet," the patrolman whispered. He stood, donned his slicker and went out the front door. In a moment, he was back. "Just wanted to watch his tail lights disappear up Lawai Road. You can't trust that sonofabitch as far as you can throw him."

"He was a perfect gentleman to me," Liz said, entering the room behind Manny, still towelling her hair. She was wearing a silk beach robe open over a tank top and running shorts.

"Have a seat, Madonna," her father said. Liz's attire had been a sore spot with Andrew since she had reached puberty. "We were about to—"

"T'anks God you come back jus' now, Miss Lizzy," Artemis interjected. Liz smiled at the sobriquet, which Artemis had coined as he was carrying the Chase bags to Bungalow 13. "Yo' faddah start act li' one prosecutor, and my cousin here begin da night by shoot me,"—he displayed his injured hand—"and now he accuse me of peepin' tom."

"What I said, Artie, was that you were about to make a phony confession that you were a peeper. That's what I said—let me finish!—and the fact that it was me who said it and not you saved you from lying to a cop."

"How you ever prove lie, pig? See, Miss Lizzy, yo' dad and my cousin, da nightstick, here, dey tryin' get me killed. If I say I come over here fo' look in your window, da right t'ing dat should happen is, your faddah say, well, lucky fo' you dat no one home 'cept me, but don't show yo' *okole* around here no mo.' And den, da right thing fo' cousin Manny to do is 'scort me back to my car, ri' down da street dere, and give me some bad-ass law 'forcement speech and some, you know, disgrace-to-da-family blah-blah. Den let me free, li' dat. But no. Not dese guys. Dey say, "We don' b'lieve you.' Dey can't seem to figure out dat if I'm willin' to admit some pervert t'ing li standin' in da rain jus' fo' see some private parts, den da truth must be somethin' dat might hurt me real bad if I tell."

Liz put a hand over Artemis' forearm. The sensation of size and strength beneath her fingers was overwhelming, but the emotions he was expressing were soft. "You know, guys," she said, "the rain stopped as Race and I passed through Koloa Town. The moon is poking through the clouds. Why don't Artemis and I take a little walk, and see if we can't find a new perspective on this?"

"Ma'am, this guy's not anyone you want to stroll around in the dark with."

"Daddy?"

"What's the point, Liz?"

"I think it's just possible that Artemis would relate better to me than to either of you. You haven't been very nice to him."

"*We* haven't been nice to *him*? This is no time for foolish risks, daughter."

"I don't want to take any risks, Dad. You two should come along. Just don't crowd us. Right, Artemis?"

Andrew considered the proposal. Manny Gabriel's cousin seemed to feel that Liz was on his side, for some reason. What could it hurt to let her talk with him, so long as he and the cop were within easy reach? "Well, Manny, I guess I'd rather have the information than put your cousin in the slammer. If we ended up not pressing charges—I mean why would you arrest him, really? It's worth a try isn't it? Unless—well, you tell me. He's your relative."

"Ah, he's got no place to run to, I suppose," the policeman responded. "And if he laid a finger on your daughter—" Manny Gabriel pulled out his service revolver and laid it on the table, finger on the trigger, muzzle pointed at Artemis' midsection. "Walk her down to the Stouffer's, Buggah," he growled. "We'll be right behind you in the cruiser."

Liz and Artemis strolled up to the Lawai Road, Artemis barefoot, having lost his zoris while attempting to run away in the dark. Behind them a discreet distance, Manny Gabriel's cruiser rolled slowly along, its headlights illuminating them from behind, so that they stepped into their own shadows as they went. To the left about a mile was the Pakala Inn. The pedestrians turned right, however, then right again onto Ho'onani Road, at the other end of which lay two large beachfront hotels and a sprawling condominium development. They crossed an old wooden bridge over a stream, its babbling just audible over the crash of surf against the rocks farther along. Lit by moonlight and by the moving police car, the whitewashed framework of the bridge was like a monument to a simpler time.

As the sound of the ocean grew in their ears, Liz weighed in. "Let's not dance around this, Artemis. Just tell me, okay?"

"If I tell you, you go tell da police."

"What makes you think that?"

"Well, I—I—Because, de police are doin' somet'ing' for you ri' now, dat's why."

"Don't make too much of that, Artie. I like that nickname. 'Artie.' It gives you a cozier image."

"You t'ink I wan' have one cozy image, Miss Lizzy?"

"Oh, no, a brawler like you. Course not. On the other hand, from a woman's perspective, Artie, it's a whole different thing. Women are probably afraid of you, you know what I mean? Same as most men probably are. So a cozy nickname like 'Artie' would be attractive to a woman. It'd tell them that behind that rough exterior you have a lot of qualities they'd like. The sound of it. 'Ar' from 'archangel': 'Art' from—"

"Artis'."

"Right. Shows you're sensitive in a sophisticated way. And then 'Artie' itself: the tongue moves from the back of the mouth to the front as you say it, kissing the palate along the way. Very sensual."

"Yeah?"

"Oh, yeah. Definitely. Listen, Artie, I don't have to tell the police anything. Stella's going to walk back out onto that trail tomorrow, wet and bedraggled and sorry she ever tried to lose herself in the rain forest, and that will be the end of my involvement with the police. So you can tell me the truth. I happen to think you should also tell your cousin the truth, but that's up to you."

They walked a few paces in silence. Then, "Look up," Artemis grunted, pointing skyward. Small cumulus clouds, the last tatters of the departing storm, were racing silently past the moon. They eclipsed it briefly one after another, and as they did so, their penumbral boundaries shone silver, then faded. To either side, the streams of clouds drifting near the moon but not in front of it formed a celestial hallway in shades of gray, along which the sainted ones passed for their instant of glory.

"Oh, gosh," Liz exclaimed. "It's magical."

"An' look." Ahead of them, where the road curved left, waves were smashing against the stone breakwater, throwing spray and spume high above the modest barrier wall. In these ice-white, towering ephemera, droplets caught tiny quanta of moonlight as they rose shimmering off the stones and then fell to die on wall or roadway.

Liz shook her head. "So beautiful."

"An' look down dere." Artemis was leaning over the barrier wall to the right of them. Following suit, Liz could see the inlet to Koloa Landing, buttressed with large dark stones on both sides and terminating in concrete slabs laid on the steep bank to allow the launching of trailer-ported boats. Next to the landing, the stream over which they had passed flowed through a steep, leafy bed to the salt water. In the middle of the inlet, three large, indistinct balls of deep yellow light floated in seemingly random patterns beneath the surface of the water.

"Omigosh! What are those?"

"Night SCUBA."

"Amazing. There are little wonders all around us tonight, it seems."

"Dat's Hawaii," the blocky Filipino replied, apparently satisfied that he had displayed a sensitivity worthy of his nickname.

He would ask for a date next, Liz was certain, if she didn't slow him down. Men are such playable instruments. "Artie," she said. "You are so sensitive. I can't believe you're a drug dealer. Or was your cousin just making that up?"

"You t'ink *pakalolo* is bad stuff? Bad to get a li'l high, have a li'l joy in life?"

"Hey, I'm not sitting in judgment here. I get high, too, but in a different way. Bad? Maybe not. But illegal, Artie. Criminal. Gets a nice guy like you involved with the wrong company. Maybe leads you doing the wrong things."

"I ain't no criminal, Miss Lizzy. A real criminal, I mean. I ain't dat," Artemis said softly.

"Mmm. I'd like to believe you. But then—" Liz stopped and turned to face him. "What were you doing outside our windows tonight?"

He gave a moment's thought before answering. "You no tell Manny?"

Liz felt the moonlight against her face as she shook her head. "I promise," she breathed.

"Tryin' to see if yo' sister back."

"That's it?"

"Yup."

"That's all? Seeing if Stella had turned up? But why? Not out of concern for her, I'm sure."

"Nah. I was paid to do it, by—" He wavered. "See, dat's da hard part."

"Telling me who paid you."

"Yeah. Maybe not so good fo' me. Maybe not so good fo' you, either, li'l sistah. I don't know fo' sure. Just being, like, caution, you know?"

They had rounded the curve in the road. To the right, ocean mist from the crashing waves fell over them intermittently. To the left, darkened low-rise houses and condominiums sat waiting for morning. Ahead, on an artificial excrescence of land that jutted into the sea, the Sheraton hotel sprawled, many of its guest rooms still lit. Palm trees lined the road down to the hotel. "Okay, let's hold that question for now, then. Tell me why they paid you."

"Yesterday afternoon, dese people wen' Bungalow 13, looking for Smilie, da guy who—I know dat's not his real name."

"No, I guess not."

"Anyway, dey come askin' fo' him, right? An' I told dem he check out, but maybe he stay back dere anyhow. I di'n't see 'em again, but dis morning dey call me, right? Said when dey wen' in, dey found da guy dead in dat closet, same li' you did. Do I believe 'em? I dunno, but dat's what dey said. So dey come out Numbah 13 and, bingo, see da two French kids starin' across da lawn. Now, dey have nothin' to hide, supposively, right? But anyway dey bolt 'roun' back an' out t'rough da bushes. Di'n't wan' get involved, dey tol' me."

"And they know somehow that the French couple disappeared and Stella did, too, and if Stell had come back, they wanted to—to what?"

"Talk to her."

"Just talk to her?"

Artemis shrugged. "Dat's what dey say."

"And you knew these people?"

"Hell, no. Dey Oahu folks. I ask 'em show me picture ID before send 'em back to da bungalow."

They had reached the Sheraton, two low-rise buildings separated by the road. "Da beachfront building wen' beat up by Hurricane Iwa maybe ten year back. I t'ink dey just finish one big renovation dere, but no check it out yet."

"Yeah, you have hurricanes out here, too, don't you?" The television pictures of Hurricane Andrew, which had devastated south Florida less than three weeks earlier, were fresh in Liz's mind.

"Well, dere's hurricanes in da Pacific every summer. But it one big ocean. Iwa come in eighty-two, but before dat, no real hurricanes here I can remember. So, yo wanna go out wi' me one day while you're here? I give you one supah tour of da island."

Liz turned to her escort and smiled in the moonlight as if she hadn't heard that line just hours before, as if a million women visiting Hawaii over the past decade hadn't heard a line like that before. As she opened her mouth to speak, there was a shuffling sound to their left, and a figure materialized in the intersection they were passing. Artemis stiffened, and took half a step in front of Liz.

"What you look at, Braddah" the stocky Filipino demanded. The figure walked toward them out of the shadows.

Liz peeked around Artemis' sturdy shoulder. "You've been eavesdropping on us, haven't you?" she said to the new arrival.

"Force of habit," the figure responded, moving into the illumination thrown by the cruiser's headlights.

Liz stepped between the two men. "Artie," she said. "Do you know Race Kendall?"

September 9, 1992

The *Honolulu Advertiser* predicted sunny weather for the day. "Thunderstorms near Kauai are moving northeast," it reported, "and should not affect island weather. Tropical Storm Iniki, 570 miles southeast of Hilo, is moving west at 16 mph and intensifying. Iniki's winds have risen to 70 mph with 85 mph gusts." It often rains on Kauai on days when fair weather is predicted for the Hawaiian Islands generally. Kauai is, after all, home to the "wettest spot in the world."

7

"She's not out there."

While the sun, still below the horizon, was lighting the morning sky with warm sunrise colors, Barry Saga and George Akamai stood talking quietly in front of the dank grotto known as Waikanaloa Cave. Along the road in front of them, police and other emergency personnel were making ready to comb the Na Pali coast on foot, by helicopter and in inflatable boats. Shouts, engine noise and the clanking of equipment filled the air. Saga sipped black coffee from a plastic cup before responding to Akamai's assertion. "You mean this whole cliff search is for nothing, George. I'd be happy to call it off right now. Our budget doesn't need the stress."

"Barry, you know I make no guarantees. It's just an opinion."

"What's your logic?"

Akamai gave a little laugh, and reddened slightly. "Logic? No logic, Captain. I had a dream last night."

"A dream? George. We're here to do police work, not psycho-analysis."

It was a game they'd played many times before—Akamai laying out an extrasensory hunch and Saga challenging it. The outcome was always the same. "In my dream, I was in bed, asleep. Then I heard my name being called. After a few seconds, I recognized the voice as Stella's. She was sitting on a hill by a stream. Alone. The walls of a steep valley rose around her. I asked if she could hear me; she said she could. I said, 'Tell me where you are.' She said that they had climbed up from the trail with the sun at their backs, and descended into this valley."

"They?"

"She, Chantal and Luc. But something happened to the French kids, I think. Stella was definitely alone."

"So what valley are we talking about?"

Akamai looked at Saga equivocally before answering. "It's got to be Limahuli, Barry."

The captain of detectives swallowed his coffee wrong and began to cough. Akamai tried to smack him on the back a few times, but Saga waved him off.

"Limahuli, lieutenant! That's impossible. That means they'd have to scale the ridge."

"I know, Barry. It's crazy. But they did it. Or at least Stella did."

"Your intuition's not always right, George."

"No, it's not." Akamai shrugged. "But I'm going up the old valley trail this morning, captain."

Saga looked down the road to where, in the distance, the stream that had patiently created the Limahuli Valley over a thousand millennia was overflowing a swimming hole used by the locals to rinse off after swimming at Ke'e Beach, in preference to the *haole* showers. The water ran across Highway 560, flooding a short section of the road. "The stream's way up this morning," he said. He inhaled deeply, and exhaled in a low whistle. Then he nodded. "Okay, George. Take one EMT, but that's it."

"I could use at least one more, Barry. In case we—"

Saga held up a hand. "You can radio for more support if you need it. Or—why don't you see if the girl's father will go with you?"

The small search party set off ten minutes later. Andrew began perspiring almost as soon as they were underway. It seemed much warmer than yesterday, and there was less of a breeze. The air was heavy and close around him. It pressed itself steamily against his body, crowding him, stealing his breath, pushing his attention inward where there was only fear and confusion.

The paramedic was the same young Hawaiian woman Andrew had met the day before. Niki Makana wore a bikini top, cutoff denims that exposed the lower curvature of her buttocks, an electric green sun visor, thick wool socks and hiking boots. She carried a big backpack that obscured the whole of her torso above the hips. Beneath the pack, her lower half sashayed in graceful, rhythmic motion, like a sensuous metronome. The effect on Andrew was more hypnotic than erotic. As he trudged the badly-maintained trail single file behind the swaying backpack, his mind was on what things they might discover that morning, and, when he couldn't bear to think about that any longer, on his other problems.

After a few minutes, Niki shouted over her shoulder that she had met Liz the night before.

"Oh?"

"Yeah. She came to the restaurant where I work the dinner shift. She was out with that rascal Race Kendall."

"Rascal, you say?"

"Rascal, yeah, Andy. He's a nice enough guy, a friend of mine, really, but he thinks he's carrying God's gift to women around between his legs. Which would be okay if he were, I suppose, but he's not." Andrew wasn't sure how to respond.

"Thanks for the tip," he muttered. What could he do about it? He had been unable to influence Liz's taste in men for as long as he could remember.

The trail followed the stream. Matted grasses and natural debris along the banks left evidence of yesterday's flood, though Andrew did not know how to read the evidence. In any case, he was so lost in his own thoughts that the tropical wonder of the Limahuli Valley slid past his consciousness unnoticed. The lushly-foliated walls rising above the rushing stream; the white-tailed tropic birds soaring on invisible air currents that rose toward the ridgelines; the yellow guava hanging from the trees or fallen and torn open to reveal the pink fruit and translucent seeds within; the native *i'iwi* and imported cardinal, their crimson feathers competing for attention in the forest depths: he perceived none of these things. Stella, his unsuccessful relationship with his daughters, his unrequited feelings toward Janet, his loveless sex life, the implosion of his law firm, the meeting with Chamberlain scheduled from Hong Kong for that afternoon that he should have cancelled—those morose subjects blotted out all external sensations, except occasionally his own footing. He did not own hiking boots, and in his sneakers he had to be careful about his ankles in the uneven and rock-punctuated terrain.

He wasn't being careful enough. Preoccupied with his troubles, he stepped onto a smooth, wet stone. His foot slipped into a mud slick and kept moving sideways until he wobbled and fell forward, spread-eagled. He shot his hands out in front of him, more to quiet his fall than to break it. At the expense of his wrists, he succeeded in avoiding a wholesale crash and attracting the attention of his companions. Quietly, he regained his footing and his composure, but the misstep stuck in his mind as a metaphor of what he must not do again on this trip. Earlier that morning, as he, Janet and Liz had stood together next to the foot-deep flood through which police cars, ambulances and blue-lighted volunteer vehicles were slowly passing, he had first expressed the caution. "All this police stuff is a godsend, and I'm sure we'll find Stella in no time," he said with a semblance of confidence, "but we can't just leave the family's safety to the police."

Janet frowned. "What are you talking about, Andy?"

"The police have the whole island to worry about. They'll find Stella, certainly, but after that they can't justify expending all their attention on the Chase family. I'm hiring a security service to guard the house for as long as any of us is here. Now, if you girls do leave before—"

"Not 'if,' Andy. 'When,'" Janet insisted.

"Okay. When you girls leave, I'll hire a service to protect you back home."

"So you've come around to my view of things?"

Andrew took a deep breath. "Well, I—I love you, Janet, and you, Liz, and Stella. I had hoped that when we found Stell, things would—you know, normalize. But last night I realized that there wasn't going to be any normalizing on this trip."

"Can I tell her, Dad?" Liz asked in the awkward silence that followed her father's uncharacteristic expression of affection.

"Be my guest. You're the heroine of the tale."

"Dad caught Artemis Gabriel prowling around the house last night."

"Artemis! Artemis? What on earth was he up to?" Janet asked. Liz recounted the walk she and Artemis had taken. "Do you think he was telling you the truth?" Janet wanted to know.

Liz nodded.

"The important lesson for us," Andrew urged, "is that it was Liz who got the information out of the guy, not the police. Based on what I saw last night, I'd have to say it's doubtful the police ever would have got the truth out of him. And that's why I say we have to be in charge of figuring out for ourselves whether and when we're safe. The cops can't do that for us. We all have to be resourceful. Vigilant. Careful. And we can't let up until we're out of this thing, whatever it is."

Revisiting that conversation as he picked his way more carefully now, Andrew shook his head. *Right,* he thought as he passed beside the Limahuli Stream. *Resourceful, vigilant and careful, and the first thing I do is fall flat on my face.*

Half an hour in, they found Luc's body. It was floating face upward in a pool formed by the stream beneath an overhanging rock ledge. Andrew couldn't see how George Akamai had sighted it from the trail; it was totally obscured from his own view until he joined the others at the water's edge.

Akamai grabbed his arm. "Let's pull him out and lay him up on the bank, Andy. We'll send a team in to collect him later."

"You could radio back now, George." Niki suggested. "You know, the flies—"

"No, no," Andrew interjected. "We can't radio this kind of news back until we find Stella."

Akamai nodded and motioned Andrew into the stream.

The water temperature and the air temperature were about the same, so that the pressure of the flow against Andrew's legs felt like a strong, sultry wind. Akamai took hold of Luc's legs, and Andrew grabbed his wrists. The young man's flesh was bloodless, cool and flaccid, like supermarket meat. Andrew held it with a mixed sense of reverence and revulsion, thinking more about his daughter than about the lifeless young man. After he and Akamai had set the body down on a relatively flat area, he tried to speak: "George, do you—?" but he could say no more.

Akamai walked over to him and gripped his shoulders. "There was a flood on this stream, Andy, you can tell by the way the banks look. Luc didn't make it. I believe Stella did. If I'm right, we should find her very soon."

As they moved off, Andrew Chase began to face facts in a way that he hadn't before. *She might have drowned,* he thought. *She might be dead.* His mind began a now-familiar race toward panic. This trip had been his idea. It was his fault that Stella had met the French couple. The fact that Stella had gone missing on the Kalalau Trail was his fault for not being more watchful. Even the fact that Stella separated herself from him on the trail was probably his fault: she was trying to avoid yet another grilling over her life choices. What had he thought he was accomplishing, he wondered now, by quizzing her, questioning her intelligence, challenging her beliefs? She was out of the nest and would fly as she wished. Wittingly or unwittingly, he had helped set her on the path she had taken, and it was too late for him to try to turn her aside. He finally saw all too clearly that the role of a parent of adult children was vastly different from that of a parent of minors and prayed that he had not come too late to that obvious conclusion, prayed to a God in whom he did not believe that his daughter was safe. *If she's dead,* he told the Lord, *I will probably go mad.*

A few agonizing minutes later, he heard Akamai cry out, "Here's the other one!" Chantal's body lay on its side in the Limahuli Stream, in currents no longer strong enough to move her off the rocks between which she had come to rest. Her head, badly battered, lay half in, half out of the water. Tugged by the current, her short hair aligned itself in the general direction of the sea. The two men waded in slowly, clumsily. The stream pressed arrhythmically against their ankles, and the rocks were slippery and irregular beneath their feet. Cautiously, they lifted the French woman's body out of its stony cradle. Its spiritless weight seemed more than could be accounted for by its slender proportions. "One step at a time," Akamai warned. "Make sure you have a solid footing before you shift your balance."

For Andrew, the awkward journey across five feet of stream bed and up onto the shore was a communion with unseeing eyes from which he could not look away. They deposited the hapless young woman in a grassy bower formed by breadfruit trees, young figs and vines. The lawyer sat down next to it, dripping with sweat and shaking.

"I can't go further, George," he said weakly. "I'm just not up to it."

"You can't stay here, either, Andy. Chantal left this body yesterday; now it's nothing but decaying mortality. Get up, will you?"

Andrew shook his lowered head. "No, George. You go on. If Stella's alive, we'll all—re—rejoice. If not—then maybe by the time you bring her back I'll have learned how to—to talk to—dead children."

Akamai looked around. "Where's Niki, anyway? Iniki," he shouted. "I need some *kokua* here."

A muffled shout came from further up the trail. "I'll be right back," Akamai said, and ran off. Andrew Chase turned to the corpse. He touched its bruised cheek with the back of his hand. The half-open eyes stared upward into the leafy canopy. He tried to close them, but the lids would not stay shut. The lips, too, were parted, as though Chantal had something more to say. *Who were you?* he wondered. *What were you doing on Kauai, and why did you end up like this?*

"Andy."

Akamai had returned. He bent down and grabbed the lawyer under his shoulders to lift him to his feet. His strength seemed superhuman. "It's Stella," he beamed, his face not six inches from Andrew's. "She's alive. She's fine. She's fine!"

When her father arrived, Stella Chase was seated on a rock by the side of the trail, wiping her hands and face with a paper towel impregnated with disinfectant. Niki, backpack off, hovered over her, dabbing at the crown of her head with a cotton swab that had been soaked in a purplish fluid.

"Dad!" she shouted, and rose to meet him. He rushed over and threw his arms around her, hugging and rocking her, feeling the life in her, sharing an unaccustomed moment of wordless joy with his daughter. "I'm okay, Dad. I'm okay!"

Niki grabbed each of them by the arm. "Stella, please sit down for another minute. I just want to check you out a bit, to be certain you can walk. Andy, if you don't mind."

George Akamai came up beside Andrew and stood watching Niki at work. "I had a dream about you last night," he said to Stella as the paramedic checked her reflexes.

Stella glanced up at him and gave a half smile. "I dreamt about you, too, George. You were looking for me, and somehow, I was able to let you know where I was. And now, here we are." She turned to her father. "Some luck, huh, Dad?"

"For the moment, Stell, I'm prepared to believe in miracles," Andrew laughed.

"What a shame about the other two," Akamai offered.

"At first, I didn't understand, George" Stella replied. "There was a flash flood. It just roared down on us. It's incredible, the destructive power. There's no stopping it—you can't argue or reason with it. But I saw it coming, and got up high enough, just barely high enough. I'm sure Luc and Chantal saw it, and they should have had enough time, too. I thought maybe I was in their way—you know, that it was my fault—"

"Follow my finger, please." Niki held a digit up in front of Stella's eyes, and moved it from side to side, then closer and farther.

"A huge branch knocked me out and then saved my life yesterday," Stella continued. "It conked me on the head. Would have split my skull, except it snagged in the tree I was clinging to on its way down. While I was out of it, I was wedged in between that branch and the tree trunk, so even though the flood was still pulling at my legs, I didn't get sucked in. Another miracle, Daddy?

"I might have been unconscious for a few seconds or a few minutes, I don't know. When I came to, I pushed the branch off and waited for the water level to drop. Then I went to look for Luc and Chantal. They weren't around." Stella stopped for a moment. Her gaze dropped toward the ground, and she took an unsteady breath.

"Not being able to walk much," she continued after a moment, "because of my head and because it was pouring rain, I found the driest place I could, under a shelf of rock, and dozed until morning. Then I came down here and discovered Chantal in the water—her body in the water. I had a premonition that the two of them were dead, so I was ready for it. I went out to try to lift her, but I couldn't do it alone. So I decided to wait up here, on this stone, until you came."

"You said you didn't understand at first what happened to them," Akamai reminded her. "Do you understand now?"

"You mean, you didn't see?" Stella asked, surprised.

Akamai shook his head.

"See what?" Andrew Chase asked.

"There's a bullet hole in the middle of Chantal's back. Luc's, too, I'll bet."

Andrew sank to his haunches, bringing his eyes level with his daughter's. "What?"

In the superheated waters south-southeast of the Big Island, Iniki became a hurricane. The circling cluster of storms had formed an interconnected ring of inward spiraling rainbands. Near the center of the spiral sat Iniki's eye, an area of very low pressure held in place by a huge, well-defined wall of violent thunderheads. Above her, in the stratosphere, conditions were favorable to her viability. High winds could have killed the hurricane by disturbing her cycle of rising vapor, condensation, falling rain and release of latent energy. Instead, a relatively gentle anticyclonic circulation perched like an exhaust fan atop her eye, helping to radiate condensate water out into her body and increasing the upward draft through her cloudless core. Iniki was thus free to gorge herself on water vapor and to grow in size and power.

At sea level, winds of over eighty miles per hour were chasing one another around the spiral. Had the hurricane encountered land, winds of that force would have snapped the tops off softwood trees, toppled shallow-rooted trees, shattered large pane glass windows and lifted an occasional roof from its moorings. But this virago was far from land, still following the trade winds across balmy waters, well south of Hawaii. She was also far from what she would become.

That the life force of a massive hurricane should be something as simple and benign as humidity may seem strange; yet that is the case. On the surface of the sea beneath Iniki, moisture-laden air was now being ingested in prodigious volumes into the fifty-mile wide maw at the base of the eye. This ethereal power source, deliciously full of warmth and energy, gave Iniki the gifts of growth and motion, through the elementary processes of condensation in the cool upper reaches of the ferocious toroid of thunderstorms, and outward radiation by the mild anticyclone.

Waves beneath the hurricane churned up more warm water from the depths, providing a ever-replenishing supply of nourishment. South of the hurricane's central body, the inward-coiling surface winds created spiral bands of storm clouds that clung to Iniki like reverse pilot fish, feeding their host with energy instead of feeding from it. Iniki was now measured at Force One, lowest on the Saffir-Simpson five-point scale for assessing a hurricane's destructiveness. So long as she remained in the thrall of the trade winds, she would gather strength. If she drifted to the north into the waters near the Hawaiian Islands, though, the meteorologists believed that she would likely die.

Over the islands, a persistent subtropical high pressure region fosters high rates of evaporation from the ocean's surface, but little rainfall. As a result, the surface waters become increasingly saline. Saltier water is denser than less salty water and eventually sinks, to be replaced by cooler water from below. Hurricanes venturing into these cooler waters are deprived of vapor fuel. They weaken and dissipate, which is why the instances of hurricanes actually striking Hawaii are so rare. Rare, but not impossible.

At noon the Chase family was reunited for lunch in the rented—and now guarded—house in Poipu. It was the first meal they'd taken together in Hawaii. The day was gloriously sunny. Andrew had laid a charcoal fire in the barbecue pit, and was waiting for the coals to subside from red hot to cindrous white so that he could cook the hamburgers and, for Stella, veggie burgers.

Janet and Stella were in the kitchen, slicing local tomatoes and Maui onions, and looking up plates, glasses and utensils. Liz was in her blue bikini, doing what she had come to Hawaii to do: being an object of the sun's fury. She lay on a chaise lounge on the deck, not far from the grill, eyes closed and arms stretched out along her well-greased torso.

"Dad?"

The deck was two steps above the back lawn. Andrew was seated on the bottom step, wearing a bathing suit and a tank top and still worrying. He couldn't decide whether the shooting of the French couple was a bad sign or whether the fact that Stella had not also been shot was a good sign. Unfortunately, there was no way to tell. All that was sure was that violence was swirling around his family. "Yes, honey?" he answered without looking up from the cooker.

"I just want to thank you for the confidence you showed in me last night."

He turned around, surprised, and found himself facing the bottoms of Liz's feet. He almost said something sarcastic like, "You know, in some countries, it's offensive to display the soles of one's feet," but caught himself. "You—you mean, with Artemis Gabriel?"

"Yes," Liz replied, rising up on her elbows to look at him. "I was so proud that you supported me; that you felt I could make a contribution."

"Well, of course—and you made quite a contribution, in fact."

"I did, didn't I? It really felt great to be able to, you know, draw him out. Win his confidence and get him to tell me what he knew."

"You didn't feel as though you were—you know, exploiting him, did you?"

"Oh, not at all, Dad. It didn't hurt Artie in any way to tell me about those two people. In fact, it was better for him, because once he told me, he was then prepared to tell his cousin, which probably saved him serious difficulty with the law."

Andrew nodded, wondering if his daughter could discern the line between pursuing mutual interest and flat-out manipulation. "You've always had power over the men in your life, Liz."

Liz lay back down on the chaise. "Is that a compliment, Dad?"

Just then, Janet and Stella emerged onto the deck, carrying trays laden with the makings of a meal. Andrew stood up. "Anyone want grilled onions?"

While they were eating, Stella accounted for her absence. Luc and Chantal had been hiding on a plateau above the Kalalau Trail, she said, afraid for their lives and at a loss as to how to save themselves. When they saw Stella walking down the path, they thought a way to salvation might have been opened to them. "They literally pulled me into the underbrush," Stella declared, animating her words with energetic pantomime.

"What were they so afraid of?" Janet asked, suppressing her inner hurt over the fact that Stella's disappearance seemed to have been voluntary rather than forced.

"Being arrested, obviously, Janet," her husband proffered.

"No, Dad. That's what everybody thought, but it wasn't true. They were afraid of whoever killed Adibi."

Liz put down her hamburger. "But why, Stell?"

"Two reasons. One, they had seen two people leaving Bungalow 13 on the afternoon of the murder, and those people knew Luc and Chantal had seen them—"

"—A Caucasian man and a Chinese woman, the same people Artie Gabriel told me about?"

"Artie, that's cute. Right, a tall, blond guy and a slinky woman, from what they told me."

"Saga has an idea who that couple is," Andrew put in, "but he wouldn't tell me."

Janet put down her hamburger. "There's something—I wasn't listening very carefully yesterday, but I think Mr. Chamberlain mentioned that his realtor was a woman. Her name sounded Oriental to me."

"Did he say where she worked?" Liz asked. "Artemis told me the two people he sent back to the bungalow that afternoon were from Honolulu."

"Yes," Janet answered. "Yesterday is kind of a blur for me, but I think he said she was from Honolulu and so was the guy, who is his lawyer."

"Which means they're the same couple who asked Artie to find out about Stella's whereabouts, which means your meeting could be very interesting today, Dad," Liz observed. "Maybe you should have some company."

Andrew looked at his daughter, trying to betray no signs of concern. The family had had enough of a fright already. Yet if Chamberlain's lawyer and his realtor had murdered Adibi, and perhaps Chantal and Luc as well, there was ample room to be apprehensive about meeting them. Take it a little further and imagine that they were acting on orders from Chamberlain, and there'd be good reason to cancel the meeting. The problem was, it was all too farfetched. "From what I know, Liz," he said, "Chamberlain's lawyer and his realtor—her name is Low, Janet—are very smart, very successful people. If they wanted Adibi killed, they'd be far more likely to hire someone to do it for them, and there's no way they'd have showed up at the Pakala Inn on the afternoon when the deed was done. Let's stay with to Luc and Chantal for now. Why didn't the poor kids just go to the police, Stella?"

"They didn't trust the police. We talked about that, and worked out a plan where I would speak to George on their behalf. I didn't expect that I'd be gone overnight, Dad," Stella added, answering a question her father hadn't asked. "The police choppers frightened Luc before he was comfortable with the plan, and then we heard what we thought were gunshots. I guess they were—weren't they?—given what happened afterward. I asked—um—well, let me just say it. I asked for guidance as to whether I should leave them at that point."

"You mean, you reflected," Andrew interjected automatically. Stella's attribution of her own decisions to direction from God was a source of such great annoyance to him that he could not restrain himself from correcting her.

"Oh, please, Andy. Not now," Janet objected.

Liz was sitting across the table from her father. She moved in her chair to catch his eye, and when he glanced at her, she gave an infinitesimal, sympathetic shake of her head.

"Okay, Janet," Andrew sighed. "For now, let's assume that God is responsible for the agony you suffered overnight, not Stella."

"God is responsible for everything, Dad," Instead of playing further on her father's turf, Stella picked up her story. "Anyway, I stayed with them. They were frightened, and I *decided* they needed my help—happy, Dad? So I left the swan sign on the trail, expecting Liz to find it quickly and to know that I was okay. What I thought at the time was that I would bring Luc and Chantal back out within a couple of hours. It just didn't work out that way."

"Maybe there was static on the cosmic connection that garbled the word from on high," Andrew suggested. He accompanied his words with a warm smile to make clear that he was not trying to make fun of Stella, but attracted a kick in the shin from Janet nonetheless. "What I mean is, it seems odd that you would put yourself in such danger for people you hardly knew, and scare the bejeezus out of your family as well."

"But it wasn't just foolish bravery, Dad. I had no idea how treacherous the ridge would be. And the shootings—I don't know. Maybe I was meant to be with them for that, because otherwise no one would know that they'd been killed." Stella fell silent for a moment, and then gave a tremulous sigh. "The rain forest seemed so beautiful, so pure—"

Her eyes began to tear. Janet moved her chair closer, put her arm around her daughter's shoulders, and put away her own pain. "It's okay, Stell."

"Thanks, Mom," Stella sniffed. "I thought about you the whole time, how worried you'd be. I was worried, too, believe me. With the clouds and all, it was pitch black last night. Scary. But then, at a certain point, I felt that George somehow—" She looked at Janet almost apologetically.

Janet nodded. "George is a *kahuna*, according to Bar—Captain Saga."

Andrew looked from mother to daughter. He knew that Janet basically shared his views about Stella's numinism, and that she was extending herself for her daughter's sake, but he did not have the emotional wherewithal to do the same. "George somehow what?" he asked, trying not to sound offensive.

"My dream and his dream, remember? I know you can't relate to this, Dad," Stella said, "but I felt we were communicating."

Liz sighed but said nothing.

"Telepathy?" Andrew felt the unfriendly squeeze of Janet's fingers on his thigh and read the message on his ex-wife's face. "Later, Stell, I'd like to hear more about that."

Stella nodded resignedly. "Dad?"

"What, daughter?"

"I said there were two reasons why Luc and Chantal were afraid of Adibi's murderer."

"Right."

"The second reason was that Luc and Chantal were working for France-Orient."

Andrew Chase froze with a glass of lemonade halfway to his lips. "Well, well. And they thought—what? That one of the other bidders was trying to eliminate the competition—literally. Is that it?"

"Uh-huh. Luc and Chantal were a sort of advance team. They had done a lot of investigative work for France-Orient regarding this huge plantation called the Makai Ranch. They weren't hippies at all. The whole story they told me about themselves the night of the murder was untrue. They weren't from Lyon. They were Parisians living the expat life in Vietnam. They told me that Adibi was working for a company interested in the same property. Luc had given him the list of potential buyers that he and Chantal had found out about through their snooping, and so when he was killed—"

"What company?" Andrew was still holding his lemonade aloft.

"I think it was called XIL."

"Xerxes Industries, Limited."

"Yes, that's it. What's the matter, Dad?"

Andrew came out of his state of suspended animation, brought the glass to his lips and took a sip of his drink. "I'm just wondering what all this means. Adibi was working for Xerxes, which isn't on the list. Chantal and Luc were working for France-Orient, which was on the list; and all three of them are dead." He scowled and then shrugged, unable to put the pieces together yet. "Have you told the police?"

"No, I didn't really have a chance. I have to see George after lunch, to be debriefed or to debrief him, however you say that."

"Why don't you just beam it to him now?"

"Andy!"

"Just joking, Janet. I just meant, the sooner the better, Stell."

"I know. Dad, I don't expect you to believe what I believe. For your own sake, though, you should try to be a little more open-minded."

"I should be. Unfortunately, I've got more immediate problems. One of the guards will take you up to Umi Street, Stella."

"I think a squad car is coming for me."

Andrew nodded. "Oh. Okay, that'll be fine. So you're out for the afternoon. And I have that meeting. What about you two?" Andrew looked at Janet and Liz. "Staying here at the house, I assume."

Liz shook her head. "I'd like to get out. Race Kendall offered to show me some tricks of the private eye trade. Maybe I'll take him up on it. He's kind of obnoxious, but—" She didn't finish the thought.

Andrew raised his palms into the air. "I don't know why I hired those guards."

"Not to keep us prisoner in the house, Dad. Don't worry, I'll be safer with Race than with those two superannuated ex-cops out there."

"Niki Makana says that Kendall's a fast mover," Andrew warned.

"I've yet to meet a man whose moves are too fast for me," Liz said. "Besides, he's doing some work for the Hawaiian sovereignty movement that I'm kind of interested in."

"Janet, what about you?"

"Well, I don't want to stay here alone again. I'll probably go up to Lihue with Stella. We can do a little shopping afterwards, or maybe stop in at the Kauai Museum. They're supposed to have a good exhibit on the history of the island."

"Can—can we talk about that meeting of yours, Dad?" Liz was hunched back in her chair.

"Talk about what? It's a client meeting. I can't say any more than that."

Liz straightened. "Dad, wait a second. You're going to the Makai Ranch to see that fellow Chamberlain that Mom met yesterday afternoon. Your client, Paracorp, wants to buy the land, just like France Orient probably does. People working for France Orient have been murdered. And this thing with Xerxes and Adibi looks the same. And now with what we know about that Low woman and the lawyer, I'm worried about you."

Andrew Chase rubbed a hand across his mouth. "You're right to be worried, Liz. I'm worried, too, a little. It's the list that bothers me. Why was it left in Adibi's hat? It wasn't a hit list, because Xerxes' name wasn't on it. Most likely, Adibi wrote it down when Luc gave him the names. The killer may not even have seen it."

Janet gave him a skeptical look. "You mean the poor man had an ice pick shoved into his ear while he was wearing his hat?"

"No, the killer could have done the deed, picked up the hat by the crown and then placed it back on Adibi's head without ever seeing the list. I'm not sure we're focusing on the right facts yet. Don't forget that there was another connection between Adibi and the French kids: marijuana. We can't be sure they weren't caught up in some kind of drug war that involves the ranch somehow. But even if it's a straight land war, Luc and Chantal were industrial spies. Maybe Adibi was, too. I'm not a spy, I'm a lawyer."

"Lawyers bleed, Dad," Stella chided.

"Lawyer's bleed," Liz echoed. "And the island bleeds. The sovereignty folks are afraid that wholesale development of the Makai Ranch could change the character of Kauai forever."

"Who said anything about wholesale development, Liz?"

"Well, okay, exactly what are Paracorp's plans, Dad?"

"Paracorp is a financing company. It doesn't do land development."

"So the land would stay in sugar, then?"

Andrew stared at his eldest daughter, then at the other two women. "Honestly, I don't know. I assume they'd lease it to someone, but they haven't told me anything about that aspect."

"What do you know about France-Orient, Andy?" Janet asked.

"Well, they're a lot like Paracorp. A huge finance vehicle for wealthy French people who want to invest in Pacific Rim properties. Not an operating company."

"They'd probably lease the land to someone else, too?"

"Probably."

"And Xerxes Industries," Stella prompted.

"Now, they're a different kind of animal," Andrew offered. "Laundered Iranian money. It's tricky for Americans to do business with Iranians, but not impossible. They do large-scale building projects, everything from refineries to power plants to resorts. I haven't heard their name in connection with Chamberlain's property until you mentioned it just now, Stell."

"You wouldn't represent just anyone, would you, Daddy? I mean, there's certain businesses that you would turn down as a matter of principle, right?" Liz eyed her father.

"Where are we going here, Daughter Number One? Let me try two different answers, and see if they're what your after. First, I'm a partner in a law firm. The firm has its principles, sure. We don't represent violent criminals, or tobacco companies, or gambling establishments."

"Or polluters?"

"Polluters." Andrew screwed his mouth into a thoughtful pout, and drew a breath before responding. "Every manufacturing company produces environmental waste, Liz. But we would not take on a new client that wanted us to help them violate the environmental laws, no. So that's one thing. And secondly, I do have my own principles, too. I wouldn't knowingly represent a party to a deal that would destroy the beauty of this island, if that's your question." He hated having to use that weasel word, "knowingly," and he hated Harry Wong for having put him in that position.

Liz didn't like that word, either. "Dad, your client is just a facilitator in the Chamberlain deal," she replied. "You don't really know what the ultimate use of the property will be."

"That's true, honey. But I know Paracorp management; I've been representing them for over a decade. They're—honorable people." It was a statement the truth of which depended on a very special definition of the word "honorable." Andrew Chase hoped that his deepening sense of guilt didn't show on his face.

Stella was staring at him as though examining an object she'd never seen before. "You mean they're not the type of people who would join with this Xerxes company on a big development deal?"

The notion caught Andrew by surprise. What was most surprising was that Stella, and not he, would have seen the possibility of a link-up between Paracorp and Xerxes. "Look, kids, for all I know, Paracorp's going to buy Chamberlain out and then turn around and lease the ranch right back to him. A very common transaction for people in Chamberlain's position, lots of assets but poor cash flow. I—I'll try to find out this afternoon and let you know as much as I can ethically—let's just say, as much as I can. And likewise, anything any of you learn this afternoon, we share tonight. Okay?"

The front doorbell rang out a few notes of *Aloha Oe*. It was the first time the Chases had heard the sound. Under other circumstances, they'd have found it amusing, but not so on this particular afternoon. They looked at one another. "Who's expecting company?" Andrew asked. No one answered. "Maybe the guard has a question. I'll get it." Before he could stand up, the front door opened, and a voice called out.

"Hello. It's C. B. Freeman. Anybody home?"

"Local newspaperman," Janet murmured. "He came by here yesterday. Seems nice enough." Then, more loudly, "Out here, Mr. Freeman." She pushed her chair back and rose to greet him.

Introductions were made and an extra chair placed at the table. The journalist eyed the Chase family. "You're having a hell of a vacation," he said.

"The fun part hasn't really started yet," Janet replied.

Andrew saw no merit in chatting with the press, either from his family's viewpoint or from his client's. "What can we do for you, Mr. Freeman?" he asked.

"C. B., please. Actually, I came over to see if I could do anything for you folks with what Janet called the 'fun part,' now that your ordeal is over."

"That's most thoughtful, but I think we'd just like to be left alone. The last thing we want right now is to help you sell newspapers."

Freeman chuckled. "Oh, I don't need your help, sir. Three unexplained murders in three days? We'll sell out until they catch the bastard—excuse me, ladies. No, I only thought you've been through a lot in the short time since your arrival, and you're not here indefinitely. If there's any way I can assist you to begin enjoying yourselves, I'd be pleased to do it."

"That's very kind of you," from Janet, and "We'll be fine, thanks," from Andrew, tumbled out at the same time.

"Well, for example," Freeman persisted, "up Lawa'i Road here less than five minutes is a salt water geyser, a lava shelf and some quite interesting shopping booths, all in one spot. I'd be happy to take you up there."

Andrew looked at his watch. "I'm sorry, I have an appointment in a little while. Liz, I think you'll be leaving soon. And Janet and Stella, you have plans, too, don't you?"

Janet scowled and shook her head. "Stell and I have some time. This place is right up the road, C.B. I guess our main concern is, will we be safe enough if a guard escorts us up there?"

Freeman spread his hands. "It's a tourist attraction, Janet. There'll be plenty of company."

Andrew stood up abruptly. "I'm sorry, I really must be going. Janet, would you give me a hand inside, please?"

In the bedroom, Andrew put his hands on Janet's shoulders and pushed her into a seated position on the bed. "This is no time for southern hospitality," he lectured her. "You understand what he's up to, don't you?"

"I understand what you're up to, Andy dearest. Look at you. Standing over me like a slave-owner, talking down to me. Do you really think I'm going to a listen to a word you say in this posture?" Janet motioned to a small arm chair that faced the bed.

"What I would give to have the old Janet Chase back," he moaned.

Janet pointed a finger at him. "It was you who killed her."

Her erstwhile husband sighed and sank himself into the chair. "He just wants to get information out of us," Andrew complained, "information that he can print in the next edition, to keep the story alive, make it look as though his paper's investigators are producing results even before the police do."

Janet leaned back on her elbows, and made a face at her former husband. "You won't believe this, I'm sure, but I was able to see through his clever ruse."

"W—well, then, why are you being so compliant with him? My assignment for Paracorp here is a secret, Janet. It's bad enough that the cops know about it; but if it's plastered on the front page of the newspaper, I lose a big client, something I can ill afford right now."

"Don't worry, darling. This man was kind to me when I was falling apart yesterday. I want to be nice to him. Stella and I are going to enjoy this one tourist site with our neighbor and one of the guards for maybe half an hour. C.B. will be gracious and gallant. Afterwards, he'll ask a few questions, and I'll ask a few questions. He's been doing some digging, too, you know. Maybe we'll learn something interesting for you. And we promise not to give away any of your secrets." Janet leaned forward, braless under her batik sundress.

Andrew Chase stared at his former wife. Their relationship had certainly not improved on this trip, even after a crisis that should have brought them closer together. "There's no hope for reconciliation, is there?" he asked suddenly.

Janet looked as if she'd just been struck by lightning. "Reconciliation!" There was a long pause. "Where the hell did that come from? Jesus, Andy, even if everything was sweetness and light between us here on Kauai, that was never in the cards. You asked me if we could vacation together to give our kids a sense of family. You said we wouldn't bring the old entanglements with us. Remember?"

"Well, yes, that's the way it was supposed to be," Andrew answered, backpedaling. "Instead we had a—an emergency. It got me thinking. I mean, hell, I don't know if I want us to get back together. I don't even know why the question occurred to me. It might be interesting to discuss the pros and cons, mightn't it? Just a dispassionate conversation?"

Janet Chase folded her arms, unfolded them, and then repeated the action. She shook her head slowly and sighed. "Look," she said. "I suspect the kids will be out for dinner tonight. Why don't you and I eat in? I'll pick up a nice bottle of wine and some groceries, and we can talk about whatever. And don't worry. It will definitely be dispassionate." She pushed herself up from the bed. "Oh," she said to herself, responding to a rogue thought.

Andy raised his eyebrows expectantly, hoping for a positive signal.

"I don't know whether this means anything, Andy," Janet continued, "but yesterday while we were at the Makai Ranch, Captain Saga thought he saw Chamberlain's son. Chamberlain told him he was mistaken, but a few minutes later Captain Saga almost came out and accused Chamberlain of lying about that." She walked past him toward the door, adding, "I thought you should know."

Andrew slumped in his chair. "Yes," he called out after his disappearing ex, "well, thank you for that."

"Captain?"

Barry Saga looked up from the case file open on his desk. "Hi, George. Any news?"

"Oh, yeah. We've got the car, all right. You didn't do badly for somebody firing blind. Actually hit it once, in the left rear quarter panel."

Saga smirked. "Not my finest moment. What about prints?"

"Plenty of them. Every Makai Ranch employee with a driver's license, and many without, have touched that vehicle."

"It was reported stolen Monday?"

"Afternoon, around three. The mechanic at the Ranch garage phoned in the report. The folks there weren't real careful with the vehicle; the key was in the ignition all day, and anyone on the property could just jump in and drive it around."

"So someone on the Ranch borrowed it to terrorize the old man?"

"Or else Web set up a little play when he saw you pull up in a cruiser. Or somebody not associated with the Ranch stole the car. I don't have any intuition about this one yet, Barry. Given that we're talking about attempted murder, all the workers at the Ranch will be questioned, but—" He raised his shoulders and turned down his mouth.

"What about the forensics on the gunshot wounds to those French kids?"

"So far, all they can say is that the weapon was a 30.06 hunting rifle, Winchester cartridges, range fairly close for that kind of weapon, maybe a hundred yards. With the noise of the flood and the natural cover, there was no need to stay too far away. But because of that, the gunman had more firepower than necessary. Had the kids not been wearing backpacks, the bullets would have gone straight through them."

"Suspects, George? The chief is all over me. The mayor and the councillors are all over him."

"Hey, we're not lacking for suspects, Barry. What we don't have is a theory or any hard evidence that would allow us to narrow the field."

"Okay. Listen, draft up a report I can give to the chief, will you? What we've got so far, the leads we're pursuing. No wild-assed speculation. And don't feature the real estate stuff for now. We just don't know enough—"

"Right. You'll have it in half an hour. Say, are you around for a while? Stella Chase will be here in about an hour, and apparently her mother is coming with her. Shall I buzz you when they arrive?"

"No, George. I'll be with the chief, but when I get done I'll stop in and say hello, if they're still here."

Below the observation area at Spouting Horn, a deck of gnarled lava extended about thirty yards into the ocean. Inside that hardened ebony flux there was a hollow tube, once a channel of cooled lava through which red-hot magma poured into the sea. Now the tube was a tunnel for the sea itself, drawing incoming waves into its dark recesses. There, the salt water raced past a blowhole in the lava shelf, making it roar, and then crashed into a wall beneath a second blowhole, exploding up through it in intermittent geysers. Janet and Stella heard the angry, hollow blast sounding over the crash of the waves against the lava cliff, and seconds later saw a plume of water shoot forty feet into the air. A minor wonder of nature, the like of which can be found in many other coastal venues, Spouting Horn's allure was enhanced by the views in both directions up and down the palm-fringed southeast coast of Kauai.

C. B. Freeman leaned against the railing, watching the play of the waves against the cliff, the emptying and filling of the treacherous breathing hole that lay like an open mow in the lava shelf, and the periodic water-flares themselves, mounting as if shot in bursts from a fire cannon, and then falling back in ringed splashes against the dark, irregular promontory.

"Everyone has the same reaction to the noise," he said over the natural din. "Dragon. And indeed, their reaction is consistent with legend. The story is that this coast was once guarded by a gigantic dragon, or *mo'o*, as the Hawaiians called it. People who came down to the shore were at risk of being eaten by the *mo'o*. A fellow named Liko was fishing here one day, when the *mo'o* attacked. He had a spear, which he flung into her mouth. In the fray, he fell into the water and swam into the lava tube. She tried to follow him, but got stuck down there, and what you hear out there are her cries from under the ledge."

Stella nodded and smiled at the folk tale, but Janet was more concerned with what was going on below them. "Should those kids be out there?" she asked, pointing out two teenaged boys who were making their way across the water-slicked lava projection toward the blowhole.

"Definitely not!" Freeman cried, and cupping his hands to his mouth he yelled at the teenagers, to no avail. "Two people have slipped into that blowhole since I've been here," the publisher told his guests. "One was pulled out pretty quickly, badly cut up from just a few seconds' of being smashed by the water surging against the jagged edges of the hole. The other was sucked into the lava tube, shredded up and taken out to sea by the rip current. Madame Pele's torture chamber," he added, inclining his head toward Spouting Horn. As the three watched, one of the teenagers slipped and fell, cutting his arm on a sharp irregularity. His cohort picked him up, and the pair retreated.

Janet shivered. She was in no mood for grisly tales or grisly sights. "Pele is the goddess of the volcano," she returned distractedly.

"Pele is the spirit of Hawaii, a wild fire deity whose power and influence overshadow any other force, human or natural, in the islands."

"Speaking figuratively, of course," Janet said, just to make conversation.

"Figuratively? Not at all. Pele walks the forests and beaches, she ruins crops or causes them to thrive, she pushes people who disobey her off of cliffs and saves from certain disaster those who comply with her wishes. Pele is as real to the people on these islands as you are, Janet Chase, or you, Stella. She's just about that real to me, and I, originally, am from Missouri."

Seeing that the two women weren't sure how to respond to his brief soliloquy, Freeman changed the subject. He pointed to the grassy hill behind the viewing area. "This is a great place to shop. You can get

Ni'ihau shell jewelry here at half the Lihue prices and a quarter of the Honolulu prices. Other things, as well. Shall we explore the booths?"

The high ground on the grassy hillside was commanded by tented stalls shaded by canvas flaps that reached to the ground and formed a kind of arcade. Inside the stalls, ranks of vendors hawked monkeypod and koa woodcarvings, polished sharks' teeth, tee-shirts with tropical themes, and jewelry. The adjacent parking lot was about half full of cars—"a good crowd for a Wednesday afternoon," Freeman said. Shoppers in bathing suits, sarongs, or shorts and tee shirts jockeyed for position in front of the glass-topped display cases, behind which salespeople touted the superiority of their own wares over their neighbors.'

The shell pieces turned out to be necklaces woven of pastel-toned snail shells the size of apple seeds, for which the raw materials were said to be found only on the beaches of Ni'ihau, a small private island off the southwest coast of Kauai where a traditional Hawaiian life-style was maintained. The simple beauty of the necklaces appealed to Janet, and she decided to buy a some for herself, Stella and Liz. Surprised but not daunted by the prices, Janet tried to haggle.

The vendor held up the necklace Janet had chosen for herself. "Look at this," she demanded, her brown eyes flashing against olive-toned skin slightly dewy from the heat inside the tent. "There is maybe three thousand tiny shells in this lei. Each one of them has to be found on the beach; they don't get delivered by the postman. My auntie, who make this one, only look for the shells at night after high tide, because she think if she get 'em next day aftah they sit in the sun, the color gonna fade. So she bend over with a flashlight, or down on hands and knees, picking up these teeny things one by one and deciding whether take or no take. Then, at home, she sort by type—*momi, laiki* or *kahelelani*—by size and by color, into her jars. She can't start make the lei until she got enough of each kine she gonna use. After, she clean the sand out of each one of the little buggahs with a tool like a pin or something. Then make hole in each for stringing. Auntie is good, but even she break more than half her shells trying to put hole in. Then finally set the pattern and string the shells, not just, you know, slip them on one after the other, but slip, knot, slip, knot, slip, knot, turn, to make like this one. You buy the three we been talkin' about here, I can do ten percent. That's all. You want 'em, fine, but I don't sell my auntie cheap."

Janet bought. On the way back from Spouting Horn, Freeman asked the guard to stop the car in front of a residential compound enclosed by a wall made of dusky lava rocks. "This is my place," he announced. “Like to see it?” Janet and Stella followed him through the gate. The property consisted of a main house and two guest bungalows, situated on a level quarter acre of land, shaded by royal palms and separated from the ocean by a yellow-sand beach. The interior of the main house was finished in exotic woods: teak, koa and mahogany, and window walls giving out on the ocean from each room.

“You must be very happy here,” Janet said.

“It’s hard to complain,” Freeman agreed. “The publishing business has been good to my wife and me. We started a little magazine twenty years ago called *Stargazing*—”

“Omigosh,” Stella exclaimed. “Really?”

“Oh, yes. It was just fluff, really, still is, but by the time we sold it four years ago, well, you know how successful it was. So here we are. We put out the *Progressive* once a week, and otherwise just roam the island looking to meet interesting people like you.”

“Actually, we’re pretty ordinary,” Janet replied.

He looked at her and then at Stella.

“I disagree. I’d like to interview you and your daughters.”

“I don’t think so,” Janet replied. “We’d prefer to be anonymous tourists again.”

“You can’t unscramble the egg, Janet. You and your family have been touched by three murders. Your daughter disappears and is found the next day in the company of two cadavers. That simply doesn’t happen to tourists here. Like it or not, you’re special. Newsworthy.”

“I’m sorry, C. B. We can’t.”

Freeman shrugged. “I understand,” he sighed. “It’s Andrew. He took you into the house and raised hell with you. Not that I blame him. We’ve looked him up. Reputable New York lawyer, does a lot of international work. Maybe that’s what he’s doing here. That meeting he’s going to this afternoon. You wouldn’t care to tell me—No, I suppose not.”

Janet Chase glanced at Stella, and then around the capacious living room, and finally back at Freeman. “Your paper comes out on—”

“—Tuesdays.”

“Tuesdays. So the next edition is next Tuesday.”

Freeman nodded.

“Well, I could see the possibility of some quotes from Stella about climbing over that ridge, which I gather has been rarely, if ever, done; about being caught in a flash flood on the other side, that kind of thing. Maybe Liz would have something worth printing about what it was like to find Adibi’s body. Fluff, as you call it. But we’d have to discuss it first—the family, I mean.”

"Of course," Freeman answered. "And it would work both ways. If my people came across something that it would be important for you to know—"

Janet nodded soberly. "We understand one another, C. B. Any information you can give us that would keep us out of further trouble would be much appreciated." She looked up into the rolling hills that stretched toward the central mountains. "That's all sugar cane up there, isn't it?"

"Yes, and everything you can see up there is part of a single plantation."

"Really? I've heard that the sugar business in Hawaii is in trouble. Is that true?"

"Quite true. I think we'll find the large plantations closing before long."

"Large as that one?"

"Funny you should ask. Rumor around the county office building is that it might be on the block."

"Could the problems in the sugar business have any bearing on the killings, do you think?"

"Could be. For now, our assumption at the *Progressive* is that the killer is a local. We could be wrong, you understand. My reporters are probably biased by the fact that the only kind of ground-level investigation we can afford is one based right here on Kauai. If they're right, though, the investigation shouldn't take long, because only a very small percentage of the island's population is disposed to premeditated murder. A number of the violent types have connections to the sugar business. The police know who those people are and so do we."

"And—who are they?"

"Generically? Marijuana growers, users of hard drugs and other low-lifers; people who would be willing to hire out as hit men."

"But what kind of connections would people like that have to the sugar industry?"

Freeman scratched his head. "Well, marijuana growers use the cane as cover for their plantings; they trespass on the land and salt the fields with their own crops. There's a certain amount of addiction to hard drugs among cane workers—it can be a hot, difficult, boring and even painful occupation. And your generic low lifer preys on the cane workers, who are largely immigrants and a vulnerable population. Gamblers, pimps, drug dealers—those are the kind of people I have in mind."

Stella stirred, eager to move on to Umi Street. "But these crimes only just happened," she said. "You can't be very far along in your investigation."

"You're right, young lady. In fact, we're still planning our attack." The publisher led the two woman back to the car. "Where are you off to next?" he asked.

"To see George Akamai," Stella told him, earning a reprimand from her mother in the form of a surreptitious pinch on her upper arm.

The publisher wagged a finger at them. "Now that fellow comes from an interesting family. Just about as pure Hawaiian as you can find on this island any more."

"You know him, them, then?"

"Yes, Stella. We did a story on him once after a shootout with some marijuana growers up north. His family lives on Maui. Simple, working class people. Going way back, his family ran a big chunk of the island. They were royalty, posterity of a fellow named Kukona, one of the wisest of the ancient kings of Kauai. To understand George, you have to appreciate the trajectory of his family's history."

They got into the car, and Freeman continued. "One of Kukona's kids had the ability to communicate with the gods."

"A *kahuna*," Janet offered.

Freeman held up a finger again. "Right. An exalted personage, someone who could make the unknown known and see the future. That power stayed in Akamai's family for generations."

"Maybe it's still there," Stella said, now more interested in talking with the publisher.

Freeman swivelled in the front passenger seat to look at her. "You've spent some time with him. What do you think?"

"It's possible," Stella said with a slight smile.

Freeman nodded. "I think so, too."

"But something happened to the family?"

"Oh, yes. Something rather sad. Their faculties had earned them chiefly status. They sat at the right hand of the kings of the island. For generations the Akamais were one of the most formidable clans on Kauai. Things started to go wrong for them when Captain Cook's expedition in search of the Northwest Passage sighted Kauai in 1778, thereby 'discovering' Hawaii or what he called the 'Sandwich Islands' after his patron. His two ships, the *Resolute* and the *Discovery*, were unlike anything ever seen by the natives before. One of Akamai's ancestors concluded that they must be the floating *heiau*, or temple, of the Hawaiian god Lono, which of course got the relationship between the Hawaiians and the whites off on a basis that distinctly favored the whites.

"There followed a long period of interaction in which the *kahunas* had continuing difficulty in interpreting the role of this new race in the lives of the islanders. Eventually the whites took over Hawaii and the indigenous royalty crumbled. The invaders' religion was viewed as more powerful, and its monotheism more seemly, than the Hawaiian religions. The *kahunas* were derided as savage buffoons by the whites and ultimately lost almost all influence with their own people. George Akamai is a noble, graceful and, I think, frustrated descendant of this star-crossed lineage."

Staring out the window in the back seat as they rode back to Puuholo Street, Stella Chase tried to imagine a time when people who communicated with God were revered, not scorned.

8

Andrew Chase turned off Highway 50 onto a red-earth road, and passed beneath an arched sign displaying the words "Makai Ranch" in rope-like script. He had the vinyl top of the convertible closed and the air-conditioner on, so that he would arrive unruffled and unwilted for his appointment with Webster Chamberlain. The long driveway wound upward through fields of green sugar cane that shook in the insistent easterly breeze. Here and there, the monotonous thickets of long, spiky-leafed cane were punctuated by service roads, irrigation ponds, uncultivated microforests, pumping equipment and piping.

About ten minutes into the climb, a cane truck, large, blocky and yellow, came barreling down the driveway toward him, hauling a heavy-ribbed trailer filled with burnt stalks to a height almost double the height of the truck itself. Its exhaust pipe blasted a brown miasma into the air above the cab, and the road behind it was obscured by a thick cloud of dust thrown up by its oversized tires. As the distance closed between the two vehicles, it seemed to Andrew that the diesel might be out of control, or worse, intentionally aiming at him. He swerved sharply into the stands of cane at the side of the road. The truck did not slow down. It careened toward him. He held his breath. The vehicle was nearly on him. He envisioned the impact crushing his skull, the massive wheels flattening him and his car to the thickness of the aluminum foil. He opened the door, with the thought of running into the cane field, but by then it was all over. The cane truck passed with a menacing but harmless roar. In its wake, the convertible rocked back and forth on its shock absorbers.

The lawyer sat still, feeling his heart race, staring at yellow-green stalks of growing cane, while a fine, dry rain of oxides settled onto his windshield. Fearless in his own environment—the business meeting, the conference room—he doubted he would ever be able to summon up that same level of courage in moments of real physical danger.

After fifteen minutes of bumping along the cane road, the gleaming white plantation-style house loomed before him on a grassy rise, an oasis of civility in a sea of rude agrarianism. In the gravelled circle in front of the house, just past a walkway leading to the pillared front porch, a luxury sedan was parked. Its license plate read "Makai-2." He pulled in front of it, parked and grabbed his briefcase. As he walked into the sweltering afternoon, he was greeted by a breathtaking vista of the south coast of Kauai lying at the foot of the plantation. In hazy remoteness to the southwest, the smokestacks and blocky buildings of a sugar mill punctuated the shoreline. Rooftops of a small town dotted the greenery directly below him on Highway 50. A series of foliated ridges rolled away to the east and west, fading to blue with distance. To the southwest, seventeen miles from the closest point on Kauai, the island of Ni'ihau sat low in the Pacific, with a single fluffy cumulus cloud resting on its shoulder like a guardian angel.

The visual extravaganza was the only greeting Andrew was immediately accorded. No one came out to meet him. He mounted the steps of the capacious porch and rang the doorbell beside the glass-paned doors. After a moment, a figure approached on the other side of the glass, a man past his prime, moving slowly. He motioned for Andrew to let himself in.

The entry hall, lit only by indirect sunlight through the front doors, was dark and cool, with cream-colored walls and large polished coffee-colored tiles laid in a diamond orientation. There were several pieces of Asian furniture, a large mirror in an ornate gilt frame and numerous small paintings in styles ranging from early nineteenth century maritime to late twentieth century post-modern. Andrew Chase strode over to the elderly gentleman and held out his hand. "Mr. Chamberlain?"

"Yes. Mr. Chase, is it? How do you do? Won't you come in, please." Webster Chamberlain led Andrew into a large room panelled in koa and open to the roof above the second floor, from which skylights allowed shafts of light to descend at an angle to the surface of a high wall, where they shattered into a diffuse mist of radiance that settled into the room. A table suitable either for dining or for meetings sat in highly burnished glory in the reflected light, attended by eight gracefully carved wooden chairs.

At the other end of the room, two people put their coffee cups and saucers down on a mahogany sideboard, and approached the new arrival. One, a tall fellow in a tan, tropical-weight suit, with mane-like blond hair turning white at the temples, introduced himself as Carter Robinson. The other was a striking Chinese woman of moderate height, rather younger, with close-cropped black hair and wearing a form-fitting red silk suit that was hemmed almost a foot above her knees. "I am Li-Ann Low," she said. She pronounced her last name more like "law." From the hard look she gave him, Andrew could tell that he would not be able to charm her into taking seriously Harry Wong's lowball bid.

The three representatives exchanged business cards. Chamberlain invited them to sit at the table. "Leave your briefcases in the corner for now, and let's just talk for a while," he suggested. "Coffee's on the sideboard if you'd like some, Mr. Chase."

Chamberlain sat at the head of the table with Robinson and Low to his left and Andrew Chase to his right. After a few minutes of anemic conversation, the "just talking" wound down. Chamberlain looked at Andrew. "Mr. Wong sends his regrets," Andrew began, excusing his client's absence with studied gravity, even though Chamberlain had no reason to expect Harry Wong to attend. "He was unable to join me, and felt it inappropriate to send any lesser Paracorp executive in his stead. He asked me to assure you that he is available by phone at any time during our discussion today, and that he will move heaven and earth to meet with you in person should our discussions proceed to a point where that seems appropriate."

Chamberlain chuckled. "Thank you, sir. Please tell Mr. Wong that I'm sure he's bought properties worth many times more than the Makai Ranch without ever speaking personally with the principals on the other side, and therefore I am quite grateful for his kind assurances. Now, unless you have something else to say at the outset here—no?—well, then, if it is agreeable to you, I'd like to stimulate our conversation this afternoon by having Ms. Low present some information about the Makai Ranch that she has stored on her Thinkamajigee." He nodded in the realtor's direction.

Li-Ann Low rose from her chair and swung her slender body on stiletto heels over to the wall ten feet or so away, where she bent down at the knees to retrieve her laptop. The motion exposed the whole of her left thigh. Staring brazenly at the Paracorp lawyer, she rose easily out of her crouch, returned to the table and sat down. Andrew remained impassive, but he was thinking how fortunate it was that Harry Wong was not present; this woman would appeal to his most uncontrollable weaknesses. She could eat him alive. He stared steadily back at her and by entering into her game even in that small way, unconsciously evidenced the extent to which she had begun to exert dominion over him.

The realtor opened her computer and slid it toward him across the table. Unbuttoning her jacket, she leaned forward to reach the space bar. "The Makai Ranch is the lower half of a pie-shaped wedge of land running from the top of Mount Wai'ale'ale down to the sea," she began, in a clipped, businesslike tone. An aerial photo of the southern quadrant of the island appeared on the screen, with the boundaries of the property superimposed on it. "At thirty thousand acres, it comprises about twelve percent of the privately owned land on the island. In ancient times, it belonged to a Hawaiian royal family. Minor royalty. The property passed into the hands of Mr. Chamberlain's ancestors in the 1850s. It is fertile, well-drained and, like most of the south of the island, reliably sunny."

The ensuing description of the Ranch's history physical attributes was lost on Andrew Chase, since he had no idea how Paracorp intended to use the property. He did notice, though, that each time the realtor leaned in his direction to advance the presentation by touching the space bar, her breasts beneath her black camisole-like blouse brushed against the tabletop. An intentional effect, Andrew assumed. *Nice touch.* His admiration was blunted by the realization that he was seated across the table from the pair that had been seen running from Bungalow 13 on the afternoon of the murder—the couple who had sent Artemis Gabriel prowling around the Poipu house the night before. Andrew straightened up in his chair, intending for his posture to remind him to remain vigilant. It seemed inconceivable that Webster Chamberlain's high-priced lawyer and main-island realtor were multiple murderers, but he did not intend to take chances.

The sales pitch ran on for about fifteen minutes. Finally, the realtor sat back in her chair. "So, as you can see, Mr. Chase, the Makai Ranch is a unique property, amenable to numerous uses. It is a particularly good agrarian parcel, and although sugar may be a less profitable crop than it once was, the land will support plantations of macadamia nut, coffee, and many types of vegetables that could become a reliable supply for the hotels on all the islands. It is also perfect for resort development, having its own beaches, as well as rolling lowlands for golf and highlands for tropical touring and honeymoon-type settings. One can imagine many other uses consistent with the character of the land. In the right hands, this would be a very rewarding investment." Her small but full-lipped mouth closed in a thoughtful pout, and she stared across the table, waiting for a response.

Andrew nodded politely, but made a point of not responding. Instead, he turned to the sugar magnate. "What are your objectives in selling this property, Mr. Chamberlain?"

"My objectives?"

Carter Robinson interceded in a blatant attempt to move the focus of inquiry away from his client. "I think you've got the wrong end of the stick, there, Mr. Chase. My client has put a truly unique property on the market. You've just had a presentation describing its manifold advantages. The question for discussion now is whether the property meets the buyer's objectives and what the buyer is willing to pay."

Professional courtesy dictated a response, though not necessarily a cordial response. "Thank you, Mr. Robinson. Are you saying that the buyer's objectives are relevant but the seller's are not? Is there some new philosophy of negotiation in currency out here of which I'm not aware?"

Chamberlain's lawyer reacted as expected: he took the questions personally. "I think it would be best, sir, not to try to talk down to the seller and his representatives."

Andy ratcheted back smoothly. "Oh, dear. I've given offense. I apologize. I've worked in New York for twenty-five years, you know, so I tend to be an in-your-face kind of negotiator. All I really meant was that in my experience, a successful negotiation requires that the parties understand one another's motivations, so that their energies are directed toward a mutually advantageous set of deal points. You wouldn't disagree with that, I imagine."

"I think all of us can agree with that," Robinson returned, subsiding a little. "But we've made our opening remarks, if you will. Now it's your turn. What is it about this property that interests Paracorp?"

Web Chamberlain cleared his throat. "If you don't mind, Carter, I'd like to answer Mr. Chase's question."

Perfect, Andrew exulted privately. *Divide and conquer.* Looking at Robinson, he asked, "I wonder if it would be appropriate to proceed on a first-name basis." The Honolulu lawyer nodded sourly, but did not speak.

"Good, so it's Web, Carter, Li-Ann and Andrew, then," Chamberlain announced, obviously pleased with the turn toward informality and, presumably, away from rancor. With the notable exception of his dealings with Harry Wong, Andrew's experience was that clients hated the rancor on which lawyers tended to thrive—a useful fact for a strategic negotiator to keep in mind. He settled back in his chair and looked at Chamberlain.

"My objectives in selling the Makai Ranch are threefold, Andrew. I want to convert my estate into liquid assets. My only child no longer lives in Hawaii, and the land, even though it has been in the family for almost a century and a half, means little to him—certainly far less than the equivalent value in stocks and bonds, off the income from which he could live after my death. Also, I want to get out of the sugar business, which grows harder for me to operate profitably every day. And number three, I want to assure that the Chamberlain name is not besmirched by my successors in interest; that is, that the purchaser uses the land in such a way as to redound to the benefit of the people of Kauai, and does not change its essential character."

"Thank you, Web. I think we should mark those objectives down as deal points for the seller." Andrew pulled a little pad from his hip pocket, and scribbled on it with the small pen that had been tucked inside. To himself he noted that price was not explicitly among those deal points, which might mean that there might be some hope for Paracorp's niggardly offer after all. "Li-Ann, I understand that there are several actual or potential bidders for this parcel."

"We are in discussions with six companies, Andrew. Two are at the offer stage, if we properly anticipate Paracorp's position here today."

"The other offeror being France-Orient?"

"Please, Andrew. Don't play games with us."

"Okay. So, there are six players beside Paracorp?"

"No, six including Paracorp."

Andrew Chase put his fingers to his lips, and glanced from the realtor to Robinson and back. "France-Orient, Nihon Investments, Chung Bank." He ticked them off on the fingers of his other hand. "Singapore/Vision, ROC Overseas. Paracorp. Xerxes Industries. That seems to be seven. Correct?" At the mention of Xerxes, Robinson had stiffened a little, and Li-Ann Low's eyes had widened for just an instant.

Robinson folded his arms against his chest. Li-Ann Low tapped her fingernails against the tabletop. "I don't think that even in New York you would expect a seller in a deal of this magnitude to identify other interested parties," she replied coldly.

"I'll take that as a Yes," Andrew returned cheerily. Again he glanced at Robinson and back at the realtor, unsure what to make of the discrepancy.

"We are not here to play 'twenty questions,' Andrew," she answered.

"Excuse me, Li-Ann," Chamberlain interjected. "What about that last company mentioned by our new friend here? It doesn't sound familiar to me."

Thanks again, Web, Andrew thought.

Carter Robinson cleared his throat. "I think it would be fair to say that no company by that name has expressed interest in buying the Makai Ranch, Andrew."

"Well, I guess I had bad information," Andrew replied. Robinson had chosen his words very carefully. They did not exclude the possibility that Xerxes was a potential lessee working with one of the buyers.

"Yes, well, then, let's get to the bottom line. Are you prepared to make an offer on behalf of Paracorp today, or does your client need more data from us, or what?"

Chamberlain pushed his chair back and got to his feet. "Hold on, folks," he commanded. "Methinks that—as Milton put it—more is meant here than meets the ear. On reflection, I think this bargaining table format is too confrontational. It didn't work that well with France-Orient, either. Oops, I guess I shouldn't have told you that, should I, Andrew? In any case, why don't we go out back, sit in the shade and have a cocktail?"

The planter led his guests down the central hall of his capacious abode and out the rear door. Behind the mansion the grounds had been professionally landscaped to look accidentally beautiful. The centerpiece of the setting was a pond that reflected an angular ridge rising sharply upward perhaps a mile away. A canal entered at the rear of the clearing, made its sinuous way into the pond, and exited the pond not far from the house over a small dam. The lawn was a brilliant green border to these water treatments, and here and there thickets of tropical foliage were placed so as to please the eye. At the far end of the pond, domesticated geese and ducks swam and fluttered and sounded their unmusical calls. To either side of the dominating ridge, low mountains shrouded in haze decorated the deep background.

On the grass near the back of the house, shaded by a large banyan tree, there were six white, slat-backed wooden lawn chairs, on four of which Chamberlain and the others seated themselves. Roots of the banyan reached from the branches above them to the ground below, forming a natural maze behind the chairs.

Andrew surveyed the property, then raised his eyes to watch the small clouds that caressed the top of the ridge. "How can you let go of this place, Wes?" he wondered aloud, continuing his effort to avoid talking about Paracorp.

"Ah, I was raised in this house, my friend. I've seen this view almost every day for over six decades. I think I'm ready for a change."

A dark young woman in a modest frock had come out to join them. Chamberlain took her hand. "This is Emma. She will bring you whatever you want to drink. But I should tell you that she makes an absolutely delicious and quite healthful planter's punch. She'd be happy to bring us a pitcher, wouldn't you, dear?"

While they waited for their punch, Chamberlain recounted tales from his youth on the Ranch—some ribald, some hair-raising and some interesting only to Chamberlain himself. Robinson added his own perspectives on the Hawaii that barely existed any longer, Hawaii before mass tourism. Andrew was happy for the interlude, and for the injection of alcohol into the meeting, which could only be helpful to his uphill struggle, so long as he himself didn't overindulge, which he intended not to do anyway for security reasons.

Eventually Emma brought a full pitcher and four glasses that were already brimming with punch. She presented the tray to the guests and to Chamberlain, offering each a glass and a napkin. Then she placed the pitcher on a low table next to her employer. "I just heard on the radio that Hurricane Iniki is gonna pass south of Kauai day after tomorrow, Mr. Chamberlain."

"How close, Emma?"

"Not very, I guess. We gonna get lotsa rain, though, and real strong winds."

"On this island," Chamberlain said to the others, "that means power outages. Emma, dear, make sure we've got extra ice and candles, and that Jojo has got plenty of gasoline up here for the generators." He raised his glass—"cheers"—and took a long draft, watching his guests as he did so to assure they were following suit. Andrew wasn't. "Come on, my friend," the planter chided. "Don't reject my hospitality."

Andrew nodded cheerfully, and without a blink or other sign of reservation, lifted his glass to his lips. *Just one swallow.*

He inhaled the bouquet, expecting fruitiness and experiencing instead a breath of rum so strong that it stung the insides of his nostrils. Still smiling, he drank as long and as eagerly as Chamberlain did. The concoction was surprisingly sweet and smooth, a kind of ambrosia of coconut, mango, passion fruit and guava that masked to the tongue the alcohol that could not be concealed from the nose. In a matter of seconds, a warm, comfortable sensation began to radiate through his body. With a satisfied sigh, the proprietor of the Makai Ranch hoisted his tumbler again and, looking heavenward, recited a phrase from childhood. "He plants his footsteps in the sea, and rides upon the storm."

"We had hurricanes in New England, too, when I was a kid," Andrew mused. "Big ones, or maybe it just seemed that way to me. But that's changed. I think the last big one that made it into our area was back in the seventies some time."

"I remember when Hurricane Dot hit us in the mid-fifties, and there was one a couple of years before that," Chamberlain replied. "The island wasn't so developed at the time, but those of us who were here got roughed up pretty badly. Then Iwa in eighty-two. Wasn't even a direct hit, but it caused a lot of damage because of the shoddy construction that had gone up all over the island in the sixties and seventies. Other than those two, it's been a long time since a hurricane made landfall anywhere in Hawaii. It just doesn't happen often."

"They go roaring by to the south, like Iniki is doing," Robinson added, "or sometimes to the north. Wet us down, do some moderate wind damage on one of the islands, maybe; that's pretty much it."

"Florida is where I wouldn't like to be," Li-Ann Low put in. "Looks like that hurricane in south Florida last month created a few hundred thousand homeless people overnight. No electricity, no water, no nothing. And they get hit every year down there, just about."

They drank Emma's punch and chatted more or less easily for half an hour. Chamberlain refilled their glasses once, and then again. Andrew Chase found to his dismay that his attempts at abstinence provoked objections from Chamberlain, which was counter to his strategy of ingratiating himself with his host. Because he had no other choice, he allowed himself to conclude that the best course would be just to go with the flow and drink along with the others. The passing of the afternoon was marked by the slow clock face of nature: drifting clouds and lengthening shadows. Conversation became vague and unconnected. Under the influence of the sublime ambience and the rum, Robinson's nervous caution dissipated, and Li-Ann Low's hard edge softened. Eventually, she turned to Andrew, mugging her usual stoniness.

"So, Mr. Big New York Lawyer. Are you gonna make an offer this afternoon, or are we just gonna sit here and drink ourselves into a stupor?"

Andrew gave a throaty chuckle. "Both, Li-Ann. First the stupor, then the offer." The little joke threw Li-Ann Low into a fit of giggles. "I did a deal like that in Osaka once, actually," Andrew continued once the laughter ebbed. "It was a dinner meeting, and I knew that by the end of the evening everyone, including yours truly, would be hopelessly shitfaced. Excuse me, Ms. Big Honolulu realtor."

"S'Okay. I use the word myself on occasion, usually to describe someone in your present condition."

"Ha! *Touché!* So anyway, what I did—you'll like this, Carter—I prepared the papers ahead of time, making, you know, a guess, basically, as to what the position of the parties would be at the end of the evening. Where I didn't know, I made up a position that was fair, let's say, but not disadvantageous to my client. Then I gave the papers to a young associate who was not attending the dinner, and instructed her to have the waiter bring them into the dining room along with the cognac. Well, by then everyone was blind drunk, of course, and we all had a merry time passing signature pages around and executing them. The next day, the Japanese realized what they had done, but were constitutionally incapable of retracting because they felt they would lose face to the *gaijin*." He threw the Japanese word for foreigner, with its pejorative overtones, at Li-Ann Low, who gave him a been-there-done-that smile.

"Based on that, Web, you'd better cut the rest of us off," Robinson warned with a little snicker, "but keep this shyster drinking until he's drunk enough to make his offer."

"Unless you're ready now, Slick," Li-Ann added.

"Yeah, sure, I have an offer for you, or rather for you, Web." He turned to Chamberlain. "Thirty million. A thousand dollars per usable acre. Cash. How's that sound to you?"

Li-Ann Low tittered derisively. "No wonder Harry Wong stayed home. Thirty million? You're one funny man, Andrew Chase."

Web Chamberlain leaned forward in his chair, a hand on his chin. "Let me put it somewhat differently, Andrew," he said thickly. "Thirty million dollars is a lot of money. I don't think the Ranch has produced that much profit if you added up all the years I've been running it. It's a sum that would allow me to retire quite comfortably, to settle a nice inheritance on my errant son and to make some very important charitable contributions here on my home island. Please thank Mr. Wong for his offer, which I, at least, do not take as a joke. Unfortunately, it's our belief," he waved his hand in the direction of his representatives, "that the other offers, when they come in, will exceed thirty million by a factor of two or more. Three or more, Li-Ann? No, no, I'm a little foggy. Two or more."

Andrew nodded deliberately, then shook a finger at Chamberlain. "You know, you could be right, Web. Makai Ranch may be worth sixty million, even eighty million to someone. Who can say? The problem, as I see it, is that assets like this don't come up for sale often enough to establish a market price. So maybe there's that perfect buyer out there, the one who will see the true potential and worth of your Ranch that no other buyer sees. Maybe that buyer is sitting in Singapore, or Bombay, or London, Sydney, Johannesburg, I don't know, and some day or some year something will bring you two together."

He took a breath, almost losing his train of thought in the process. "On the other hand, here we are, September ninth, nineteen-ninety-two—election year, vote for Bush, everybody—here's Paracorp, bringing you what you need. What you want. Is it worth waiting three, four, eight, ten years for that perfect buyer, when you could stop worrying tomorrow? A thousand an acre for raw land ain't bad. In my briefcase," Andrew looked around him, blearily anxious for a second. "Oh, yeah, it's inside! In my briefcase, there's a binder check for five million dollars. I think you should take it."

Chamberlain's lawyer stirred. "What use would Paracorp propose to make of the property, Andrew?"

An indication of interest? Carelessness? Or is it the rum? Andrew wondered. "I'm not at liberty to say at this time, Carter. Surely we can separate the questions of price and use."

Li-Ann Low slapped her hands gleefully against the arms of her chair. "You bet we can, Andrew. Harry Wong's price is doo-doo, no matter how you intend to use the Ranch. Web doesn't have to wait ten years. We expect to have another offer in a week and are negotiating with several other active prospects."

Andrew Chase spread his arms wide. "Li-Ann, you should come to New York. It is your destiny, your true milieu. You and I could do such deals together."

"In your dreams, Brah!" The realtor collapsed in laughter.

"You know, I hate to bring this up." Andrew was not sure he would bring it up if he were sober. "There's a shadow over this land. You've got representatives of potential bidders or otherwise interested parties being murdered here. How that will affect—"

"Whoa, there!" Carter Robinson sat up in his chair, chin forward, eyes glazed and narrowed. "What are you talking about? Murders?"

"Yeah, murders, *mon cher colleague*. Two French people doing G-2 work for France-Orient, shot in the back yesterday. I saw the bodies myself. A fellow working for Xerxes Industries killed down in Poipu. My family saw that body. Maybe you did, too." Andrew made the veiled allusion to the pair's visit to Bungalow 13, even though he knew it was probably unwise. He wanted to know why these two seemingly respectable people hired Artemis Gabriel to stalk his daughter. Having spent the afternoon drinking with them, he was willing to gamble on his conclusion that Robinson and Low were not dangerous, and that asking in an indirect way about their connection with Adibi would precipitate an interesting side bar with Robinson.

Robinson's stony visage suggested that Andrew might have misjudged the depth of goodwill in the garden that afternoon, and he was attempting to overcome his wooziness in case trouble arose, when a voice behind him brought the conversation to an end. "Funny you should raise that issue, Andy. That's just what I was wondering."

Webster Chamberlain stood up as gracefully as his state of inebriation would allow and walked unsteadily over to the new arrival. The others turned to see who it was.

"Captain Saga!" Chamberlain declared as he clapped the police officer on the shoulder. "Does this mean the shooting is about to begin again?"

"Where are you taking me?" Liz Chase glared out the window of the old MG. She and Race had just driven past the grounds of the large but understated Hyatt Regency, which, sitting at a distance from the road, looked like a long, stucco hacienda with an aquamarine tiled roof. Since the hotel was the last developed property before entering a sea of sugar cane, Liz had expected Race to turn in. He hadn't. Now the roadway had become a hardpacked, rutted dirt track that led into the plantation and toward some odd dome-shaped hills.

"I told you," Race Kendall replied over the noise of the wind and the engine. "To the beach."

"This does not look like the way to the beach," Liz shot back.

"There are spectacular beaches here, Liz. Trust me."

"Sorry. The members of the Chase family are not into trusting other people at the moment."

"You'll love it. Guaranteed."

"It's not that I don't want to be alone with a strange man on a godforsaken spit of sand, Race," Liz yelled back. "It's that I don't want to be alone with you on a godforsaken spit of sand."

"You won't be alone with me. These are public beaches," Race shouted back, flashing his handsome but maddening smile.

They reached a crossroads, trails going off in directions that led, as far as Liz could tell, to nowhere. Race turned right and in a moment a building that looked like either an abandoned guard shack or a forlorn, sunbleached outhouse loomed on their right. Race stopped the car in front of it, and to Liz's surprise, an elderly man wearing a baseball cap, jeans and a work shirt stepped out of the dilapidated structure and handed her a clipboard with a one-paragraph liability waiver on it. "Just sign your name," Race barked.

As soon as Liz handed the clipboard back to the drowsy attendant, Race threw the car into gear and spun off in a cloud of dust. Liz twisted in her seat, grabbed the emergency brake with both hands and jerked it up abruptly. The MG stalled and skidded to a halt. "Explain this, please," she demanded when Race turned to her goggle-eyed.

"O-kay. Just let me extract my front teeth from the steering wheel." He pantomimed their retrieval and reinsertion. "You see," he began, whistling the sibilant, "all the beaches in Hawaii are open to the public. In fact, not only are they open, but the public must be given some way of reaching them. The Maha'ulepu beaches, where we're going, are part of the McBryde sugar plantation. That guy back there was a McBryde employee, getting a release from liability in exchange for permission to pass through the plantation to the beaches. There are three nice beaches down here. We'll go to Gillin's today. Maybe Kawailoa Bay, too." He stopped and stared at Liz for a minute. "So, are you with me?"

Liz stared back. The story sounded legitimate. There was something about McBryde on the waiver—She waved a hand to indicate that Race should proceed.

They reached Gillin's Beach after a short bumpy ride. It was a long stretch of sand, shaped like a reverse "J," backed by palms and shrubbery and terminating in a little cove. Under the surface of the water, reefs and hardened lava sheets appeared as dark masses. Race suggested that they put their beach bags down and take a walk; he had something he wanted to show her. "Keep you zoris on," he advised as Liz started to pull off a flip-flop. "The sand is hot, and we have to negotiate some rocks."

The land bordering the cove rose sharply. Where it met the water at the far side of the cove, steep cliffs faced the incoming tide. Behind the sandy crescent itself was a dome-shaped hill, and between the cove and the upper beach, a stream—or perhaps an irrigation ditch—flowed into the sea. They splashed through the stream, and Race led the way through a thicket of brush onto a narrow path that followed the curve of the dome. In a few moments, they were behind the hill. "Here we are," Race said, pointing to an opening at its base.

"What is it? A cave?"

"No, a tunnel. Come on, and watch your head."

Liz hung back. "Race—"

"Oh, come on. This is in all the guidebooks. Trust me, will you?"

He marched toward the opening, ducked a bit and disappeared into it. Liz, suddenly alone in the middle of nowhere, took a deep breath and followed. The tunnel curved a little, but once her eyes adjusted the visibility was adequate because the tunnel, though curved, was only about thirty yards long. Half a minute later, they emerged into a natural amphitheater. What had appeared from the outside to be a hill was actually a topless, hollow shell. The upper walls of its interior were almost vertical, and the rocky residue of centuries of erosion lay at the base of a roughly circular area thirty or so yards in diameter. The vault of the sky arched overhead, with light clouds floating into view and then out again.

Though the sun was high, two large banyan trees filled the space with dappled shade, which fell across the tall grasses, flowers and bushes that occupied most of the ground here.

"Wow," Liz breathed. "Is this a sacred place or something?"

"Gives you that feeling, doesn't it? I don't really know. Let's ask Niki."

"Niki?"

A path traced the inner circumference of the enclosure. Race set off counterclockwise, with Liz after him. Halfway around, sitting in a patch of sunshine, reading a book called *Kauai: the Separate Kingdom*, was Iniki Makana. She was wearing a flowing brown-and-white wrap tucked into itself at her breast.

"I asked Niki to join us because you wanted a chaperone," Race teased, drawing ocular daggers from Liz. "Just kidding," he chortled. "I thought you'd be interested in hearing more about the sovereignty movement. What're you reading there, Niki? *Haole* history?"

"Just getting into the mind of the oppressor, white boy. Sit, sit," Niki urged Liz, patting a flat-topped rock next to her in the sunshine.

"Is that what *'haole'* means—'oppressor?'" Liz asked before settling down.

"Not officially," Niki replied. "It means 'foreigner'. Over time, it's been used mostly to refer to white people. By now, it may have overtones of 'oppression' just by the force of history, I guess. So, shall I tell you all about our impossible little movement?"

"That's the thing, isn't it? The thing that makes the idea so romantic and poignant? Sovereignty is so just, and at the same time so impossible." She sat down and immediately found the proximity a little close for her taste. She leaned back against the rock wall and held her right leg up with her hands to keep it from resting against the Hawaiian's left leg.

Niki smiled. "Maybe so. The chances of wresting the land back from the overlords are slim to none. But, you know, even if we can't succeed, the movement has other benefits. It gives us Hawaiians back our identity, our sense of pride; it focuses us on our history, our culture, our diet, our environment. And the fact that until the movement fails there's at least a theoretical possibility that it will succeed gives us hope—which is, you know, a lot better than despair."

"But are the objectives of the movement to throw out the foreigners, or what?"

"No, that's a typical *haole* misconception. What we want is an independent nation. Anybody of whatever race who was born in Hawaii could be a citizen of the Hawaiian nation."

"But then—I don't understand. Is sovereignty a movement of the Hawaiian people, or a movement of people of whatever race living in Hawaii?"

"It's a little complicated. Kendall tells me you're interested in environmental issues. Well, then, you know how much more environmentally conscious and friendly the cultures of the American Indian tribes were than those of the European invaders. It's the same here. The historical culture of Hawaii is the culture of the Hawaiian people, which is based on deep reverence for the land. That culture would be the basis for life for all the people of whatever background living in independent Hawaii. Returning to an aloha culture, an aloha economy, would change these islands so much. So much!"

"I thought the Hawaiians were actually a fierce people," Liz put in.

"Fiercer than any other people? I don't know about that. I would say that, sure, the testosterone level of Hawaiian men is certainly not lower than the level in men of other races. The ancestors did battle with one another, and our society was a better one under the queens than under the kings. But our men also wore flowers in their hair. Been a couple thousand years since European men did that. And the aloha culture emphasizes the positive aspects of our heritage, Liz, not the negative. Want to hear the list?"

"You bet." Liz nodded perfunctorily.

"No, you have to pay close attention, now. I didn't come here to listen to myself talk. Commit them to memory, so you can help spread the word."

"Me? Spread the word?"

"You bet, sistah. Ready? Here we go. *Malama 'aina,* caring for and appreciating the land, or conservation. *Aloha 'aina,* loving and being committed to the land, or in modern terms, environmentalism. *Kokua,* helpfulness. *Koko'o,* supportiveness. *Akahai,* modesty, gentleness, even meekness. *Lokohi,* togetherness, or what we might call today inclusiveness. *Ha'aha'a,* humility; *'Olu'olu,* kindness. And *ahonui,* patience. Hopefully, all our citizens will be able to live by those principles; anyway, they would be the basis of the national culture."

"I could live by them," Liz said, "except maybe for meekness."

Race Kendall was leaning against the trunk of a small tree that struggled for sunlight under the umbrella of one of the banyans. "Isn't there a more fundamental question, Niki?" he interjected. "How the hell could Hawaii survive economically as an independent country?"

Niki kicked a naked leg in Race's direction. "You've always got money on your mind, Brah."

"Not always. Sometimes I think about surfing—or sex."

The brief exchange seemed relaxed, intimate. Liz wondered what the relationship was between Race and Niki. She felt a kind of unfocused jealousy. Though Race was a great diversion and apparently wealthy, he didn't seem to be her type. Too much a surfer dude. Anyway, she had Harlan at home. But Liz had never been comfortable taking second place to another woman in any man's eyes. She didn't know how to play the part. Just then Niki looked at her as if to say, "Isn't this guy too much?" It was a knowing glance between women, between friends. Liz smiled back, her envy defused as quickly as it had arisen.

"If you take away the money we get from the U.S. government—the nonmilitary money, I mean," Niki said, in answer to Race's question, "we wouldn't lose that much. The Hawaiian economy is already based largely on private foreign trade: agricultural exports and tourism. That would continue; maybe it would even increase, 'cause we could trade with countries that the U.S. won't allow us to now. Naturally, if the U.S. pulled the military out, it would hurt pretty bad for a while. But the U.S. has military bases in lots of foreign countries, so they might not do that. And, see, even if they did, we would be able to get by with less, because the aloha culture would be less materialistic. Materialism is based on a belief that humans are separate from their environment. The aloha culture is based on the opposite principle."

Liz put her leg down. Her thigh brushed against Niki's. "I really like this concept," she said. "What occurred to me as you were talking is that Kauai is, like, a metaphor for the earth. It's isolated in the ocean in the same way the earth is isolated in space."

"And so, if the aloha culture could succeed here—" Niki put in, carrying Liz's thought forward.

"—then the whole world could learn from Hawaii's example. This is really, really interesting. To me, anyway."

"I'm glad," Niki answered, and laid her hand on Liz's forearm. "I—I need to tell you something, Liz. A confession. When Race suggested I meet you here, I had an ulterior purpose for agreeing. The fact that you are in tune with what the Kamehamehas stand for, that we sort of, well, we're sistahs, right? Well, it makes it easier to ask you." Liz hadn't moved her arm.

"So ask," she replied, looking steadily into the woman's lovely dark eyes.

"It's about your father. I feel as though I know him a little, because of the time I spent with him looking for Stella. Well, anyway, I'd like to talk to your dad."

"About the Makai Ranch?"

"Yes. He seems like a very nice man. Sensitive."

"Sensitive?"

"Well, the tears in his eyes when we found your sister—"

"Really!" Sensitivity was an emotion Liz had never seen in her father.

"It was touching. So I thought if I could tell him our story, maybe he would tell me Paracorp's story."

Liz lifted her arm out from under Niki's hand and clasped her hands over her head. She wasn't offended and didn't feel as though she was being used. She did want to be prudent, however, when it came to her family. She thought for a moment, staring out into the banyan trees. Then she turned back to Niki. "Let me ask you a question. Would you be willing to die for the sovereignty movement?"

"Whoa! Where's that coming from?"

"I need to know what kind of a movement this is, that's all."

"Gee. Do I think there will be martyrs before we're done? Could be, and I'm not afraid to be a martyr for sovereignty, if it comes to that. But I'm sure not looking for an opportunity."

"Would you be willing to kill for the movement?"

Niki drew back. "Oh! Now, I see where you're head is."

"Can you blame me?"

"No, under the circumstances, I guess not. Look, the Kamehameha Society is committed to peaceful change. There are way fewer of us than of foreigners in these islands, so violence makes no sense. But we're not a nonviolent movement, in the sense of swearing off the use of physical force to achieve our goals. We don't advocate violence, though, and we do advocate gentleness. Besides," she exclaimed, poking Liz in the side, "if I intended to kill your father, I wouldn't be dumb enough ask you to set up the meeting, would I?"

Liz smiled tenuously, but then looked away again. The rock wall rose up like a sandstone canyon above them. Overhead, a large, metamorphosing cumulus cloud roiled by. At the tops of the banyan trees, leaves rustled in the onshore breeze. Where the threesome were sitting, though, all was becalmed and muted. Liz asked Niki the question she had asked Race some moments ago. "Is this a sacred place?"

Niki sighed. "Not anymore. Now, there's a lot of *pakalolo* smoked here at night, a lot of beer drunk. That's about as sacred as it gets. It'd be nice to change that."

"The aloha culture," Liz murmured. She turned back to Niki. "I understand what you want. Philosophically, I'm with you a hundred percent. Maybe two hundred. But this is a weird time for my Dad, and the rest of us Chases, too. Let me think about it for a little while."

Race gave a sigh of relief and rubbed his hands together. "Well, now that we've got the female bonding out of the way, why don't we walk up the beach and around the point to Kawailoa Bay. The swimming's a lot better, there's shade and maybe an opportunity for some male-female bonding."

They walked single file back through the tunnel, along the footpath and onto the beach. The sun beat against the radiant sand, making the beach a hotplate. The three of them ran to the water's edge, and trudged the length of the beach in the scudding waves. As they were rounding the point, Liz asked what she thought was an innocent question.

"Have you guys ever heard of Xerxes Industries?"

The other two wheeled on her, glaring, as if she had uttered a gross obscenity.

"Oh," she gasped. "I guess you have!"

Downtown Lihue was a low-rise, low-speed environment that time left behind in the nineteen-fifties. Anyone with nostalgia for a simpler period in history could find great satisfaction there. Two principal streets sat perpendicular to one another, coming together at the site of a working sugar mill, with tall chimneys that eructed sweet smoke into the municipal air. The town had considerable charm, but this lay chiefly in its people, not its buildings, which were, with few exceptions, plain as soda biscuits. Janet and Stella spent an hour at the Kauai County police station, where Stella gave a full accounting of her trek with the ill-fated French couple. Afterwards they strolled over to the Kauai Museum—not a soda biscuit but a two-story cut stone edifice with a salmon-hued tile roof and a presence that was at the same time formal and atavistic. There they read, in photos, writings and artifacts, the history of the settlement of Kauai by successive waves of immigrants from Polynesia, Europe, China, Japan, the Philippines, Puerto Rico and elsewhere. Then Janet walked Stella back to the police station again, where she went in to meet George Akamai for dinner.

As Janet was getting into a cab, she saw Barry Saga stepping out of a police car, in the company of a distinguished-looking Caucasian man and a sexy and very angry Chinese woman. Saga spotted Janet as well, and came over to her while a sergeant escorted Carter Robinson and Li-Ann Low into the station house. "You know who those people are?" he asked.

"I think so. Weren't they meeting with Andy this afternoon?"

"Yes, that's where I found them. I thought we should invite them in for a chat. Jan, do you know whether you will still be here tomorrow night?"

"Yes, it looks as though we're staying another day and a half. Andy won't leave until he's finished dealing with Chamberlain, my daughters won't leave until their father leaves, and I won't leave without them."

"Well, if you'd like to come out—I mean, it is the other side of the island, so I'd understand—"

"Don't be silly, Barry. I'd love to *see* that part of the island, rather than sleepwalk through it, as I did while Stella was missing. It seemed quite beautiful."

"Why don't I check with you tomorrow, then." Saga waved, and Janet got into the taxi, feeling more or less like a teenager. She had not divorced Andrew in order to date other men, and since the divorce she hadn't met any other men for whom she'd felt anything. Until now.

Stella asked the receptionist to page George Akamai, and sat down to wait. On the Formica-clad coffee table, the jumble of dated magazines did not particularly invite perusal, but as she was captive there until Akamai arrived, Stella picked them up and shuffled them absently. The least uninteresting was called *Kauai Business.* She flipped the pages idly, and discovered an article on alternative health practitioners on the island, which absorbed her interest until Akamai appeared. He was wearing civilian clothes—khakis and a subdued aloha shirt; muted floral patterns against a soft gray-brown field.

"I like that," Stella said, standing to greet him.

"What, this shirt?" Akamai looked down at his chest, as if surprised.

"Yes. It's so Hawaiian."

"Actually, it's not a very ancient Hawaiian tradition," Akamai said as they were walking out the door. "The idea of this kind of shirt came from the mainland in the eighteen-hundreds. From California. I think maybe it started there during the gold rush. Local people added the tropical designs, and some enterprising Chinese character on Oahu commercialized the concept in the nineteen-thirties. He even came up with the name, 'aloha shirt.' A Chinese guy!"

"Whatever, it looks great on you."

They got into his car, an enclosed jeep. It was neatly-kept inside, but the inescapable red-dust of off-road travel had dyed the carpet, dashboard and other surfaces. "I thought I'd show you the Makai Ranch,"

Akamai said, "to give you an idea of what's at stake in this situation you and your family have wandered into."

They headed south on Highway 50. "Are you okay, Stella?" Akamai asked, glancing at her as he drove. "You've been through quite an ordeal."

"I'm okay," Stella said. Then, after thinking a moment, added, "Why, George? Don't I seem okay?"

Akamai glanced at her again. "I don't know. I was a little surprised at how little emotion you showed this morning. Out on the trail, I mean. Your own ordeal in the flood, your two friends shot in the back; fairly intense experiences, to put it mildly. Yet it doesn't appear to have—I guess 'stirred' you, is the word I'm looking for."

Stella stared at her hands, startled to see them wringing themselves. Yet another opportunity to explain her world view. *Does he understand me, or doesn't he?* "It has to do with my faith," she said. "I believe that what happened to me in that valley was the flow of my karma. The same with Chantal and Luc. Their karma determined their fate in life, and their actions while they were alive determined what they will experience in their next lives. I grieved for them, of course, but after all it was, you know, kismet."

"Is that what you feel, Stella, or are you just reciting dogma?"

"What I feel? It's what I believe. It explains why my internal mood might be more complex and less—what? Out of control, histrionic?—than you might have expected."

They had stopped at a light. Off to the left, a sign a little distance down the road advertised the Kukui Grove mall. She had seen the sign on her way into town with her mother, the irrepressible shopper, but had neglected to mention it. *I must remember to tell her,* she thought. When she turned back to Akamai, she saw that his lips were pressed together in thought.

"What is it, lieutenant?"

Akamai took his hands off the steering wheel, spread his fingers wide, then grabbed the wheel again. "It's just that it sounds as though you're rationalizing rather than letting your feelings out. I'm not sure that's healthy."

"You're sweet to be concerned," Stella said earnestly, "but believe me, I know myself a lot better than you do. It's not that I don't have feelings. I do, but I process them internally in harmony with my beliefs. I don't have to hang them out for everybody to see."

Akamai didn't respond, and soon they were in motion again. The island's community college drifted past on the right, low tan buildings with red tiled roofs. They descended into a valley, where tall, wild trees draped with flowering vines rose beside the road, and then sugar cane. The windows were open, and as the jeep came up to highway speed, wind noise made the conversation less intimate. "So," Akamai called out, "you really think that Luc and Chantal's spirits are in the process of being recycled?"

"Recycled," Stella shot back. "If you weren't a spiritualist, I'd be insulted. No fooling, George, you do have an understanding of the Buddhist concept of karma, right?"

"It's not just a Buddhist concept. The Jainists also believe that actions in life accumulate karma, and that you have to clean the karma out by successive rebirth and proper behavior so the spirit can be liberated from the cycle. Actually, from what I read, the notion of karma probably goes all the way back to the ancient Vedic religions."

Stella stared at the brown-skinned Hawaiian. *Maybe he knows more about karma than I do,* she thought. She'd had no formal training in Buddhism, after all, just several months of weekly group sessions with a hirsute gentleman who used the sobriquet Swami Shivalinga but whose real surname was Seidelman. "And you think these are silly notions?"

"No more silly than any other religion."

"What do you mean by that, for goodness' sake?"

"Just that there is no one true religion. All belief systems are imperfect attempts by imperfect humans to define a relationship with a greater power. Because of their imperfections, the attempts are all silly to some extent. It'd be surprising if they weren't, wouldn't it?"

They passed the turnoff to Poipu. Beyond the cane fields to Stella's right, verdant mountains rose to catch the low-hanging clouds tinged yellow by the late afternoon sun. Mountains on a mountain, Stella thought, picturing Kauai as a volcano risen from the sea, holding up the mountains at which she was looking. Surrounded by ever-moving, ever-changing waters—water, the wellspring of illusion —the island was an illusion, as were the mountains, the road ahead of them, the jeep, George's body, hers....

"Is your religion silly, George?"

"Oh, sure. Really silly. The pantheon of gods; the rules of *kapu*, or taboo; the sheer terror that the *kahunas* could cause in the old days. But it's a way of thinking. I respect it. I practice it."

"You have spiritual powers, don't you?"

He glanced at her. "Do I? I can see some things and do some things that others apparently can't, and I seem to be able to call on these powers by invoking the names of the gods. But is that what's really happening?" Akamai shrugged. "Maybe it's just some genetic quirk."

Stella leaned back in the corner between the bucket seat and the door and smiled. "But of course your genes are just the expression of your karma."

That comment elicited a rolling chuckle. "Zen and the art of molecular biology. Here we are."

They turned off the highway and onto the earthen road that led to Chamberlain's estate. "The Makai Ranch straddles the highway in both directions from here," Akamai explained. It extends all the way down to the ocean on the other side of the road, and part way into the mountains ahead of us. That's why it's called *'makai,'* or 'toward the ocean,' rather than *'mauka'* or 'toward the mountains.' Akamai waved at the plantation workers assigned to guard duty as part of Web Chamberlain's belated emphasis on security. They knew him, and they knew he had free run of the ranch. "Up ahead is where the owner lives," he told Stella, "but we'll turn off before reaching the house. I want to show you the whole picture."

They abandoned the driveway for a narrow track that wound through sharp-leaved clots of mature eight-foot cane stalks. Looking up at the towering cane, Stella felt like an ant traversing a grassy lawn. They drove upward at an increasing angle and soon encountered a series of switchbacks that challenged the passenger's inertial guidance system. Endolymphic fluid sloshed around in the vestibules of her inner ears, making her slightly queasy. After twenty minutes of serpentine tracking, Akamai stopped the car. "Hop out," he said. We're going to take a little stroll."

"I hope 'little' is the defining word, George. I've had enough hiking already."

"It's not far."

There was a footpath through the cane. Akamai told Stella not to get close to the plants, which could cut her. The way was fairly steep, although nothing like the Na Pali ridge she had climbed the day before. As she walked, she could feel the muscles in her abused thighs and calves tightening in protest. Her skin dampened in the muggy heat of the late afternoon. After a few minutes, they came to a boundary between the plantation and the forest. Stepping into the shaded brushland, Akamai said, "Now we're on state property." The path became muddy, then rose sharply so that they could make their way only by searching for handholds on branches or treetrunks and footholds in the rocks protruding from the clay-like earth.

"George, this is too much like what I did yesterday."

"When we're over the top of this hill, we're done."

"Great! My skirt will be done, too. I didn't dress for the occasion, I guess, but then I didn't—oof—know what the occasion was going to be."

A few moments later, they emerged onto a plateau. Akamai reached down to help Stella up. A thunderous roaring greeted her, and a sight so beautiful it brought tears to her eyes and made her knees weak. She sank to the rocky ground, still holding Akamai's hand, forgetting how dirty and hot she was.

It was a waterfall almost four hundred feet high dropping over a gleaming face of wetted black lava. To either side, the forest hung like curtains. Sunlight caught the view full on, bringing the whitewater chute into luminous relief against the inky cliffside. The falls began as a pencil-thin beam high above them, gradually widening in its plunge, then divided at a protruding ledge, creating two subsidiary chutes and a mist that drifted off on an amiable breeze. One leg of the falls split again against an upward-jutting crag, throwing into the air a fine spray that also floated gracefully away. The three watery strands continued earthward in free fall until they crashed against the base of the cliff in energetic splendor, exploding into clouds of flashing droplets that spattered like rain into a clear, dark pool.

"Oh, George," Stella sighed. "This is unbelievable. Enchanting!" For the first time, she was aware of her hand in his. She gave a tug, and he pulled her up.

"Now turn around," he said. From the plateau, they could see the entire southern coast of the island. "Way over in the east there, the Naupu Ridge reaches to Nawiliwili Bay, where the big boats come in. When you pass that ridge on Highway 50, you can see a rock outcropping that's supposed to look like the face of Queen Victoria lying on a pillow. You can't make it out from here, but look for it next time you go that way. Just this way from the ridge, what looks like a little settlement there is Koloa Town, where we had breakfast with your family; and *makai* from there, the Poipu section and its beaches. The house you're renting is in there somewhere. The Lawai Valley is the long scoop you can see cutting down into the plantation and all the way through to the ocean. There's a lovely botanical garden in there, called NTBG, where they try to propagate endangered tropical plants from all over the Pacific.

"The next valley to the right is Wahiawa, and that town you can just see nestled in there is Kalahea. Used to be that mostly Portuguese laborers lived there. There's still a strong Portuguese influence. The valley after that is Hanapepe. The little village is a funky, artist-colony kind of place. The haze makes it hard to see beyond that point, but if you look up on the right there above the hills, you can just see the west wall of Waimea Canyon. Some people like the views better than the Grand Canyon, although it's nowhere near as large.

"Up above the canyon is Koke'e State Park, a different world from what you see from here—highland forests and a sort of prehistoric swamp. Behind us, the land rises another couple of thousand feet to the highest point on the island, Mount Wai'ale'ale. Now, put your arms out like this." Akamai held his own arms out in a V.

Stella followed suit. The Hawaiian moved behind her, and sighted over her shoulder. "Wider," he said, and again, "wider. Okay, right there. Your position pretty much defines the boundaries of the Makai Ranch. All that shaggy green stuff you see in there is sugar cane. There's a macadamia plantation down on the other side of the highway, and some coffee that Chamberlain is experimenting with. The dark green spots in amongst the cane? That's marijuana. The *pakalolo* growers know which fields are not going to be harvested this year—there's a two-year cycle for sugar—and they poach on those fields. The bigger spots, we'll go after and tear out, but the smart guys plant in small clumps and keep good maps.

"Now, imagine a triangle with its top on Mount Wai'ale'ale and its arms running like yours down the mountain and through the plantation, and ending at the shore. Are you with me, as that Perot guy says?"

"Yes. I've got the picture."

"All the land you're imagining belonged to my ancestors. This gorgeous slice of the island was in what became the Akamai family for several hundred years. We lost it in the last century as the whites took over the economy. Now the state owns the high part, and old man Chamberlain owns the rest."

Stella dropped her hands slowly to her sides. "My gosh. I'm trying to fathom—well, to have this vast, beautiful domain, and then—"

"Yes. The past hundred years of my family's history is full of alcoholism, suicide—very dark things."

"It wasn't just the loss of the land, was it?" Stella ventured. "Mr. Freeman told us your family descended from one of the great Hawaiian kings, and were *kahunas*."

George Akamai stared out over his ancestral lands to the ocean. "C. B. Freeman said that? Funny what impresses people. My family history doesn't make me any better or any worse than the next person. As for my ancestors, I guess the higher you fly, the further you have to fall. The transition to white rule destroyed a way of life that had sustained itself for more than half a millennium without changing this land, and replaced it with a way of life that required herculean clearing of much of the island; yet the new way of life was only able to sustain itself for a hundred years. Now, somebody wants to buy the makai part of the former Akamai lands and no doubt impose yet a different way of life. Condomania? A dozen golf resorts? Who knows? Another transition, destroying a pattern of living and changing the face of the land again."

"Sad."

"Sad, and scary, if the murders this week are connected with that transition. You know? Someone wanting either to advance it or hold it back."

"Do you think my dad's in danger?"

"Look at the Makai Ranch, Stella. Is it the kind of land that someone might kill for? There's a motive for the murders right there in front of us. Your dad is one pawn on the chessboard in a game in which the Ranch is the prize. So, could he be in danger?" Akamai took both her hands in his. "Yes, and his family could, too. Great danger."

"I guess we should have been on tonight's flight after all?"

Akamai shrugged and thrust his hands into his pockets. "Maybe it's not the kind of danger that you can leave behind."

"So then we should stay?"

"There's no right answer, Stella."

"Great danger, you said, George."

"Because the police don't have control of the situation yet. Three killings in two days, and not the kind of cases likely to be solved quickly. Then yesterday, when Saga and your mother stopped at the Makai Ranch to see Web Chamberlain, some goons drove up in one of the Ranch's own cars and fired pistols at them." Akamai took a deep breath and turned back toward the waterfall.

"What is it?" Stella asked.

Akamai didn't respond. He was facing the falls but didn't seem to be looking at them.

"George?"

"Oh, something else happened at the Ranch during that visit. Barry Saga says he saw Nate, Chamberlain's son, who was a good friend of mine for many years. Chamberlain denied that Nate was there."

"So?"

"So nothing, really. If he's on Kauai, Nate should've called me; but he didn't. Yet somehow I think Saga was right, and it gives me a queasy feeling."

"Because of all the stuff that's been going on?"

Akamai nodded.

"You think Chamberlain's son was involved in the murders, do you?"

"There's no evidence that he was, no theory as to why he would be. What bothers me is that I'd have a hard time thinking objectively about the Chamberlains, even if some evidence did turn up."

"Well, sure you would. But Adibi's the key, isn't he? At least, I feel as though he is. What do you know about him?"

"Not much yet. Greek passport. Born in Tehran, had an apartment in Lihue, worked in Kapa'a but was using the Pakala Inn for meetings, apparently."

"What kind of job did he have?"

"He worked up at Sunshine Resources, a small import/export business in Kapa'a, that little town you passed along the coast going up north. Nice company, very community-minded, well-known for their philanthropy. According to the manager up there, Adibi was not their employee but some sort of contractor from a foreign corporation."

"Xerxes?"

"Why—yes. Where did you get—from Chantal and Luc?"

Stella blushed with embarrassment. "I forgot to tell you earlier. Sorry."

"Well, while you're at it, you can apologize for asking me questions to which you already know the answers."

"Objection," Stella protested. "That's a false accusation. I didn't ask you whose employee Adibi was; I asked what he did for a living.

Akamai nodded. "Got me on a technicality. He was apparently an all-purpose administrator, a special projects manager, whatever that means. Could have been a hit man, with that kind of job description."

"And the marijuana? A sideline?"

"That's going to take a while to ferret out. Apparently he liked to gamble. Flew to Macao every month or so for a long weekend. He may have gotten into the drug business to support his habit."

Stella turned to the waterfall again. "Sit down a minute, George." She sank to the ground, watching light play on the narrow fans of living water and on the angelic mists that hovered over the scene. The Hawaiian lowered himself, and looked at her. "I don't want to leave Kauai," she said. "Could the island stand one more *haole*?"

Akamai grinned. "No problem, once this case is solved. If you stay, we'll get one other *haole* to leave. But you might want to think on that notion a while. This place is a long way from the rest of the world."

"Hey, I'm a long way from the rest of the world, too," Stella murmured. "Inside, I mean." She gazed at him steadily. "Everything I need is right here."

The import of her words was clear. George Akamai started to respond, but said nothing. Stella knew she had put him in an awkward position. After what she had been through, could he say that he wasn't interested even if he wasn't? And if he was interested, but not as aggressively as she, how would he phrase a response?

Their silence embarrassed her. She took a deep breath. "The night before last, as I was sitting in the darkness and the rain, in a place I'd never been before, my thoughts flew to you across—How far would you say it was?"

"Twenty miles, more or less."

"—across a distance of twenty miles, separated by mountains and a huge storm. And you answered, George. I heard you."

"Stella—"

"—No, hear me out. That's not all. The next day, without any material clues as to where I was, you set out in an improbable direction and came straight to me. This is the first time I've experienced anything like that. Maybe it happens to you all the time, but can you appreciate what an affirmation it is of my spirituality—of our spirituality?"

"Stella, Stella!" Akamai lifted his hands in front of him. "Were we communicating, or was it coincidence? If there is a spiritual plane, the one sure thing is that communication over it is unreliable at best. When I talk to the Hawaiian gods, my side of the conversation is clear enough, but theirs is always murky. With the Judeo-Christian god, both sides are murky. Can I really heal people? Can I foretell the future or reconstruct the unseen past? Sometimes it seems to work, sometimes it doesn't, and I'm left not knowing whether my heritage is magical or fraudulent. Frankly, if the heritage weren't such a powerful a part of the native culture of this island, a culture that needs to be kept alive, I'd have stuffed it all a long time ago."

Stella sighed. She reached out and smoothed his shirt, as a mother might do for her son. "Life is a quest for enlightenment, Lieutenant Akamai. Whether we'll ever actually achieve it in a given cycle is another question. More likely, there will always be doubts, doubts that have to be filled by belief. Do you—" she gulped at the boldness she was about to display "—are you romantically involved with anyone, George?"

Akamai's eyes widened. "Stella Chase," he said. Stella held her ground, unblinking. "Well, no, not at the moment. I—um—Going off to Dartmouth for four years cut me out of the social scene on Maui, where I grew up. Then going into police work plus moving to Kauai, just seemed to make it harder—"

"—And you were probably waiting for the right native Hawaiian woman to come along."

The question hung there for a moment, while the waterfall thundered and birds called overhead.

"You are surprisingly perceptive," Akamai said.

"We're very different, I know that; and yet there's something about us together that's special. Right now, it's just a potential, but I'd be willing to try to develop that potential, if you are."

Again, an awkward silence while Akamai tried to come up with an answer. Stella slumped a little and looked away. *Maybe being so open was a mistake.* Her eyes followed the waterfall wistfully from bottom to top. As she watched, a pair of white-tailed tropic birds, snowy radiances in the sunlight, swooped down from the precipice, the feathers of their long, forked tails flowing like streamers behind them. They began a languorous aerial pas-de-deux in the updrafts along the cliff. Spiraling upward, diving, their wings outstretched, their direction changing with the slightest adjustment of their tip-feathers, the two parted as if moved by a common inspiration, then came together, close enough to kiss for an instant, then parted again and met again. Now they stood out in brilliant relief against the lava cliff, now they disappeared in front of the incandescent waterfall. She beamed, and pointed them out to Akamai.

He watched them soar, a half smile on his face. "We really haven't known each other that long," he said.

He didn't say, "We really don't know one another." Stella shrugged. "But there's a resonance, isn't there, George?"

Akamai followed the pair of birds with his eyes as he tried to sort out his feelings. Maybe he and Stella would be a good match. He viewed love in the same way that she viewed enlightenment—as a quest rather than a condition. At what point are two people "in love"? No one could say, but two compatible people living together, growing in shared experience, raising children, would likely develop that jumbled sense of affection, trust, desire and willing sacrifice that is as close to the ideal of "love" as anything gets. He tended to agree with Stella that the two of them had the potential to build a loving relationship; but there would be complications. Their children would break the pureblood lineage of the Akamais. His family would be deeply unhappy. And yet, would the racial interruption be so bad, really? Stella had strengths of her own from which the family line could benefit—

"What are you thinking about, lieutenant?" Stella asked softly.

He turned his face to her.

"Children."

Stella Chase caught her breath. "Oh, George." She rose up on her knees, leaned toward Akamai, put her arms around him and kissed him on the mouth. He embraced her in return, feeling the surprising force in her slender frame. Clumsy, he seated and she kneeling, they fell over.

They laughed, feeling each other's movements at every point at which their bodies touched. When the moment passed, Stella—her head resting high on Akamai's chest—cleared her throat. Her mother had taught her that, in life as in dancing, the woman must often take the lead or nothing worth experiencing will happen.

"Did you bring me to this romantic spot just to look at the scenery?" she murmured, "or did you have something more in mind?"

"It was the only French wine I could find," Janet called over her shoulder as she set the table. All the doors on both sides of the living area in the rental house were open. Ceiling fans provided the breeze nature had withheld all day. Outside, thick clouds rolling in from the east caught the deep blush of the setting sun and broadcast it all over Poipu. The sound of waves breaking against the rocky fortifications of Koloa Landing was audible above the rustling of the trees and hedges in the yard. A man in uniform sat under an awning at the far end of the deck. Another sat under the tiny overhang at the front entrance.

Andrew Chase looked at the label. It was a non-estate white Bordeaux. There would be no bouquet to speak of, a wateriness in the mouth. Little to object to, but also little to enjoy. "That's okay, Janet. After that scare over Stella"—and, he did not add, his own scare in the house the night before—"somehow I don't think I can worry about acidity, finish and nose."

"Andy," Janet exclaimed. "Do you mean that?" Her former husband had made a second career of vinophilia, a passion she found pretentious. During their marriage, she would have had difficult identifying an activity that consumed her former husband more than selecting the proper wine to accompany a meal.

"You bet," Andy answered as he uncorked and poured the mute little white. "I'm telling you, out on that trail, just before we found Stella, I really lost it. I felt like—I'll tell you exactly what I felt like. You know the big cicadas that used to climb the spruce tree in the front yard to molt? They left behind those paper-thin larva-shaped shells that clung to the tree and shuddered in the wind? I felt just like one of those shells. Thinking about it, I'm shaking again. Look." He held out a glass to Janet with a trembling hand.

"To our family," he said.

Janet looked at Andrew and lowered her glass, then raised it again and struck it lightly against his. "May we always be as close as we are now," she returned over the muted clink.

She had invented a salad of greens, tomato, sliced mango, Maui onion and walnuts in a dressing sweetened with a little guava juice and liquefied papaya. The combination worked beyond her expectation. Andrew complimented her, something that happened rarely enough to be further evidence of a change in him.

As they ate, she raised the question uppermost in her mind: the family's safety. "I don't think you have to worry," Andrew answered. "The house is guarded twenty-four hours. The service that Saga recommended is the same one the government uses to help with state visits, and the same that movie people use to guard their vacation homes here. Stella seems to have a personal police escort, and Liz has a randy but probably effective voluntary bodyguard."

"I don't have to worry? We're like a family in a witness protection program here. Stella was almost killed, Andy."

"We don't know that."

"I don't mean that she was shot at. It's true that we don't know that, but only because she's got no bullet holes in her. She did almost drown, and she could have fallen down that ridge. And somehow this real estate thing is at the heart of it." Janet raised a hand to cut off Andrew's interruption. "I know you think some kind of drug war is behind all this, but I don't. The truth is, if it weren't for the fact that the kids won't leave you here alone, and the fact that you won't leave until Friday because of your damned client, you'd be sitting here toasting yourself tonight."

"Yes, and I'd be sitting in one of the loveliest places on the planet, in a situation where there's still no indication that these murders have anything to do with us—"

"Well, tell me: how are we going to be able to tell whether they do or not? Maybe if one of us has her throat slit, then we'll know."

Andrew was determined to keep the evening from spiraling into acrimony. "I've been trying to figure out why you're being so tough on me, Janet. I accept that this whole mess we're in is my fault, and if that's the reason, fine. And I accept that I haven't exactly been a knight in shining armor rescuing my family from danger. If that's the reason, I can understand that, too. But if you're doing it to build a wall between us, to—to protect yourself against feelings toward me that might otherwise arise—you know what I mean. You can't touch me, you recoil if I touch you—Then I don't think that's fair, and it just makes a bad situation worse."

Janet opened her mouth but stopped herself from making the fiery retort. Instead, she folded her hands in front of her instead and stared at them. When she looked up, the anger had gone from her face. "It's probably all of the above, Andy. I haven't been fair to you, I admit that. After all, you're not Rambo, and I—Well, I wouldn't have married you if you were. I guess where I think you're letting us down is in trying to balance our best interests against Paracorp's."

"Honey, we're in an ambiguous situation, I don't deny that. It's why I hired the guard service. But we'll be out of here in a day and a half. One more meeting with Chamberlain, day after tomorrow, and we're gone."

Janet clapped her hands to her head. "That's another thing, that meeting. The lawyer and the realtor will be there. They're also a connection between the murders and us."

"I doubt it. After meeting them at the Ranch, I called the police station and asked Akamai at what time of day Adibi had been killed. He told me that the forensics lab placed the time of death at around eleven a.m., shortly after the guy checked out of the Inn. Artemis told us last night that Robinson and Low had appeared at the Pakala Inn at around two-thirty, well after the deed. Plus, having met them, I'm convinced that Robinson, at least, could not have been involved in that murder or any murder. He doesn't have the guts."

"What about the realtor?"

"I—um—she's another story," Andrew said, his eyes cast downward. "Very gutsy—but a killer? I don't think so."

Janet waved her hands. "I'm sure they're lovely people across the table, but those two also sent Artemis down here to snoop around. I'm not convinced, Andy. As I say, if I could persuade your daughters to leave you behind, we'd be on the first flight for home."

"You could do that." Andrew shrugged. "It's only money."

Janet leaned across the table. "Andy, is that what this is about? That you've already paid for the house? I—Well, I may as well say it, because it's another reason I haven't been all sweetness and light with you. Since the divorce you've become a real scrooge. Don't look at me that way. I know what you're thinking, but it's not just me. The girls have noticed it, too. And the idea that we should stay here and risk our lives here simply because the house is paid for—"

"Janet, please don't fly off the handle. I meant that it's only money, so by all means, do it if you want to. Can I tell you why I think we're safer here than anywhere else?"

"I don't think even William Jennings Bryan could convince me of that, but give it a try—"

"Here's the logic. Either the murders were connected with the Makai Ranch deal, or they weren't. If they weren't, then they have nothing to do with us, and we needn't worry no matter where we are. Am I right? Okay. On the other hand, if they were connected with the deal, then maybe I'm at risk, too, and you and the girls may be at risk because harming you would be a way of getting to me. Suppose the killer—or whoever hired the killer; say, another bidder—wants to get to me for some reason. First of all, he's making a big mistake, because Harry Wong doesn't give a good goddam about losing a round-eyed lawyer who's billing him at four hundred U.S. dollars per hour. But put that aside. What makes you think that the killer is going to forget us if we leave Kauai? This plantation is going to sell for about fifty million dollars. The cost of a hit man in Portland or Manhattan or Greenwich is minuscule by comparison. It wouldn't be given a second thought."

Janet made a rolling motion with her hands. "Get to the bottom line, counsellor."

"Imagine that a hit man in Portland has been hired to shoot Stella. Don't fight me, just imagine it, okay? Now compare your comfort level in that scenario with your comfort level here. We're all together. We know the police here, which I'm sure Stella doesn't in Portland. Not only do we know them, but they seem genuinely concerned about our safety."

"George Akamai advised me to leave Kauai the morning we picked you up," Janet said.

Andrew lifted his wine glass and took a long draught, as if it were a mug of beer. Janet could see disappointment on his face. He had been hoping for a pleasant, maybe even a healing, interlude with her, but she would not oblige him. Yes, there were signs of change, a softening of the hard edges the practice of law had carved into Andrew's personality. Yes, he had suffered on the Limahuli Trail, just as she had suffered while waiting in the Ke'e Beach parking lot. But the scale was far from balanced; she could be less caustic, she supposed, but she was not prepared to break the hard shell she had constructed around her heart.

"Not to cast aspersions at George," Andrew ventured, "but if we're off this island, we're not his problem any more."

"What a terrible thing to say, Andy. That man has gone out of his way to help us, time and again."

"I agree. I'm not impugning his motives, Janet. But you've just made my point. On Kauai we have the attention of the police. If we're not on Kauai, who knows? Plus, the people killed have been Iranian—or Greek, however you count Adibi—and French. The percentage of tourists who visit Hawaii from Iran, or Greece, or even France is so low you can hardly see it. On the other hand, the percentage who come from mainland U.S. is about half. If whoever is responsible for the murders has a brain, he'll recognize that the murder of Americans on Kauai would result in a vigorous manhunt, in a way these other killings won't. You think that's farfetched? Consider this: Over a third of Hawaii's tourists are Oriental, and most of the new investment money flowing into Hawaii is Oriental. A couple of Paracorp employees were roughed up here some weeks ago—don't yell, I just learned about this. The point is that they were mugged, not killed."

Janet bristled. "Oh, that's just great! We've come to a pretty sorry pass, Andrew Chase, when you have to argue that a mugging of a member of this family would be a good thing. As usual, you're elevating logic over common sense. You should know by now that I run on intuition, not logic. What you say may hang together like a Supreme Court brief, but it doesn't persuade me in the least."

"Okay." Andrew put his hands up in surrender. "Sure. What the hell are we arguing about, anyway? A day and a half. I can't leave until Friday morning, Janet, I just can't; but we'll be on the first plane out of here then. Promise." He picked up the wine bottle. "A little more?"

"Here, let me clear the salad plates." Janet looked around the room. It was getting dark. In the hallway an illumination-sensitive night-light had just come on. "Light the candles, will you?"

"Ah. Romance, darling?"

Janet had known it would come sooner or later, and she knew she what she had to do. "Just aesthetics, Andy," she replied.

The main course was grilled fish, garnished with slender green beans and a ready-made *ratatouille* from a health food store.

"It's called *ono*," Janet said, when Andrew asked about the fish. "The word means—"

"I know, it's a homonym for the Hawaiian word for 'delicious.' And it is delicious, too. This is lovely, Janet. So nice of you to cook for me."

"I don't know what got into me," Janet said, treating the compliment as a joke. She saw that Andrew was suddenly lost in reverie. He was staring at her. "What?"

"That feigned-modest thing you just did. You've been doing that ever since I met you. It takes me back to our first date."

Janet's eyes widened. "Omigod! Sentiment? Is that what I just heard, sentiment? Am I seeing a new Andrew Chase here?"

"A new Andrew Chase? In more ways than you know. I—I'm even writing a novel." The admission embarrassed him, and Janet knew he was pulling out stops he would have preferred to keep shut in order to move her.

"A novel. You? I don't believe it. What's it about?"

"Well, I don't exactly know. I'm not that far along. It starts out in Hawaii, so maybe, with everything that's happened to us on this trip, it'll be about the family."

"Oh, God, I hope not. I wouldn't want to see all our private problems on America's bookshelves. But a novel! Andy!"

Andrew nodded. "Let's talk about our private problems. The scrooge factor, for instance. I plead guilty to being more money-conscious since the divorce, okay. You may think it's malice or, let's put it this way, attitude. In point of fact, though, it's something quite different." A breeze blew in through the nearby screen door, putting out the candles on the table. "Wind's picking up. We're probably going to get some more rain," Andrew said as he stood to close the doors.

"Leave the ones on the far side open, Andy. That breeze feels good."

Andrew relit the candles and sat down. "At around the same time that our marriage fell apart," he began, "Fowler and Greide started falling apart, too. Business declined some, and my income declined a lot, as you know from my tax returns. A new generation of partners began to wield the balance of power in the firm, and they have got things screwed up to a fare-thee-well. All they care about is money. Their own money. You're nodding, but I don't think you've got it yet. That's *all* they care about. Nothing else has any value to them. Civility, quality of work, quality of life, respect, compassion—forget it. Lawyers five to ten years senior to me, as well as folks in my tier, are being hounded into taking huge cuts in their already-reduced shares or, worse, into leaving the firm. Associates are being worked hundred-hour weeks for months at a stretch, on mindless stuff. Mindless—just to inflate billable hours. So at either end of the scale, the senior partners and the associates, there's extreme bitterness. And in between are these lunatic young turks, intent on keeping their incomes in seven figures no matter what the cost. If they can't do it at Fowler and Greide—and they can't at the moment—then by God they're willing to jump ship and take our clients with them, which is what is about to happen. There's a big defection under way right now, and I sense another one on the horizon. Believe it or not, I could easily see the firm closing its doors in a couple of years."

"Oh, come on, Andy. Surely—"

Andrew halted his knife and fork in mid-cut and shook his head. "There is no 'surely' any more, darling. A couple of major defections will destroy the firm's economics, and its reputation. After that the only question will be whether to leave the respirator on for a while or cut our losses and disband."

Janet all at once felt like a balloon punctured by a pin. The financial basis of her independence was the alimony provided by her ex-husband in accordance with the divorce decree. She had already experienced a reduction in monthly payments because of the downturn in his financial fortunes, but she had never considered that—except in the event of death or incapacity, both of which were insured against—the entire flow of funds could be in jeopardy. "Well, if Fowler and Greide were to close," she said very slowly and quietly, "what would you do?"

"As soon as I have a plan for that," Andy replied, refreshing the glass she held out to him, her own hand now vaguely trembling, "I'll let you know. I sit and imagine all the legal headhunters in Manhattan filled with Fowler and Greide lawyers, and ask myself how I'm going to stand out in the crowd."

At that instant, there was a brilliant flash of light in the sky outside the house, and, seconds later, a loud crack as thunder roared in from over the ocean. The first torrent of raindrops from the storm blew into the living room, and the two of them ran to close the French doors at the front of the house and towel the puddles off the marble tiles. "I thought you said it never rains in Poipu," Janet protested.

"It never has, until tonight," Andrew shot back, on his hands and knees as he wiped the floor. "What you're witnessing is not a mess, Janet. It's a miracle!"

Dessert was chunks of lightly steamed and then chilled mango and pineapple in a guava sauce.

"How many bottles of that unobjectionable white did you buy, darling," Andrew asked as they were bringing the fruit and plates to the table.

"Oh, don't open another for me, Andy. I'm fine."

"I'm going to have a little more. I think it might be quite good with your dessert, actually."

When they were seated again, Andy poured a glass for himself and topped off Janet's. "I hope you don't mind my asking what you already know is on my mind," he said cautiously, "but do you ever think what it would be like if we got back together?"

Janet closed her eyes and rocked back and forth for a moment. Lightning flashed red inside her lids, the strike so close the ensuing thunder made the house shake. "Andy," she said when it was quiet enough again, "I'm not going to sleep with you, tonight or any other night on this trip."

"You're so quick, Janet. So quick to leap to conclusions."

"Didn't you and Galen and Harry Wong have enough friction on your units last week in those Hong Kong whorehouses?"

"You've never understood—well, I should leave aside those old arguments." Andrew looked off into space for a moment. "You sound jealous, Janet," he remarked pensively, as if to himself. "Jealousy would suggest that you still care."

"I don't care, Andy. I'm just telling you that, for many reasons, I'm not one of your multiple sexual partners now, any more than I was after I first found out...." Janet's voice had begun to quaver, and she stopped in mid-sentence.

"I'm not trying to seduce you, Janet. Gave up on that years ago. I'm only asking you to share, you know, your feelings about us remarrying."

She looked at the candle before answering, watching it melt in the heat from its own flame, its substance dissipating into the air or dripping down and congealing against the brass holder. There was no point in hurting Andrew, really, and yet she could not help but hurt him, if he insisted on an answer to his question. "Why on earth would you want to remarry me, Andy?"

"I never wanted a divorce in the first place. It was your idea. I liked being married to you."

"Oh, right! Well, then, why do you think I divorced you?"

"Because I was, you know, having—you know, going out in Hong Kong—"

"Wrong. If that had been the only reason, I'd have fought back, forced you to stop."

"Well, all right. Because you were miserable being married to me."

"You're just reciting a phrase you heard me say. Why was I so miserable?"

"Well, because—because I was inattentive. I was wrapped up in my work—"

"Let me say it in my words. The man I married was a witty, attentive, sensitive guy, a law student who had a truly positive outlook on life. We had fun together, we met life's challenges together. When we made love, it was just that, a deep expression of love. The man I divorced was a cheerless, sour, self-absorbed guy—still handsome, I have to admit—"

"—I picked a career that gave us a good life, Janet. It was a tough career. It forced sacrifices on both of us."

"You picked the career that you wanted. I don't blame you for that. But whatever the reason was, you lost passion for me, Andy. In the end, we were just going through the motions. That was the main thing. Without love, a marriage is an albatross around the neck. You get to a certain point in your life: the kids are gone, your days are filled with community activities or work or hobbies or friends—whatever it is that replaces a moribund love—and it just doesn't make sense to carry the dead bird around any more. I think it would be a bad idea to try to get back together again. A really bad idea. Enough said, darling?"

Rain beat against the roof above the peaked ceiling. Electricity and shock waves split the dark skies over Poipu. Andy sighed, and for a moment, seemed resigned to defeat; but then he shook his head deliberately from side to side. "No," he shouted over the din. "No, it's not enough said, by God, because I don't think it's such a bad idea at all, Janet. I mean, Christ, we lived together for over two decades pretty happily—don't interrupt. Toward the end—well, you know my feeling about that. Toward the end, for whatever reason, we had those arguments, and the more we argued, the angrier it made us, and the angrier we were, the more we argued, until finally we were so pissed off at one another that any hope of reconciliation was lost. But even then, Janet, I still loved you. And I do now."

Janet shook her head in melancholy wonder. "Words of love, Andy. After it's all over, you've learned to say them voluntarily."

"I'm telling you, I've learned a lot of things. When your world falls apart, you learn a whole lot of things. This scrape on my throat; I haven't had a chance to tell you the whole story. I was sitting there in the Cathay-Pacific lounge, half asleep, when all of a sudden everyone else in the room was screaming and racing for the door. I looked up, and there was this sheet of plywood coming right through the window, with a big piece of corrugated sheet metal waggling along behind it. Heading straight for me. There was no time to get up, really. I could have dropped to the floor, but there was this little Chinese kid at my feet. I couldn't protect both him and myself. I picked him. Why? Not out of bravery, Janet. You know I'm not the heroic type. Out of disgust with myself, for what I'd let Harry Wong turn me into. In a way, I hoped my life would end there and then."

Janet put down her knife and fork, and sat looking across the table. "Well—" she began, but the words caught in her throat. Her eyes moistened. "Well, just so you know, Andy." Janet stopped herself, shook her head and winced. "It's incredibly hard for me to say this, to admit it, but I still love you, too, and I'm sure I always will. But I can't live with you, sweetheart. It's like with your parents, don't you understand? You love them, but after you go through that stage of teenage psychological warfare, you can't live with them comfortably. Since we broke up, I've changed, too. I'm not this meek, silent shadow following you around any more."

An electric click, a bright flash and a blast of thunder heralded a close strike. "This is ridiculous," Andrew shouted, raising his hands to heaven. "It's like trying to have an intimate dinner inside a kettle drum at the end of the 1812 Overture."

"It's fine, Andy. Don't get excited. I can hear you perfectly well."

Andrew gave an exasperated nod. "It's just that now we're getting right to the heart of the matter, the part that we really need to talk through." As Andrew was composing himself again, all the lights in the house went out, leaving the couple in wan candlelight. "Jesus," he cried, jumping to his feet, "that hurricane is not going to come within two hundred miles of us, but it's intent on screwing up our vacation anyway. I should check with the guards."

He walked to the front door, opened it, and in the intermittent lightning saw the guard, apparently asleep, sitting half in and half out of the rain in a slicker and waterproof boots. When he shook the reposing figure, the man's body fell over heavily onto the brick entry way. "Dear God," Andrew gasped, and rolled the fellow over onto his back. Rain poured onto the guard's face, but did not revive him. There were no visible signs of violence. The man was breathing as if in a deep sleep. Andrew pulled him into the shelter of the overhang and ran back into the house.

Too late. The candlelight revealed a tableau that stopped his heart. A woman in a black, hooded raincoat, water from her outer garment streaming onto the marble floor tiles, was standing over Janet's prostrate, motionless body. Though he couldn't see the woman's face, he recognized her calves immediately.

Should he rush her? It would be about six steps, six noisy steps, and he had no idea what kind of weapon she was carrying. "Li-Ann!" he blurted out, in his best simulation of a menacing voice. Instead of turning around, the woman leaned quickly over the table and blew out the candles, plunging the room into darkness. Sweat formed on Andrew's upper lip and under his arms. He had to do something. He knew there was a vase holding birds of paradise and haleconia on a low table by his left hand. He scooped it up and hurled it ahead of him as he lunged for the intruder. Unbalanced, the vase did not fly true. Instead, it thudded against a wall and shattered on the tile floor. Simultaneously, there was a flicker of lightning, giving Andrew a brief glimpse of the woman in black, in motion near the sofas in the middle of the room. What should he do? By the time he reached the sofas, she'd have moved again. It occurred to him, though, that Li-Ann Low had the same problem he did. Neither of them knew when lightning would flash again nor where the other would be when it did. More than anything, Andrew wanted to see what Janet's condition was, and in the sightless moment he took the chance. Dropping to his knees, he crawled along the open floor to where his former wife lay. He felt her warm with life; the pulse at her throat was strong. "Thank you," he said silently, to a deity with whom was suddenly becoming intimate for the first time since childhood.

In the next instant, the room was lit up as if by sunlight, and there was a tremendous, crackling crash. Looking up quickly as the light faded, Andrew saw no trace of the realtor. It struck him then that she had not shot at him, despite three opportunities to do so. If she had no gun, she'd need to get close to him to do him any harm.... He decided to stand near Janet, and do his best to defend them both. As he moved to rise, there was a faint illumination from some distant lightning jumping between clouds. It was just enough to give him a view of Li-Ann Low propelling herself full force at him, teeth bared and fury in her eyes.

She caught him off balance and fell on top of him onto the floor. The back of his head struck hard against the tile, and in his momentary disorientation she pinned his arms to his sides with her sinewy thighs and forced his head back with a hand pressed under his chin. Now she was covering his nose and mouth with a cloth. The way she was gripping his chin, he could not shake his head. A noxious, volatile vapor filled his nostrils, then his lungs, and then his bloodstream. His subduer was saying something to him, but she sounded as though she was at the bottom of a well, so that he couldn't make out the words. The room flickered bright again for a heartbeat, and he saw Li-Ann Low hovering over him, her terrifying image rippling psychedelically as if on the surface of a pond. And then he lost his grip on consciousness.

"Investigative work is heavily oriented toward nighttime," Race Kendall explained as he and Liz sat at the counter in the Hamura Saimin Stand, located in a dark and dreary alley off Rice Street in Lihue. U-shaped Formica counters thrust themselves into the long, narrow room that constituted the dining area, so that visitors faced strangers rather than each other while they ate. The decor was haphazard and tatty. Still, all the counters were fully occupied, visitors in new aloha shirts sitting shoulder to shoulder with locals in droopy tank tops. Along the outer wall, people of all sizes, shapes and ages stood awaiting their twenty minutes in saimin heaven. The mature women that ran the shop moved in and out of the service areas formed by the undulating counters, bringing the patrons steaming, brimming bowls of broth-covered noodles and vegetables, with optional seafood, chicken or pork. The counter area was open to the kitchen, and Liz watched the women cooking soft noodles by the handful, chopping the meat, seafood and vegetables and stirring and ladling soup in a culinary ballet performed with the confidence that came from mounting the same show each night, and the pride that came with knowledge of the public's appetite for their work.

"Uh-huh. So what kind of investigative work do you have in mind for tonight?" Liz asked. The high level of ambient noise in Hamura's shop allowed the two to converse freely. "Why don't we check out this Xerxes Industries subsidiary?"

"Ah, I don't know. That could be tricky."

"Yeah, but you're a tricky guy, aren't you?"

"Tricky, but prudent. I was thinking we'd do something safe for your initiation. Say a real estate office. Just to show you some techniques, you know."

Liz tapped her spoon against the lip of her bowl impatiently. "Here's the problem," she said. "My family has a mystery on its hands, and we need to solve it fast. So I'd just as soon skip the initiation, because for me, a 'tricky' breaking and entry isn't any more of a risk than the Chases are already running. If I can find out who's responsible for the murders, not to mention doing what you and Niki want me to do, which is to keep my father from being a servant of environmental plunderers, I'm up for whatever it takes."

"Maybe I wasn't explicit enough." Race stared at Liz solemnly. "The Xerxes people are *very* dangerous."

Liz stared back equally solemnly. Then she turned back to the counter, picked up her chopsticks, scissored them into her bowl and captured a cluster of Japanese noodles. She pulled them out of the liquid, bent her head slightly toward them, and brought the working end of the chopsticks to her mouth. Then she slurped the noodles as she had learned to do in *soba* shops in Tokyo. "As dangerous," she asked while she chewed, "as jumping out of an airplane at eleven thousand feet without a parachute?"

Race straightened and sat speechless and, except for the blinking of his eyes, motionless. He inhaled, whistled and inhaled again. "You did that?"

Liz nodded. "With my skydiving team. We were videotaping some stunts. You free fall with a group, and fly over to a buddy before her chute opens. Anyway, are you getting the message here?"

Race put a hand on her shoulder, and she swivelled her stool to face him and also to slip his grasp without being obvious about it. "Yeah," he allowed. "I get the message. But I've never jumped out of a plane, either with or without a parachute. So the best I can do right now is agree to drive you by the Xerxes place, and see how things look."

The Xerxes operation on Kauai was called Sunshine Resources. The company bought tropical flowers from growers in the islands and exported them by air freight to Japan, Korea, Canada and elsewhere, where they were used primarily to adorn hotel lobbies. It also imported dates, pistachio nuts and other foodstuffs from the Middle East for local consumption. A modest business at best, and yet Sunshine Resources had been generous in support of island institutions, particularly those associated with conservation and with ethnic Hawaiian causes. During the three years since it had established itself on Kauai, the company had been an active and visible promoter of recycling, a major contributor to hula schools and Hawaiian cultural programs, and a sponsor of the cleanup program for several mile-long sections of the main road along the periphery of the island. The president of Sunshine Resources, Rafi Palahved, had taken a particular interest in the Kamehameha Society when it was just an underground movement, and helped fund its rapid growth into a mainstream charitable organization pursuing numerous initiatives aimed at reviving Hawaiian traditions, combating drug and alcohol abuse among Hawaiians and educating tourists in the folklore of old Hawaii. Liz learned these things from Niki and Race after she had asked her unintentionally provocative question that afternoon. She had also learned that, at least for a time, Palahved and Niki were more than just patron and beneficiary.

"You know," the alluring Hawaiian had confided while she and Liz sat on the sand watching Kendall surf, "the first Hawaiians brought with them the Polynesian penchant for free sex. Even though it's not a cultural tradition that makes sense in this day of AIDS, it's kind of inside us." She touched the space between her breasts with her fingertips. "This guy Palahved has got the sexiest eyes. I think eyes are the sexiest part of the body anyway, but this guy had penetrated me so many times with his eyes that getting into bed with him was almost anticlimactic. Well, it was pretty climactic, actually, but—you know what I'm saying."

"Um, yeah, I know." The subject matter was a little too intimate, in Liz's view, given the brevity of their acquaintance, yet it was not uninteresting.

"Anyhow, on general principles, I didn't want the Kamehamehas to be taking money from unknown sources, so when Sunshine started pouring real money into our community activities, I asked Race to check them out. He did some dumpster diving, some computer hacking, whatever, and discovered that Sunshine was a subsidiary of Xerxes Industries, and was then able to find out a lot about Xerxes, because they're a huge operation."

"And?"

"*Auwe*! Did I feel, like, *hilahila*." She put her hands over her face, and peered out through her fingers sheepishly. "This Xerxes outfit, they are bad, bad actors. Big construction projects all around the world. They low bid everything, so they get the third world business big time, usually funded by some international aid agency. Some of the stuff, they get to keep part ownership in. Also, they got into the refinery business, and petrochemicals when one of their project partners went bankrupt. Well, they liked that so much because of the profits, they've been in it ever since. Their record on pollution is terrible; safety on the work site, real bad, too. They dispute their property taxes everywhere they do business. I forget where their main headquarters is, somewhere in the Middle East, but their profits go back to Iran."

"So, you were had by this Palahved guy."

Niki nodded sadly. "In more ways than one. I kicked him out of my life a few months ago, but he's still performing that good guy act of his all over the state. Softening folks up for whatever it is that Xerxes has in mind."

"The bastard. So why don't you expose him?"

"Because of his eyes, again. There's this other look he gets when he's angry that's like—I don't know, like looking at your own death. I never want to see it again."

As she drove north to Kapa'a with Race that night while the MG's windshield wipers struggled to maintain the view ahead, it occurred to Liz that though she now understood why Niki had reacted so negatively to the mention of Xerxes Industries, she wasn't sure what caused Race's reaction. "Why do you suppose it is," she ventured, coming at the question indirectly, "that Xerxes has set up this island-friendly trojan horse on Kauai?"

Race shook his head. "That, I haven't been able to find out. 'Course, now, with these murders, it seems as though it has something to do with the Makai Ranch situation."

"No shit, Sherlock. Even I've got that far." Liz knew instantly that she had cut too deep. It was an unshakable habit of hers, which was one reason why she had ended up with Harlan, a thick-skinned New York swellhead who let her barbs roll off him like water off a duck.

"Oh, you have, have you?" Race replied, making a sour face. "Well, maybe I should just drop you off at the Sunshine building and let you have at it on your own."

"Ums has a touchy spot, does ums?" Liz reached under the driver's arm and tickled his rib cage, taking a calculated risk that the act of familiarity would soothe Race's ego without stirring his libido. "You know I'd be completely helpless without you. As a private eye, that is." For the time being, she abandoned her inquiry.

As they crossed the concrete bridge over the Wailua River, the storm began to abate. The dark ride from Lihue out to and along the coast road gave way to a drive illuminated by hotels, modest shopping malls, gas stations, and ultimately the town of Kapa'a, a strip of wooden storefronts, restaurants and bars. Strollers ambled up and down the little strand and a steady current of cars, jeeps, pickup trucks and the occasional tour bus flowed by. Near the north end of town, Race turned *mauka* from the main road and suddenly all was dark again, as if Kapa'a were a thin veneer on the surface of an untamed wilderness. They drove up a long hill, and when the road levelled out again, he pulled the MG to the side of the road. The rain had subsided into a fine mist. "Across the street and up the road there, you see the sign?"

Through the moving wiper blades, Liz could see about thirty yards ahead a concrete-framed placard made of varnished wood, with the name, "Sunshine Resources, Inc." carved into it in block letters. Behind the sign was a warehouse-like building with a corrugated metal roof, prefabricated panel walls and no windows.

"That's it, then?"

"That's it."

"Okay, let's go."

"Go where?"

"Go in," Liz answered. "What's the matter, Race? Is it this Palahved guy? Are you afraid of him, too?"

"Afraid, no. Respectful, yes. This is a smart cookie with powerful forces behind him. Me, I'm just an above-average surfer and part-time PI. Some woman in Sausalito thinks her deadbeat husband is hiding out in Kauai; I'll find the sonofabitch. Somebody's stealing melons from Mr. Yakitori's truck farm? Great, I'll stake the field out for him. But heavy-duty multinational shit going down, people getting shot in the back and stabbed through the ear? Out of my league."

Liz put on a disappointed face. "Oh, dear. My idol turns out to have feet of clay. Can't we at least rut around in their dumpster? That would be fun."

"It won't be much fun tonight if they didn't close the top. Everything'll be wet and smelly," the investigator rejoined, "but, yeah, if you want, we could do that much, I guess."

They left the MG and walked up the street, Race wearing a backpack that he had retrieved from the trunk. The mist that signalled the end of the storm had turned to fog. Ethereal balloons of radiance glowed around the spotlights at the corners of the building and the sign in front. In the far corner of the parking lot, the dumpster was a dimly-visible hulk. "We're okay," Race observed. "The top's closed." Their footfalls were smothered by the profound haze, and they did not speak as they approached the receptacle. The surfer-cum-investigator inspected it, and then whispered, "It's a divided cover. I'll boost you up there, and push half the top up so you can grab it. You pull it over, and I'll catch it on the other side so it doesn't clang." He crouched and locked his hands together to form a stirrup.

Liz stood in front of him, put a heel into his hands and bounced upward. In time with her motion Race exhaled loudly and lifted, his cheek opportunistically brushing along Liz's back and buttocks as she rose high enough to clamber onto the metal cover.

A moment later, they had dropped themselves inside. The dumpster was almost half full. Crouching, Race removed his backpack and extracted two flashlights. He handed one to Liz. "Okay," he whispered as he swung the other light around the inside of the container. "As you can see, there's all sorts of crap in here. Office paper, broken bulk packing for the fruit, the remains of bag lunches, used paper towels from the rest rooms. You're sure you want to do this?"

"Hey, Race, what I wanted was to get inside the building. It's the same as if I wanted to go to a fancy restaurant for dinner, and you took me to the restaurant dumpster instead, and said, 'You're sure you want to eat this garbage, now.' "

Race frowned as he extracted two pairs of rubber gloves from his backpack. "Here," he said brusquely, handing one pair to Liz. "Wear these."

They sat down and set about their work. Race gave no instruction, but from watching him, Liz deduced that she should make two piles, one for interesting stuff and the other for rejects. After a quarter hour or so of silence, her dive instructor spoke. "So, why aren't we getting along better?"

"What do you mean?"

"You're acting as though you don't think much of me."

Liz put her hands on her hips. "It's not an act. Do you expect all women to just melt in your presence?"

"That's what typically happens. What, are you wearing asbestos underwear tonight?""

"You want the truth, Dude? I'm sitting here seething. After talking to Niki this afternoon, I realized that you have information you're not sharing with me." She shone the flashlight in his face until he waved her off. "My family may be in jeopardy, okay, and you've been holding back on me. You've been in this dumpster before, probably in that building before. You've cracked Sunshine's computers. Now, instead of telling me what you know, you've got me going through this charade, as though, wow, if I do well here, maybe I'll win a code ring."

Race Kendall looked up into the fog overhead. "Douse the flashlight," he whispered, "and be quiet for a few minutes." He pointed through the open cover of the dumpster. Liz did as he instructed, and in a moment she could see the ray of a searchlight. It moved into their field of vision and out again a couple of times. An automobile engine was faintly audible at the other end of the lot. The dumpster divers waited wordlessly, listening to the sounds of one another's breathing, watching one another's shadowy outlines. The seemingly interminable moment passed when the engine growled and then faded to nothingness as the car pulled back onto the road.

Race leaned forward on his hands to respond to Liz's accusations. "I think you're being unfair. I was the one who told you about Paracorp bidding on the Makai Ranch, remember? I mean, it was last night, so maybe you've forgotten."

"I haven't forgotten; but for all you knew, my father had already clued me in on the business he was doing here. Why don't you give me something I can't get elsewhere? Tell me what Xerxes' involvement with the Makai Ranch deal is."

Race inched closer. Liz lit her flashlight again to keep him in his place.

"I told you," he hissed, "I don't have the answer to that. You don't always find the smoking gun in this business. You can't just dive into the trash and pull out a plum like what's-his-name."

"Jack Horner."

"Jack, yeah. Sometimes you have to piece together little shreds of evidence until you can see the pattern. Phone records, expense accounts, orders or bills, calendars, a note here, a contract there. I haven't seen the pattern yet."

"Well, no time like the present, don't you think?"

"If I were to break in, Liz—and it's a big if—it would be some other time. And alone. I'll tell you what, though. Let's spend an hour in here so I can update my file, and then if you want, we can go over to my place and see what's new in Sunshine's e-mail system." Race Kendall switched on his light and shone it on the papers in front of Liz so he could see the look on her face.

The look was skeptical. "What was that, some electronic version of 'Would you like to see my etchings'?"

"Damn. I can't win for losing with you, can I? My computer is at my home, believe it or not. There's nothing suspicious about that, is there? But, hell, if you don't want to come home with me, we could do it right here. Bet that would be a first for you."

"Do it? Is that what you said? 'Do it?' Either in this dumpster or in the fanciest suite at the Westin, *that* is a degree of degradation to which I do not aspire, thanks. 'Do it!' Jeez. Let's just get to work, okay?"

They spent a little more than an hour in the dumpster. After a while, Liz's olfactory mechanisms had become desensitized to the aroma of rotting food, which made it possible for her to concentrate on the papers she was reading. She found a lot of chaff in the office waste. Race showed her how to read the accounting printouts and other business records, but her perusal of that kind of documentation produced nothing of value, as far as she could see. In fact, only one document held any interest for her. Labelled "Project Thermopylae, Draft 001," it was an outline written in English, and apparently then partially translated into an unreadable language—Farsi, Liz guessed. Her crossword puzzle books listed Farsi as the official language of Iran. Intuition also told her not to draw Race's attention to the paper, so instead of reading the outline, she put it on the reject pile and later, when her escort was turning over the upper layer of trash to look for more reading material, she slid it behind her, under her blouse and into her shorts.

When they finished their dive, Liz had no documents in her "interesting" pile, while Race Kendall had a fist-thick stack. Before they clambered out of the dumpster, he riffled through Liz's rejects and selected a few to add to his collection. "I'll tell you why I picked these when we're in less degrading surroundings," he muttered as he stuffed the papers into his backpack. As he was slinging the pack on again, Liz began clambering over the top of the dumpster. "Hey, wait, let me—" Race murmured, but Liz swung herself over the edge unaided.

When he landed on the asphalt again, Race saw that Liz was walking toward the darkened rear of the building. He jogged after her.

"Where are you going?"

"It looks as though there's an entrance back here," Liz replied matter-of-factly.

"There is. So what?"

"One of the techniques you said you were going to show me was lockpicking. I thought we might do that here."

"Oh, yeah? Like the President says, lady, 'Read my lips.' I'm not taking you in there. If you want to learn how to pick a lock, fine, let's just go right up the street. There's an empty house we can practice on just a couple of minutes from here."

No amount of cajoling, browbeating or humiliation was going to induce Race to take Liz into the Sunshine building. After an energetic attempt to do so, Liz gave up, and settled instead for a training session at the house up the road, where, according to Race, they could unlock and lock the door as many times as they pleased.

The ride took rather more than a couple of minutes and led them along the margin of a cane field to an unpaved road on which there were a few modest wood-frame homes hidden behind a hedge of alien decorative shrubbery of the sort that was beginning to change the island's ecosystem. The MG pulled into one of the driveways. Its headlights gave a misty lambency to a small, pale blue ranch house on a cinder-block foundation. The driveway ended in an attached carport which, like others Liz had seen on Kauai, was used not to shelter cars but rather as an open porch. This one had an old sofa in it, some folding chairs, a card table and a refrigerator.

They walked to the front door. Race asked Liz to retrieve a tool kit from the compartment at the bottom of his backpack. He opened it. "Shine your light on these," he said.

Inside the hinged box lay a set of what looked like lengths of stiff wire, the ends of which had been hammered into blades shaped like diamonds, disks, or triangles. There was also a tool that looked like a small screwdriver with a rubber handle and a shaft bent ninety degrees near the working end. All these were held in place, like miniature silverware, by little elastic ropes that wove over and under the cloth-covered cardboard tray inside the box. "Where did you get these, Race?" Liz asked.

"Made 'em. You could buy something like this, or even an electrified version, from a locksmith supply house, but that would probably get you on a list that you don't want to be on." Race took out the wire with the disk-shaped end and the bent screwdriver. "Try the door," he said. Liz did so and found that it was locked.

"Okay, shine that light on the lock."

Race held his tools in front of the lock so Liz could see them. "This," he said, waggling the length of wire, "is a picking tool. It's called a scrubbing pick. This one," he added, motioning with the screwdriver, "is a torque wrench. Here's the idea. This lock, like most door locks, is a cylinder inside a hole bored in the outer hull of the lock. Without the key, the cylinder won't turn, 'cause there's these little pins called tumblers—maybe half a dozen or less of 'em-that stick out of holes in the hull and into holes in the cylinder. Got that much?"

"Yeah. I think I had that much before. You're sure there's nobody home here?"

"I'm sure. So, now, if you think about what a key does in a lock, it really does only two things. First, when you slide it into the cylinder, the key pushes the tumblers back into the hull to a point where they get out of the way so the cylinder can turn inside the hull."

"I had that part, too, Kendall."

"Okay, fine. Y'know, some women aren't that good with mechanical things." Liz gave him a dirty look, which was lost on him in the darkness. "Here comes the more advanced lesson. What's really going on there is that the tumbler consists of two pins. One is called a key pin. The key pins are in a little tube inside the cylinder and they can be different lengths. The other pin is called a driver pin. The driver pins ride on top of the key pins, and they're attached to springs on the other end. Shine the light over here now."

He made a partial fist, and stuck the index finger of his other hand down through two fingers of the fist. "The driver pin keeps the cylinder from turning, because it sticks part way out of the cylinder and into a little tube in the hull, where the spring is. When you push the key into the keyway, it lifts the key pins up just enough to push the driver pin clear of the cylinder." As he spoke, he pulled his index finger clear of his fist. That's why, when you push the key in, the lock will turn. The tumbler lock's been around a while. It was invented by the ancient Egyptians, according to the guy who taught me."

"Then these tools you have—you use them to push the key pins up out of the cylinder."

"You got it, Liz. Watch this."

Race slid the pick as far as it would go into the lock, and pushed the blade of the torque wrench into the space underneath the pick in the keyway. Then he ran the pick back and forth in the lock a few times, all the while adjusting the torque he was applying with the wrench. After the sixth pass, the plug turned free, and there was a muffled click as the bolt retracted into the door. "Try the handle," he said.

"It's open," Liz said in a low squeal, suitably and sincerely impressed. "But how did you keep the key pins from sliding back into the cylinder?"

"Push the button on the inside handle to lock the door again, and I'll show you."

"You're sure nobody's in there?"

"Positive."

Liz opened the door gingerly, then reached in and pressed the button on the handle. When the door was closed again, Race took out his own flashlight and shone it into the lock at a slightly upward angle.

"Peek in there," he instructed. "Can you see the key pins protruding down?"

She could. Race explained that the job of the lock picker was to move each tumbler up until the driver pin cleared the plug, and to keep it from falling back down by applying just enough torque to the cylinder. This could be done tumbler by tumbler, he said, or it could be done by jogging all the tumblers at once with the pick, as he had just done, so that they all jump. By gently torquing the plug at the same time, one might get lucky and clear two or three tumblers at a time. "Scrubbing takes experience and instinct. You have to feel the innards of the lock through your tools, apply the right amount of pressure with the pick and the right amount of torque with the wrench." Liz crossed her arms. "I've got to say, I had pretty much written you off, but now I can see that you're not a total waste after all."

"Why, thank you so much for that ringing endorsement. Coming from a New Yawker, that's high praise, I guess. Here, take these. You can try it, but don't expect results yet."

Liz pushed the pick into the keyhole with its disk end in an upright position. She scraped the disk over the upper region of the inside of the plug, and could clearly feel the tumblers. She pressed the edge of the disk against one of them, and felt it move. Then she ran the disk back and forth as she had seen Race do, and with the torque wrench turned the plug gently until the tumblers blocked its motion. She cleared one pin, quite by accident, but found that she had to relieve the torque, because the next pin wouldn't move otherwise, and that caused the cleared pin to fall again.

"That's just going to frustrate you at this stage, Liz. Put the scrub pick back and take the one with the triangle on the end. We're going to do this one pin at a time."

It took about three quarters of an hour. The process was simple. Because of the vagaries of the lock manufacturing process, one of the driver pins will always bind before others do. With light torque, the bound pin can still be raised with the pointed pick. Raise it, and the torque will cause the plug to turn ever so slightly, binding another pin. Repeat the process until all the driver pins have cleared and the plug turns free. That was the theory. In practice, Liz experienced the false starts, missed cues and clumsiness that was to be expected of a beginner. She was determined to succeed, though, and her determination paid off when the plug finally rotated into the open position.

"I did it!"

Race let out a little whoop and clapped her on the back. "How does it feel?"

Liz savored the sensation for a moment, trying to put a descriptor on it. "You know what I'm feeling?"

Race smiled broadly and nodded. He crooked his right arm and flexed his biceps. "Power," he growled.

"Power. It's as if I could walk through walls."

"Exactly. Once you can pick locks quickly and reliably, you're a superhero."

"Or a super villain."

"Well, that's just a matter of how you use your power, right?" Race reached inside the open door and flicked a light switch, bathing them both in light. "Let's go in." He stepped across the threshold.

Liz didn't follow him. "Oh, I don't—"

"C'mon," her escort chided. "Power unused is like sex unused. Barren. C'mon, walk through that wall."

She followed him in, and he closed the door behind her. The modest living room was a mess. Decrepit furniture, clothing strewn everywhere, fishing poles, surfboards, snorkeling gear just dropped on the floor at whim, it seemed. Still, it was someone's home. "This makes me very nervous, Race."

"Imagine how you'd feel if we had walked into the Sunshine building."

"I think that would be different, somehow. Hey, those tools of yours. Where can I get a set?"

"These? Here; they're yours." He handed her the box.

"No, I couldn't—"

"Take it. I've got several sets. Now, why don't we celebrate your achievement?" Race disappeared into the tiny kitchen. There was the sound of escaping carbonation, and when he returned, he was holding two open cans of beer.

"What on earth are you doing?" Liz exclaimed.

"You mean you haven't figured it out yet? Use your deductive skills, Lady Dick."

Liz stared blankly at him. Then she blushed with embarrassment, and blushed even more because she realized her embarrassment was showing. "You rotten—" she began.

Race raised his arms in a shrug. "It was the safest place to break into." He handed her a beer, and as he did so, muttered, "Congratulations," put his other arm around her back and kissed her on the cheek. Liz neither returned nor pulled away from the kiss, hoping it would be over quickly. His skin was damp against hers in the sticky ambience of the small house. She felt the Project Thermopylae plan just below his forearm, and stood as still as she could. As men will do, Race misinterpreted her lack of resistance, slid his enfolding arm up until his hand was behind her neck and kissed her full on the mouth.

Still holding a beer in one hand and a box of lock picker's tools in the other, Liz was not well positioned to defend herself. She let go of her beer. Hearing it thud and slosh on the floor, Kendall assumed that his irresistible embrace had transported her. He dropped his beer, too, and bore down with intensified ardor, molding his body to hers. At the same time, Liz reached into the pocket of her shorts. There was only one thing she could do now. It was partly her fault for mishandling the evening, but whatever the reason, she had no alternative left. She wasn't sure enough of him either to let him see the document or to let the moment get any more intimate. His hands moved down her back. Her hand moved toward his face.

"What's this?" he mumbled as he felt the folded document at her back.

"Never mind that," she replied, her lips still encumbered by his. "What's this?"

When Race leaned back and opened his eyes, he saw a small aerosol can with the nozzle pointed at his face. A jet of pepper-charged fluid shot straight at him, bathing his eyeballs and nostrils in intense pain. He staggered backwards, tripped over a surfboard and fell onto his back. "Oh, Jaysus," he cried, barely able to speak intelligibly. "Wha' the hell you—? Chris' almighty! O-oww! You bitch, tha's the way you trea'— What the fu'g was tha' paper, you—"

He was writhing and screaming alone in his living room. Liz had already sprinted out the door and down the road toward the lights of Kapa'a. She was deeply sorry for what she had done. Race had his faults, but he was basically a considerate person. And handsome. And apparently competent at some things. More interesting but less accomplished than Harlan, more self-assured with less reason, more muscular but less brainy, equally untidy but far more exciting physically. As she ran, she decided that she could learn to like the guy, in fact, except for one thing: she still didn't trust him. Not that he would hurt her or cause her to be hurt; but information was his stock in trade, either protecting it or selling it. She wasn't paying, and she wasn't getting any information; but maybe someone else was.

Headlights far behind her suddenly cast an anemic light over the telephone poles at the roadside. Even though she knew that the object of her musings was still lying immobilized on the floor of his living room, Liz stepped into a cane break until the vehicle had passed. Its taillights safely ahead of her, she resumed her run and her rumination. Why didn't she trust Race? She couldn't put her finger on it, exactly. In part, the coincidence of his appearance and Stella's simultaneous disappearance on the Kalalau Trail had planted a seed of suspicion that had quickly taken root, even though those events now appeared to be unconnected. In part, his overt interest in sexual conquest had turned her off, just on general principles. In major part, though, it was exactly as she had told him: she felt that he was hiding knowledge about Xerxes Industries from her, and, it seemed, from Niki, too. Particularly after she had found the Project Thermopylae draft in less than an hour's sifting through the Sunshine dumpster, she couldn't believe that he had learned nothing about Xerxes' connection to the Makai Ranch situation in the course of his work for the Kamehamehas. Clutching the tools of her newfound craft in one hand and the purloined document in the other, Liz Chase jogged downhill, looking forward to the next day, which, she strongly sensed, would bring greater enlightenment.

Despite the amount of rain that had fallen on the Chases since their arrival, Hurricane Iniki had not had much of an effect on Kauai's weather yet. The storms since Monday had been caused not by Iniki but by a large but much weaker disturbance over the Pacific to the north and west of Hawaii. If one were to search for traces of Iniki's presence on the weather in Kauai between September 7 and September 9, one would find them only in the temperature and relative humidity for that period, which had increased to above-normal levels because Iniki was disrupting the typical high pressure pattern over the island. These changes, though subtle, had their effect on the Chases. The sultry, enervating environment gave the violence and death they had encountered a preternaturally evil quality, and oppressed their spirits, enhancing the sense of distraction, vulnerability and foreboding that dogged them all, but especially Janet and Andrew.

Though her effects on Kauai were so far principally psychological, Iniki's capacity to do mayhem was rising. About an hour after Liz abandoned Race Kendall to his suffering, the Central Pacific Hurricane Center in Honolulu upgraded the hurricane to Force Two. Hurricane Iwa, which had caused so much damage on Kauai in 1982, was a Force One hurricane. After Iwa caused over two hundred million dollars in property damage even at that low level of force, the local building codes had been tightened significantly. Unfortunately, the county government allowed property owners a grace period so that they could return their homes and workplaces to livable condition quickly; an understandable short-term decision, but it allowed most of the damaged buildings to be restored in a fashion that did not comply with the new ordinance.

Force Two hurricanes, packing sustained winds of between ninety-six and one hundred-ten miles an hour, with an accompanying storm surge of six to eight feet, would under any circumstances be expected to do extensive shoreline damage and to keep the roofing trade very busy in their aftermath. On Kauai, where much construction remained below code, and where the upsweeping topography could intensify wind speeds, Force Two storms could be expected to cause even more severe damage. Iniki, however, was still almost four hundred miles south of the Big Island, on a west-northwesterly course that would pass well south of Kauai, a course that had held reasonably steady for two days. Although she was growing larger and stronger by the hour, the beast's movements minimized concern over her increasing destructiveness.

As energy poured into her already seething, circumducting eyewall, Iniki's power to draw storm cells under her spiralling skirts increased, allowing the hurricane to sweep clean the weather patterns at the fringes of her influence. By staying well south of the island chain, Iniki was also remaining in nurturing warm waters that would feed her as much energy-rich moisture as she could devour. This year, those waters were more torrid than usual, as a result of an El Nino current in the eastern Pacific. A decade earlier, another El Nino had invigorated Iwa, and it was more than unhappy coincidence that Hurricane Andrew had raked over South Florida three weeks earlier, Typhoon Omar visited havoc on Guam on August two weeks earlier, and four other hurricanes stalked the Pacific at the same time that Iniki was prowling the waters south of Hawaii. Iniki and her siblings were the destructive spawn of the artificial warming of the Earth during the last half of Twentieth Century.

September 10

"Hawaii suffered another day of hot and humid 'hurricane weather' yesterday as meteorologists cast a wary eye south and said a big blow called Iniki would miss the Islands if it stayed on course," according to *The Advertiser* for this day. Iniki was blamed for the record ninety-one degree heat, but forecasters expressed the view that on its present course and speed Iniki would have little effect on the Islands other than heat and some high surf. Iniki's forward speed had slowed from sixteen to fourteen miles per hour, but its cyclonic winds were now reported to be one hundred miles per hour, with gusts up to one hundred twenty. It had passed well south of the Big Island, and was at press time moving into the longitudes of the northern Hawaiian Islands.

The Advertiser predicted sunny, hot and humid weather for the day.

9

"You two must have had quite a fight." Liz Chase surveyed the damaged wall and shard-strewn floor through half-closed eyes as she walked into the living area in the low morning light.

"Your father threw the vase at one of his new girlfriends last night," her mother responded from behind the kitchen counter.

"I heard that," Andrew shouted from the edge of the deck, where he was sitting with his head in his hands. "Your mother refuses to clean up the mess, in case she decides to call the police."

"Coffee?" Janet asked her eldest daughter, whose eyes were now fully open and scanning the room inquisitively as she slid onto a ladder-backed stool.

A door opened down the hall, and a groggy Stella shuffled in. "What happened here," she mumbled, on her way to the counter.

"Your father had a fight with one of his crazed admirers," Janet replied.

"That wasn't funny the first time!" Andrew yelled. He sighed, stood up and walked back into the house. "Last night, during the storm, Web Chamberlain's realtor came over here while your mother and I were having dinner. The guards were in place outside the front door and in back. Both those areas were lighted, so the guards were highly visible, which you would think was a good thing, but it wasn't. A lesson learned, I guess. In the storm, she was able to get close to the guards without being heard. She had some kind of anesthetic fluid impregnated into a cloth. It was very powerful, as both your mother and I can attest."

"My head is still killing me," Janet moaned.

"She jumped the guards one by one. They both had the same instinctual response, which was to suck in their breath in surprise, and that's the last thing they remember. After she put the boys to sleep, she rolled the garage door open, which we didn't hear because of the noise of the storm. Inside, she found the fusebox, and flipped the main circuit breaker."

"When the lights went out, your father went to the front door," Janet put in, "and discovered the unconscious guard. At the same time, Li-Ann Low—that's her name—slipped in through the kitchen door. I heard the rain coming in, and thought the wind had blown the door open somehow. Just as I was getting up to close it, this madwoman swooped around the corner. The next thing I remember, she was running smelling salts under my nose and apologizing profusely."

The Chase daughters had been mute to that point in Andrew's story. Now Stella asked uncertainly, "Is—is this woman in jail, now or what?"

"Yeah," her sister contributed numbly.

Andrew shook his head. "Whether she is arrested or not is up to your mother. I'm not pressing charges, and neither are the guards."

"Why not?" Liz demanded, holding her coffee cup under her nose with both hands as if it, too, were smelling salts. "This is really scary, Dad."

"Let me finish the story, and you'll see why not. I came back into the house, which was dark except for a couple of candles on the table. I saw your mother on the floor, and Li-Ann standing over her. Li-Ann doused the candles as I was picking up the vase, and when I threw it, she had moved. She jumped me, too, and when I woke up, she was sitting on top of me."

Coming to with the smell of ammonium carbonate in his nostrils and his head still buzzing from the ethyl ether in his blood stream, Andrew Chase had been a captive audience. Li-Ann Low towered over him. The black cowl of her raincoat still covering her head made her look like a mythical figure, some sort of malign goddess. "I am so sorry, Andrew," she had said, as she lowered herself so that her haunches rested on his pelvic bones. "I give you my most humble apologies, and hope what I have to say will compensate for my terrible rudeness."

"Rudeness," Andrew had repeated slowly, thinking what an odd word that was for what the woman had just done. "How is my wife? I mean, my—"

"—She's asleep. It's just a general anesthetic, Andrew."

"Why are you sitting on me? If you're trying to rape me, I don't think it's going to work."

The Chinese American put a hand to her mouth to suppress her laughter. "Oh, Andrew," she sighed, bouncing up and down on his lower abdomen. "That's really sweet. I'm not sure how to answer. I guess I should say, Not tonight."

The humor left her face. "No, no. Tonight, I have a message for you, as the mouthpiece for Paracorp In-ter-na-shun-al." As she enunciated the latter word, she thumped on the lawyer's chest with the fingers of her right hand. "I want you to tell that evil sonofabitch Harry Wong that if he fucks with my client or me any more, he'll be sleeping at the bottom of Hong Kong harbor faster than he can say *'wo xiong-kou tong.'*"

The way she had spoken the Anglo-Saxon obscenity—forming the opening fricative by curling her entire lower lip under her incisors and popping it out defiantly, then drawing out the plosive-sibilant ending into a separate syllable—and the way she spat out the Mandarin phrase, which, if Andrew's mental translator was functioning properly, meant something like, "I'm having chest pains," bespoke a particularly active animosity toward his client. He could not think of anything meaningful to say, so he simply mumbled, "Pardon me?"

Li-Ann Low cocked her head. "Oh. Maybe you would understand better if you were sitting up?" She helped the lawyer to his feet. He was unsteady, so she lifted his arm over her shoulder and walked him to one of the sofas.

"Thank you," he muttered as she turned him so he could sit down. All at once she pushed hard on his chest. He fell into a seated position, and she leapt onto his lap, pinning his arms to his sides with her knees. The vigorous motion caused her miniskirt to hike up, revealing her lace panties. "M-must we be in such—p-proximity, Li-Ann?" he stammered.

"No," she said brightly. "I could tie you up. Would you like that better?"

"Maybe you could—j-just say what you came to say as quickly as possible, and then we could s-see to Janet and the others?"

"Sure," she replied. She grabbed him by the throat and pushed his head back against the cushion, so that he had to look down his nose to see her. The effort caused his eyeballs to ache. "Your client, Harry Wong, has had his goons terrorizing and killing people who work for other companies bidding on the Makai Ranch, and for a potential lessee. Through you, he arranged for me and Carter Robinson to be hauled in for questioning as suspects in those murders."

"I had no—"

Li-Ann Low pressed her hand against Andrew's Adam's apple, closing his larynx so that he could not breathe. "I did not come here to argue," she said, and only when Andrew showed signs of serious distress did she relax her grip. "It's simple. Paracorp is trying to scare off the other bidders and intimidate Xerxes, so that the ridiculous bid that Harry Wong asked you to put in will be the only bid on the table. He's trying to destroy my credibility and Robinson's, so that we can't protect Chamberlain's interests. And you, you stupid round-eye! You come to Kauai, you ingratiate yourself with Chamberlain, and then without the slightest idea what you're doing, you help that old gangster Wong steal the Makai Ranch. Now do you understand why I am so furious with you, asshole?"

"C-can I say something?" Andrew inquired hoarsely, moving his chin slightly to indicate discomfort.

"Speak, puppet." Li-Ann Low removed her hand from his throat, and wiggled herself back toward his knees an inch or two.

"First, I'm nobody's puppet," he said through his teeth. The assertion was rewarded with scornful laughter. "Second," he continued, "you are accusing my client of conspiracy to commit murder. If you have proof of that, I'd like to know what it is."

"No proof. But isn't it strange that your daughter wasn't shot along with the France-Orient agents the other day? Or that you haven't been attacked?"

"Do you know Mr. Wong, Li-Ann?"

"I know all about him. His family and mine both moved to Hong Kong from Fukien Province a hundred years before the British annexed it. For three centuries before that, his ancestors were well known thieves and extortionists in Fukien. Those were the skills that his family brought to Hong Kong, and those are the skills that brought Harry Wong his fortune. He's an unprincipled, predatory cri-mi-nal." More punching at Andrew's chest.

"Wh-what do you want from me, Li-Ann?"

The realtor bared her teeth and brought her face forward to Andrew's nose with such ferocity that Andrew feared she might bite it off. "Number one, I want you to go away, back where you belong. And number two, I want you to tell Harry Wong that Mr. Chamberlain rejects his bid, and will not accept any further bids from Paracorp."

"Are you—" Andrew was afraid to ask the question, but he had to. "Are you authorized to make that representation on behalf of Chamberlain?"

Li-Ann's breath smelled like fresh mint, her perfume like lilacs. Her legs were smooth, strong but not sinewy, and her face was mesmerizing in its every expression. If she were only acting, Andrew might have been aroused by her dominatrix simulation. But she was not acting, and his only sensation at the moment was impotency.

"I'll be authorized tomorrow, puppet," she said.

"O-one more thing, Li-Ann." Andrew drew a deep breath. It seemed to help clear his head, so he did it again, maintaining eye contact with the manic realtor. "W-Web Chamberlain claims never to have heard the name Xerxes Industries before I mentioned it to him. Yet you and Robinson were inside Bungalow thirteen at the Pakala Inn on the afternoon that the Xerxes Industries agent was murdered there. Why were you there?"

"Mr. Adibi invited us to meet him there." Li-Ann Low spat out the words. "That's all I know." Though her countenance remained fixed, something in her gaze wavered as she said the words.

She left Andrew with the smelling salts and told him to point out to the guards that if they turned her in, the story of their incompetence would spread throughout the islands, and they would never do serious security work again. He revived Janet and the two men. The guards immediately recognized the wisdom of LiAnn's position. Once he was sure that Janet was all right, Andrew allowed that he would not press charges, either. If Li-Ann was right about Harry Wong—and he knew the man well enough not to dismiss her allegations out of hand—it would be dangerous to his career to engage in a public process having anything to do with the Makai Ranch.

"What about you, Mom?" Stella asked, when her father ended his explanation.

"I'm torn. On the one hand, that woman is clearly a psychopath. She ought to be locked up, without a doubt. On the other hand, if her story turns out to be true, then she's not the killer, and we should probably not shoot the messenger, even if her method of communication was felonious. She didn't kill or even wound anyone last night, when she certainly could have. And I definitely wouldn't want to provoke her further. I don't know. The whole experience was horrifying."

Andrew Chase walked over to the counter and put his arms around his daughters. "You girls know as much as we do. What do you think about Li-Ann's Paracorp theory?"

Liz slid off her stool and headed for her room. "I have something that you might want to read, Dad," she said over her shoulder. She returned with the Project Thermopylae document, opened it flat on the counter and pressed her finger against a page. "See, here. 'Potential lessors.' And the names underneath? It's the same as the list in Adibi's hatband."

"Whoa, Nellie," Andrew said. "What is this?"

Liz explained the document's provenance.

"Does your friend Race know you have this?" Andrew asked.

"No, but he knows I have a document that I wouldn't show him."

Andrew leafed through the draft. "This is incredible. It appears to be an outline of a plan for construction of an industrial city. A refinery....They're talking about chemical plants....A port for tankers.... Good-bye, Garden Island." He sank onto a stool. "And the reason XIL wasn't on the bidder's list is that it isn't bidding directly, but only through the financing companies."

"Did you have any idea, Dad?" Liz asked.

Andrew Chase shook his head. "None, honey. I swear. Stella thought of this angle before I did." He flipped through the pages again and shook his head. "God! What have I been doing here?"

Janet reached across the counter and slipped her hand into his. "You couldn't have known, Andy," she murmured.

He was too stunned to appreciate the small intimacy in her gesture. "Thanks, Janet. Maybe I couldn't have known. Clients never tell you everything; but in this case Paracorp wouldn't tell me anything. It's conceivable that Harry Wong isn't aware of the scope of the Xerxes project either, though I can't think of any other reason for him to be so secretive. Damn! I should have insisted. At least I should have refused to represent him on this deal."

Stella moved behind her father, put her hands on either side of his neck and began to massage the muscles of his upper back. "There's a reason for everything that happens, Dad. There's a reason why you weren't made aware of the Xerxes plan until now, and a reason why you're the one here representing Paracorp rather than some other lawyer."

"Hadn't we better get going?" Janet said. "We've got all morning to talk about this." She lifted a styrofoam cooler to the countertop. Her daughters looked at her without comprehending. "Your father and I thought we ought to clear our heads by taking a walk—in a public place. You're coming, too. Last tour before we leave tomorrow."

"Is that still the plan? Leave tomorrow?" Stella asked.

"After last night," Janet declared, "it's not even an issue." The phone rang next to her, and she picked it up. "Hello. Oh, hi. It's for you, Liz." She mouthed the name, "Race," as she gave her daughter the handset. The other Chases could hear only one side of the ensuing conversation.

"Hello. I-I'm sorry about—Yeah. Well, I'm used to fast company, but, you know, I do have a boy—No, no, just a boy friend—

Sure, all's fair, but I don't like being treated like—Yeah. Anyway, how're your eyes—Really? What, do you just cut the aloe leaf and let the juice—That's amazing. Well I'm glad—Tonight? I don't know if that's such a good idea, Race—You would do that? Promise? Hold on." Liz turned to Janet. "Mom, you're still going to Captain Barry's place this afternoon? Is it okay if I go out with Race? I mean, if this is our last night—"

"I don't know, Liz," Andrew fretted. "He didn't bring you home until the wee hours this morning."

"Dad, he didn't bring me home at all, but that's another story. So it's okay, right?"

The Chase family was on the road by eight-thirty. The morning was glorious: sunny, warm and drier than it had been all week. The sky was dotted with high, puffy clouds that drifted out of the northeast like petals on a heavenly stream. In the open convertible, conversation was difficult, and instead the family spent the next hour and a half pointing out sights to one another with intermittent shouts. They travelled west on Highway 50, stopping at a grocery store on top of the hill in Kalaheo, engagingly called the Menehune Food Mart. The Mart was a lot less cute than its name suggested, but had adequate fruit, trail mix and water for a morning's hike. Then they took the highway parallel to the coast, across forested ridges and through lush valleys. It bisected several small towns in which one or another of the Chase women saw an establishment worth shopping, had time permitted. Eventually, the road flattened out and approached the shore. Vast fields of sugar cane carpeted the rolling land on the *mauka* side, and ahead in the distance a huge plume of yellow smoke rose several hundred feet into the air, like a lazy, stationary tornado, before metamorphosing into a cloud that drifted out toward Ni'ihau.

"It's a cane fire!" Andrew shouted, recalling the fascination he had felt for these powerful conflagrations during his childhood visits. "They burn the cane before harvesting the stalks, to get rid of the dry leaves. You should see one of these at night. Like a volcano!"

Janet was relieved to have her family around her. Oddly, Li-Ann Low's deranged visitation the night before had left her less concerned than she had been. If Li-Ann was right about Harry Wong, the Chases were not facing the same risks as the representatives of other bidders; and if she was wrong—well, as Andy had said, they weren't going to be in any greater danger in Koke'e State Park than anywhere else.

She gazed at her former husband, the lovable but insufferable one. Even Andy's presence was a positive addition to the day. The turns his life had taken since the divorce were making him more human, more interested in things other than work, including his family, apparently. In another few years, he might even be able to sustain another long-term relationship. In the open convertible, the balmy air pulled at her body like the urgent caresses of an invisible lover. To one side of them as they drove, the ocean was almost always in view, living out its restive, monotonous life in their sight. Waves broke atop enormous swells that seemed to be a kind of breathing. To the other side, a magical terrain rose, born in fiery torment millions of years ago, but eroded by rain and wind into a remarkable, undulating surface on which, first, nature had planted her wild gardens and later, humankind had substituted its tamer cultivations. For the first time since the night she arrived, Janet could actually enjoy her surroundings.

A sign announced that they had reached the town of Kekaha. Andrew made a right turn that took them past level streets filled with modest houses reddened by dust from the iron-rich earth. There was a sugar mill here. The big trucks worked the fields just beyond the little town and hauled cane down dirt roads and across the main street to the mill. As they did, they ground the plantation's unpaved roadbeds to a powder with their man-high tires and flung that powder into the air, creating a pall over the settlement.

Andrew stopped the car across the street from the mill, which was a large rectangular building painted yellow, with huge openings on the side and in front. Through the side opening, a conveyor belt delivered cane in bunches into the upper regions of the works, where a steamy spray filled the air as it washed the cuttings before they entered the two story machinery of cane production. Outside, a parade of trucks, overflowing with great mounds of burnt cane, waited their turns under the giant, toothed pincers that would relieve them of their burden. The noise was riotous, truck engines groaning under the weight of their loads, pincers moving into position and scooping up mawfuls of cane, the spray echoing loudly inside the mill and the machinery, behind its clunky, dark, oxidized exterior, chopping and turning and moving the cane. All of it, the massive machinery, the oversized piping, the pincers, the trucks, all of it was rusted. The building itself, and the storage tanks behind it, were coated with red dust, and so looked rusted, too.

"This industry is so antiquated," Andrew said.

"It sure looks archaic," Liz agreed. "Shouldn't they have scrubbers in that chimney?" She pointed to the top of a smokestack that was pouring a continuous, tawny cloud of steam and carbon waste into the sky.

"Maybe not. That probably stays aloft until its well out into the Pacific."

"Oh, good. Then it's only polluting the ocean."

The ascent to the state parks took the Chases from sea level to almost four thousand feet, in a series of looping switchbacks that bore them into increasingly less tropical vegetation: koa trees dotted the ridges, and higher up there was redwood. Glimpses of Waimea Canyon and its tributary gorges shot by on their right. Their first stop was at an easy walk over a hillock to a lookout point above those marvels of erosion. They stood leaning against the railing, enjoying the cool air of the higher altitude and gazing out over the rim of a canyon a mile wide and three thousand feet deep. Its walls were largely pastel in hue, and sculpted into shapes not dissimilar from those found in their more massive counterparts in Arizona. The view to the north was of a canyon divided at a point where two rivers had met countless millennia earlier, after the collapse of part of the shield of the central volcano. In the saddle of land between the two canyons, a third river poured itself over a precipice in an imposing waterfall.

"I don't really want to leave tomorrow, Mom," Stella murmured as she watched a tropic bird navigate the air currents in the canyon.

"Neither do I," Liz said.

"I don't see how you can say that, girls," Janet countered. "In less than three days on this island we've seen more violence than most people we know are exposed to in a lifetime."

"Mom, you and Dad may have led uneventful lives, but I never told you half of what happened on those summer trips you sent me on when I was in college. I mean, the Amazon was nothing but danger the whole time."

"But you were travelling with seasoned explorers."

"Scientists, Mom. Scientists. Other than gathering, examining and cataloguing specimens, they were worse than helpless. We kids kept them alive, not the other way around."

"It's true, Mom," Stella said. The important thing about those trips wasn't the scenery, or the culture. It was learning how to cope on our own in an alien environment. That time I missed the boat out of Sardinia and had to stay over the weekend with no money? If I ever told you that whole story, your hair would fall out."

"This isn't negotiable, girls," Andrew said. "Even though Iniki's going to miss us, there's another hurricane blowing right now, called the Makai Ranch deal, and it just doesn't make sense to stay outside in a hurricane."

"It's okay for you, Dad," Stella said, struggling to find an explanation other than the one that was in her heart. "You've seen Kauai before. It's different for Liz and me. I mean, this is so beautiful—"

"And it's interesting," Liz added. "So many different races intermingling. The whole question of native rights. How the land should be used—"

Janet slapped her hands against her sides. "It'll be just as interesting next year. We can come back. It's nice that all this beauty brings you to the brink of tears, Stell, but at this particular moment, we have more pressing considerations."

"Let's get up to the lodge, shall we?" Andrew said. "I need to make a phone call."

Andrew found a pay phone on a post in the lawn between the Koke'e lodge and the natural history museum, two log buildings at the entrance to the largest state park on the island. It was just five a.m. in Hong Kong, but he knew that Galen Khoo was an early riser. "Good morning, it's me. Sorry to call you so early, but there are a few questions."

"That's fine. This is not a secure line?"

"No. I'm out in the wilderness. No names, okay?"

"Is everything all right?"

"Yes and no. I'd like to know if your employer is in negotiations to lease property for large-scale industrial use."

"Anywhere in the world? Sure."

"You know what property I'm talking about, goddammit."

"We told you we weren't going to disclose—"

"Listen, friend, we're talking about life and death here, me and my family. So don't play games with me."

There was the sound of a breath exhaled. "Okay, okay." There was embarrassment in Khoo's voice, and resignation. "Yes, we are."

Andrew had hoped against hope that the answer would be negative, because of its implications, among which was the fact that neither he nor his firm was involved in the negotiation with Xerxes. "Whom are you using for counsel on the lease, if I may ask?"

"We're doing it internally."

"Internally? Jesus!" Khoo was lying, but Andrew had to react as though it were the truth. Harry Wong had forced Andrew's former classmate into a position in which dissembling would cause Andrew the least pain. "That's a mistake we can talk about later. No reflection on the competence of your department, you understand. There are serious foreign asset control issues here, because of the lessee's identity, and you need an American lawyer involved." *Which firm is it,* he wondered. *Probably Dillon, Cafferty. The bastards have been putting the rush on Paracorp from their Hong Kong office ever since the National Law Journal article about discontent at Fowler & Greide.* "Uh, let me tell you something else. This lessee is probably working with some or all of the other bidders, too. Were you aware of that?"

Silence on the other end of the line.

"Were you?"

"No."

That answer was not a lie. "Okay, one more thing you should know. The seller is going to be advised today that your employer has resorted to violence to frighten off other bidders." Andrew paused, waiting for a reaction.

After a moment, Khoo said, "You're full of surprises today, my friend."

"Is that all you have to say? That's a pretty fucking serious allegation, don't you think? I mean, I'm out here on the pointy end of the spear—"

"Oh, come on. That charge is bullshit. The boss plays hardball, I don't have to tell you that. But he likes his lifestyle too much to jeopardize it by doing something illegal."

"Mm-hmm. Well, the seller's going to be counseled by his broker to reject your offer because of your employers alleged actions. You may want to take instruction on this, and call me tonight. I'm setting up a meeting with the seller tomorrow morning and will hang around for the day in case there's a need for follow-up, but then I'm leaving Kauai."

"Leaving? It's that bad?"

"How the hell do I know? It's been terminal for some people. I can't justify staying. Look, my friend, the equation balances like this for me. There's been violence around my family here; I haven't told you everything about that, but believe me, it's enough to rattle any sensible person. On the deal side, the seller thinks your employer's bid was about half what the property will sell for, and I think he's right. The offer is not viable unless all the other bidders disappear. The allegation of violence fits right in with that view of things. It makes an already difficult situation impossible. Given the limitations on my understanding and authority, there's little I can do for you here anymore."

"I understand, my friend. You should definitely do what you think is right for you and your family. I'll try to smooth it over with the boss, but I—well, I can't guarantee success. I'll call you tonight."

After hanging up, Andrew stood motionless at the phone, wondering what was happening to his law practice. Dillon, Cafferty, or whoever, had been handed a big project for which he wasn't even invited to compete. Galen Khoo couldn't guaranty that Harry Wong would not fire him for abandoning a hopeless cause for exigent personal reasons. He took a deep breath. He could only do what he could do, he decided, and picked up the phone again. The call to Carter Robinson was very chilly, very businesslike, with no mention of the issues that had been raised, or rather, stuffed down Andrew's throat, by Li-Ann Low the night before. He asked for a meeting with Web Chamberlain the next morning. Robinson made no promises, but said he'd call the Poipu house later in the day and leave a message.

When Andrew relinquished the phone, Liz grabbed it and rang Niki Makana. "Niki, it looks as though we're leaving tomorrow. If you want to talk to my Dad, you'd better do it today."

"So you'll set it up. *Mahalo nui loa,* Sistah. Where is he now?"

"All of us are up in Koke'e. We're going to hike a bit and have a picnic."

"Okay, tell your family I recommend the first part of the Pihea Trail. When it starts to dip down into the swamp, turn around and come back; it gets really messy from that point on. Picnic down by the lodge, and I'll meet you there."

When Liz finished, it was Stella's turn. She called the police station looking for George Akamai. He was "not reachable," so she left word that she wanted to see him that evening.

Then the family drove up the paved access road to a spot called the Pu'u o Kila lookout. "Brace yourselves," Andrew said as he got out of the car.

The view from the overlook was transcendent. There may be more dramatic natural spectacles: the Grand Canyon at sunrise from Yavapai point, the Canadian Rockies from across Lake Louise, Everest from below the northeast face, Ayers Rock at sunset; but there is no place more enthralling than the view of the Kalalau Valley from this spot. The Chases stood mute at the brink of a vertical drop from which the valley emerged between two long, craggy ridges; a broad, fertile, emerald-cloaked, two-mile wide scoop in the earth, it fell in an ever more gentle incline some three miles to the sea. The ridges to either side were rippled, folded and sharp-edged. They framed the view with geological finality. At the far end of the valley, waves dashing themselves against the cliffs and sliding onto the long beach could just be seen as a shifting white line, beyond which the ocean merged with the sky where offshore clouds and mist occulted the horizon. Vertiginous, expansive, elemental, exotic and pacific, the Kalalau Valley revealed itself to the visitors, from their four-thousand foot vantage point, to be a paradigmatic Hawaiian place.

The scene worked its magic on them. After a few moments, Andrew made a suggestion. "Why don't we talk for a while about what we've got ourselves involved in, that's going to take us away from this gorgeous island tomorrow."

"A fight over a gorgeous piece of land," Stella offered.

"A fight over a way of life." This from Liz.

"A fight between rich and greedy men," Janet contributed.

"Okay. At least you all agree that we're in the middle of a fight. Maybe we should do this more systematically. Let's take Xerxes first. A heavy duty petrochemical and construction company, with a plan for industrializing a big chunk of Kauai. Incredibly, it appears that they're working with companies that are competing with one another to buy the Makai Ranch. Why would they do that? Why wouldn't they just team with one? Doesn't what they're doing assure a higher sale price and therefore a higher land lease rate to Xerxes."

Janet and Stella stared blankly back at him, but Liz shook her head. "The price would be higher only if Xerxes was the only potential lessee. If there's competition among lessees as well as lessors, then there might be even more of a bidding war—right?—so it might make sense for Xerxes to try to lock up all the lessors if it can."

Andrew blinked. He reached over and tousled his daughter's hair. "And I thought that 'D' you got in economics reflected your understanding of the subject."

"Gee, is that a compliment?"

"I, uh, guess I could have said it more positively. Brilliant, Liz. How's that?"

"I like the sound of it, Dad."

"Me, too," Andrew said, surprised at how good it felt. "Let's keep going. Now, would Xerxes have any motivation to kill Adibi, one of its own employees, plus Chantal and Luc?"

"My book club read a mystery novel once," Janet mused, "in which a corporate raider killed a rival, and then murdered one of his own employees in order to deflect suspicion."

"So poor Adibi might have been a sacrificial lamb? It's creative, Janet. But weak. Any other ideas?"

"Adibi was meeting with the seller's agents," Stella offered. "Maybe he was double dealing."

"Wow." Andrew gave his younger daughter's shoulder a loving punch. "Now there's a theory, Stell." He reflected a moment. "But it raises another question. Chamberlain told me he had never heard of Xerxes Industries. If that's true, then why were Robinson and Low meeting with Adibi?"

"Maybe they were double-dealing, too."

"Whoa, Stella. Even a good theory will tear if you stretch it too far."

"But Dad, it makes sense, doesn't it?"

"Not unless Robinson was prepared to be disbarred from the practice of law. But okay, it's something to be looked into. Shall we move on to Paracorp? The general counsel says that Harry Wong would not do anything illegal. That may be something of an overstatement, but I tend to agree that he wouldn't embrace murder as a negotiating technique."

"He might not, but maybe the kind of pressure he puts on his people would lead them to do it," Stella suggested.

"You're losing ground, Stell. This isn't a life-or-death deal for Paracorp. It's just a typical purchase/lease."

"A very big one," Liz said.

"Okay, a very big one."

"Maybe big enough either to ruin or to nail an executive's position in the company?"

"Fine. If both of you girls like that scenario, we'll hold it as a definite maybe. Of course, it does give us a little problem, because executives of other bidders would be under similar pressure. And if we tie in your mother's book-club theory, we can't even eliminate France-Orient. We're not narrowing the field, I'm afraid."

"So far," Liz said, "we've only talked about people interested in buying or leasing the Makai Ranch. What about people interested in blocking any sale or lease?"

"You mean your sovereignty friends," Andrew asked.

"Well, no. I don't think they—I had in mind the owner's heirs, for example, or neighboring property owners. I guess," Liz added, wondering suddenly about the wisdom of having alerted Niki to the family's whereabouts, "you could add the Kamehamehas to the list of suspects. Speaking of which, Dad, Niki wants to talk to you. She—she's coming up here this afternoon." Liz winced.

"Well, well, well," her father murmured. "You can tell me a little more about that while we're hiking, okay? Have we completed the list of suspects? Oh, wait. 'Heirs!' Here's one more possibility, based on what you told me yesterday, Janet. At my meeting with Chamberlain, he mentioned that one reason he was selling the Ranch was to create an inheritance for his 'errant son,' which I took to mean that the son couldn't be relied on to run the Ranch, or maybe even fend for himself, and needed income-producing investments to live on."

Janet frowned. "But if the son were in for a big inheritance from the sale of the Ranch, why would he be scaring off potential buyers?"

Andrew gave her a look that said he had no idea. "Maybe he and his father disagree on the selling price?"

Stella raised a hand. "Another group that could be opposed to selling the Ranch are the marijuana growers. They've planted their crops all over the property, right in with the sugar cane."

"And according to C.B. Freeman, they are prone to violence," her mother added.

Stella nodded. "George told me that they sometimes use firearms to keep Ranch employees away from their plants."

"Seems as though there are bad guys all around us," Andrew half-joked.

Janet swept her arms up from her sides. "That's why we're leaving, Andy!"

Liz mentioned Niki Makana's suggestion that they hike the Pihea Trail. Andrew considered the proposition, recalled the route vaguely but agreeably from a youthful visit, and concurred. They set off, Andrew feeling an unaccustomed inner warmth in the realization that whatever danger they were in had at least drawn them closer together.

The first part of the trail was a road to nowhere, a controversial, aborted project to provide a connection between Koke'e, which is only accessible from the south, and Hanelai in the north. A wide, compacted, red-earth track led the Chases along the top of the ridge, where they were rewarded with additional views of the valley. Under the open sun, in a quiet breeze and out of the sea-level heat, the hikers walked together for about three quarters of a mile, reminiscing about hikes that some or all of them had taken elsewhere in the world.

Where the road ended, there began a narrow, twisting, hilly track that had been carved into the clay-like, rocky soil. The expansive views of the coast petered out, and were replaced by limiting views of the encircling foliage, and an occasional peek out over the exuberantly vegetated, ancient caldera. *Mokihana* trees, small and berried, *maile* vine with shiny little leaves and tiny white flowers, tree ferns growing to a height of ten feet, *ohia lehua*, its branches decorated with tufted flowers rather like those of the bottlebrush tree, and exotic grasses; these and other varieties of flora surrounded them as they made their way. Farther along, the path became a muddy reminder of the recent rains. Puddles so large that ankles disappeared into them seemed to materialize on the windward side of every rise. In one or two places, the going became so steep that handholds on sapling trunks or protruding stones were a necessary aid to passage. In less than half an hour, their arms, legs, shirts, shorts and shoes were ornamented with stains of burnt sienna, and when the initial shock of being filthy wore off, it left Janet laughing giddily with her daughters at every misstep, slip or splash that adorned her with a new badge of hiking ignominy.

At length the trail led them down gradually into the Alakai swamp. Ferns began to predominate, and trees were more deformed and moss-laden. The landscape here looked distinctly Cretaceous.

They had passed the turn that Niki had mentioned to Liz. The elder Chase daughter had not failed to recognize it; rather, she had decided to say nothing, because she was curious as to what a swamp on top of an almost mile-high mountain looked like.

A low-pitched mechanical whine and the sound of hammering reached their ears. Walking toward the source of the noise in single file, Andrew in front, they were all at once nervously vigilant again. They climbed up out of a messy gulch onto a hilltop. In the low-lying area ahead of them, a small crew was laying a boardwalk. Nearby, a supply of pressure-treated planks sat on a large palette that could only have reached the site by helicopter. The workers were fastening timbers to metal rods that were being inserted into bedrock with the aid of oversized drills. The family approached the closest crew member, and Andrew asked about the project.

"We're just starting," the woman explained, her lavender tank-top darkened with perspiration. "Eventually, this will connect with the Alakai Swamp Trail and take you right on out to Mohini Road. Y'know where that is?"

They didn't, but it didn't matter. Liz gestured at the boardwalk. "Makes the swamp less of an adventure, more of a tourist attraction, doesn't it," she remarked.

"Yeah, you're right; but it's better for the ecosystem over all. Right now, hikers are widening the paths to avoid muddy parts, and that compresses the ground. This is a very delicate environment, and the boardwalk will help preserve it."

"A worthy cause." Andrew clapped his hands together. "Well, shall we head back?"

"Wait! Are we in the swamp yet?" Liz asked the carpenter.

"Not yet, but you're not really dressed to go in there, anyway. You need high boots, preferably waterproof. Those running shoes'll just get sucked off your feet in the muck. The muck, by the way, will be up to your ass in some places."

"Maybe another time, Liz," Janet said decisively. "Let's go."

It took another hour and a quarter to re-slog the Pihea Trail and drive back to the lodge, where the family used the restrooms to wash up. The liquid soap from the dispensers wasn't strong enough to remove the russet stains from their skin and clothes, but when they were as clean as they could get under the circumstances, Andrew drove the car over to a grassy glade nearby. Janet and her daughters chose to walk there across the sunlit lawn. By the time they reached the picnic area, Andrew had unpacked the cooler onto an old redwood table. The luncheon conversation, in which Stella did not participate unless prodded, dealt with the question whether they should try to spend next week together somewhere else, or just return to their respective homes and make reservations on Kauai for early next year. By the end of the meal, it was clear that there would not be a consensus, and that a command decision would have to be made later.

As they were packing up the cooler, Iniki Makana appeared at the upper end of the access road and strolled toward them. Ahead of her, a moa rooster, its black body and autumn-colored wing and tail feathers glistening, ran to and fro for a while, then dove into the bushes and disappeared. The lissome Hawaiian ambled under the sugi pines that lined the road, wearing a short wrap skirt and a bikini top that celebrated her bosom. Shadows slid easily over her chest and shoulders as she moved. Not wishing to appear overly interested, Andrew busied himself with emptying the trash and loading the cooler into the trunk of the convertible. Niki joined the women, and in a moment Andrew closed the trunk and walked over to the foursome.

"Hello again, Niki," he said cheerfully.

The young woman with the same name as the hurricane looked at him with timeless eyes; eyes shaped by a thousand ancestral years of isolation in Hawaii; and before that, a thousand years of habitation in Tahiti; and before that, a thousand Southeast Asian years; and still before, unknown thousands of years in China. "There was another death today," she said, unblinking. "I heard it on the radio coming up. An executive from ROC Overseas. Died in his room at the Wai'ohai."

"What of?" Liz asked.

Niki shrugged. "They didn't say." She turned back to Andrew. "I'd like to talk with you for a while."

"Liz told me." Andrew looked at his Rolex. "Two-thirty. We should be starting back, Janet, if you want to be home by four to get ready for the captain." He tried to sound as though it didn't bother him that his former wife had a date that evening. "What are you girls doing tonight?"

"I'm going out, Dad."

"Me, too."

Niki smiled at the lawyer. "Why don't you give Janet the keys to your car, and let the girls get home so they can, um," she made a shooing motion with the backs of her hands, "get the crud off. I'll drive you home later." Janet flashed a worried scowl at Andrew. Niki noticed it, and Andrew saw that she noticed. The Hawaiian raised her eyebrows in a sign that might have been either surprise or dare. In his mind, he heard her say, *What's the problem? Didn't I find your younger daughter, and minister to her? Haven't I sent your older daughter home safely to you when I had the opportunity to do otherwise if I were so inclined? Why is this woman worried about me? Or is she just jealous?* Niki was as beautifully seductive as Kauai itself, and the uncertainty of the moment, too, was seductive. He fished in his pocket for the keys.

"You girls can find your way back? Fine. Here, Darling. I'll see you at the house later on."

Janet gave him a look that could have broken glass. "Have a nice chat," she said as she took the keys.

At quarter past five, Barry Saga's auto rolled into the short gravel driveway of the Puuholo Street house. In her bathroom, Janet Chase heard the crunch of wheels on pebbles. She checked her makeup, pulled a brush through her hair a few final times, slipped a simple gold bracelet onto her wrist, pulled the shoulders of her floral-patterned blouse up and let them drop. The doorbell rang. "I'll get it." She adjusted the outline of her lipstick with a finger, rubbed her hands on a towel and walked to the front door. Shrugging at Liz and Stella, who had a thousand-piece puzzle laid before them on the coffee table, as if to say, "Here goes nothing," she opened the door. "Hello!"

"Hello, Jan. Are you ready?"

"I'm ready. Come in a moment and say hi to my daughters." The Chase siblings stood. Barry Saga walked over and shook their hands. He glanced at the puzzle box on the coffee table. "'Tropical Terror?'"

"It's one of those mystery puzzles," Stella said. "You find the clues as you put it together. Mom, um, brought it with her because," a nervous giggle punctuated her explanation, "she thought we'd have fun solving a murder that takes place on a tropical island."

Saga raised an eyebrow. "Just in case real life here wasn't exciting enough for you?"

Janet touched Saga's arm. "We heard there was another killing today."

"Well, 'killing' assumes evidence we don't have yet," the police officer responded guardedly. "The body was found in bed by a housekeeper late this morning. There were no signs of violence, but I expect the autopsy will show that Mr. Song was assisted unwillingly into the afterlife."

"Li-Ann Low told us last night that the head of Paracorp is behind all this madness," Janet said, to see how Saga would react. "She said that's the reason Andy is still alive."

"Did she come over here? She wasn't in a very good mood when we were done with her yesterday afternoon."

"We noticed."

"Mmm. Well, she gave us that story about Mr. Wong, too. Yesterday, it was just a theory, no better than any of the others we're playing with. Today, it's moved up in the ratings a little bit."

"Does that mean my father is under suspicion again," Liz put in.

"Not under suspicion, no; but we'll probably want to talk to him in more depth about his client before you leave tomorrow. Shall we go, Jan?"

Janet flashed a self-deprecating smile at her daughters. "Have a good evening kids," she called.

After the door was closed, Liz mugged. "'Jan?'"

"Hey, whatever. She's reinventing herself. How do you feel about, you know—" Stella asked, motioning at the front entry.

"You mean Mom going on a date? It's weird. Really weird, but then it has been two years."

"That's the way I see it, too. I suppose we've both been hoping that Dad and Mom would get back together."

Liz sighed. "I think Dad had been hoping that this trip would.... Well, anyway, it doesn't seem to be happening, and she does have a life to live." She looked down at the coffee table. "We're never going to finish this puzzle before tomorrow afternoon," she said after a pause.

"No point even trying," Stella replied. "Why don't we get one of the guards to walk up the Lawai Road with us. I'll show you Mr. Freeman's house."

They strolled the beach road, past a jarring assortment of houses sitting cheek by jowl on a slice of what had been a beautiful beach before the builders arrived, past some four-story concrete condominiums, past a restaurant set on an elevated lawn and shaded by mature palm trees, past the small crescent beach where they had walked with Janet on the night they arrived, and past the Pakalolo Plaza on the *mauka* side. After that, a second strand of homes materialized along the shore, some spectacular in setting and realization, like the Freeman compound, some just funky beach houses. Then the road began to rise toward Spouting Horn, and they turned back.

Half an hour after they returned to the house, George Akamai appeared at the door. Stella greeted him with a demure kiss on the cheek, which she made sure that her sister could see.

"Things are really heating up, girls," Akamai said. "You've heard by now, no doubt."

"You mean the man from ROC Overseas," Stella replied.

"Yeah. I've never seen anything like what's been happening this week. We're going to have to assign guards to everybody involved in the Makai Ranch sale, it seems."

"For the record, George," Stella said, "my father was home all last night and with his whole family all morning."

"Duly noted," Akamai replied with a smile. "We'll take him off the suspect list." He turned to Liz. "Are you staying here tonight, Sister?"

"No, I have a date, Lieutenant."

"With that Kendall character?"

"I'm afraid so. Why, isn't he safe?"

"It's not that he's unsafe. It's that he does things that could get him arrested, and I wouldn't want you to find yourself on the wrong side of the law." He tapped his chest.

"Don't worry," Liz returned, shooing Akamai and Stella toward the door. "I won't let him do anything I wouldn't do."

Left alone to wait for her date, Liz turned to the puzzle. As she moved pieces idly around on the table, a pattern of color and shape began to emerge. It was a portion of an image, but not enough to allow her to identify it. Searching for more matches in the quiet house, she began to feel lonely. Stella was out with the latest — and, her sister swore, the best — love of her life. Instant romances were not Stella's thing, so she must have discovered something very special in her police lieutenant. Andrew was overdue from his meeting with Niki; knowing what she now did about Niki's persona, his tardiness could well bespeak a seduction. It was a thought she did not let linger. And even their mother—even Janet, for God's sake, who had been death on men only three days ago—was spending her last evening on Kauai with a date that had brought a flush to her cheeks. For Liz, there was only Race Kendall, with whom she might share a nocturnal trespass, but not romance. Feeling sorry for herself, she stood up, fetched the telephone from the counter back to the coffee table and called Harlan at his studio in Manhattan. It was not yet one a.m. in the Big Apple. He was no doubt in the middle of some serious production work, but he'd take a break to talk to her.

She had to hold for several minutes before he picked up. "Hello," he said, in a purposefully businesslike tone.

"Hi. I just wanted to say that I miss you."

"What? In the middle of a session?"

"Yeah. I miss you in the middle of a session. I miss you all day and night."

"Well, I certainly appreciate knowing that, Liz. But, of course, you're the one who went away for two weeks, not me."

"Did I catch you at a bad time, or just in a bad mood?"

"Both. I can't really talk now."

"Oh, right, just lay a guilt trip on me and hang up, after I call to say I miss you. You know, you travel all the time, Harlan."

"I travel on business. That's different. You're using all your annual vacation time to go away with your parents, for Chrissake, like some coddled preteen."

"Harlan, we're trying to work out our family relationships, and—Harlan?" Liz found herself speaking into a dial tone. *Oh, great, Harlan. Wonderful. How can somebody so smart be so immature.* He hadn't even asked how the trip was going, hadn't given her a chance to tell him about the murders, Stella's disappearance, lockpicking or the sovereignty movement. Disgusted and dejected, she went back to the puzzle. As she sat there moving pieces around mechanically, her mind was stuck on Harlan. From a distance, she could see more clearly what a peculiar couple they were. She worked days, he worked nights. He was emotionally needy, she was not emotionally generous. She liked the outdoors and travelling. He liked to stay indoors, and to stay in Manhattan. *Opposites attract, but why?* There was love, but there was also a lot of bickering, and so far there was no hint of permanence. It really was far from a perfect match. Where were they going in the long run?

Coming out of her funk, she found that she had made three more fits without paying much attention. She stared at the image segment, which was now complete enough to recognize. *Strange coincidence*, she said to herself.

It was a lifelike rendering of a marijuana leaf.

"It's not that I don't like sex," Andrew Chase heard himself saying. "It's that I don't think much of the concept of sexual excitement. It's the cause of a lot of trouble in the world."

He was sitting on the floor of a simple housekeeping cabin in a wooded area near the Koke'e Lodge, leaning against a bedraggled sofa. Next to him, Niki Makana inhaled deeply from a hand-rolled joint, and passed it to him. While she held her breath and looked at him in bemused expectation, Andrew explained.

"See, Niki, the sex drive is a primitive urge that unthinking living things, like squid, or dung beetles, or guinea pigs—" he laughed at his own short list, "that dumb creatures need to have, or else they wouldn't reproduce. People are different. They have a strongly developed ability to reason. They can project a desired result, and engage in a means to obtain the result, whether or not the means in itself is fun. In other words, if a man and a woman want a baby, they know how to make one, and they don't need some irrepressible impulse to impel them to do it. Understand?" He was feeling relaxed, a little foggy. "So, for humans, the sex drive is a throwback, unnecessary. You have these organs that the opposite sex can use to deprive you of your senses. They lead to rape, divorce, death, madness—" He stopped. Niki was clearly not convinced. He took a drag on the joint and changed the subject. "This is unbelievable stuff," he rasped, and added, chuckling, "but it's not part of the aloha culture, is it?"

Niki shook her head as she exhaled. "Technically, no. The Polynesian narcotic is kava. You grind up the roots of pepper plants to make a beverage. It tastes really bad, though. This is a pretty good substitute." She took another toke, and sat silent as tetrahydrocannabinol seeped from her lungs into her bloodstream. After half a minute, she blew a stream of smoke into the room, and said dreamily, "Now, what were we talking about? Oh, yeah. Poor Andy. Poor, poor Andy. You've got it all wrong. Sex isn't a throwback, Silly. It's a transcendental experience. It's an escape from space, time, gravity, matter—all the physical burdens of life, a way to let the spirit soar free and be... well, be everything there is." She looked at him. "Okay, sure, the organs of sex can be misused or can screw up rational thought, I've experienced that, but that's no reason to repudiate...is that the word? Repudiate them. The hand can be misused, too,"—she made a punching motion—"and the mind. The very fact that people spend most of their time reasoning and thinking and projecting and being civilized and... and li' dat, as we say here, is what makes sex so important. It connects us with God, and at the same time with the rest of the living world. It's the power that drives the human species forward, and all your civilization is just a sad attempt to keep that power in check."

Andrew drew himself up and looked at the young woman. Her face floated before him, its features slightly distorted by the effects of cannabis, so that she seemed a Gaugin portrait come to life. Although her words had already started to blur in his mind, he knew that they had been more eloquent than his sermon, and more human, too. "Is that what you really think," he asked, "or are you just, you know, trying to upstage the white guy?"

Niki stared at him for a moment, and then rocked back in laughter so contagious that it started Andrew off as well.

When the silliness subsided, Niki sighed and snuffed out the joint. "I think we've had enough of this junk," she declared. She ran a finger along a mud streak on Andrew's leg and held her soiled fingertip up in front of him. "You're a mess," she complained. "Why don't you take a shower and rinse out your clothes. I'll light a fire—it's already cooling off up here—, and put out some food." She stood up and put out a hand to help the lawyer to his feet.

"Um, I don't recall bringing a change of clothes," Andrew said, feeling all at once that he had unwisely let control of the evening slip away from him.

"Oh, we'll make a wrap for you out of one of the spare bedsheets. Across your chest and over your shoulder: you'll be just like Julius Caesar visiting the remotest corner of his empire."

Niki and Andrew were relaxing in one of the dozen rustic cabins maintained by the state at Koke'e. In heavy demand, the cabins could rarely be rented except on several months' advance request. This was particularly true during trout season. The Pu'u Loa Reservoir, a few miles from the Lodge, was stocked annually, and residents of the other islands came to Kauai in August and September to fish its waters. In September, however, fishing was only allowed on weekends. Niki's uncle, who lived on the Big Island, had reserved a small cabin every weekend that September, beginning on Thursday nights so that he could jet in early Friday morning, get settled by noon and do a little hiking before spending the rest of his time flycasting. After the call from Liz, Niki had manage to coax the use of the cabin out of her uncle until he arrived the next morning.

She had brought Andrew to the cabin after Janet and the girls were gone. His modest interest in exercise had been satisfied on the Pihea Trail, and he was content sit in the presence of the comely islander and listen to whatever she wanted to tell him. Was it possible that she would attempt to strangle him in the cabin, or cut through his jugular vein with a kitchen knife, or that other members of the Kamehameha Society would burst in on them and bludgeon him to death? He'd thought seriously about those possibilities, and decided that the odds were so strongly against it that he might as well worry about a meteor falling on his head. If the Kamehamehas were found to have resorted to murder in the furtherance of their cause, it would be the end of their movement as a political force in the islands; and the openness with which Niki had met him and his family, and later negotiated the key to the cabin from park personnel, substantially assured that no mishap would befall him while he was in her company. So, as they had settled onto the lawn chairs underneath tall Norfolk pines in front of the one-room cabin earlier that afternoon, Andrew was as much at ease as anyone could be who had been physically assaulted the night before by another seductive woman.

What Niki had wanted to discuss with him, it seemed, was the sovereignty movement. He didn't understand why, and when he asked, Niki said only, "I want your help."

"What help can I be? Ah, a contribution, is that it?"

"No. Well, sure, if you like. But I want you to do something for us, too. Let me try to sell you on the concept, first."

"You mean, if you asked me straight out, I wouldn't agree." Niki smiled.

"You could surprise me, I suppose. You're such a nice man, Andy. But I'd rather not take the chance." She moved her chair around to face him, and sat with her knees together and her hands folded in the lap of her miniskirt wrap. "You know parts of this story already, but I don't know which parts, so please bear with me. We're going to start way back in time." Her eyes brightened with enthusiasm. "About twelve hundred years ago, give or take a few hundred years. That was when the people we call the Menehune arrived on Kauai from the Marquesas Islands, almost two thousand miles away."

"I thought the Menehune were mythical people, like elves or leprechauns."

"They were, on the other Hawaiian islands. But here on Kauai, they were real."

"How do you know that?"

"Are you going to interrupt me at the end of every sentence?"

Andrew winced. "I'm a lawyer. Sorry. I'll try to restrain myself."

"How do we know? There was a type of *poi* pounder found on Kauai, but not anywhere else in Hawaii; a stone tool with special indentations in it for holding onto. That same type of pounder was found on an island called Uahuka in the northern Marquesas. The scientists dated it as being between fourteen hundred and seven hundred years old. There are also ancient similarities between the Marquesan and Hawaiian languages.

"So, anyhow, several hundreds of years after the Marquesans settled on Kauai, the Tahitians appeared here. There's over a thousand miles of ocean between Tahiti and the Marquesas, so these people were not exactly neighborly. Actually, they didn't get along at all. It appears that although Tahitian men took Menehune wives, and Marquesan culture left its mark on the culture of Kauai, the Menehune warriors were not integrated into the society and eventually left the islands altogether.

"For several hundred years after the arrival of the Tahitians, Polynesian culture flourished here. The land, being volcanic and ancient, was defined by tall ridges and deep, eroded valleys that, like, radiated out from the middle of the island. Because of the topography, the people tended to settle in dispersed groups in the separate fertile valleys, rather than establishing cities. They grew the foods they brought with them: taro, banana, coconut, chicken, pigs. They fished the waters around the island. They had their gods, their chiefs, their priests, the spirits of their ancestors, their kapus. This island and the other Hawaiian Islands were alive with mysticism and magic. There was some fighting, in the sense of occasional raids by warriors from one territory or island on the people of another; but the tribal economies were low-tech and low-budget, so large-scale or persistent warfare just couldn't exist. The great chief Kamehameha became King of all the Hawaiian Islands by winning a few tactical battles, really.

"Clothing was simple to nonexistent. The great beauty of the surroundings was recognized, incorporated into song and revered in ceremonies. The Hawaiians developed a culture of their own, based on harmony with nature and the spirit of aloha. At its peak, the Polynesian population of the islands never exceeded four hundred thousand. From the first coming of the Menehune, the Hawaiian culture had over a thousand years to develop in the glorious isolation of these islands.

"Then, a little over two hundred years ago, an English explorer named James Cook accidentally sighted Kauai on his way from Tahiti to the northwest coast of America in search of the mythical Northwest Passage to the Atlantic."

"Now we start the downhill slide," Andrew predicted.

"You think this is funny?"

"No. Heavens, no." Her sensitivity caught him by surprise. He wanted to say something sympathetic, but not knowing what she would consider appropriate, he subsided.

"All right, then. In your history books, they call Cook's accident the 'discovery' of Hawaii, even though Polynesians from two separate island groups had clearly arrived here long before Cook. He came back from his unsuccessful search for the Passage a couple of times and was generously provisioned with food and women for his crew. The Hawaiians wrongly thought that, because of his wondrous sailing ships, he must have been a superior being. Two years after his first arrival, he provoked a fight with the ruler of the Big Island over the theft of one of his ship's boats, and was killed.

"One death, though, even the death of such a great, if misguided, explorer as James Cook, could not stop the tide of Caucasian expansionism. Within ten years, I think, American traders, who were desperately searching the Pacific for foreign trade to replace the commerce they lost with England in the revolution, discovered that Honolulu harbor was deep enough to serve as a port for their large trading vessels, and began wintering there, bartering with the locals for provisions and later for sandalwood, which they could sell for a good profit in China. This western trade destroyed Hawaii's sandalwood forests, a crime in which, I'm sorry to say, Kamehameha cooperated in exchange for a vast accumulation of western guns and cannon."

Andrew Chase had been paying more attention to the way Niki Makana's mouth moved as she spoke than to what she was saying. There was a hint of childlike awkwardness in the way she formed her words, as though unaccented English had been a capacity acquired after her formative years. "So King Kamehameha found it desirable to trade with the evil *haole*, then," he mused.

"The king recognized the superiority of the evil *haole* weaponry," Niki shot back, her eyes flashing, "and the need to get his hands on it in order to be able to stand against them. Besides, anyone can be seduced, even a great king. Even Caesar, as I recall. That doesn't absolve the seducer of guilt."

The lawyer held up his hands in a gesture of submission. "You're right, of course. I apologize." *Anyone can be seduced,* he repeated to himself.

Niki drew a breath to calm herself, and then continued. "The next big excitement for the *haole* intruders happened in eighteen-nineteen, when, a whale was caught in Hawaiian waters by an American vessel. That started the Hawaiian whaling industry and turned the Hawaiian economy into an offshoot—that's not the word. What's the word for when something is, like, a dependent part of something?"

"Uh, I don't.... Appendage, maybe?"

"Yeah! Whaling turned the Hawaiian economy into an appendage of the mainland economy. The next year, the greatest scourge of all, the Christian missionaries, arrived. They converted a third of the population to a foreign monotheistic religion within a generation. By then, a political conversion had taken place, too. The royalty adopted a Western-style constitution, thanks to their *haole* advisors, and accepted the concept of private property, an advanced notion that—most conveniently—made it possible for foreigners to acquire huge pieces of these islands.

"The whaling business collapsed after the discovery of petroleum in the Eighteen-fifties, and the islands might have reverted to a more natural state, but, no. The combination of private property rights and the American Civil War, which destroyed the sugar business in the southern mainland states, gave rise to a new industry in the islands based on sugar cane. Of course, by then diseases introduced by the *haole*—primarily smallpox and venereal diseases—had ravaged the hell out of the native Hawaiian population, so there wasn't enough indigenous slave labor to work the fields owned by the whites. It became necessary to import foreign workers, mostly from China at first. The Chinese brought their own favorite diseases with them, too, like leprosy and cholera. Within a century of Captain Cook's arrival, the descendants of the first Polynesian settlers numbered less than forty-five thousand, a little over a tenth of what the population was a century earlier."

Andrew shifted uncomfortably in his chair. Neither he nor his ancestors had anything to do with this shameful history, and he didn't believe he bore the burden of the misdeeds of his race or country; nonetheless, he felt guilty and embarrassed.

"Now Hawaii had been transformed," Niki continued, "from a self-sufficient, rural, agrarian, tribal economy into a plantation export economy. When the Civil War ended, the demand for Hawaiian sugar declined, and the Americans living in the islands began to lobby the mother country for reciprocity, which meant duty-free treatment for Hawaiian sugar in the States, in exchange for duty-free treatment of some American products in Hawaii. Once reciprocity was established in 1875, the sugar business grew again, and really came to dominate life in the islands. The planters became the rulers of Hawaii, in fact if not in title. Twelve years later, they rose up against the monarchy, forced a new constitution on the king that limited the vote to property owners—few of whom were native Hawaiians—and gutted the powers of the monarchy. The next step was annexation, and the planters formed a secret organization in 1892 to begin the process.

"The Hawaiian monarch at the time was Queen Liliuokalani. She was a courageous fighter for a return of the islands to Hawaiian rule. In 1893, she dissolved the planter-controlled legislature and prepared to proclaim a new constitution. But the planters, with help from American troops, took over the government buildings, forced our great queen to surrender her powers and eventually held a humiliating show trial and sentenced her to house arrest in her palace. Annexation followed a few years later, when the Spanish-American War led the United States to covet Hawaii as a Pacific stronghold against the Spanish presence in the Philippines.

"The consequences of annexation were disastrous for the islands. First, the children of all the immigrants brought in by King Sugar obtained the right to vote. And second, Hawaii became an important military base and therefore a military target for enemies of the United States, like Japan. The final two steps in the subjugation of Hawaii were statehood and jet travel, which turned the islands into a playground for American and other foreign tourists."

"A cake that, having been made, can't be unmade," Andrew observed.

"We're not out to 'unmake' any 'cake'," Niki responded frostily. "We're not dreamers, hoping to turn Hawaii into some sort of utopian third-world country. We want to throw the cake away, and replace it with a modern version of the aloha culture, a more human culture that evolved before the white man first set his inhuman boot on this island."

"And what would that look like?"

Niki sighed and stood up. "I have a standard speech on that subject. Do you really want to hear it? Okay, let's go in."

They stepped into the cabin. The small windows were shaded by overhanging eaves, and the pines blocked the afternoon sun. It took Andrew's eyes a moment to adjust to the darker environment. Niki motioned him to sit on the couch. It was lumpy and unyielding. Andrew sat quietly as she took a deep breath and began to pace the room. "The aloha culture," she recited mechanically, as if she were nervous about sharing her mission with Andrew. "The aloha culture would be based on conservation of our precious land, environmentalism, helpfulness, supportiveness, gentleness, inclusiveness, humility, kindness, and patience."

Andrew followed her with his eyes, drinking in her graceful movements, the way her leg muscles flexed and shuddered delicately under her skin with each step, the angle of her breasts under the bikini top, the way her hair floated from side to side along her back as she walked. Niki gave the short form of her argument for Hawaiian sovereignty: the advantages it offered not just for native Hawaiians but for all Hawaiians; the iniquities of the present economy and government of the islands; the viability of an independent Hawaiian nation; and the benefits to be gained by pursuing sovereignty whether or not it could ever be achieved. Andrew asked a few simple questions, all of which she had been asked many times before and had ready answers for. When she was done, she leaned against the jamb of the open front door and said, "So, what do you think?"

The lawyer stood up, trying unsuccessfully to mask the stiffness left in his legs by the morning's hike, and gazed at the silhouette in the doorway with a mixture of admiration and longing. Admiration for a woman of such a young age with so strong a commitment to a cause, and so mature an understanding of the reasons why she should be committed to it; and a longing to have his youth back, a youth during which he had—mistakenly, as Niki's passion made so clear—failed to seize the opportunity to commit to any cause, despite the fact that he had come of age during the turbulent sixties. "Shall I tell you what I really think," he asked warily.

"Sure, Andy," Niki urged. "Hit me with your best shot."

"I think two things. One, we're on the brink of a Pacific century. The strategic importance of Hawaii to the United States is going to grow for the foreseeable future, not shrink, so your cause won't get much sympathy on the mainland. And two, even if you succeeded in establishing an independent Hawaii, the aloha culture, as you described it, would quickly be devoured by the more predatory cultures around the Pacific."

"Whew," Niki sighed. "That's all? Apart from those two things, you're with the program?"

"Well, wait a minute. Those two things are show stoppers."

Niki sauntered toward him. She took his hand and pulled him toward the door. "Come on. The darkness in here is putting you to sleep. Why don't we take a stroll along the Nualolo Trail. The trailhead's right outside. Oh, wait." She let go of him and returned to the interior. "Let's see if uncle laid in some cold drinks." Niki peered inside the refrigerator, and wrinkled her nose at the contents. "Only beer. Is that okay with you?"

Two bottles stuffed into her backpack, Niki led Andrew out of the cabin and down a trail that separated the cabins from the lodge. It began as a level path. To either side, mature trees shaded the hikers from the late-day sun. As the forest deepened around them, Niki spoke of the experiences that had led her to become a sovereignty advocate: her undergraduate years at the University of Michigan, a school with a long tradition of welcoming students from Hawaii, but a school at which the weather and the strange attitudes of the student body about life and work made her realize that she would never be comfortable in mainstream American culture; then her work as a bank economist in Honolulu, where she came to see that the capitol of Hawaii was just a mainland city with exotic faces, everyone intently engaged in the money chase, and made less human for it; and finally, the night she attended a sovereignty rally with a boy friend, and discovered what it was that her instincts had been telling her.

"You know, until recently I wouldn't have understood your aversion to what you call the money chase," Andrew admitted at one point, "I've been a career-oriented person all my life. That's strained my relationship with Liz and Stella, who have much different views of work than I do. It also probably did my marriage in—focusing so single-mindedly on my career, that is. I don't know why I'm sharing this with a kid I hardly know, but...." He left it at that.

The trail wound its way out of the forest and descended toward the sea. The growth along the trail gave way periodically to views of the deeply-eroded Nualolo Valley, now being shrouded by lengthening shadows. It had the feel, to Andrew, of a silent repository for ancient mysteries. Half an hour later, they found themselves sitting on an eroded outcropping, sipping beer and looking out over the ocean where a glowing orange orb was beginning to sink behind the bank of cumulus clouds that rose from a lavender horizon.

"Based on what's been happening around me on this trip, I should be worried that you might push me over the cliff here," Andrew mused. "But I'm not."

"I guess I should take that as a compliment," Niki returned dubiously.

"You sound like Liz. It's a high compliment, believe me. But tell me this. Separatist groups tend to have two factions, at least: a political wing, with articulate, moderate spokespeople like you, and a paramilitary wing, with members that are armed and dangerous. Is there a radical fringe of the sovereignty movement that I should be worried about?"

"Yes, there is a lunatic fringe, Andy. We had to kick half a dozen people out of the Kamehamahas because they advocated armed insurrection. They're still out there, and if they knew who was involved in the Makai Ranch deal, they might well get it in their crazy heads to try to assassinate some of the players. But these guys, by your standards and mine, are boneheads, marijuana growers, and I don't see how they could get information on the bidders, let alone kill the bidders' representatives, without leaving traces."

Andrew shrugged. "Okay, some risk, but not much, is what you're saying," he said. Feeling the need to be more aware of his physical surroundings, he glanced up and down the trail.

Niki watched him. "Do you really think of me as a kid, Andy," she asked softly.

The question surprised him. He turned to look at her. "What? You mean what I said back on the trail? Well, come on. Compared to me—"

"Oh, hell, I know I'm a lot younger than you, but a kid.... A kid's someone you don't trust, you don't take seriously."

"Oh, Niki," Andrew said, with a sudden hoarseness. "No, no. I trust you. And I take you very seriously." He put an arm over her shoulder in what he intended as an avuncular gesture. As soon as his hand touched her skin, and his fingertips fell across the bikini string, however, he knew that she would not take the gesture as avuncular, nor did it feel that way to him.

Her face was close to his. He felt her breath on his lips, and then her lips on his. The embrace was almost tentative, and very sweet. Niki was at once soft and firm, tender and urgent, earth and fire. A real kiss, not the workaday contact he paid for in Hong Kong. Andrew felt a rush unlike any he had experienced since adolescence.

And then they parted. The moment afterward was saved from awkwardness by the mute splendor of the western sky. From behind the gilt-lined clouds, rays of soft pastel light shot across the celestial meridian. In front of them, the sky itself was the color of tangerine skin; behind them, the color of a robin's egg, and somehow these two disparate hues blended together over their heads. Puffy clouds sailing into view above the forest at their backs were set aflame by the setting sun.

"I think I should tell you what I want from you," Niki murmured. "I can't imagine there'll be a better time."

Andrew nodded, his body still tingling, while Niki collected her thoughts.

"See, the history of the white race in Hawaii has been one of exploitation, subjugation and desecration. Criminal behavior on a grand scale, really. And more than any other factor, sugar is responsible for the suppression of the aloha culture in these islands. Webster Chamberlain is a sugar planter whose ancestors were active in all the bad stuff—reciprocity, insurrection, annexation, and statehood, the Chamberlains were right out there—so his guilt is genetic as well as individual. Wouldn't it be a wonderful way of.... What do you call it?"

"Expiating?" Andrew saw with dismay where Niki was going.

"Now *there's* a lawyer's word. —of expiating his guilt for him to donate the Ranch to the sovereignty movement. Maybe not the whole thing," Niki added quickly. "He could keep a chunk for himself and that no-good kid of his. But most of the Ranch to us, along with a little trust to pay the taxes."

Andrew tried to respond, but all that came out were stuttering sounds. The idea was so staggering, so remote from Chamberlain's objectives, that it beggared comment.

Niki leaned to him, locked her hands together on his shoulder and spoke seductively into his ear. "And I thought you might agree to suggest this to him on our behalf. Think of it, Andy. A place where we could build a community, experiment with ways to make it viable. Show others how the aloha culture can bring a better life to all the people of Hawaii."

Andrew took Niki's hands from his shoulder and held them in his own. He knew he had to treat her proposal respectfully.

"Niki, Niki, Niki. Look, it's a breathtaking proposal, okay. Bold and breathtaking. But there are couple of big, big problems with it. The first one is that right now, Chamberlain is expecting a windfall of tens of millions of dollars. Giving the property away is the farthest thing from his mind."

"But don't you see," the Hawaiian countered, "that's because making money is his way of justifying his existence and the burdens he places on others. It'd be up to you to convince him that the purpose of his existence is to ex—exp—"

"Expiate."

"Atone for the sins of his family going back five generations. I mean, does this man want to die surrounded by municipal bond certificates and be forgotten in twenty years, or does he want to die loved by a million people and mentioned in every book on Hawaii written for the next five hundred years?"

"It's a powerful argument, all right?" Andrew continued to measure his words, to give Niki the impression that she was being taken seriously. "The only thing I'm saying is that you're coming to the game too late. If the bidders weren't being bumped off one by one, the deal might already be—" He stopped in mid-sentence, suddenly realizing the portent of what he was saying.

Niki Makana saw his guardedness return. "Andy, it's not us. I swear to you."

He looked into her eyes, and realized that he might never know for sure; he had to take the risk. "Yeah, okay. But even if Chamberlain were as open-minded as I am—don't look at me that way. Even if he were, there's another problem. I already represent one of the bidders, Niki. I can't represent you. It would be a blatant conflict of interest."

"Why?" Niki leaned back against the rock. Her posture reminded Andrew of the way Liz had laid back on the chaise lounge in Poipu, and brought on a twinge of shame at the feelings he was having toward someone his daughter's age.

"Why," he echoed.

"Uh-huh. We don't care who gives the land to us. If Paracorp wants the publicity and the tax deduction, they could buy the property and then give it to us. Then you'd have no conflict, would you?"

Andy ran his hands through his thinning hair. "Under the Code of Professional Responsibility— Oh, hell, Niki, let's not get into it, please. I simply can't represent Paracorp and the Kamehameha Society at one time. Period." He stood up and brushed off the backside of his shorts. The sun, sinking into the horizon, found a gap in the deeply-grayed magenta and cobalt blue clouds that were lying there, edges aflame, and shot a lava-red beam toward them through the hole. Higher up, patches of cirrus clouds caught the sunlight through thinner air; they shone like enough golden fleece to tempt a flotilla of heroic Greeks. Around the cirrus puffs, the sky was the color of blood, and beneath it all, the sea was an ultramarine wash against which the fronts of the waves danced royal purple. Nature's light show had reached its climax. A minute later, the spectacle was over and it was time to head back.

"What did you mean," Andrew asked idly as the were retracing their steps along the darkening path, "by your reference earlier to Web Chamberlain's 'no-good kid'?"

"Chamberlain only had one child, a boy. The kid was born of Chamberlain's Hawaiian wife, and growing up, he ran with the Hawaiians most of the time. He's only a couple of years older than I am, and has been trying to put the make on me since I was ten. The dude was always lost, you know; wanted to be a regular guy, but had all this money! After he came back from college, or maybe while he was away at college, he began to do drugs in a big way. Anyhow, he sank further and further into that culture, until finally he disappeared from the island altogether a couple of years ago."

"Mmm." Andrew tucked that bit of knowledge away, certain that it would be useful in some way in his next meeting with Chamberlain, although he didn't yet know how.

People sometimes find themselves in quite abnormal circumstances as a result of a chain of small, very normal decisions and events. That is the situation that Andrew Chase found himself in after his hike with Niki. For a prestigious member of the New York bar and an officer of the courts of that state to be sitting on the floor of a wooden shack, in the caldera of an extinct volcano, smoking pot and talking about sex with a woman half his age whom he had just met that week and who advocated secession from the Union made no sense at all, even though it resulted from individual steps that were in themselves more or less ordinary. Being in an extinct volcano was unusual, but not abnormal, and it was not unexpected given that he was in Hawaii. The same could be said for being in a wooden shack. Sitting on the floor was not normal, for Andrew, at least, but given the decrepit condition of the sofa, it was not abnormal, either. These were small steps. Being alone with a separatist woman half his age whom he'd just met was a big step, and highly unusual, and arguably abnormal. Yet it was explicable by his interest in learning what involvement, if any, the sovereignty advocates had in the Makai Ranch intrigues. Smoking marijuana? Unusual and quite abnormal. But his legs had cramped on the uphill hike back to the cabin, causing him severe pain; by accepting the joint from Niki, he felt he was only entering the ranks of those suffering multitudes for whom marijuana is prescribed as an analgesic. In any case, the fact that, however it came about, what he was doing made no sense was now lost to him in a cannabis-induced haze.

Following Niki's suggestion, he ensconced himself in the tiny bathroom, and showered his person and his clothes. When he emerged a few minutes later wearing one of the spare bedsheets, his nakedness under the wrap should have made him self-conscious, but his head was not clear and the only thing on his mind was: sex, would she, should he?

"I just realized," he announced to Niki, who was setting plastic jars of takeout food on the table, "that now that my clothes are wet, I can't go home."

"This just occurred to you?" Niki put her hands on her hips. She was no longer wearing her bikini top.

"D-don't blame me, Niki," Andrew stammered, looking away. "It was your idea." He should have asked her to put her top back on, and was acutely aware that the weakness keeping him from doing so had left him defenseless.

"Uh-huh. Did that just occur to you, too," Niki asked. "Are you uncomfortable in the presence of nakedness, Andy? You are, aren't you. Just like the missionaries. They passed brassieres out to the poor heathen Hawaiian women. It was typical of the acts of the missionaries, completely out of step with the local culture. The women couldn't figure out what the lingerie was for. Over on Ni'ihau, they cut the hooks off them to use as clasps for their necklaces." She moved toward him, smiling slyly.

Andrew backed away, raising his arms, no longer conscious of the fact that they had been providing crucial support for the bedsheet. "N-Niki, I-I'm not really prepared to—" he blurted out, and his drape fell to the floor.

"I can see that," the Hawaiian replied, eyeing him as he reached madly down to retrieve his modesty. "But I am." She fished a condom out of her skirt and held it up in front of the defrocked lawyer. "We have these printed especially for us," she grinned. "It's a big money-maker." On the shiny black wrapper, in fluorescent script lettering, were three words that Andrew had seen scribbled in restroom stalls, first at the county lockup, and again at the Koke'e lodge: "Fuck da Haoles."

Barry Saga found it easy to talk to Janet Chase, and so she found it with him as well. In consequence, the police radio was turned down as they made their long drive from Poipu to Haena. Had the volume been up, they might have heard the dispatcher relay a report that Hurricane Iniki had changed course. Although she was still some four hundred miles south-southwest of Kauai, her western motion had slowed somewhat and her northerly motion had increased somewhat. If she kept to her present vector, she would pass near enough to Niihau and the west coast of Kauai to brush the islands with her rain bands. A hurricane watch had been issued at around five p.m. for those two islands and the little island of French Frigate Shoals still further west. The CPHC now categorized Iniki as a Force Three hurricane, with sustained winds of over a hundred-fifteen miles an hour. At Force Three on the meteorological scale, a hurricane will typically denude their trees of foliage, cause even large trees to topple, occasion serious flooding and destruction of smaller buildings in coastal areas, demolish mobile homes, and damage windows, doors and roofs. It will cut evacuation routes in low-lying areas a few hours before the eyewall even arrives.

The police captain's house was about as *makai* as one can get and not have beachgoers walking through the living room. The beach began not thirty feet from the front door. In summer, it was a broad, long, bowed expanse of sand that faced the open ocean. In winter, Saga told Janet as they walked at the water's edge, most of the width of the beach disappears, and the gradual slope it now had transforms into a steep decline.

"Where does all the sand go?" Janet wondered.

"Out there somewhere." Saga swung his arm at the ocean. "The amazing thing is, it always comes back."

The house was partially screened from the beach by a row of ironwood trees. Their wispy, needle-like leaves moved gracefully in the light breeze. Visible, edge on above the treetops and behind the house, a ridge ascended steeply on the other side of the road and, curving into floating mists in the distance, gave an intermittent view of a slender cataract falling across the face of a thickly-vegetated precipice.

"My great-grandfather came to Kauai in eighteen eighty-five," Saga said over the sound of the surf breaking against the reef fifty yards or so from the shore. "The sugar growers had visited Japan a few years earlier hoping to recruit several thousand laborers. They were apparently looking for an alternative to bringing in more Chinese workers. The Chinese were industrious, as you would expect, and very cheap labor, but they kept to themselves, had these secret societies that scared the whites, and brought opium and disease to Hawaii. I suspect what worried people most, though, was that they tended to leave the plantations as soon as their contracts were up and go into business for themselves, also very industriously and cheaply, creating troublesome competition for the merchants. Why the growers thought the Japanese would be any less enterprising, I don't know."

"Did your great-grandmother come with your great-grandfather?" Janet asked, imagining a creaking sailing ship floating in a peaceable harbor while a couple in exotic garb huddled on the deck, waiting their turn to disembark.

"Oh, no. Great-granddad wasn't married then, but very few women came with the men anyway. After working the cane for several years, my ancestor exchanged letters and photos with a young woman from Yokohama. A semiformal matchmaking program had grown up by then in order to find wives for the immigrants, and these exchanges were part of that program. Great-grandma was what they called a 'picture bride.' Their letters are still in the family."

They walked back toward the house. "Grandpa Saga was an auto mechanic, and later an auto dealer as well. Not a big business on Kauai, but he and my grandma were comfortable. When they retired, they bought the little piece of land we're walking on, and built the original house." The house they were approaching was a simple wooden contemporary on four-foot concrete stilts, with a prow-like glass facade.

"This is obviously not that house," Janet observed.

Saga laughed. "No, indeed. The original place was completely destroyed by a tsunami in nineteen forty-six. Gramps rebuilt it right away, but eleven years later there was another tsunami and the house was swept away again. This time, unfortunately, my grandparents were in it. After that, the land just sat here until Riko and I had our second child."

He led her up the wooden steps and into the house, Janet pondering the wisdom of oceanfront habitation as she climbed. Two tidal waves in eleven years was a completely unacceptable risk, but afterward—what was it?—thirty-five years of well-behaved ocean. Were the two tsunamis just freaks of nature—or was the long, placid time?

The living area was open, much like the Poipu house, but more rustically finished in unpainted wood. The furniture was simple and in the shape one would expect for a household with two boys, a busy father and no mother. The soaring glass walls gave out through the ironwood stand onto the beach and sky. In front of the windows, a young gymnast curled herself backwards on a balance beam, supported on the toes of one foot and the fingers of both hands, with her other leg stretched horizontally through the air, toes pointed.

Janet walked silently over to her, and ran her hand along the curve of her body. "This is exquisite," she said.

"It was her last work," Saga replied. "After the gymnast, she got too weak to work the material—this is koa wood, very hard. The blocks had to be pieced first, you can see the sections there; they're all bolted together. Then she did the carving and finishing and polishing."

"I-I don't know what to say. I just feel so inadequate. This figure—it's not just an exquisite rendering." She traced its outline with her hand. "The concentration, the resolve, the pain and the joy of this young gymnast, they convey the feelings of the artist about her work, don't they? It's so evocative."

Janet caught herself and looked over her shoulder. Saga had turned away from her. She went to him and touched his arm with shuddering fingers. "I'm sorry. I didn't mean to cause you pain."

"It's not that," Saga responded, his eyes moist. "I've become numb to her passing, really. I-I'm moved that you recognized Riki in the work, that's all. Come on, there are some other pieces up in the loft."

An hour later, the two of them were seated in sling-backed chairs on the deck that ran the width of the house's facade. A bottle of wine sat between them on a low table. The same sun that Andrew and Niki had watched was setting unseen behind the hills to the west, creating a dome of crimson below the meridian, while out of the ocean to the east a fat, liver-colored moon was beginning to climb. The first stars were visible overhead through the wispy ironwoods. Janet Chase drank in the scene, letting its simple beauty restore her equilibrium.

"I had no idea that seeing Riko's work would be such an emotional experience," she confessed. "If I had, I don't think I would have come."

Barry Saga put his glass down. "I'm glad you did. Riko was so much a part of me—still is, really—that I can't altogether let go of her, but I do have a life to lead. You're the first person outside my family that's been in this house in two years."

"Well, I-I'm sorry I won't have a chance to meet your boys before we leave tomorrow," Janet returned, in quest of a less charged subject. Barry Saga's sons were camping out overnight with his brother in an interior valley. The little adventure had been arranged a week earlier, and the last weather report before they had set off was the hurricane warning, which predicted that no effects from Iniki would be felt for another thirty-six hours.

"Me, too," Saga said. "They're great kids. I do think there's wisdom in your leaving, though." He stared into her eyes. Light from inside the house illuminated one side of her face directly, and also reflected softly off the iron woods to give the other side a warm, diffuse glow. Her looks were appealing though not classically attractive. About his age, maybe slightly older, Saga judged, she had seen so much more of the world, done so much more, that she could easily have made him feel like a naive country boy. But she didn't. "It's funny," he added. "I've only known you for three days, but I have a feeling I'm going to miss you."

The glass suddenly felt as though it were going to fall out of Janet's hand. She lowered it to her lap and closed her other hand around its stem. "It is strange, isn't it?" she offered, keeping the emotion out of her voice with some effort. "Once in a great while you meet someone to whom you instantly relate on all sorts of levels, from the most superficial to the deep—the most meaningful. I'm sure Stella would say that you and I had probably met in a prior life." She laughed awkwardly. "Anyway, I'll miss you, too, Barry. You're the first man I've spent all night in a car with since my senior prom."

They cooked *a'u* steaks on the grill, along with sweet corn still in its husks and slender eggplants from Saga's modest garden. The moon shrank and turned yellow and then white as it rose. The sky filled with stars, and with that immense, irregular sigh of light called the Milky Way. The scourge of earthlight, which had taken the delight out of stargazing over much of America, had not yet reached the north shore of Kauai, and the heavens seemed close, more substantial and much richer in design than Janet had ever seen them.

When the marlin was almost done, she went into the house, reemerging a few minutes later with a tossed salad. There was a small circular table on the deck and, in the middle, a fat candle in which the wick sat at the bottom of a glass cone. Saga lit it, restraining himself from repeating his earlier mistake and telling Janet that it was the first time since Riko's passing that he had done so. When his guest was seated, he rolled one of the glass sliders back a bit, reached inside and with the flick of a single switch doused the interior lights. "More Hawaiian this way," he said.

Across the table, Saga looked tense to Janet. Was the candlelight revealing something she hadn't noticed before, or was it simply distorting reality? "This case is weighing on you, isn't it?"

Saga exhaled through partially closed lips and drummed his fingers against the tabletop. "It's the politicians more than anything else. They expect instantaneous results, and they expect us to prevent further homicides. That's all well and good, but each one of these three cases is difficult in its own right. The victims were not locals, but foreigners; although Adibi had worked on Kauai for a while before he died, virtually all of his life had been spent in the Eastern Mediterranean. So it's hard to come up with a motive. The Makai Ranch deal appears to be a common thread to the story, but it's not clear why. As of today, we're still at sea as to motivation. Then, too, the *modus operandi* of the murders—assuming the death today was a murder—was different. Two people shot, one possibly stabbed, one possibly asphyxiated. It's going to take a while to solve them, and who knows what else is going to happen in the meantime? If everyone interested in the Makai Ranch would register with the police before they arrived, maybe we could protect them. But of course, they won't."

"You're suggesting that the killer has information about the identities of the bidders and their representatives? Doesn't that mean the killer's someone involved in negotiations on the Ranch side?" Janet scowled, recalling Andrew's wanting to meet Chamberlain and his advisors the next morning.

"Maybe. I can see you're already wondering about Li-Ann Low. So are we, but our preliminary check on her and Chamberlain's lawyer is negative. They are pillars of their respective professions in Honolulu, with no skeletons immediately popping out of their closets. Ms. Low is a little mercurial. She's had episodes before, apparently; but she has a big and respectable Chinese family in the islands, and would not want to lose face by getting involved in criminal activity."

Janet wondered whether Saga's view of the realtor would change if she told him the whole story of the break-in at the Poipu house the night before. "Well, if not them, then who?"

"Maybe somebody working at the Ranch, as you suggest. Chamberlain sent a driver to pick up Song—a practice we're going to ask him to discontinue. He would have done the same for Andy, but Andy was meeting you at the airport, so he didn't take advantage of the service. If the driver were the source of the information, that could explain why Andy and the rest of you have been left alone: Andy's name would never have been mentioned to him. Of course, the hypothesis has its flaws. In particular, it fails to account for the first three killings."

Janet drew a line on the candle thoughtfully with her fingernail. "Does Chamberlain have a personal secretary?"

Saga smiled. "You're not looking for a job as a detective, are you? Sorry, he doesn't. You know, another possibility is that the only hard information the killer has is the information on Adibi's list, and the rest he gets by bribing hotel personnel to keep a look out for names on the list. Which might also explain why you folks haven't been bothered. There's a problem with this angle, too. Neither Xerxes' nor Adibi's name was on the list."

"Also, the girls and I stayed in the same hotel as Bouchard and Minot."

"For one night, without Andrew, without an advance registration, and you were out the next morning. Well, at any rate, none of our theories is watertight yet."

After dinner, two people with large empty spaces in their lives stood in the small kitchen area, cleaning up.

"Where's the plastic wrap," Janet asked, holding a plate with the leftover fish on it.

"In the cupboard behind you. It's a mess in there, though, I'd better—" Saga moved away from the sink to open the cupboard door. At the same time, Janet turned around. Twisting to avoid bumping him with the plate and spilling the fish, her chest brushed against his arm.

"Excuse me."

"I'm sorry."

Saga took the plate from her and set it on the counter. Then he took her hands. She held her breath.

"How long has it been?" he asked.

"Two and a half years, I guess," she said with a brief, painful smile. "You?"

"A little more than two years. How do you feel? I'm not a man who would force himself on you."

Janet squeezed his hands. "Does that mean you're not going to throw me onto the countertop?"

The puzzle was half assembled when Race Kendall arrived, and Liz was half asleep. The doorbell roused her, and she got up from the sofa and let him in.

"Gosh, you don't look so bad," she exclaimed, scrutinizing his face. But for a puffiness around his eyes, and a redness in the eyeballs themselves, there was no discernible effect from the pepper spray.

"Yeah, I'm a walking advertisement for *aloe vere*. Here, I brought you a peace offering." He drew his hand from behind his back and handed Liz an exuberant bouquet of exotic flowers.

"Race! I should be giving you flowers. Tell me why on earth I deserve this?"

"Oh, Jesus, Liz. I was a real asshole last night. I know you think I'm kind of an asshole in general, but.... The flowers are a way of showing you my kinder, gentler side, as the Prez would say."

"Hey, are you a Bush supporter? You should talk to my father. I'll just put these flowers in a bucket of water for now."

Liz waited until the car was moving to ask him why he was so late.

"The later we do this, the better," Race shouted back. We don't want any company. In fact, we're still a little early."

On the way through Kapa'a, Liz noticed that supermarkets in two of the shopping centers were still open and doing a brisk business. "Is that normal for a Thursday night," she asked.

"No. Iniki's changed course."

"So they're stocking up?"

"Yeah. In case the utilities go out. Canned food, bottled water, candles, that kind of stuff. Camp stove if they haven't already got one. Maybe tape for the windows, in case there's a high wind."

"Go back!" Liz yelled.

"What?"

"Go back! I want to get some stuff for the Poipu house."

"Liz, you're leaving tomorrow, aren't you?"

"Only if the planes are flying."

The shelves in the Big Save were already largely depleted of canned foodstuffs. The reason, according to an elderly Japanese woman that Liz asked, was indeed that the hurricane was going to pass closer to Kauai than previously predicted. Though no one seemed to know how close, customers were buying supplies faster than the night staff could replenish them. The only edible goods Liz could find were broth, canned okra, corn meal and soy milk. It wasn't much. To make sure the rest of the family did some shopping, too, she called the Poipu house and left a message on the machine. Then Race drove her out to the north end of Kapa'a town where they killed time in Jimmy's Grill, first on stools on the sand-covered ground floor, sipping drinks—non-alcoholic, at Race's insistence—and afterward, since Liz had not had dinner that evening, upstairs having salads on the open balcony. "No heavy food," he had counselled. He was edgy, Liz sensed, not as full of himself as usual. They made small talk, until at one point, with the meal almost finished, Race put down his utensils in a sudden fit of pique. "I've been waiting for you to tell me about that document you stashed in your shorts last night. Don't you feel as though you just might owe me an explanation there?"

His intensity caught Liz by surprise. She sank back in her chair and thought for a moment. "You haven't known me very long," she answered at length. "If you had, you'd know that I very rarely feel as though I owe anybody anything. It's usually the other way around. A character flaw I inherited from my father, I guess."

"Well, Jesus H. Christ! See, the difference between you and me is that when I act like a jerk, I'm willing to admit my mistakes and apologize. Like I did tonight. But chuteless-jumpin' Miss Liz Chase, I guess she don't have to apologize to nobody."

"Being willing to apologize doesn't justify a practice of acting badly. I wasn't sure I could trust you, Race. I told you last night, I felt you were hiding information. But it's more than that. There's something about you—an Adonis complex, I guess it is. I think maybe that's the root of the problem."

"What the hell are you talking about?"

"Don't be angry. I'm trying to get my feelings out here; it's not something I do a lot. See, to me, a guy who is major self-centered is dangerous. Likely to put his own interests before mine at the wrong time. Just for your information, a lot of women probably share that view, in case you're wondering why someone so perfect as you has had difficulty in forming long-term relationships with the opposite sex. I'm right about that, aren't I? So, anyway, here I am, along with my family, tangled up in some very serious shit. I have to be careful, Race. I have to be really careful, and I don't think I can trust an Adonis."

Race Kendall glared at her for a moment. Then his gaze wavered. The expression on his face softened. He looked down into the street below, and then back up. "It's funny," he said, "I could never have put it into words the way you just did, but somehow I knew why you did what you did. That's why I called you this morning. That's why I'm sticking my neck out tonight. As for not telling you everything I know, hell, for all I know, you'll tell your father, I'll get hauled in to Umi Street again, Palahved will find out I've been snooping around his office, and I'll end up with a second smile cut into my throat."

Liz had been leaning on the table, supporting her chin with her hands. Race's answer caused her to roll back against her seat cushion. *So that's it,* she said to herself. *He was afraid, and he didn't want to admit it.* She flashed her companion a tight-lipped grin, then leaned forward again and, reaching into the back of her shorts, pulled out the Project Thermopylae draft. She dropped it on the table and resumed her pensive pose.

Race stared at the paper without touching it. "You mean you were going to let me—" He shot his index fingers toward the document and back again, like flippers in a pinball machine.

"Not necessarily."

He began reading. As he did so, his eyes widened and his mouth fell open. When he was done, he growled. "I don't believe it. I've spent five nights in that dumpster, and never saw anything more exciting than phone bills. You spend an hour in there and pull out the plum?"

"Just like Jack what's-his-name. Seems to me dumpster diving is like panning for gold, Kendall," Liz said with a wiseguy accent, holding her spoon up between her thumb and index finger like a cigar.

A little past midnight, they drove up the hill to the Sunshine Resources site. Race parked the MG in a darkened side street and donned his backpack. As they walked over to the windowless structure, Race explained the obstacles they would have to overcome.

"The lock on the back door of this building is not much different from the lock on my front door. We shouldn't have any trouble with that. The challenges are inside the building. There's an infrared beam shooting from wall to wall right behind the back door. Open the door, you cut the beam and an alarm rings at a central service. The interior is one big open space, with half-high partitions for office cubicles and a big area for shipping and receiving, packing and such. Way up on the ceiling, there are motion detectors. Every time you move, a signal goes to the central service."

"Have you got something in your backpack that solves those problems?" Liz asked dubiously.

"In my backpack, and up here." Race tapped at his temple. "Grab a flashlight, would you?"

They had reached the rear of the building. Liz fumbled in the pack and retrieved a long-handled flashlight. "Over there, on the side of the loading dock? That enclosed shed."

Liz's flashlight illuminated a three-sided wooden structure that had been built against the rear wall of the building, with windows giving out onto the loading platform. "The shed has a southern exposure," Race explained, "so being cooped up in there a good part of the day would be pretty beastly without air conditioning. But you don't see any air conditioner stickin' out of there, do you?"

Liz considered that fact for a moment, and what it might portend. When the answer came to her, she grabbed Race's upper arm. "Oh, no you don't. I've seen this done in the movies, and I'm not interested." Race flexed the muscle under the sleeve of his polo shirt.

"What're you talking about?"

"I mean, the part where we take our flashlights and crawl through the air conditioning ducts into the building. If that's what you have in mind, you can forget it, and figure out a better way to get us in and out of there without being caught."

"That's not what I had in mind. Come on."

They climbed the steps to the shipping/receiving office. The lock proved to be a simple tumbler type that yielded easily to a scrubbing by Race. Inside, there was a small desk covered with papers, an old swivel chair, a wall telephone and a low file cabinet. As Liz had anticipated, an air conditioning vent broke the surface of the warehouse wall near the ceiling of the shed, and there was a return duct near the floor. Race stood on the filing cabinet and unscrewed the upper vent cover. Inside the hole, there was a short horizontal section of duct, and then a vertical section rising to the ceiling of the warehouse, where the main building ducts were suspended. "In the pack, Liz, there's a wireless drill and a box of bits."

She retrieved them and handed them up. "What are we doing, exactly?"

"We're going to set off the alarm." He fitted the drill with a three-eighths inch bit, thrust the tool inside the vent and drilled a hole in the wall of the vertical duct. "There's a car radio antenna in the pack, a stapler and a notepad." Liz handed Race the items, and he fashioned a kind of flag with them, which he waved at her. Liz, bemused, watched him roll the paper flag tightly around the telescoped antenna and slide it into the vent.

"I'm just going to slip it through the hole I made and wave—"

The alarm went off, violating the silence of the night. Race handscrewed the vent cover on quickly, then said, "We're out of here!" He jumped down, stowed his tools and ran out the door. "Shut it behind you and follow me!" he shouted to Liz.

They dived through a line of tall shrubs into an open lot next to the Sunshine building, ran along the back of the lot, then across the unlit road and down to the car. When they were safely inside, Race turned to Liz and, still catching his breath, asked, "So, what do you think?"

"Clever," Liz panted. "Primitive, but clever. How long will it take them to get here?"

"The central station will call the police. The closest patrol car will respond first. There's a cop cruising the Kapa'a area somewhere. There should be someone here in a few minutes. Somebody's got to come up from Kapa'a with a key. Ten minutes for that, maybe."

"They'll think it was a false alarm?"

"Unless they notice the hole I drilled, which isn't likely. I don't know what the statistics are for Kauai, but nationwide over ninety-five percent of the central station alarm signals are false. It's a huge problem for police everywhere, and I'm sure Chief Nagato has some guidelines in place to deal with it. We may have to do this a couple more times, but eventually either the central station will stop calling the police or the cops will stop coming on their own."

Race kept watch through the rear-view mirror. After a few minutes, he said, "The law's arrived." Turning around, Liz could see the cruiser crawling through the parking lot, its roof lights flashing and its searchlight playing on the building and the property around it. Shortly after, a second car arrived. The policeman and a private security guard entered the building. They emerged again five minutes later, stood briefly chatting in the pulsing light from the police car, and then left.

"If we're lucky," Race commented, "they'll decide there's a rat running around in the building. Let's do it again."

After the second alarm call, the patrol car returned and reconnoitered the building, but left quickly. After the third call, no one came. The fourth alarm call occurred when Race Kendall opened the rear door of the warehouse and he and Liz walked in, their flashlights scanning the interior. It was now almost three a.m., and Liz had by then learned a great deal about the business of private investigating, at least as described in the MG by Race Kendall. It relied heavily on two traits of character that Liz did not have: a capacity for shmoozing, and an ability to lie with a straight face. The way Race acquired his knowledge about the Sunshine building's alarm system was exemplary of the use of those characteristics. When Niki Makana asked him to look into Palahved's activities he called Sunshine, claiming to be a Hawaiian

Electric Company representative. He was connected to the administration manager, and asked her whether Sunshine had installed some new electrical equipment, or had otherwise changed its operating procedures such that its usage of electricity would have quintupled. When she answered in the negative, Race offered to send a technician over to check the facility for possibly dangerous short circuits. He then asked a friend who worked for HECo for the loan of a company jacket, made himself a phony HECo ID card, and showed up at the Sunshine facility carrying an ammeter and a clipboard. He tested all the outlets, made notes about every piece of electrical or electronic equipment on the premises, ascertained the location of the circuit breaker box, the alarm sensors and controller, the light switches, the computer setup and the telephone system console. While the administrator didn't know much about the technical details of any of these installations, she had the general concepts of each firmly in mind, and with particular regard to the security and computer systems, which she had selected herself, was happy to share her knowledge with an interested and admiring, if unsophisticated, visitor.

Now, as they entered the building, Race said, "I have to disconnect the security system from the phone line, otherwise every time we move there'll be another alarm signal, and they'll send an electrician out." He strode over to an electronics cabinet, which was inadequately protected by a simple disk lock. Liz stepped after him. "Same principle as the pin lock. Just requires a different pick." The door yielded, and he pulled out a module and unplugged the phone cord.

"Okay, which way is Palahved's office?" Liz demanded. In an interior darkness relieved only by the narrow beams of two flashlights, she was beginning to succumb to claustrophobia. This was not like skydiving at all. There was no greater feeling of openness than the sensation that comes from leaving an airplane door at twelve thousand feet; whereas walking in pitch blackness with a range of vision limited by a flashlight's beam left most visual information closed off, and she felt trapped. Dwelling on the sensory deprivation was not a good idea, because the more nervous she became, the less help she would be. Instead she began to take deep breaths, and concentrated on being alert to what little she could see. Race led her to the front of the building, where the only proper office had been built: a large, sheetrock box protruding into the warehouse space from a corner, with a teak wood door set into it. A combination lock secured the door. It had a lever-style handle next to it, such as one would find on a safe. Race shone his light on the lock, examining it closely. He began nodding his head, penguin like. "This will take a few minutes."

"Don't tell me. You need to sandpaper your fingertips."

"No, Babe, these digits," Race declared, shoving the flashlight under his arm and wiggling the fingers of both hands in the air, "are just naturally sensitive."

Liz illuminated the lock, while Race grabbed the handle with one hand, pulling it down slightly. "Just enough to stick the pin," he said. With the other hand, he turned the knob to the left until it stopped moving. The number five was under the little pointer on the outside of the dial. "The first number is ten," Race muttered. "Five more than what's indicated on the dial, for this make of lock, anyway." He released the handle, spun it a couple of times and then turned it to the left until the pointer reached ten. Then he pulled on the handle again, turning the knob gently to the right until the handle fell slightly and the knob was hard to turn. "Second number is six." He let go of the handle again, spun the knob and then entered the first two numbers. Now he applied pressure to the handle as he moved the knob one digit at a time. When he reached the number nine, the handle moved easily in his hand and he swung the door open.

"Can we turn the lights on in here?" Liz asked as they crossed the threshold.

"I'd rather not," Race answered. "Light leaks. You can never be sure. Even these damn flashlights can be a problem. Desk or credenza?"

The desk was devoid of clutter. Its proprietor was clearly not a man distracted by details. Liz settled into the plush swivel chair while Race manipulated the disk lock on the front of the desk. The peak of her anticipation and the height of her claustrophobia had arrived simultaneously, and she swung her light around the room until she had seen all of it. It was drab and undecorated, except for a large oriental rug in front of Palahved's desk. Pieces of used industrial furniture punctuated the empty white space. No windows. Linoleum floor. A metal credenza behind the well-polished, but used, wooden desk. An inexpensive setup that didn't reek of insuperable power. Her spirits started to lift. Claustrophobia wasn't fear, but discomfort. With a lightly shaking hand, she shone her light into the top drawer of Rafi Palahved's desk, reached in and pulled out a sheaf of papers.

At a quarter to midnight, Stella Chase and George Akamai burst into the Poipu house. Stella ran to the bedrooms, and returned in a panic. "Nobody's here, George!"

"Where the hell are they?"

"Do you see any notes out there?"

Akamai looked around the great room. “Nothing.”

“It must be that no one’s come home yet.”

“Is there an answering machine?”

“Yes, in my father’s bedroom.”

The message light on the machine was blinking. Stella pushed the button. An electronic voice barked from the loudspeaker. “You have four messages. Message number one was received at eight thirty-two p.m.” “Hi, it’s Dad. Looks as though I’m going to be stuck in Koke’e tonight. From my discussions with Niki, I think we can cross the Kamehamehas off our list of suspects. There may be some ex-members who would have the inclination, but probably not the smarts. However, it seems that Chamberlain has a son who was in with the drug crowd before he left the island a couple of years ago, and we ought to look into that. I’ll see you all in the morning.” Stella tugged at her hair with both hands. “I don’t believe it. My father’s shacked up with Niki Makana.”

“They probably haven’t gotten the news about the hurricane up there,” Akamai guessed.

“What about Chamberlain’s son, George?”

Akamai gave her a melancholy smile. “He was my best friend for a good part of my life; almost a brother, really—”

The answering machine interrupted him. “Message number two was received at ten-fifty-seven p.m.” “It’s Liz. Is anybody home? Hello-o.... Guess not. Well, Race and I are in Kapa’a to do some sleuthing. Won’t be back until very late. Don’t worry, Dad. This is not a contact sport. Did you guys hear that the hurricane is gone to pass pretty close to us now? Better get to the grocery store and stock up, in case we can’t get out tomorrow. Oh, and by the way. Guess why Race hasn’t been more forthcoming with me about Xerxes. He was afraid, poor baby; afraid that the head of their Sunshine operation here would slit his throat, no exaggeration; which tells you what kind of guy is running Sunshine. Interesting, huh?”

“What could they be doing in Kapa’a, George?”

“Getting into serious trouble, if she’s with Kendall.”

“Message number three was received at eleven-forty-one p.m.” “Why isn’t anyone picking up?” Janet’s voice fussed. “It’s so late. We just heard about the hurricane. Barry’s kids are out camping, and we can’t really get them for a few hours. Rather than have Barry drive me back, I’ll stay here. Once we pick up his kids, we’ll head straight for the airport. I’ll have to meet you there, so someone please pack for me. By the way, it seems to me the police should figure out who knows when the bidders' representatives are coming to Kauai; not including Robinson and Low, I guess."

Stella looked at George Akamai, who was staring back at her, utterly flabbergasted. She blushed.

"What's going on here?" he barked. "Has the Chase family opened up a detective agency?"

"We're just trying to look after ourselves, lieutenant. Now what were you saying about Chamberlain's son?"

The fourth message interrupted Akamai's response. It was for Andrew from Carter Robinson, confirming a meeting for next morning, weather permitting. He would not be there, but Li-Ann Low was already on Kauai, and would join Chamberlain.

"Let's call Saga and your mother back," Akamai suggested. "We can talk shop later."

"The kitchen phone has a speaker," Stella said, grabbing his hand and hurrying him out of the bedroom.

"Barry, looks as though we're in for a messy day tomorrow," Akamai said when Saga picked up.

"Where are you, George? I've been trying to reach you."

"I'm down at the Chases'. Stella and I just got in from dinner."

"Stella, I'm here, too!"

"Hi, Mom. I guess now we have a hurricane to worry about, on top of everything else."

"I need a vacation from this vacation! We have to be at the airport early tomorrow, Stell, or we won't get off the island."

"It's more complicated than that, Janet," Akamai cautioned. "Your husband and your eldest daughter are out for the night, and unreachable. They may not know about the storm, so they may not be making plans to get back to the house at all tonight." He could feel Janet's discomfort at the other end of the line. "If Iniki keeps its current vector, the coastal areas will probably be evacuated some time tomorrow morning. If you folks aren't at the airport by the time that happens, you can forget about getting out of here."

During the evening, Hurricane Iniki's course had undergone a radical change. Almost as if the monster storm had selected its prey by glancing sidelong as it passed south of the Hawaiian Islands, then turned sharply on its unsuspecting target, Iniki was now on a northerly course that would take it very close to Kauai. Heavy rains, high winds and high seas were expected to rake the island the next day. In meteorological terms, the sudden discontinuity in Iniki's track was caused by a massive low pressure sector now sitting to the north of the island that was sucking the hurricane out of the flow of the trade winds.

"Where are the other Chases, George?" Barry Saga demanded.

"It sounds as though Andrew is up in Koke'e, and Liz is in Kapa'a with Race Kendall. What's this about your boys?"

"Oh, they're camping out with their uncle. I'll go after them as soon as there's enough light in the morning. Meantime, I think it would be a good idea to get some sleep, Lieutenant. You may not have that luxury tomorrow night."

"Yeah. You, too, Captain."

After hanging up, Stella and George Akamai sat at the kitchen counter, waiting for water to boil. Stella put a bag of herbal tea in each of their cups.

"How bad do you think it will be?" she asked.

"Too soon to say. The storm just made one unpredicted move; maybe it'll make another. It could turn around again, or it could angle in closer to us, or angle out the other way. If it passes by us on the west, as they predict, it could still be messy. Hurricane Iwa did that ten years ago. Wasn't a direct hit, yet it savaged the place. This storm is stronger than Iwa. In fact, I think when we've had our tea, you should come up to my place."

Stella folded her hands on the counter top. With the news that the rest of her family would not be returning that night, she had in fact assumed that she and George would spend the night together, but in the Poipu house.

"Why not stay here?" she asked.

"I can't stay here tonight, Stella. If this hurricane is going to hit some time tomorrow afternoon, there are things I need to do at my house before I go to work in the morning; which means tonight."

"Maybe you could tell me what I need to do here, too, then."

"The owners probably pay somebody to do those things. Besides, I think you should come with me."

"I couldn't abandon this place. I mean, who knows when my Dad and Liz will be drifting in. Liz'll be good for nothing after being out all night, and I shudder to think what shape my father will be in. Somebody's got to be around who can organize the trip to the airport."

"I don't think you should be here alone. Big weather is hazardous. There could be fifteen-foot surf pounding the shore by the time you wake up. The street might be flooded. If it gets windy, debris could make the streets impassable. And besides, no matter what the weather is in the morning, I wouldn't leave you alone tonight."

Stella shivered. "Why? It's that Taiwanese fellow, isn't it? He was murdered." Stella pulled the now-singing teapot off the burner and poured the blustering water into their cups.

"No doubt. We have to wait for the lab report, but I felt the horror still emanating from the body when I viewed it."

Stella's head swung slowly from side to side as she sought guidance from within as to what to do. She couldn't ask George to forego securing his house. There was also the question of her own security. If his concern for her safety was well-founded, she'd be better off leaving the Poipu house. Her inner voice wasn't coming, and she couldn't sit there like a lump waiting for it. If her family was not able to take off tomorrow, she would be just as happy—happier, really. Besides, she was anxious to see the lieutenant's residence; it would speak to her about its owner in ways her intuition or their brief familiarity had not. Maybe, she mused, the fact that she was not being told to stay in the Poipu house was the guidance she was seeking.... "Okay," she said finally, "Let's go up to your place."

The house was situated in the hills *mauka* of Highway 50, in a hilly residential area with views of the distant ocean. It was a mixed neighborhood. One of Akamai's neighbors had a fifteen acre-wooded estate with a manor house, stable, paddocks and horses. Another was a truck farmer with a shambles of a house close to the road, a couple of rusting automobiles and an old refrigerator slowly being eaten by vines in the side yard, and several ill-disciplined mutts—"poi dogs," Akamai called them. There were winter homes for snow birds, retirement homes, plantation houses like Akamai's, starter houses for young families, shanties and substantial estates—all nestled in the rolling uplands off winding arteries that branched from the entrance road.

The policeman's house lay off a long gravel driveway at the northern end of the neighborhood. The property sloped dramatically upward, and the house, illuminated now by the headlights of Akamai's jeep, looked like a ship riding the crest of a swell. A one-story single-walled shotgun affair, painted a deep green with white trim, it had a corrugated tin roof and a covered front porch on stilts. To Stella, it seemed from the outside to be an archetypal island home. According to Akamai, it was originally built by the Makai Ranch for a Portuguese plantation supervisor in the early 1900s. The whole neighborhood was given over to housing for cane workers and supervisors at that time, he told her, but over the years most of the original houses had surrendered to bad weather, lack of maintenance or real estate developers. Few of them still stood, and those that did had been heavily remodelled, with the exception of the one toward which they were now walking.

Akamai opened the door and turned on the light. Stepping in, Stella was disappointed. There seemed to be little of George Akamai in the fabric of the place. The front room, which ran the width of the house, was sparsely furnished with mass-produced pieces; there was no decoration except for a hunting rifle on a high shelf, no curtains at the windows, no rugs on the floor. The room was neatly arranged and clean, which was more than might be expected of a bachelor pad, but the neatness only added to the undefined nature of the place. Physically, it had a certain inchoate charm, a potential for hominess, but Akamai had done nothing to exploit its virtues. *My job,* she thought.

"Where's all your stuff, George?" Stella asked.

"What do you mean?"

"You know—stuff. A shell collection, or some of those glass fishing balls, maybe a net, a ukulele, some photos, an heirloom or two or three, vacation souvenirs. Stuff."

Akamai shrugged. "No stuff, Stella. To me, this is a place to sleep at night, like a hotel room." He walked her toward the central hall, flicking light switches as they went. "Here, want to see the rest?" Behind the living room, there was a tiny kitchen to the right and a two-person dining alcove to the left. Next, a bathroom on the right and a sizable closet/cupboard on the left; and last, a bedroom on either side of the hall, each with a single bed. Throughout, the walls were the same roughsawn board that enclosed the house, painted in a creamy white.

After the brief tour, Akamai rummaged in the closet and brought out a large utility box. Into its several compartments, he threw various items as he collected them from around the house: a shortwave radio, a couple of handheld portable radios with headphones, several packages of batteries in various sizes, two flashlights, a handful of small boxes of matches, four butane cigarette lighters, fifteen or so bags of dried or powdered camping food, candles, a first-aid kit, a roll of toilet paper, a shaving kit, bars of soap, a small bottle of shampoo, a few changes of clothing and a can of tiger balm.

"Grab the camp stove out of the closet, would you, please Stella?"

He carried the emergency kit out to the jeep. Stella brought the stove and went back for the lantern, the kerosene and the propane canisters, while Akamai cleared out the rear of his vehicle and secured the evacuation items there. That done, they walked to the rear of the yard, where a spotlight at the edge of the roof revealed a modest in-ground pool, into which four impact-resistant plastic deck chairs and a plastic-topped table holding a striped umbrella cast long, shimmering shadows.

"I'll take the umbrella into the house. You toss the chairs into the pool."

"What? Toss these—?"

"It'll keep Iniki from blowing them through the neighbors' windows."

Stella picked up one of the chairs. Its lightness surprised her. She held it over her head, looking at her underwater shadow on the bottom of the pool. It was a baleful image, like the silhouette of a pinheaded murderess about to smash her victim's skull, and it frightened her. Nothing happened by accident, she knew, even the casting of a shadow. She flung the weightless bit of furniture, breaking her evil doppelganger into a million pieces that flew concentrically out from the point at which the chair entered the water. Repeating the act three times, Stella felt as though she were part of an ominously surreal stage play. Never having prepared for a hurricane before, the act of submerging the chairs was a spooky affront to civility.

George joined her on the patio. They lifted the table and swung it in after the chairs, like two vandals.

"Fun, isn't it?" George laughed.

"Weird," Stella replied.

"I've got plywood covers for the windows. I'll put them on while you fill the plastic jugs on the floor of the closet with water and set them in the jeep wherever you can fit them. That'll give us a few days' supply."

"Boy, you're expecting a real catastrophe, aren't you?"

"Better to say I'm preparing for a real catastrophe, which I would do whether I expected one or not, given the weather forecast. After you put the water up, just sit on the porch for a minute, quietly. Maybe you'll get a sense of what I'm anticipating here."

After filling and lugging the water jugs, Stella sat on the front porch stoop. The moon was obscured by clouds, and the muggy night air stirred listlessly around her. She could hear George in the house applying masking tape to the insides of the windows, against the possibility of pressure changes that could snap them behind the plywood.

She tried to cleanse her mind of extraneous thoughts, to feel the flow of energies around her, to sense Iniki moving over the ocean. With her eyes closed, she felt as though she were suspended in space, her face and arms caressed by a ruffle not in the local atmosphere but in the infinite ether. The porch faced south, and as she waited patiently she began to feel the ocean heaving and surging, salt spray swirling and foam-capped waves crashing under the influence of a powerful disruption. On the face of the disturbed sea, the disruption was a dark vortex, drawing the energy of the sea into itself and at the same time, weighing heavily on its surface as it coursed toward Kauai. It was approaching not at a glancing angle, as the radio reports had described, but on a direct assault. She could see it now, rising to such a height that there was no telling where its power ended, and stretching to such a compass that despite its distance from her she could not find its boundaries. Its might was more than palpable. Stella had been caught in violent thunderstorms before, and had an internal calibration of the scope of their fury. Iniki was something else entirely. The strongest thunderstorm was to this hurricane as a fly to a fighter-bomber. Its energy field was so fearsome, so titanic that, sitting in its path, Stella felt like a mote, a cipher, facing a threat beyond fear or resistance.

Akamai came up behind her and put his hands on her shoulders. "Got the picture?" he asked.

Stella swivelled around. "It's a monster. Nothing we're doing tonight will necessarily have any effect. George, I think it's coming right at us."

Akamai stopped massaging her shoulders. "Is that what you see?" He remained motionless for a few seconds, then reached out a hand to help her up. "Well, either way, we've done all we can do for now. Let's get to sleep. If possible."

They walked into the living room, and into a second unpleasant surprise. Sitting in a corner, in a plaid armchair facing the door, was a curly-headed man in his late twenties. His native Hawaiian features were muted by an infusion of Caucasian genes, and he was wearing shorts and a tee-shirt bearing the words, "Go ask Alice." He was also pointing a crossbow in their direction. Stella staggered back against the policeman, who pulled her behind him.

"Nate!" Akamai growled, his pleasure at seeing his old friend apparently outweighed by concern about the weapon. "How did you get in here? Would you point that thing somewhere else, please?"

"I'd like you to sit down, Georgie." There was an unbalanced sharpness to Nate Chamberlain's voice. "On the sofa, there. Whatever that was that slipped behind you can sit on the adjoining cushion."

"I don't believe this, Nate." Akamai stood his ground. "Stella," he said evenly, without taking his eyes off the seated man, "this guy is Nate Chamberlain, my best friend in the entire world, and one of the top marksmen in the state. I want you to back up and move away from the door, because if he fires that thing at this range, the bolt'll go right through me and into you."

Breath coming in spurts, fingers numb, legs quivering involuntarily, Stella Chase stepped back three paces onto the porch and off to the side of the portal. *If he fires that thing!*

"Honey," Chamberlain called after her. "You don't want me to have to shoot my best friend, do you? Do you?"

Stella hesitated before answering. The only guidance that came to her from within, was, *Use your instincts. That's why you have them.* Her instincts told her that hiding was a sign of weakness that would only incite Akamai's lunatic friend. She stepped forward into the living room, and stood to one side of Akamai.

"No, sir. Nor would I want you to have to shoot me. I imagine that crossbow has killed does as well as bucks."

"Yes, and sows as well as hogs. Your last name is Chase, I believe."

"That's right. Your father and mine met the other day."

"Indeed. You and George are making me very nervous standing there, Doll. Would you take my friend by the hand and lead him to the sofa. Please? With the two of you standing there and me with only one bolt in the bow, I am only half as threatening as I would be if there were only one of you; on the other hand, you are a lot more than twice as threatening to me than a single person would be, if you catch my drift."

"Why don't we just let Stella go, then, Nate?"

"Too late, Braddah. Her life is in your hands, and yours in hers. Sit down."

Stella took Akamai's hand. Reluctantly, he followed her over to the sofa. Nate Chamberlain turned in his seat to keep the tip of his bolt pointed at Akamai's chest.

"Now what?" the police lieutenant demanded.

"Now we wait, Brah," Chamberlain chortled.

"Wait for what?" Stella asked. Out of the corner of her eye, she saw Akamai turn to her as if to say, "Leave this to me."

In reward for Stella's curiosity, Nate shifted the arrowhead in her direction just enough that it would be lethal to her if fired. He looked at her slack-jawed and unblinking for a moment. Then he snapped back into focus. "For Iniki, Honey. We wait for Iniki."

September 11, 1992

Early this morning, Iniki became a Force Four hurricane. Once again, its northward speed had increased and its course had corrected to assure a direct hit on the island of Kauai. The *Honolulu Advertiser* for September 11 was put to bed before these things became clear. In its weather section, it reported a high surf advisory for south facing shores, and predicted "increasing clouds with heavy showers and thundershowers" for Kauai on the coming afternoon and evening, with the "worst impact" expected to be between 4:00 p.m. and 6:00 p.m. A companion article, perhaps a little more informed of the fast-changing story, suggested that the hurricane would skid through the Kaulakahi Channel between Kauai and Ni'ihau, visiting "strong destructive winds and seas" on the two islands.

Iniki's spiraling weather system was said by CPHC forecaster Rich Lay to extend for two hundred miles beyond the hurricane's eye. Hurricane force winds were expected to strike Oahu, and hurricane watches were posted for Maui, Lanai and Molokai.

10

September eleventh on Kauai belonged to Iniki. The affairs of humankind were nothing compared to the changes wrought that day by nature's vengeful handmaiden. Matters of great significance, such as finishing the filming of "Jurassic Park," negotiating the sale of the Makai Ranch, or solving the murders of Adibi, Bouchard, Minot and Song became pale shadow plays as the great storm body made its way across the island, scouring everything in its path. In a matter of a few hours, Iniki demolished the infrastructure of modern civilization on Kauai, reducing residents and tourists alike to the status of Stone Age peasants, and teaching them how foolish it can be to rely too heavily on the complex human institutions of the post-industrial era.

The sirens began to blow at five a.m. that morning, pursuant to the county government's emergency plan established hastily the night before. Their funereal wailing would hang in the muggy, motionless air all morning. When they began sounding, Liz Chase and Race Kendall were lying in the rear of a panel truck, hog-tied and gagged. The air inside the rear compartment, not unlike the air outside, was warm and uncomfortably close. Though they had no way of knowing it, the panel truck was parked at the top of a knife-edged ridge well inland from Kapa'a. Below the ridge to the south lay a broad plain across which Iniki would soon be thundering. On the north face, the ridge fell away into a canyon the opposite wall of which was another sharp ridge. An ideal spot today for a storm-chaser in a concrete bunker, perhaps, but not for two people immobilized in a sheet-metal closet on wheels. If the vehicle tumbled into the thickly-foliaged canyon, it might never be seen again. If it were picked up and slammed against the opposite ridge by the force of the storm, it would be mangled and torn asunder.

The windowless cargo compartment provided no light except for the little that filtered around the edges of the double rear doors when the grey day dawned. In the darkness, the evacuation sirens startled Liz. She thought they meant that the hurricane was about to strike. Her attempts to ask Race what was happening were frustrated by the gags, which made speech incomprehensible; and her effort to deal with the gag was frustrated by the fact, that her hands were tied behind her back, secured by a loop of rope to her ankles. Race was trussed up in the same way, and blood was dripping from a wound on his upper arm onto the crenelated floor of the hold.

Trouble had arrived at the Sunshine warehouse at about four-thirty that morning. By that time, the two trespassers had concluded their inspection of Rafi Palahved's office. They had photocopied several documents describing the implementation of Project Thermopylae; documents that made clear the scope and nature of the undertaking. Fully realized over a twenty-year period, Project Thermopylae would transform Kauai from a garden island into a commercial and industrial center more like Singapore. Xerxes Industries did not subscribe to the notion of building on speculation. Major Asian subtenants were already lined up, subject to contingencies, as were major shipping companies and suppliers.

It was quite clear that the island's infrastructure would have to undergo massive alteration in order to accommodate the Xerxes operation. Sunshine Resources had been quietly taking options on property and snooping into the growth capacity of the public utilities on Kauai. Two non-Hawaiian members of the Kauai County Council had been given a scaled-down description of the project, along with some money, it appeared, and were quietly providing advice and guidance and preparing to champion the needs of Xerxes Industries in the council once the Ranch was sold.

Altogether, though, the amount of graft visible, or even hinted at, in Palahved's English language records was low for a project of the size that Xerxes was planning. "The juiciest documents are probably written in Farsi," Liz speculated as she and Race were preparing to leave. "Or maybe at this stage, before the sale of the property, there's not much need for bribery, except to assure the that they do get the Ranch itself."

Even so, the readable documents showed that Palahved was in regular contact with Li-Ann Low, and that the two of them had entered into some sort of letter agreement, a copy of which neither Liz nor Race could find in their early morning document review; also that Carter Robinson had been promised the lead representation of Xerxes Industries on any matters having to do with state or local permits or waivers, any real estate matters subsequent to the closing with Chamberlain, any local financing undertaken for the Thermopylae entities and any litigation arising out of Project Thermopylae. The investigators learned that while Xerxes had indeed been in discussions with all the bidders on Adibi's list, it had not reached agreements with all of them. Two, France-Orient and ROC Overseas, had broken off talks over a month ago. A third bidder had been very difficult, but until the day before, seemingly interested in striking a deal. That bidder was Paracorp. Yesterday, Galen Khoo had faxed Xerxes' lawyer a letter advising that Paracorp was not interested in pursuing a lease of the Makai Ranch to his client, and would make other plans for the property.

Finally, the intruders discovered that Adibi had been a double agent, both dispensing "commissions" to Li-Ann Low on behalf of Xerxes and supplying information on Project Thermopylae to one of the bidders for a fee. The bidder could not be identified from the English-language records.

"What we've got here is dynamite," Liz said as they were getting ready to leave. "I have to call home again." She picked up the phone and dialed the Poipu house, with Race objecting at her side.

"Don't yell at me!" she said as the phone rang. "My family's got to have this information. Particularly my dad."

"Well, how's he gonna know, Liz, if he doesn't come home, for Christ's sake?"

"One thing you can be sure of is that Andrew Chase will call in for his messages. He bought an answering machine with him just so he could do that."

They restored the office to its original condition and exited. When they switched on their flashlights to make their way across the large outer area, the whole building lit up. For a crazy instant, Liz thought there was a special high-intensity setting on her flashlight. And then they heard the voice.

"Turn around, people," a thickly accented voice said from the direction of the front door. Liz knew before looking that they were in the company of Rafi Palahved.

"We're outta here!" Race said, seeing that the Iranian was not holding a gun. He grabbed Liz's hand and ran for the back door. They could hear Palahved shouting, his words lost in the cavernous space. Liz reached the door first, flung it open and tripped over what she thought was a jamb she hadn't noticed when they came in and fell forward against a vertical wooden wall that certainly hadn't been there when they came in. Race tumbled in after her. By the time they were on their feet again and had discovered that there was no way out except back the way they had come, Palahved had reached them and was holding a box-cutter in the air in front of him.

"One consequence of having a soundproof office is that while others can't hear what's going on inside, neither can people in the office hear what's going on outside," the swarthy executive said. "I made quite a lot of noise moving that crate in front of the door."

Race Kendall started to rush Palahved, who took one step back and said quickly, "You'd better be prepared to kill me. This is a very small island."

The younger man checked himself. He had no doubt that if he succeeded in overcoming Palahved but did not kill him, the Iranian would have his revenge in due course. On the other hand, he did not want to turn a simple breaking and entering charge into a case of first degree murder.

Palahved smiled. A slender man, he was no match for Race Kendall. Even with the weapon he was holding, the outcome of a rough-and-tumble between them would have been far from certain, and with assistance from the woman, he would surely have been overpowered.

"What were you doing in my office?" Palahved demanded, glaring at Race, who did not respond.

"We were trying to find out if you intended to kill my father," Liz Chase said, trying to sound neither defensive nor defiant, but resolute.

"Forgive me," Palahved replied in parodic apology. "We have not been properly introduced. I am Rafi Palahved, head of this little business. And you are—?"

"My name is Liz Chase," Liz answered, "and my father—"

"Ah! Your father represents Harry Wong, that bastard. I might well want to wring that slant's neck, but why would I want to kill your father?"

"Other people representing bidders on the Makai Ranch have been murdered," Liz said.

"Not by me."

"One of your employees who was selling information to a bidder was killed," Liz said.

"Ach! Adibi? He was a traitor, and deserved worse than he got. Nevertheless, his blood is not on my hands, either. Will you excuse me for a moment," Palahved said, He slammed the door shut abruptly, leaving Liz and Race trapped in a crate with its open side butted up against the wall of the warehouse.

"He's going to kill us," Race said. "Let's knock this thing over. If we both run at the back of it—On three. One, two, three!" They leapt at the rear wall of the crate, crashing against it with their shoulders. It rocked, and slid away from the door a couple of inches.

"Once more!" Race shouted. The second attempt was no more successful, but there was now almost four inches' clearance between the crate and the wall of the building. The young investigators braced their backs against the door, inserted their fingers between the crate and the wall, and pushed the crate away. At the instant of their success, however, the door opened again. Liz stumbled back, and Palahved grabbed her from behind and pressed the muzzle of a pistol under her chin.

Race Kendall stood in the gap between the crate and the building, unsure what to do.

"Would you like to leave?" Palahved teased. "Be my guest. Take off, why don't you? What is she to you, anyway?" He chuckled. Race did not move. Palahved sighed. "How gallant. Well, if you're going to stay, come in and make yourself useful."

The Iranian ordered Race to take off his backpack and empty its contents onto the floor. In addition to the tools of the young man's trade, the photocopies slid out of the pack. Ordering the two intruders to lie face down on the concrete-slab floor, Palahved picked up the documents and leafed through them. "Pretty incriminating stuff," he observed after a moment. "The originals are still in my office, I assume? Good. This is quite amusing, you know. The material you copied, along with other related documents, are exactly why I came down here so early. I didn't want Iniki blowing this information all over the neighborhood."

He ordered Race to his feet again. Against a nearby wall, a large spool of twine stood on a vertical spindle, atop a blocky work table. Next to the spool was a device resembling a small paper cutter, through which the end of the twine ran.

"Go over and cut three two-foot lengths of that rope," Palahved commanded.

Race complied, moving woodenly. When he returned, Palahved instructed him to tie Liz's hands and feet. Race knelt down next to her.

"Put your arms behind you, Liz," he said softly.

"You're going to do this?" she shot back, not looking up.

"To prevent him from doing worse," Race replied, calmly but with a touch of offense in his voice.

Liz crossed her hands behind her, and felt the rough hemp bite against the skin of her wrists. When Race moved toward her feet, she lifted her head and turned it toward their captor. She could not twist herself far enough to see his face.

"This is not very comfortable, you know," she complained, already feeling the pull in her shoulders.

"If I had invited you into my building," Pahleved answered, "I would feel badly about your distress." Then to Race, he said, "Now tie her hands and feet together. Do it!"

When Liz was incapacitated, Palahved instructed Race Kendall to lie down again. He kept his distance as the young man settled to the floor. "This is tricky," the Iranian mused.

A hand truck sat about sixty feet away near a stack of cases filled with dates. With one eye on Race, Palahved moved toward it. He tried to pull the cart with one hand, but it was heavy and unwieldy and caused his gun hand to swing uncontrollably. He decided to push it instead, which meant that he had to turn it around. He set both of his hands on the handle without letting go of the gun.

Race saw a slender opportunity. Unless Palahved was an excellent marksman, the distance between them and the fact that the Iranian wasn't in firing position gave him what might be his only chance. It was a big risk, but continuing without resistance was surely lethal. He leapt to his feet, grabbing the rope that bound Liz's wrists and ankles. Running in a crouched position, he slid her unceremoniously across the floor, around the back of the partitioned area and into a cubicle. Palahved fired two shots wide of the mark, then strode quickly toward the rear of the building.

Race left Liz under a desk, injured in dignity but not body, and ran down the rank of cubicles, still crouching, and around the corner, where he raised up just enough to see Palahved and to allow himself to be seen.

"This is asinine!" Palahved called out as Race ducked out of sight. "Get back here right now, or I will kill your companion." He could neither see nor hear the young man, and began searching cubicles along the rear aisle for Liz. She was not in the first one, or the second. In the third cubicle the desk was located against and perpendicular to the front partition. To see whether Liz was hiding under it, he had to step in.

As he did so, Race Kendall dashed up silently on shoeless feet and leapt on top of him. The two of them fell against the far partition, knocking it down. In the struggle, both men were riveted on Palahved's gun, Race trying to secure a grip on the other's right hand, and Palahved struggling to keep it free.

In the hollow of the desk, Liz was beside herself. Debilitated by her fetters, all she could do was wait for life and death to contend beyond her sight. Depending on the outcome, her own life might be next on the line. Though she was not afraid of death, she was not about to lie around waiting to be shot, either. With the two men striving against one another across the toppled partition, she rolled onto her side, and by leveraging her head against the desk, impelled herself onto her knees.

Palahved was slim but wiry. Race was finding it difficult to stay on top of him and hold the gun hand at a harmless angle at the same time. In order to take the weapon away, he enlisted both his own hands in the task of prying the Iranian's fingers off its handle, and sought to control Palahved's other arm with the weight of his body. It didn't work. Palahved was able to wriggle his left hand free. He slid it into his pants pocket, and brought out the box-cutter. Awkwardly, because both his body and Race's were in violent jerking motion, he managed to slice the blade through Race's shirt and into the flesh of his arm. It was not a deep cut, but it was effective. Unsettled, the private eye loosened his grip, and Palahved smashed his cheek with the butt of the pistol. Race rolled onto his side, allowing the Iranian to break free and jump to his feet.

He swung the pistol toward Race's midsection. In the heat of the instant, Liz did something for which, even afterward, she could not explain the inspiration. Taking short, rapid-fire steps on her knees, she flung herself against the backs of Palahved's legs. The President of Sunshine Resources gave a dumbfounded yell and tumbled onto his back on top of her. She turned her head to protect her face from smashing onto the floor, and took the blow against her temple and ear.

Both men jumped up at the same instant. Liz could see only Race's bare feet. She heard Palahved say, "Hold it—Hands on your head, now." She heard Race breathing heavily. She saw him shift his weight onto the balls of his feet. The moment crackled with nervous energy. Then, from Palahved, "Okay, let's cool down, shall we?" There were a few seconds of silence. Then, again, Palahved: "Just walk slowly over to that hand truck, all right?"

Race stood his ground for a heartbeat, but directly Liz saw him rebalance onto his heels and step away. She heard Palahved shuffling behind her, keeping his distance. "For what it's worth, Miss Chase, you probably saved your escort's life just then, for a few hours, anyway." After the two men left her, Liz maneuvered herself out of the cubicle and down the rear aisle in order to see what was happening.

At Palahved's direction, Race pushed the hand truck over to the bench that held the spool of twine, cut three lengths, which he left on the bench, and then slid under the hand truck, face down, until only his feet were exposed. Palahved grabbed the twine and, resting the gun on the floor next to him, bound the young man's ankles together. That done, he moved the hand truck down over Race's legs. Palahved then sat on the back of the young man's neck and proceeded to immobilize his hands with the rope in the same manner as with Liz.

"Are you going to kill us?" Race asked.

"No, no. I'm only going to take you for a ride," Palahved said. It was an honest enough answer, as far as it went.

When he was done securing Race, Palahved looked up at Liz and said, "Just waddle over to the back door, would you, Miss Chase? We'll join you there."

Three-quarters of an hour later, Liz and Race lay on their sides in the dark, staring at one another's dimly discernible silhouettes, their ears filled with the piercing call of the civil defense siren down in Kapa'a. In a moment that gave her so little cause for gratitude. Liz found herself thankful that she and Race could not converse. She wasn't sure what she could say to him. For one thing, neither she nor Race knew what was about to happen to them. Were they going to die within the next few minutes? Or hours? Were they going to be left to starve to death over the course of the coming days? Or was she being used as a chip in a game Palahved meant to play out with her father? For another, her attitude toward Race Kendall had become confused as a result of his actions over the past several hours, during which he had displayed aspects of character she hadn't imagined that he possessed: a capacity for contrition, decisiveness, true courage—as opposed to mere surfer machismo—and ultimately, self-sacrifice. Here was a man worthy of better treatment than she had accorded him. She was mortified to think that the two of them would not be suffering whatever sorry fate now awaited them had she not insisted on breaking into the Sunshine building.

The rear doors of the truck swung open, washing the interior with ghostly predawn light. With difficulty, Liz shifted her body to bring the opening into view. Palahved was standing there, his face bruised from the scuffle with Race, but cheerful. Though a fine rain was falling, the shrubbery behind him was motionless in the lull before the storm.

"Please accept my humble apologies," he said. "I have not handled this particularly well. I wasn't expecting to find anyone in my office this morning, and so everything since then has been completely improvised and, frankly, clumsy. For example, I should have used packing tape on your wrists and ankles instead of twine—equally strong, but less painful. I'm just a businessman, after all, lacking in experience in such matters." Liz raised an eyebrow, and Palahved was moved to elaborate. "You are perhaps thinking about Adibi. But, you see, even there it was not in me to do him violence. He had certain allergies, poor man, and I mentioned the fact to a colleague of mine when we were discussing—well, what to do about him. My colleague apparently took matters from there. Bee venom caused Adibi to swell up like a balloon. His neck would almost disappear—I saw this when we were immigrant kids in Greece—and his larynx would be squeezed almost shut." He glanced at Liz again. "The ice pick, is that what's on your mind, Miss Chase? My colleague felt it was a device that would send a message to other potential double dealers and put the police on a false track." He shuddered. "A revolting but, he thought, necessary deception. Anyway, in the case of Adibi, it was not murder so much as it was a dispensation of justice."

Race Kendall growled behind his muzzle.

"You are saying something about the gun I turned on you?" Palahved smiled. "Except perhaps at that one point where I had lost control of the situation and was afraid of you, I don't think I could have used it, really; which is why I'm hoping that Iniki will solve this problem for me. Well, good-bye. I'll be back after the storm to see if anything more needs to be done."

The doors closed. They heard a key turning in the lock, followed by a sound like metal sliding across the skin of the doors. Race mumbled something unintelligible and began to strain against his bonds.

"That's useless," Liz tried to say, and realized their gags were not a blessing after all. She and Race needed to communicate in order to free one another.

The gags were shop cloths like those sold in bulk at superstores around the country. Palahved had held them by opposing corners, spun them onto themselves, pulled them across their mouths and knotted them at the back of the neck. The first step to freedom, Liz decided, would be to untie them.

She used the wall of the compartment to raise herself into a kneeling position, an action that increased the pain in her already aching shoulders and thighs. The pain deepened as she inched herself over to where Race lay on his side, facing her. She shouted grunts at him every time he attempted to sit up. Eventually he got the idea and stopped, and she fell forward onto him. Catching his shoulder under her chin and sliding backward, she coaxed Race onto his stomach. That done, she rotated onto her back—shards of pain cutting through her arms and sides—and positioned the knot of her gag over Race's bound hands.

"Untie it," she said. Although he couldn't make out the words, he understood what she wanted. But understanding and accomplishment were two very different things. Race's fingers were limited in their mobility because of the bindings, and they were beginning to go numb from lack of blood. Lying backwards over Race as he fumbled with the knot put Liz's muscles, ligaments and joints in painful tension, and she had to roll off every few minutes to rest on her stomach, catch her breath and cry quietly. It was not working. After half an hour, Race had made no progress at all because he couldn't feel the direction of the knot and he couldn't use the strength of his arms to pull at it.

The interior of the enclosure had brightened somewhat as light from the advancing morning seeped in around the doors. He could see a stack of furniture-movers' pads at the front of the compartment, but no objects that could help them. In his pocket was the thing they needed: a Swiss Army knife. He felt it pressing against his leg, and the feeling frustrated him to the point of distraction. The wind was now blowing steadily over the panel truck. Occasionally, an abrupt gust exploded against the cargo compartment, causing it to sway. With Liz in agony and his ability to move even his fingers dissipating, the presence of the knife and his inability to reach it became his only focus. It was the knife or nothing.

The next time Liz slipped off of him, he turned himself over onto his side, and waited. When Liz signalled that she was ready for another try, he began thrusting his haunches in the air and yelling, "Pocket! Pocket!" To Liz, it sounded like, "Ah-eh," and she thought Race had reverted to type and was proposing some peculiar form of sex, a final round of sadomasochism before they were done in. Absurd as it was, the idea was reinforced when Race, seeing that she was not responding, slid toward her and began rubbing his upper thigh against her knee. When she objected loudly, though incoherently, he stopped moving and instead pressed the knife as hard as he could against her kneecap, saying as clearly as he could, "Knife."

Though Liz heard only "Aaaa," she now appreciated that it was the thing in his pocket, not the one between his pockets, that he wanted to bring into service. *Why do I always think the worst of him?* She pushed against the base of the object with her knee, but the action did little but move the knife sideways. She turned herself around, and tried to get at it with her hands, but those normally willing agents were no longer obeying directions from her brain. For a time, she lay there, stumped, but at length the only other method she had at her disposal came to her. She wriggled herself into position along Race's upper leg. Her lips and teeth projected beyond the gag, and she could use them to force the knife into slow, controlled motion. This process, too, took an excruciating amount of time, but by degrees the green-casketed knife made its way to the top of the pocket and clattered onto the metal floor.

Race was on top of it immediately, shifting positions until he felt it under his hands. He had a plan in mind and wanted to execute it as quickly as possible. Blown leaves and small branches were smacking broadside against the walls of the truck, which had begun to shudder in the wind and, worse, to slide sidelong now and again when hit by a vicious gust. They had to get out of the truck fast. In no time, he was lying on his stomach, with the knife held securely in his hands and the blade extended upward, its business edge facing away from Liz. He jerked his head in a nodding motion.

Liz understood. She adopted the torturous, backward-leaning position again, lifting her head forward this time so she could slide the blade between the knotted cloth and the back of her neck. Pressing down on Race with her elbows, then releasing the pressure, she managed to saw at the gag. Before long, she felt it parting, and a moment later, "Mmff! Aaah! Oh, God, oh, God! Okay, Race, quick. Your turn." Her hands were not as strong as Race's. The knife fell out of position several times, and Liz cut herself once, blood dripping onto the back of her shirt; but eventually, the second gag yielded.

Focused more on escape than on small talk, Race said only, "All right! Now, I'm going to grab the knife between my teeth and cut through the twine around your—Jesus!"

There had been a loud thump against the panel truck and a violent shake that caused the rear of the vehicle to skitter off the center line of the ridge. The floor of the cargo compartment was now tilting toward the rear.

"What on earth was that?" Liz cried over the mounting wind noise.

"Sounds like the debris is getting bigger," Race yelled back. "The way this rattletrap is vibrating, I'd say the wind must be sixty, maybe seventy mph out there." He bent over Liz's hands and between them they managed to transfer the butt of the knife into his mouth without cutting off his nose. The twine parted easily. A quarter of an hour later, they were rubbing their arms and legs and shaking themselves out. The truck was quaking convulsively, pelted by driving rain and forest rubble, along with asphalt shingles, the odd two-by-four and an occasional swatch of sheet-metal roofing blown up from the plain at the base the ridge.

"We've got to get out of here and below the ridge line now!" Race shouted, "If the wind gets any stronger, we'll be killed moving around out there."

There were no handles on the insides of the doors, and the little tools on his knife were not suited to the task of disassembling the locking mechanism. "I'm gonna have to kick the damn things open!" he shouted. Lying on his back, he cocked both legs and gave it everything he had. The doors did not budge. He hit them again, and was rewarded by a cracking sound in the region of the lock. On the third try, the doors parted a couple of inches, but did not fly open, and now they could see why. They looked at each other in despair. Palahved had slipped an iron pipe between the handles.

Race braced himself to begin kicking again. "I should be able to hit hard enough to tear the handles right off the doors," he cried. As he delivered the first blow, however, a tremendous gust of wind burst like a bomb against the side of the truck, lifting its rear end and swinging it in the air a quarter turn before dropping it. The rear wheels bounced to a landing down the leeward side of the ridge. Race Kendall came to rest standing on the doors and staring through the opening between them down a steep grade to the valley floor some six hundred feet below. Liz slid into him, followed by the furniture padding.

"Time's up!" Race said. "We're going down with the ship. There's only one thing to do. Let's get a couple of those pads open on the floor." They stood at opposite sides of the compartment, laid one of the pads out on the slanted decking, and then opened another on top of it. Race ordered Liz to lie down at the edge of the padding and rolled her up in it. "Our only hope is to survive that fall," he yelled, as he tied the roll into a sausage above Liz's head and below her feet. Then he felt for Liz's face, pulled the padding away from it and gingerly sliced away at it until she could see. "Now," he shouted, "I'm going to slit this thing near your waist, so I can pass a cinching rope through it." He made two cuts in front and two in the rear, then passed a length of twine in and out, finally sticking the ends inside where Liz could grab hold of them. "Pull tight and tie it," he instructed at the top of his lungs.

She did so, but then tugged at the opening in front of her face with both hands. "How are you going to wrap yourself?" she screamed.

"Watch me!" He grabbed the remaining twine, spread out two pads, lay against them and, gripping them by an edge, rolled across the floor. Liz could see the knife blade emerging from the padding at his waist, making the requisite holes. Race passed the twine through the holes quickly and then tied it. She smiled despite herself. *This guy just won't give up.*

Presently, the blade appeared again, cutting horizontally across the upper part of the grey cocoon. "Hi!" he hollered through the opening. What she saw of his face evinced both determination and apprehension. "You okay?"

"I'd prefer a regulation coffin to this giant tampon, but, yeah, I'm okay." Inside the musty padding, Liz felt claustrophobia attacking her gut. She was overheating, and the mobility of her arms and legs was limited. Truth was, she was anything but okay.

"So this is worse than skydiving?"

"Hell, yes. In diving, you control your destiny, more or less. Here we have no control at all. You scared?"

"Pretty much. How about a good-luck kiss before lift-off? I deserve that, don't I?"

He did. Liz pulled the slit padding down so that her lips were exposed. She, too, was eager for a tender touch in the darkness of the moment and didn't mind at all that it was Race rather than Harlan who was there to provide it. Two padded sausages came together in a brief moment of cylindrical tenderness.

The fall into the valley did not occur right away. With its grill now facing the wind, and its body partially protected by the crest of the ridge, the truck sat in place for what seemed hours. All around them, the fury of the hurricane roared, an unearthly sound that combined elements of jet engines, high-speed freight trains, roaring lions, howling wolves, stampeding cattle, artillery barrages and carpet bombings. Bursts of wind exceeding a hundred miles an hour drove debris at the vehicle, shattering the windshield and the headlights, weakening and then tearing off the grill. Still, the little panel truck held its position, like the steadfast tin soldier.

Inside it, the demented howl of the hurricane would have made conversation impossible even had Liz and Race not been encased in their full-body cushioning. Liz had ample time to think about what was going to happen to her. She had seen the steep angle of the ridge and knew that the ride down would be swift and chaotic. Most likely, despite the desperate brilliance of Race's protective packaging, they would not make it. Conditioned to mortal risk by hundreds of leaps into thin air, she was calm but deeply depressed. Unlike her sister, Liz did not believe in reincarnation, and had no particular convictions about the afterlife. The next big event in her life, from what she could tell, was likely to be lights out.

The closest she had been to that expectation before was in the moments before her first chuteless jump. During the ride up to altitude, her mood had been somber, though she'd hid her sobriety—perhaps not very well—behind a manic bubbliness. As soon as she left the plane, though, the familiar, magical rush of free flight had filled her with joy, and as she banked her body into a slow spiral that would bring her eventually into contact with her partner, she had gleefully imagined telling her father about her feat. Now, she could imagine no such psychic reward. Instead, she envisioned her smashed body lying at the bottom of a ravine, blood infusing the shredded padding with crimson dampness, a policeman picking up the pieces and bringing them back to her family.

In the end, it was not wind that undid them, but rain, prodigious amounts of it. Continuing to build in intensity, Iniki was laden with water, a giant wave breaking over the ridge. Runoff flowed uphill over the windward face and then down the leeward side. The ground under the vehicle became soaked, and eventually supersaturated. The dirt turned into a slurry, and when that happened, the truck let go, gracefully at first, descending backwards like an ice skater; but then one of its wheels sideswiped an exposed boulder, and it yawed sideways, tipped over and started to tumble.

Thrown about as though she were in a giant clothes dryer colliding with every surface of the compartment, Liz closed her eyes and waited to die.

Halfway down the ridge, the spinning hulk struck an outcropping with such ferocity that the cargo compartment separated from the cab and chassis, and took off on its own. Alone, the compartment had little structural integrity, and as it bounced and flew down the slope, it began to deform. The stresses caused the rear hinges to burst, sending the doors spinning into the air like a discus thrown by a titan. Race was flung out behind them, and then Liz. What was left of the cargo compartment continued to cartwheel until it slammed flat into the trunk of a monkeypod tree.

Wrapped in her musty winding-sheet, Liz sailed in an arc through what to her was black space. Her eyes tightly shut, her teeth clenched, her hands squeezed into fists, she braced for her last moment. It was an inopportune time for a revelation, but nonetheless it came to her as she felt gravity's embrace: all at once she knew why she jumped out of planes, and she knew that, if she survived this fall, she would not need to sky dive any longer.

When the impact came, it was not what she had expected. The slope of the ridge was still fairly steep, and she struck it at a glancing angle, against a bed of ferns and weeds. She bounced, and the friction of the impact set her spinning down the incline. She was jolted three more times as she fell, once on her back, once on her left side and once on her right side. No pain, surprisingly, but the shock of each collision coursed through her body like a high-voltage surge. And then she was in free fall. *Free fall? A cliff! How high....*

Before she could finish the thought, she felt the splash, the current, the bobbing—and then, as water soaked her wrappings, the sinking. She reached for the slip knot she had made near her waist, took a last breath of trapped air, pulled on the twine and clawed her way out of her now-treacherous shock absorber.

The agitated surface of the pool heaved above her. Oddly, even with her lungs full of air, she didn't seem to be floating toward it; rather something was tugging her down. The water around her was turbid, but even in the low visibility Liz could see that there was a general downward drift. It took all her strength to resist the force and propel herself up. Kicking madly and thrusting her arms against the current, she came gasping into the clear. Nearby, a cascade of rainwater was surging down a trail that descended to the conjunction of the ridges that defined the valley. At the base of the trail, the flood vaulted free of the land and poured itself into the pool in which she was swimming, and which must be emptying, Liz guessed, through an underground channel.

The cascade off the trail was laden with rocks, mud and uprooted vegetation, and she was drifting rapidly into it. There was no time to turn aside, so she dove as deeply as she could. Water slowed the passage of the stones, one of which grazed her leg as it fell. When she emerged on the other side of the chute, she lunged for the bank, where ferns grew thickly on a steep hillside. She grabbed two handfuls of fronds, dragged herself against them and quickly grappled her way out of the vortex.

Several feet above her, a rock jutted out of the earth. She scrambled toward it and then onto it, and collapsed against the green hillside, grateful for the feel of the soft earth against her back.

The noise of the flume was as nothing compared to the sound of the hurricane raging overhead. A low-frequency scream shook Liz's body and shook the earth itself, as if Iniki were furious that the speed of her passage had prevented her from descending into the valley. Winds thick with rain and flying debris careened past. Mounting the outer side of the ridge, the hurricane gained an upward momentum so that very little rain or anything else fell into the valley, except for the raw, elemental rage of the hurricane, which descended on her, filling her with an overwhelming sense of vulnerability.

As she caught her breath and fought against the apprehension of helplessness, a huge section of sheet-metal roofing came twisting across her field of vision like an amphetamine-crazed manta ray. It was large enough to have come from the Sunshine building, and Liz suddenly had a vision of the warehouse exploding around Rafi Palahved—now no less vulnerable than she—scattering his incriminating documents and trapping him in its wreckage. Wishful thinking, or a premonition? She'd find out soon enough.

She looked at the cataract again, tracing its path backwards with her eyes. Its source was a sheet of rainwater that was flowing over the crest of the opposing ridge and diverting down the trail. She saw the cliff over which she had fallen, and estimated that she had plunged about forty feet into the pool. She lay there, looking up at the infinite beast that was trashing her senses, amazed that she could be so close to it and not be devoured. She had survived, thanks to some lucky bounces—and to Race.

The thought brought her bolt upright on the rock. Race was not in sight up the ridge. She looked into the whirlpool. The invisible depths beneath its tormented face revealed nothing. *Oh, Jesus, Kendall, don't be—*

Further down the valley, a jacaranda tree stood alone, flowering in violet on the opposite ridge. Inside the enveloping leaves, there seemed to be a greyish mass. She slid sideways along the incline, until she came to the far edge of the pool, where a hillock bridged between the valley walls. Here she was able to cross over, and when she did she could see that the thing in the jacaranda tree was a drooping tube of furniture padding. Heart pounding, she made her way along the slope to the base of the tree. The trunk rose some three stories above her, and the object of her attention was halfway up, draped over a fork between the trunk and a major limb. The trajectory that had brought Race to that spot was clearly marked in stripped and broken branches. She climbed up the tree, and as soon as she was close enough, untied and peeled back one end of the wrap. Race Kendall's head hung downward before her, eyes closed. Liz ran her hand through his golden hair.

"Please be alive," she murmured. He felt warm, but he was not moving. "I couldn't bear it—"

She lifted herself up and started to attack the twine at Race's waist. His landing must have been much harder than hers, and she was afraid that he might have had suffered serious internal injuries. The slip knot was inside the roll, as hers had been, and she tore at the padding to try to reach it.

All at once, she felt a sharp pinch in her right buttock as though she were being bitten by an animal. She twisted around, and found that Race Kendall had lifted his head and clamped his teeth to her shorts. With a shove, she pushed him away and slid back down the trunk until her face was level with his. With a free hand around his neck, she bestowed on the still-captive investigator the warmest kiss she had ever given any man. For just an instant, Iniki's growing ferocity went unnoticed.

"Even upside down in a tree with your arms and legs bound, you're a pain in the ass," Liz declared. "But at least you're an endearing pain in the ass."

"Well, I shouted," the young investigator croaked, "but you didn't hear me. You know how it is. Sometimes your teeth are the only tool you've got. Did you say 'endearing?'"

11

When the sirens started blaring on the north shore, Janet Chase awoke naked in bed with a man she'd met a few days earlier and might never see again. It neither embarrassed nor unsettled her. The night before had been a different matter. For a while, she'd been both embarrassed and unsettled. Barry Saga was only the second man in her life for whom she had undressed—and the first time her tummy was flat, her thighs were lean and her nipples pointed up. Too, she and Andrew had learned how to make love from each other, and she suspected that neither of them was a particularly good teacher. Yet Saga had been gentle, caring and understanding. After an awkward start, their passion had built naturally until they were mutually consumed by a surging, throbbing lust, and neither Janet's technique nor the shape of her body mattered any more.

No, Janet was neither embarrassed nor unsettled on the morning after, but she did feel a twinge of guilt, as if she had cheated on Andrew. As if she had just done what she had been unable to forgive him for doing. In an odd way, while she lay next to Saga she felt closer to her former husband. At least now she had experienced the exquisite satisfaction and sincere remorse that extramarital passion can engender.

Outside the open bedroom windows, it was still dark. The ocean was calm, and the humidity in the air clung to her like a second skin. She felt Barry Saga stir next to her on the mattress. A light went on. She saw his muscular back, his arm withdrawing from the lamp, his jet black hair, his walnut skin.

"What does the alarm mean?" she asked, not bothering to cover herself as he turned toward her.

"It means evacuate."

"Evacuate? What about your sons?"

"Don't worry. We have several hours to collect them and get them to a shelter." He ran the backs of his fingers along her shoulder and upper arm, and then her breast. "I'm afraid it's time to get out of bed."

Janet put her hand over his and pressed it against her bosom. She kissed him gently on the mouth. "Yes, with those sirens wailing, my mind is elsewhere, too," she murmured.

They got up and slipped on their clothes. Janet stood in front of the bedroom mirror and ran her fingers through her hair. She needed makeup, but there were more urgent things to do. "Is there a risk of another tsunami, do you think?"

"Well, something like a tsunami, depending on how the hurricane hits us." Saga grabbed a pad and a mechanical pencil from the night table. Standing next to her, he drew a circle. "This is Kauai. If the eye of Iniki passes over the east side of the island," he explained, drawing another circle that intersected from the right with an arrow pointing down on top of island, "then because its winds blow counterclockwise, they can push what's called a storm surge—a mound of water carrying strong waves—onto the north shore up here. In that case, this house won't be here tonight. It'll be in pieces up in the Limahuli Valley.

"But if the eye passes over the west side of the island," he continued, "then—see here?" He drew another circle with an arrow pointing up from below the island. "The south shore takes the hit, and up north the winds actually blow the ocean away from the land. Of course, if they're strong enough, they could blow this place right out to sea."

"Oh, dear. Either way, Riko's sculptures—"

Saga looked past Janet into the living room.

"We can't go after the kids until it's lighter," he said after a moment. "Meantime, there are a some things to do here. The first is to get a weather report."

As they left the bedroom, Janet thought of her own family. "I will be able to get to Poipu this morning, won't I, Barry?"

He stopped and turned her toward him. "Here's the thing, Jan. These sirens are sounding all over the island. By the time we get the kids, bring them to the shelter here, drive down to Poipu—Your family will already be either at the airport or evacuated."

"Evacuated to where?"

"The designated shelter down there is the Koloa Elementary School, but again, it depends on how the storm hits. It might make sense for them just to move to higher ground, say, George's place. Why don't you call them, while I get an update from the station?"

The telephone was in the kitchen and the police radio in the living room. Janet punched in the Poipu number. After six rings, Andrew's recorded voice sounded over the line, asking her to leave a message at the tone.

"Where is everybody?" she demanded. "Pick up the phone!" She hung up, called back, and punched in the access codes. The answering machine began to play the stored messages.

"Hold on a second," Saga said into his microphone when Janet finally put down the receiver.

"No one's home," she said. "Stella's at George's. The other two are—" She raised her arms helplessly.

"Call Akamai," Saga said. "It's a speed dial. Just press seven."

When the phone rang, George Akamai glanced at Nate Chamberlain. "It's probably the station with the orders of the day," he said. "You'd better let me answer it, or they'll send a patrolman over here to check up."

"Do it right, Georgie," Chamberlain warned, gesturing toward Stella.

Akamai nodded curtly.

"Hello?"

"Hello, George. This is Janet."

"Yeah. Hi, Sarge."

"No, Janet!"

"Yeah, I can hear you."

Janet paused. "Is something wrong, George?"

"You bet."

"Is Stella with you?"

"Yeah."

"What about Liz and Andrew?"

"Not really. I'm just here with one of my buddies, getting the house ready for a big, wet kiss from Iniki."

Janet put her hand over the phone. "There's some kind of problem. He's calling me 'Sarge.' Stella's with him, and one of his buddies."

Saga's face dropped and he jumped out of his chair. "Jesus! Let me talk to him, Jan." He took the handset. "George."

"Mm-hmm. I know, Sarge."

"Nate's there, isn't he?"

"Sure thing. Now look, Sarge. My friend and I need a couple of hours to get the house ready, okay? Then I can pitch in with the evacuations down here."

"Shall I send a SWAT team?"

"Nah, I have it covered. Gotta go." The line disconnected.

The look in Saga's eyes unnerved Janet. "What is it?"

"I'm not sure. Here's the situation. Number one, Nate Chamberlain, Web's son, is there. Number two, George didn't want Nate to know who was calling. Number three, George doesn't want any help right now."

"Is it a good thing or a bad thing that this Chamberlain fellow is with them?"

"I don't know. As I say, he and George are close friends, but Nate turned out to be kind of a bad apple. He doesn't live on Kauai any more. I don't think George knew he was back on the island, so his visit this morning must have been a surprise."

"But, Barry, you said a SWAT team. That's what you said, didn't you?"

"Yes."

"A SWAT team, Barry. For God's sake, what are you thinking?"

"Just being cautious, Jan. There's some kind of tension down there, or George wouldn't have gone through that charade on the phone. If it were something serious, though, George would have asked for help, particularly with Stella there. Don't worry, I'll have someone stop in and check on them."

Janet could see that there was something else on Saga's mind, but since there was something else on her mind, too, she let the subject drop. "W-we still don't know where Liz and Andrew are," she stuttered.

"Yes. Is it possible that Liz is spending the night with Race Kendall?"

Janet blushed. "Are you asking if it runs in the family?"

Saga gave her a quick hug. "The more ways Liz is like her mother, the better person she is. If she did stay at Kendall's, that's up in Kapa'a. The only question there is whether the guy is mature enough to evacuate to Kapa'a High, or whether he's going to try to ride it out in his house. As for Andy, I know Niki Makana. There was a time when we were worried about her sovereignty group. Some of its members were dangerous, we thought. I talked to her, and she kicked them out. She's an okay kid, and she wouldn't let Andy get into trouble. Last I knew, she was living up in Anahola, the northeast part of the island. Maybe they'd go there." He shrugged. "She's a native of Kauai, and old enough to remember the last hurricane. She'll do something sensible. Come on, let's board this place up."

By six-thirty, a gray dawn was breaking, the work of preparing the house was done and it was time to go after Saga's children. Before they left, Saga tried calling Akamai again. The line was dead. "No answer," he grunted. "I'll try the police radio from the car. They may have evacuated."

They climbed into the auto and set off. Saga tried to get through to Akamai over the police radio but couldn't raise him. When they reached Hanalei a few minutes later, he pulled into the Ching Yung shopping center, a concrete and red-tiled structure. He suggested that Janet get them some breakfast, while he tried to reach Akamai once more.

When Janet had left for the grocery store, Saga had called the station. "Rita, I need to talk to the chief," he said to the operator. In a moment, Chief Nagato was on the line. "Saga, you going to join us down here today?"

"My kids are camping. I don't think they've heard about the hurricane. I'm going to take them to the shelter, and then I'll be right in. Listen, chief, I think Lieutenant Akamai has a situation going out at his house. I'd like you to send Lieutenant Han and a sharpshooter out there right—"

The chief interrupted him. "Saga, what the hell are you talking about? We've got a big public safety problem to deal with today. I can't be dispatching police officers on an I-think-there-might-be-a-situation basis."

"I understand, sir. But chief, unless I'm mistaken, we could be headed for a hostage situation or something even worse." He recounted the earlier phone conversation with Akamai, omitting to mention that Janet had participated in it from his place.

"Okay, so it sounds like George and his friend Nate aren't hitting it off like they used to. That doesn't make Nate Chamberlain a menace to society. I mean, my God, Captain, you want me to send a sharpshooter after Web Chamberlain's son?"

"The guy is a troublemaker, you know that. And as the only heir to the Makai Ranch, he must have some view about the proposed sale of his priceless heritage. Maybe his view of that is different from his father's, as it was on every other subject when he was living here. People have killed for less."

"Christ, Saga! That's sheer speculation."

Through the windshield, Saga watched Janet Chase walking toward him, a paper bag in her hand.

"Nagato-san, it's speculation, but I would stake my career on the conclusion that Akamai needs help right now."

There was silence on the other end of the line, followed by a sigh. "Yes, and my career, too, apparently. All right, Captain. I will dispatch Lieutenant Han and one sharpshooter down to Lawai. Just get your ass in here as quick as you can, will you?"

Saga and Janet drove east through Hanalei, eating bagels and drinking coffee. The Hanalei Valley, perhaps the most peaceful in

Hawaii, sped past on their right. A mile-wide plain flanked by serpentine ridges and peaks, all wearing mantles of verdure and veils of mist, the Hanalei Valley was a patchwork of taro fields little changed during the millennium since the days of the Marquesans. A river meandered down from the highlands, through the cultivated flats and under a one-lane truss bridge.

Just beyond the bridge, there was a turnoff. Saga headed into it and drove onto a jeep road that paralleled the riverbank. Janet saw Hawaiian ducks and mallards swimming in the submerged taro fields. The plants rose on slender stalks that drooped with the weight of broad, arrowhead-shaped leaves. The hint of a breeze set the leaves astir. The dirt road was lined with fruit trees: mango, guava, orange and pomelo. It ran past an old rice mill, restored as a museum by the Haraguchi family, owners of the largest taro farm in the valley. At the roadside, small orchid plants bearing delicate purple flowers grew contentedly and shocks of fragrant yellow ginger flourished. The road ended. Behind a gated fence, a walking trail led into the wildlife refuge. "Pop the glove compartment, would you?" Saga said.

Under a zipped leather case, Janet could see a small pistol in a lightweight holster. Saga reached for it.

"What's that for?" she asked. "Do I have to spend all my time on this vacation scared out of my wits?"

The policeman hesitated. "I'm sorry. Force of habit. Leave it, Jan; I'm not on duty yet."

They got out. A yellow Subaru sedan was parked near the trailhead. "That belongs to my brother Ken. Here," he added, handing Janet his car keys. "Take these, will you? I've got no pockets in my shorts."

Get the coffee. Hand him the gun. Carry his keys. It wasn't Saga's fault, Janet thought, but she was falling into the old pattern of subservience and dependence, somehow signalling that she was willing to, maybe eager to, cede control as worries about her family overtook her. Her posture, the anxious look on her face, the pitch of her voice, were all wrong. *Come on, Jan-not-Janet. Get a grip.*

The path beyond the gate took them through the taro fields and into an enchanting bamboo forest. Segmented trunks in shades of yellow, tan and forest green rose on either side into a canopy of slender leaves. The breeze was picking up, and the bamboo made low clattering and hissing noises around them. "It's not a native plant," Saga said, "but it's popular in the islands. Every once in a while you'll see a pickup truck carrying a few long bamboo stalks that have just been cut. It's used for making furniture and utensils and flutes—and as a building material. And of course, and we eat the shoots."

They came to a stream. Janet heard herself assuring Saga that she didn't mind if her shoes—a pair of three-hundred dollar suede pumps that she had worn specially for dinner the night before—got wet. She held his hand tightly while they traversed the slippery, stony streambed. After another bamboo forest and another stream, they came again to the Hanalei river at a point where large mango trees lined the bank. A path took them along the river and into the interior.

They were trespassing on private land, according to the signs they passed as they climbed a moderate rise into forested lands. Saga explained that the signs were there to protect the owners against liability—not to keep hikers out. Their course descended the other side of the hill, crossed an unimproved road and then ascended again.

"If it weren't for the Makai Ranch murders, would you need to go back to Connecticut, Jan?" Saga asked.

"Well, I do have a life, Barry."

"I didn't mean to suggest otherwise; only to test the possibility that you could stay—longer."

"I have a full life, Barry," Janet insisted, her shoes slipping a little as the grooves in the soles filled up with red clay. "Suppose I ask you to come to Connecticut for an open-ended period of time?"

"I couldn't. I've got my kids to think about. My job—"

"I see. So the fact that I haven't got a job and my kids are grown means that I can just pick up and ship out here? That's the same problem I had with Andy. He didn't respect me because I wasn't doing anything he considered important. That lack of respect helped him to justify all the shit he did, excuse me."

"Jan, I'm not Andy, and you had my respect before I knew whether you had a job title or not. You're on edge this morning." Saga turned to help her up a steep incline.

She looked into his eyes. In themselves, they were not particularly expressive; or perhaps she didn't know yet how to read them. His manner was easy to read, though. *He cares.* "Sure I am. I don't understand what's going on with Stella and George this morning. I'm worried about Liz. And Andy, too, damn him. My family's scattered all over the island, and this big hurricane is coming. And when I try to put aside my fears for a while, I end up thinking about you, and whether I'd have been better off if I hadn't met you."

"Ouch!"

"Oh, Barry. A loving relationship that only lasts a matter of days? Come on, it's the ultimate folly, isn't it? You spend so much more time suffering the loss than you spend experiencing the joy."

Saga clasped his hands on top of his head and rocked from side to side. "There's so much to say in response to that, and it can't be said while we're walking single file. Let's just be quiet for now. Pretty soon, you'll hear the waterfall."

A hundred yards on, she did hear it, the sound of great volumes of liquid crashing against stone. The noise made by waterfalls, Janet thought, was out of harmony with their beauty. It spoke more to their power and danger than to their picturesque elegance. The gods could have invented something more appealing to the ear, it seemed to her—something silvery and harmonic.

A few minutes later Saga stopped walking. Janet came up beside him. They were standing at the edge of a steep rockface. Not a dozen paces away was a triple waterfall. Above them, the first of the falls plummeted into a jumble of rocks and flowed to the cliff on which they stood. From there, water tumbled into a deep pool, and from the pool it leapt down into an unseen glen. Mist was all around them. It felt cool against their sweltering skins. In the pool below them, two dark-haired boys and a man were cavorting. Saga waved at them.

When the boys noticed him, they began to jump and splash wildly. Saga beckoned to them. Once they had left the water, he led Janet away from the waterfall. "The path down to the pool gets very muddy. We'll wait for them back here." They returned to the head of the lower trail, where they soon heard the sounds of juvenile exuberance filtering toward them.

"Daddy!"

"Daddy!" The shouts came on top of one another. Two scrawny boys ran up the trail, commandeered Saga's hands and tugged him in opposite directions. He calmed them down, or rather ordered them to calm down so that they were forced to simulate the state of being calm. "This is Tetsuo. Ted," he said, tousling the matted hair of the older boy, whose age Janet estimated at ten years. "And this," he added, chucking the younger boy under the chin, "is Junichiro. Nick."

A man who looked like a bookish version of Saga strode up the trail from the pool, a damp polo shirt hastily pulled on over his bathing suit. "My brother Ken. A botanist with the Botanical Garden. Spends a lot of his time having sexual encounters with flowers."

Kenji Saga shook Janet's hand and translated Saga's remark: "Among other things, I hand-pollinate indigenous plants whose natural pollinators have become extinct."

"Out in the wild, mind you," Saga put in. "He climbs mountains, dangles over cliffs, slogs through the swamp in order to give these plants fulfillment." He told his brother and sons about the hurricane and asked them to pack up quickly. They turned and headed back down the hill, and he followed them, after telling Janet to wait on high ground because she wouldn't be able to negotiate the slippery path in the shoes she was wearing.

Left alone, Janet's thoughts reverted to the whereabouts of her family and the impending arrival of Iniki. As a child in Louisiana, she had experienced hurricanes. Her recollection was that they were wind and water for some number of hours, and then they were gone, leaving the electricity off, the streets full of branches and the people who lived directly on the Gulf briefly sorry that they had chosen to do so. Unfortunately, that picture was as much like what she would shortly experience as a stick of dynamite is like an atomic bomb. While they had been hiking to the waterfall, Iniki had been upgraded to a Force Five hurricane, the highest grade on the Saffir-Simpson scale. KONG Radio had warned that Kauaians could expect sustained winds of as much as one-hundred-sixty-five miles per hour, with gusts well in excess of two-hundred miles per hour. In a radio address at ten a.m., Mayor JoAnn Yukimura ordered all traffic, including police and fire department personnel, off the street. To be outside of shelter could be lethal.

Even without the benefit of that information, though, Janet was fearful. There was no plan for the family to reunite at the airport or anywhere else that morning. Liz and Andy were unaccounted for and that Stella was caught in the middle of some kind of weird reunion between Akamai and the Chamberlain heir, who, according to Andrew's phone message, was a druggie. The worst of it was that there was absolutely nothing she could do about any of those things.

She slapped her hands against her side, spun around in frustration and came face-to-face with terror in the flesh. Tromping toward her up the trail from the parking lot were three burly men in shorts and tee shirts, all wearing ski masks. One of them was carrying a hunting rifle.

Her first instinct was to turn and run in the opposite direction, but as soon as reason recaptured her mind she realized that she would come to a dead end at the waterfall. Instead, she ran for the trail leading down to the pool. The men chased her. She beat them to the downhill path and leaped along it, screaming for Saga at the top of her lungs. Fog licked at her on the way down, and as it thickened, the ground underfoot became muddier. She was moving too fast, but she couldn't slow up enough to pick her footing carefully; the breathing, the grunting and the footfalls were too close behind her.

A puddle lay ahead. On both sides, weeds were matted down where the other travelers had attempted to avoid it, but Janet was afraid her shoes would slip on the glistening leaves. She ran down the middle of the path and found that the traction was no better in the puddle. Her feet slid out from under her and she fell on her back, hands flying over her head. One of the men grabbed her wrist roughly and pulled her up. She felt an arm beneath her knees. Wriggling, kicking and shrieking, she was swung up onto his shoulders, his head pressing into her stomach.

She heard Saga calling as he ran toward her. In front of her one of the other men lifted a hunting rifle and fired it into the air. The man carrying her turned around to face Saga.

"Boys, if you put her down right now, go back to the parking area and drive away, I'll forget about this!" Saga shouted, in a voice she hadn't heard before, the voice of a policeman trying to take command of a bad situation.

The man with the gun came up behind her and tapped his companion on the arm. He made a fist, thumb extended, and yanked it in the direction from which they had come. She was wheeled around, and as she turned, she saw the gunman raise his rifle toward Saga and back up. Then she was facing the hillside and moving up it on the shoulders of her captor.

She heard Saga say, "Put her down, now!" Then there was silence, except for the deliberate footsteps and the breathing of the three kidnappers. From her horizontal position, the forest pushing past her was disorienting. It seemed they were making the long trek back to the parking area, so she closed her eyes and tried to think. Saga would not leave things as they stood, she knew, but what would he do?

The gunman was guarding the path. Even though there was now a lively breeze whipping the foliage around, a man pushing through the underbrush was sure to be noticed if he got close. Without being able to predict exactly how, she knew that Saga would intercept them, and that she had to be ready to help him. If she stayed relatively motionless, she might be able to catch the fellow carrying her off guard at some point—perhaps pull her knee up to strike his nose, or cover his eyes with her legs and maybe bite an ear through his mask. If he threw her to the ground, she would scramble away. She had the keys to the car, and there was a gun in the glove compartment.

A gun! Would she be able to use it? Did one just pull the trigger, or was there something else that had to be done first? A "safety catch," whatever that was? In her mind, she practiced the movements that might cause the big man to drop her and tried to anticipate what his reactions would be. Underneath her, he was perspiring in the suffocating breeze. *What a mess,* she thought. Partly for effect, partly out of fear, she began to sob quietly and hung limply against her captor's neck.

By the time they reached the taro fields, the wind had become strong and unstable. It ripped through the broad-leafed plants, releasing loud, sibilant hisses; now and again it unleashed high-speed bursts that almost made her bearer tumble, then relented. On the moving air small raindrops coursed, wetting Janet's arms and legs, her hair, her muddy clothes. The closer they got to the parking lot, the tenser she got, and the harder it was for her to remain limp. Now she could see the cars: Ken's yellow Subaru, Saga's hunter-green Land Rover, and an old two-tone brown, four-door Chevrolet that hadn't been there when she and Saga arrived. The vinyl clad roof of the Chevy was torn, its body rust-ravaged. The men moved toward it. Janet could see the gunman surveying the parking lot, swinging his rifle in an arc in front of him, staggering in the powerful gusts. Janet asked herself the same question that the hooded man must be asking himself: *Where is Saga?*

Barry Saga had hiked double-time out from the falls with his kids and brother and hitched a ride with them part of the way back to Hanalei on a school bus that was picking up residents and tourists to bring them to the shelter in Princeville. Then he ran the remaining two miles along the main road and down the jeep trail. Now, he was crouched low behind a mass of yellow ginger some twenty-five feet across the narrow parking area, assessing the situation. The rifle was his greatest concern. Saga assumed that the fellow holding it would be the last one to get into the car, and that there would be one and only one window of opportunity, measured in seconds, in which to act. He began to inhale and exhale deeply and rhythmically.

The men arrived, with Janet still slung over the shoulders of the tall one. The shooter opened the passenger door wide and braced his body against the inside of it to keep it from slamming shut in the wind. He did not get in immediately, but stood guard for the others, shaking as the door was pummeled by the rapidly-moving air. The tall man carrying Janet swung her to the ground clumsily, gripping her wrist. She fired a sharp kick to his kneecap and tried to yank free, but he held tight and with a swift movement twisted her arm behind her back, pushed her into the back seat and climbed in beside her. The third masked man got into the driver's seat. The gunman turned backwards to get into the car, using one hand to prevent the door from banging his shins and the other to hold his weapon clear.

At that instant Saga vaulted over the ginger plants. With hurricane-force winds now blowing against him, he felt as though he were running under water. Fortunately, the kidnappers couldn't hear him coming, and he was halfway to the car before the gunman glanced back as he slid onto the seat. The gun, in his right hand, was still outside the car, and he aimed it awkwardly backward and fired. The bullet went wildly astray, and the shooter had to kick at the door to keep it from slamming on his hand.

He jumped out of the car, leaned against the door and swung the rifle, waist-high, but Saga was already on him. With a swift left-handed *shuto uke*, Saga deflected the weapon, which fired harmlessly into the trees. He then propelled his weight onto his left foot and executed a sharp *mae-geri* with his right foot into the man's groin. As his foot returned to the ground and the masked gunman pitched forward, Saga thrust the tensed fingers of his right hand up in a blazing *nukite* strike against his opponent's larynx. The gunman collapsed gasping to the ground. Saga snatched the rifle out of his hand and flung it over the fence into a taro field.

Inside the car, Janet's captor had loosed his grip on the arm that he had been holding behind her back. "Don't move," he said as he opened the door, and when she grabbed the door handle on her side, he uncorked a reverse punch, smashing the back of his hand into her face. The blow jerked her head forcefully into the side window. Blood erupted from her nostrils and lightning-strokes of pain obscured her vision as she slumped back into the corner between the seat back and the door.

When the burly masked figure emerged from the car, Saga stepped away. He centered himself, cleared his mind, spread his legs and bent his knees in a *shiko-dachi* stance. Iniki tried to dislodge him. *"Hai!"* he shouted to let the air out of his lungs, lowering his center of gravity and issuing a warning at the same time. The big fellow came at Saga like a Sumo wrestler, arms extended. Saga wheeled around, dropped onto his bent right leg and snapped his left leg outward in a powerful mule kick that sank into the stomach of his assailant just below the solar plexus. The impact knocked the wind out of the dark-skinned giant, but didn't disable him. When Saga swivelled back to a standing position, the other man had assumed a boxing posture. He threw a hard left jab at Saga, who executed a textbook response, striking the man's arm outward away from him with the edge of his right wrist to deflect the punch, then quickly grabbing that same arm at the wrist, and pivoting toward it so that the any right-handed blows his opponent made would fall against his back or head. The assailant struck hard, a kidney punch that made Saga falter. Still holding the man's left wrist with his own left hand, he gathered his strength, chopped sharply down on the nerve center of the upper arm with the edge of his right hand. His opponent cried out, his face inches from Saga's right shoulder. Bending his legs and then straightening them for extra force, the police captain shot his right hand up and back in a fist against the big man's chin. Before his assailant could recover, Saga stepped back with his left foot, cocked his right leg and *shokuto*-kicked into the massive belly.

The big man groaned and staggered back, almost losing his balance to the storm. Saga gave him a couple of solid body punches that brought him down with a crestfallen grunt: "Sonofabitch."

The driver of the car, apparently expecting the fight to go quite otherwise, had hung back, easing his way behind Saga. Now he leaped forward, and grabbed Saga tightly around his arms and chest. Aided by the force of the storm, he rushed Saga headlong toward the trunk of a tall mango tree.

His legs scrabbling against the ground, his arms pinned to his sides, and all his energy gone, Saga had only one blow he could use. *Ushiro atami uchi.*

"Sut!" He drove his head back as hard as he could. The rear of his skull smashed into the ruffian's left eye and the surrounding bone. The man's forward momentum stopped, and his grip weakened. Saga tore the man's thick right wrist and hand from around his chest and twisted the hand counterclockwise with all the force he could muster. The assailant let him go, and landing in a *neko-dachi* crossover stance, he pivoted to face his opponent. He stepped back with his right foot in a *zenkutsu-dachi,* trying to look as though he was drawing on an infinite reservoir of power, while in fact he wasn't sure how much longer he could sustain the fight. Iniki pounded against him and pushed him back a step. He reset his footing and stood with arms extended.

The hoodlum's battered eye was swelling shut. Now he reached into his pocket and brought out a shiny object. He flicked his wrist, and a switchblade slid into view. Saga waited. The other man waited, too. Above them, the branches and upper trunks of the trees were dancing wildly in the gale-force blasts, protesting in groans and shrieks of bark on bark. The first of the cracking sounds could be heard over the thunderous roar of the hurricane, and others soon followed. Snapped branches began to scud along the ground and fly through the air. Rain, driven horizontally, splattered against Saga's chest and the other man's back.

"Now you're talking felony murder!" Saga shouted between his teeth. "A life sentence."

A car door slammed shut. The two men continued to eye one another.

"Janet, stay there," Saga yelled in his command voice, without looking toward her.

Dazed, Janet sized up the situation, saw the two incapacitated kidnappers, saw the knife, saw Saga straining against the wind, and felt its force trying to knock her over, too, as she gripped the door handle. The Land Rover was about ten yards behind her, parked parallel to the Chevy. She couldn't think of any course of action better than her original plan, so she bolted across the muddy lot.

The storm blew her off her feet, her expensive shoes failing her once again on the slippery surface, but she got up quickly and scrambled to the passenger door of Saga's vehicle. By the time she reached it, she already had the key out. Seconds later, the gun was in her hand, heavy and scary. She wheeled around, and her heart nearly stopped at what she saw. Saga was charging at the knife wielder. She watched him grab the other man's arm and shift his stance in order to throw him. In the gale and the mud he misstepped, slipped and fell backwards onto the ground.

Before Janet could get the gun into the air, the masked hoodlum was on top of him. *This is it.* There was no time to think, no time to rebalance her morals or her fears.

She moved her finger to the trigger, and promptly discovered what a safety was, at least on the weapon she was holding. The men were wrestling on the sodden earth. She pushed the trigger guard out of the way, raised the pistol, and fired. The kick almost caused her to drop the thing. Her shot was not aimed at the kidnapper, for fear of hitting Saga; but its report was enough to divert the goon's attention. She staggered forward against the elements, as Saga wriggled free and jumped to his feet again.

The stocky assailant rose. Saga was in front of him, Janet coming up from behind. He jabbed the knife toward Saga and stepped sidelong around him. "Don't move!" Janet screamed in a voice she'd never used before, in a voice of such elemental rage that it frightened even her. "Drop the knife!"

The man took another step.

Janet stopped at the rear of the Chevy, held the gun in front of her, sighted down the barrel at the figure—*Oh, God!*—and fired.

She missed again, but the shot was close enough to spook her target. He turned to face her and let go of the switchblade. Saga stood his ground. Janet moved toward the masked figure. Something about him, something about the set of his shoulders and the stance, was familiar. "Artemis?" she cried out over the hurricane's roar. "Artemis Gabriel?"

"Shit!" The man raised his arms toward his head. "Don't shoot me, ma'am," he said, pulling off his mask. A moment later he was on his back, blinking back the rain and trying to catch his breath, with Barry Saga's foot on his shoulder.

"Do you want to do this the easy way or the hard way?" Saga asked.

"I only try keep you no find out who I was. I di'n't wan' fight one kung fu master."

Janet came to Saga's side. "If I hadn't gone after your gun, you wouldn't have jumped him, would you?"

Saga shook his head. "I was afraid—Well, I'd underestimated you." He looked down at Artemis. "You and your friends are in serious trouble here."

"L-look, I'm jus' o-one independen' contractor, Brah'," Artemis stammered. "I no got axe to grind up. Jus' take Ms. Janet an' hide her away fo' while, dat's all I was hired to do."

"Uh-huh. When my investigators retrieve that rifle, we're going to see whether you and your friends have been contracting out to kill people as well as kidnap them."

"I'm givin' you my word, Cap'n. We no do da kine stuff."

"No. But someone hired you to kidnap Ms. Chase?"

Artemis nodded.

"Who was that?"

The Filipino turned his head away. Saga's hands stiffened, and he started to crouch. Janet touched his shoulder. The storm had washed the blood from her face, but there was a pale pink stain on her tee-shirt. Her nose was swollen and felt broken, and under her eyes the skin had turned purple. Her lips, bruised and puffy, parted in a pained smile. "Let me, Kung Fu Master," she said, and handed the police captain his service revolver.

Saga winced at her in the deluge. "Kung Fu Master? In my head, I have all the moves still, but my body's getting too old to execute them."

She knelt beside Artemis Gabriel. Around them, Iniki was ravaging the countryside, torturing and mutilating the trees, tearing taro plants from their beds, and battering everything with fat raindrops like the ones that stung her face and body. "Artemis, you have no idea what you're involved in!" she said as loudly as she could. "It would be much better for you, much safer for me and my family, if you would just give us the name. Then we can all get out of here before the hurricane beats us to death." She stroked the young man's chin.

"We din't wan' hurt you, Ma'am. Da sitchuashun wen' go outa control—"

"I know," Janet replied reassuringly. "I'm surprised you're involved in this kind of thing at all."

"I do odd jobs, Ma'am, if da price right. And beside, I was afraid dat if I no take da job, maybe some real bad guys get it, guys who won't care dey hurt you or no."

Janet touched her nose, wondering how much worse the "real bad guys" could have been. "Liz told me about her walk with you the other night. She said you are basically a good person, and I believe that. But you have to tell us who hired you, Artemis."

Nearby, a limb split with a painful cracking sound, tore away from its trunk, crashed noisily to the ground and slid toward them like a speeding luge.

"Artemis!"

"It was Nate Chamberlain, Ma'am!" Artemis shouted.

Saga pulled the hefty Filipino to his feet just before the branch raced over the ground on which he had been lying. "Okay, we have to get to shelter right away. This storm's come on too fast. Let's load your buddies into my car, Gabriel, and I'll take you all with us. In case you had any doubt, you're are under arrest. You have the right to remain silent—"

The rear of Saga's vehicle was fitted out as a dog cage, so that Saga could do community policing of stray dogs even when he was off duty. When Artemis Gabriel and his groggy accomplices were safely stowed in the cage, Saga set out for the Princeville Hotel, a steel and concrete edifice on a high promontory overlooking the Pacific that was the designated civil defense shelter for the area.

They transited the jeep road without much difficulty. Twice Saga had to get out to remove tree limbs from their path, and the windshield wipers were increasingly ineffective against the intensity of the rain, but there were no other problems. The main road was a different story. To get to the hotel, they had to cross the truss bridge, and although the visibility was poor, Saga and Janet could see the trusses swaying and the suspended roadbed twisting as the wind rammed tons of rainwater along the river. "We're not going to Princeville," Saga yelled. "Even if we could make it across the bridge, we couldn't get any further." On the other side, the road rose sharply uphill and curved out of sight, but in the short piece of road visible to them, they could see three downed trees blocking the highway.

The sound inside the Land Rover was unbearable. Janet felt as though she were inside a gargantuan blender. The car was being bombarded by streaking rain. Taro leaves smacked against the windows, stuck for a moment and blew off, only to be replaced. Every once in a while, something much harder than a taro leaf struck a fender or door, causing her to jump. Although Saga was standing on the brake pedal, the car was being pushed two or three inches at a time across the slick asphalt road. Above all else was the sound—the angry, malicious sound. "But we can't stay here!" she shouted.

"We're not going to stay here!" Saga shouted back. "If we don't move ourselves, Iniki will move us." He put the car into reverse, backed onto the jeep road and reentered the highway headed the other direction, toward Hanalei. The storm was blowing in from the east and south, he said, which meant that its eye was passing to the west of them. The likelihood of flooding on the north shore was low. "I'm thinking about the Maniniholo dry cave near my house," he hollered. "It's got a northern exposure, so we should be out of the wind, and there's a second way out from there, up the ridge, in case the cave floor floods."

Above the general tumult, Janet could hear a beating sound in the rear of the vehicle. She turned around, and saw Artemis Gabriel banging on the cage to attract their attention. She clambered into the back seat and brought her face close to the wire mesh. "Tell him mo' bettah we head fo' Black Pot Beach," the Filipino shouted, "an' take da back steps up Princeville Hotel."

Janet relayed the message to Saga, who shook his head emphatically. "To do that, we'd have to cross the Hanalei River. Normally, that wouldn't be a problem. But just look out there. That's the river, right in front of us." The normally placid waterway was a boiling, muddy torrent, laden with flotsam.

Janet regained the back seat just as the limb of a koa tree, some eight inches in diameter, slammed onto the hood of the car and bounced to the ground across the street. The vehicle's rear wheels left the ground in the impact, and it spun around in the wind, almost tipping over, before dropping down again. The hood, bent into a "V" and thrown open by the impact, shook violently until it tore free of its mountings and flew off.

Artemis Gabriel gave Janet a wide-eyed explanation of what he had in mind, punctuated by nervous hand movements. His companions, who had revived by now, looked dazed and terrified. "He says," she reported to Saga as she climbed back into her seat, "there's a canoe club."

Saga gave her a dubious look. "Come up with something more realistic!" he bellowed.

There was a loud crash behind them, and a shower of tiny fragments of glass in the back seat. They twisted in their seats and discovered that the windows of both rear doors were gone. Torrential rain burst into the car as if from a fire hose, spraying everyone and everything. Artemis Gabriel, the hair on the left side of his head sparkling with tiny souvenirs of the explosion, mouthed the word "coconut," made an oval shape with his hands and jerked them from right to left in front of him. Janet felt water splashing at her feet. Looking down, she saw that a pool was forming on the floor.

"We don't have a lot of time to sit and reflect, Barry." She put her hand over his on the gearshift lever. "It's me, isn't it? You're trying to find a safer alternative for me than crossing the river." She leaned over and, as Iniki blew through the Land Rover, she moved her mouth to his ear. "We're stuck, Captain!" she said, trying to impart the supreme confidence she had in him. "I'm a good swimmer. Go for it."

They were about a mile and a half from the turnoff for Hanalei Bay. Sega set their battered conveyance back on the road and headed west. In that direction there was little forest close to the road. A few minutes into the ride they saw a lone kukui tree about three stories high collapse into the road ahead of them. To the left of the road, there was a marsh, and to the right, a steep embankment leading to a broad ditch filled with water. "It's too big for the two of us to move by ourselves," Saga shouted.

Again, the faintest hint of a human voice reached their ears from the rear of the vehicle. Janet turned and knelt on her seat. The back seat was covered with broken glass, so she stretched herself out through the driving rain and grabbed the heavy wire screening.

"Tell him it's time to deal!" Artemis Gabriel screamed.

Within seconds four strong men and one willing woman were tugging at the vanquished tree with all their might, ducking airborne debris while they strained to pull the tree aside far enough to let them past. The trunk was still gripping the earth with a third of its root system, and it was stronger than the five of them. They could lift its trunk off the ground but couldn't swing it sideways off the road. The winds were so strong that the five could hardly stand up, and the Land Rover, deprived of more than half a ton of human cargo, was skidding to the edge of the road. Saga gathered the others together. "We have to pick it up high enough to drive under," he shouted. "Jan, we lift, you drive."

She ran back to the vehicle, shielding her face from the hurricane's bite with her hand. As she did so, Iniki flicked at her with a fingerlet burst of air that knocked her flat against the pavement. She crawled the rest of the way, but when she opened the door to climb in, a second powerful gust wrenched the door from her hand and ripped it off its hinges. It was as if the hurricane were toying with her like a cat with a mouse. She grabbed for the steering wheel. The driver's side of the vehicle rose up, and Janet Chase was lifted off the ground. She pulled herself in as the one front wheel still in contact with the ground skidded off the road and the rear wheel thumped against a rock. The Land Rover turned face first down the hill, and settled back onto all four wheels, leaving Janet staring straight ahead into the ditch.

The best way, she told herself as her heart raced, *is to think about doing what you have to do, not what's going on around you.* Saga had left the engine running. She released the emergency brake and put the gearshift into reverse. The wheels spun, and, in front, began to dig into the mud. She took her foot off the gas and pushed the clutch pedal down. Looking back, she could see that the rear wheels were still on asphalt and realized that the all-wheel drive was going to work against her. She disengaged it and put the car in reverse again but kept the clutch pedal depressed.

She pressed on the gas pedal, racing the engine while she tried to decide how to handle the vehicle. When she turned around to look at the rear wheels once more, her foot slipped off the clutch. There was a high-pitched whine as the rear tires bit through the rain slick and began to burn tread against the roadway. The rear end of the Land Rover moved left and then right. On its return, the right rear wheel connected with the rock that had blocked it from sliding of the road a moment before. The extra traction was enough to set the vehicle moving backward. Janet didn't know what to do other than to keep the gas pedal floored. The smell of burning rubber invaded her nostrils as the battered vehicle gyrated back onto the road.

The men were positioned at the bases of the main limbs of the kukui tree, and when they saw Janet regain the highway, they heaved upward against its mass and against the storm. They could give her no more than five feet clearance, and that only momentarily. It wasn't quite enough, but it was all she was going to get. Still gunning the engine, she engaged the all-wheel drive again, jammed the transmission into first gear and popped the clutch, intentionally this time. Her head was buzzing and her body tingled. The tires squealed. The car jumped forward, zigzagged and then straightened out. It crashed through the opening the men had left her, tearing branches from the tree. Janet's vision was obscured for a few seconds, and then she was out the other side. The men came running up to the car, cheering loudly, and for a moment she basked in the triumph.

Saga mounted the passenger seat and pointed up toward the top, or what used to be the top, of his Land Rover. Looking up, Janet saw that much of the roof had been peeled back by a branch that had pierced it like a can opener as she drove beneath the tree. The cloth innards hung down in the back seat, and the sheet-metal top stuck up like the cover of a jack-in-the-box. She clutched at her throat as Artemis Gabriel and his companions tucked themselves back into dog cage, whooping and applauding like crazy men.

For the rest of the drive the road was littered, but all of the obstacles could either be driven over or negotiated around. They made a right turn onto Aku Road, which ran down to the bay, and then again onto Weke Road, which paralleled the beach and ended at the Hanalei River.

On these side roads, the nature of the litter changed. This was a residential area, and the streets were full of roofing tin and shingles, furniture, books and magazines, compact disks, audio and video tapes, clothing, broken bottles and jars, two-by fours, appliances and other indicia of civilized life being methodically disassembled by the unreasoning forces of Gaia. At one point, Janet drove Saga's car over the remains of a small house that had been blown off its foundation, then slid on its side out into the street and collapsed. By the time they reached the river, three of the vehicle's four tires were flat.

The final task for the all-suffering conveyance was to take the little party up the access road to the Hanalei Canoe Club. There, Saga led the way on foot, over the fence and onto the grounds, where they found their next mode of transportation. A hand-hewn oceangoing outrigger canoe sat upended on a low platform, secured to stakes to keep it from blowing away. Artemis and the man who had punched Janet—a pleasant-looking Hawaiian, it turned out, more nervous than tough—attacked the stakes in the driving rain, the wind pushing them away every time they stood up, while the other three held the canoe down. In the softened ground the spikes yielded easily, and the five of them dragged the canoe across the ground to the launching area.

Janet liked canoeing on a peaceful lake or a summertime river, with the sun high in the sky or perhaps even on a warm, moonlit evening. But not now. The little Hanalei River was out of control, commanded by a mad, alien presence that had infused it with a power too monstrous for it to handle. Even in its swollen condition, the river was not more than sixty feet across, its opaque brown flux all rapids, hydraulic holes and breakers. *Breakers!*

Inside the canoe, there were six double seats, and underneath the seats twelve paddles. No life jackets. Saga tapped Janet on the shoulder. She and their three companions leaned in to listen to what he had to say.

"Okay!" Saga shouted. "Here's the drill. We use seats three, four and five. Gabriel and I on number five, you two guys on number four and you, Jan, on number three. We put in with everybody in the canoe except me. I'll push off, and when I do, I'll be pushing the canoe around so it faces upstream. That's right, upstream, even though we want to go downstream to get to the stairway. It's the only way to control the thing in this current."

Artemis chimed in. "Captain, dere's rapids below us here. Never min' we wan' go downstream, we gotta avoid dose if we can do. How 'bout 'stead of try get downstream, we go paddle like hell, right into dem waves upriver dere, like you say, and ease lef' as we go. Li dat, we maybe slide sideways into dat one big eddy across da way dere. Den go climb da bank and walk from dere."

Saga took a good look at the river. After a moment, he nodded and clapped Artemis' shoulder. "That's your second good idea of the day. You may redeem yourself yet! So, the plan changes, Jan. I want you to take the number one seat, right up in the prow. The rest of us are going to be more or less mindless muscle on this ride. You have two important jobs. One, deflect any big debris that comes at us with your paddle, and two, shade us left a little at a time, but keep our nose from swinging downriver. To turn us left, you paddle right, and—"

Janet held up a hand. "—I think I understand that part, Skipper!" she yelled.

A moment later, they were on the river. Janet, sitting up front and at a distance from the men, felt alone and less helpful than she knew Saga wanted her to be. She couldn't see well with the rain coming straight at her keeping her eyes closed to slits. The prow was high most of the time and bobbing so fiercely that she could barely paddle. There was a lot of flotsam on the water, but because of the waves, she couldn't see it until it was almost on them. When she concentrated on being alert to the large branches, free-floating building joists and other torpedo-like hazards, the nose of the canoe tended to drift too far either right or left out of the waves, and she had to lean out and paddle hard to bring it around again—a job better done in the rear, where at the moment all energy was being expended in staying upriver of the rapids. It was the type of experience for which her psyche was not designed. *Just think about what you have to do,* she reminded herself.

A wooden ziggurat, five steps and a landing liberated from someone's staircase, tumbled out of a wave. She struck at it with her paddle, but its mass and momentum were too great. It caught the canoe on the starboard side of the prow, forcing the craft hard to port. She hear Saga shouting, "Paddle hard left!" Her arms burned as she tore at the river, but it was too late. All her strength, and all the strength of the men in the rear, was insufficient to do more than slow the deflection of the craft toward the rapids. If it weren't for the outriggers, the turning canoe would have flipped over, but it was holding upright as it began to take the currents abeam.

Desperately looking for salvation, she glanced at the eddy that had been their destination. In a recess in the shoreline, its comparatively quiet surface was broken by several saplings that probably stood out of water during normal weather. A safe place, but they were drifting away from it. She judged that there were fifteen yards of roiling water between her and the nearest sapling, not quite the length of her swimming pool.

Well, Jan, she said to herself. *You're going into the river once we hit the rapids, anyway, and by then, it'll be all over.*

Saga saw her stand up on seat number one. He watched aghast as she dived over the prow of the canoe. Only after she had disappeared did he see the line snaking out after her. The canoe continued to head for the rapids. It began to rock violently. The port outrigger came down hard on a submerged boulder and snapped off. They had lost their bilateral stability and were starting to roll over.

Janet was blinded by the silt-laden current. Her only sense of direction came from the current itself; she knew she wanted to cross it. The pressure was so strong that she instantly doubted she could do it. Laps in a swimming pool were no preparation at all for what she had what she was now struggling to do. Fifteen yards across, less than the length of her pool, and it might as well have been fifteen miles. She kept as low as she could, kicking across the current with forceful thrusts of her legs and grappling blindly in the silted water for handholds on a rocky riverbed that she could not see. Her left hand was squeezed tightly around the line, which meant she had only one hand free to pull herself across the bottom; she had to let go of one secure hold before she could search for another.

The line was still slack, and she prayed that it would not become taut before she reached safety. If it did, she would not be able to hold it, and she would have failed Saga and the others, for whom she was the only hope. All at once, a jet of erratically-moving water seized her and slammed her hard against a large boulder. Pain shot through her left side like a hot knife. She gasped and breathed water into her trachea, almost choked, and coughed up the air that had filled her lungs. Her dive had been intended as a hold-your-breath plunge for still water. Now she had to surface. The challenge of swimming against the current while she rose to breathe was almost too much, and she lost position.

When she came into the air, she saw that she had drifted downstream, and, worse, that the canoe was in the rapids and there was no one in it. Four lives in her hands, and it might already be too late. Janet dived again, kicking with a strength she didn't know she could summon. She clawed with all her might across the river bed. Pain sent sheets of light across the backs of her eyes. Oblivious to the breaking of her fingernails, oblivious to the fractured ribs that screamed for her to stop moving, she drove herself forward.

The four men had felt the canoe tipping over as the rapids took it. "Grab the outrigger and don't let go!" Saga shouted. A heartbeat later they were in the water, tossing around like flotsam. Iniki, blowing oceanward down the river valley, hurled spray, leaves and grit into their faces, obscuring their vision. The upended canoe lurched and twisted like a bucking bronco trying to throw them.

Saga looked downstream to see how far out to sea the debris from the river was blowing, but couldn't tell. His only goal now was to stay alive for his sons. It looked hopeless....

And then the stern of the canoe came around, and they were parallel to the current again. The craft swung out of the angry flow, and into the margin downriver of the eddy. They could see Janet in the calmer water waving at them, her hair slicked back and glistening, one hand resting on the taut prow line, which she had looped and knotted around a tree. The men made their way to the line and pulled themselves hand over hand to safety. When he reached Janet, Saga held onto the tree trunk with one hand, slipped the other arm around her and kissed her. She shuddered, and he said, "Still in shock?"

"No, no, it's my side," Janet responded, shifting her position. "I got banged up out there."

She came out of the water self-conscious about her clinging clothes and her appearance and wincing with pain, but jubilant. The men gave her three hasty cheers, and then, with Iniki thundering around them, they all set off. Janet took two steps and collapsed in agony from the shooting spasms in her side. Looking up from where she lay, she saw the man who had punched her standing over her. He turned and bent at the knees, silently offering her his back. She raised herself and draped her arms around his neck. He put his hands under her thighs and stood up. With the others they hastily made their way to the mouth of the river, where concrete steps led from the beach up a north-facing cliff to the Princeville hotel. Fifteen minutes later, they were sitting in the expansive lobby, recovering from their ordeal.

Iniki was tearing at the roof of the hotel, the sounds of its destructiveness echoing in the high-ceilinged hall. Before their eyes, the interior space was being transformed into a water garden, with rivulets and streams flowing out of the ceiling and over the balconies. The hurricane had ripped away part of the upper structure of the hotel, and in the process pulled apart the sprinkler system. Open pipes had pumped half a million gallons of water into hallways and bedrooms before the shutoff valves could be closed.

Janet Chase watched soggy wallpaper curl away from the walls of the mezzanine and brightly-colored sofas on the lobby floor grow stained from the dirty water cascading over a balcony. She laughed out loud at the bad joke that Iniki had made of the elegant hotel, at her mauled fingernails, at the pain that erupted with every laugh, and at the exhilaration that came from saving lives that but for her would probably have been lost.

12

"What do you mean, wait for Iniki?" Stella Chase demanded. "It's two in the morning, and the hurricane isn't expected for half a day. Are we just going to sit here?"

Nate Chamberlain leaned his head back against the cushion of the armchair. "Do you like this one, George? She seems like the bitchy type to me."

Akamai reflected for a minute. He let out a chuckle. "She's trying to work on your mind, Nate. I've spent most of the week with her, and I've never heard her talk that way."

Nate gave Stella a crooked smile. "You trying to mess with my head? You're either very brave or very stupid, Stella. Which is it?"

"Neither," Stella answered. "I'm a Buddhist. What's your religion?"

Akamai touched her on the knee lightly with one finger. Stella read the gesture, along with his laugh a moment earlier, as saying that a good guy/bad guy game with Nate Chamberlain was too risky.

"I think ol' Georgie wants you to put a sock in it, Honey," Nate sneered. "And that's real good advice, because this event is about George and me. You're of no more consequence to me than that gekko on the wall by your ear."

Stella turned her head. Nate raised the light crossbow with one hand and reached behind his neck with the other. Akamai shouted, "No!" and rose out of his seat. Nate fired, and in an instantaneous, sure motion reloaded the bow with the bolt he had just taken from his quiver. The head of the first bolt nicked the tip of Stella's nose and split the little lizard in two.

"Sit down, George! When it's time to get up, I'll let you know."

"Don't harm her, Nate, or—"

"Or what, wise one? I'll let you know when I'm down to my last bolt, and then you can begin or-elsing me. Until then, I'm in charge here." Nate turned his attention back to Stella. "Saliva is a good disinfectant, Sugar, and not a bad astringent. You may want to—" He licked his finger and tapped his nose. "There you go. Let me tell you where you stand. It's not inconvenient that you're with us. I was hoping we would find at least one member of the Chase family tonight. But the substance of this event, what I'm really here for, is between George Akamai and me. Akamai, the wise one. Did you know that's what 'akamai' means? George, the wise one, and Nate, the wise guy." He snickered. "George, the pureblood; Nate, the halfbreed. George, the impecunious public servant, and Nate, the wealthy bum. There are almost three decades of common experience, of male bonding, of love and hate, between George and me. We haven't seen each other in a couple of years, and we don't need any interruptions. So don't presume to speak, to sneeze or even to yawn tonight unless you are given permission to do so."

"May I comment, Nate?" Akamai asked.

"At your own risk, sure."

"Nate and I grew up together, Stella. We travelled together, discovered girls together, all that stuff. His father was very kind to me, very kind."

"Ever the master of understatement," Nate said.

Stella wanted to ask what Nate's aside meant. Was it a passing reference to ancient sibling rivalries, or a hint of an enduring problem between them? The arrow protruding from the wall a few inches from her ear counselled silence, though, and for his part Akamai seemed intent on ignoring the comment.

"Over the years, this guy and I have had our differences," he continued. "When we were teenagers, we went through a period when we fought some. I dislocated Nate's jaw with a roundhouse punch one time. I forget what the issue was. Do you remember, Brah?"

"I think that was when we were trying to score the same *wahine,* Braddah. The one that lived out Kekaha way?"

"That's right. Kalia. I threw the winning punch, but you ended up with her. A while later, we had a little debate about skin color, his and mine, and he hit me so hard on the side of my head that I couldn't hear out of one ear for six months. So there's a history of, what—affectionate violence?"

"Yeah," Nate said, baring his teeth in a smile. "I like that. Affectionate violence. The more affectionate, the more violent."

Akamai fell silent. He stared reflectively at Nate. To Stella it seemed that a great sadness was settling over him. Beneath the smooth skin of his cheeks, his jaw clenched and unclenched.

"Didn't you like that, Georgie? The more affectionate, the more violent?"

"It's bullshit. What's this all about, Nate?"

"Not yet, Brah."

"It has to do with the Ranch, doesn't it?"

"I said, not yet!" The whistle of the bow was like that of a sharp scythe cutting through green hay. The bolt went between Akamai's right arm—which was resting on the sofa back—and his side, putting a hole in the policeman's aloha shirt and drilling through the sofa into the wall.

"I didn't cut you, did I, George?" Nate asked, resetting the weapon with a new bolt.

Akamai shook his head as he pulled his shirt clear of the bolt's tail. To Stella, who was desperately trying to remain composed in the presence of an armed madman, her lieutenant looked unusually calm, almost serene. She hoped that it was because he knew Nate much better than she did.

"Let me tell you about Oregon," Nate offered. That's a part of my life I haven't shared with you, Brah."

"Stella lives in Oregon," Akamai said.

"Really. Portland, Sugar? Me, too. Maybe we can have coffee together some time. Wouldn't that be nice?"

Should she answer, or keep a sock in it? Whatever psychology Akamai had tried was no more effective than what she, untrained, could do. "I'd like that," she answered, "so long as you didn't, you know—" She opened her hand in the direction of the crossbow.

"—Bring my little archery kit? Cute, Sugar. But who knows, if we make it through the day—and that's a big 'if'—perhaps it would be interesting to get together. You'll have to give me your address," he added with a laugh. "Anyway, why am I in Portland? Well, after college—wait, back up a little. College—I studied surfing for the most part, minored in psychotropic drugs, but managed to con a B.A. in art out of that shit school I attended in southern California. After that, to no one's surprise, I couldn't find a decent job. The old man had supported me all through college, but after that the deal was that I could come back and work on the ranch if I wanted, or I could go anywhere else I wanted with zero money from home. As usual, old Web was using his wealth to manipulate my future. You got a slightly better deal, I think, Georgie."

"I never took any money from your dad after college. He offered to help me get started over here, but I didn't want that any more than you did."

"You didn't get any help from Web? My ass. How do you think you got onto the police force?"

"By scoring highest of all the applicants the year I applied. He did write a letter of recommendation, which I asked him if he would do. Other than that, it was a pure merit decision."

"Other than that? You can delude yourself, if you want to, but don't try to delude Sugar and me. Web Chamberlain has more influence on the police department on this island than a twenty-five foot curl has on a novice surfer, and you know it."

"You're right. All I can say is that I took no money from him, and it happens that I merit-tested best of all the candidates."

"Fine. Then your conscience is clear. Mine isn't. I came back to the big warm teat of the Makai Ranch, working for a father who was intent on making his only son into a better man than he himself was. A noble objective you say, missy?" Stella said nothing, but tried to enfold Nate's mistrustful gaze in a comforting one of her own. "Yeah, maybe. Maybe not noble enough, God knows he wasn't much of a role model."

"He loves you, Brah."

"Yeah, in his own demented way. You and I talked about that before I left for Oregon. Frankly, I don't think it matters. Love can do as much damage as hate. He fucked me up, Braddah. The constant measuring, monitoring, advising, exhorting. All I wanted to from the time I got back to the time I left was to get to a place where I didn't have to meet any expectations at all, least of all Web Chamberlain's. And that's where I am now. Living in a rat hole in Portland—since my loving pop wouldn't send any money—collecting welfare and doing some cash jobs. Running numbers, cutting heroin—righteous deeds like that. Dropping acid, spending a lot of time on the street with the derelict Indians. Good people, they are. No expectations, no pretensions."

Stella leaned forward.

"What is it, honey?" Nate said.

"I was just wondering—I don't know if I should ask—"

"I'll give you one free ticket. Ask away."

"Don't you have any expectations of your own? For yourself, I mean? Feel free to call me Stella, by the way."

"Expectations for myself, Sugar? Not that I know. Maybe I would have if the ogre of the Makai Ranch hadn't tried so hard to impose his on me."

Stella shook her head. "I guess I used the wrong word. Goals, a sense of direction, a self-definition, a quest?"

"Ach!" Nate swept her question away with a wave of his hand. "Don't give me that neoBuddhist shit."

"Excuse me," Stella returned, offended, "did you say 'neoBuddhist *shit*'?"

Akamai moved to cover her, but his friend held his hand up. "It's okay, George. It's okay. My fault. I apologize—Stella. I didn't mean to defame your religion. Truth is, I share the Buddhist fascination with enlightenment."

"The first step to enlightenment is knowing yourself, Nate."

"Now there is where you're wrong," Nate said, wagging his finger emphatically. "The first step to enlightenment is three little letters—LSD. You can spend your life conditioning yourself to be receptive to the void if you want to. Me, I've achieved enlightenment at least once a week for the past two years. You believe in a spiritual plane of being that you can achieve some day through meditation and right acts. I visit that plane whenever I want."

Akamai shifted in his chair. "Are you visiting it now, Nate?"

"Christ, no. Do I seem spaced out to you, officer?" Chamberlain opened his eyes wide and tapped with his fingers against his temple.

"Nate, you're sitting there with a loaded crossbow, acting in a way I've never seen before. I'd just like to know what I'm dealing with, is all."

"No, George. No, I'm not under the influence. It's just—well, other people, mainly my father, say they've noticed a change in my personality since I left home. I like to think it's a change for the better, but Web certainly doesn't share that view. What it is, George—after spending so much time in the ultimate reality, I've become bored with the normal plane of existence. Impatient, even contemptuous, knowing how insignificant the affairs of daily life are. You remember from growing up with me how ornery I used to get when I was bored, which was a lot of the time on this fucking rock."

Akamai did not hide his displeasure. "LSD has changed your life, is that it? You're a living testimonial, Nate."

"I don't think it would be a good idea to try to lecture me, old friend."

"Just what is that thing, Nate? The crossbow, what is it? A way of easing the boredom? Putting juice into your life? A warm-up for a confrontation with your father?"

Nate laughed convulsively. "Let's see. Yes, yes and no. How's that? Actually, you two have provided an incredible segue here. Stella, if I didn't know better, I'd think you were prescient." He laughed again. "This implement," he said, raising the crossbow and turning it in the air, "This—made it myself. Not such a hard project, really, except for the triggers. It's got two. See them? Normally, you put a multi-trigger like this on the big heavy bows, one to sort of cock the mechanism and the other to release, because otherwise the force you would have to exert to pull the trigger would be so great it would screw up your aim. With a bow this light, though, I found that a trigger that required any real force at all would also tend to move the bow too much. Same problem, for a different reason. Getting the spring loading right was a bitch of a problem."

Stella took the fact that Nate was now using her name to be a good sign, an indication that she had made some kind of personal mark, that perhaps he was displaying some feeling for her. His lack of focus, the mental drift, though, remained worrisome because of the object he was holding aloft for their approval. Nate lowered the weapon to his lap.

"The reason I came here with my little bow tonight, Georgie, was to share the transcendent experience with you, to take you part way on the journey that I've been on. Do you understand?"

"That's it? You want me to trip with you? And you thought I'd refuse and you'd have to force me?"

"That's it, Braddah."

"Either force me or kill me, Nate?"

Nate Chamberlain turned his head aside for a moment. He seemed to be looking for something inside himself, but when he turned back, his face was the same remote mask it had been when they walked into the living room and found him seated there.

"Force you or kill you. Yeah, Georgie. I guess so."

"Bullshit." Akamai stood up, pointing his finger. "That's bullshit, Brah."

"Sit down, goddammit!" Nate shouted, pointing the crossbow at Akamai's head. "Sit down!"

Akamai raised his arms and spun around to face the wall.

"Here, I'll make it easy for you. Shoot if you want to, but if you want to talk—"

The bolt shrieked past his left ear and buried its head in the wall. Holding his position, Akamai said, "About three and a half inches to the right ought to do it, Nate. But could you come over and kiss me good-bye, first?" There was no sound for a few seconds, then he heard sniffling and the sound of the bow being reset. "I didn't want to do this, George, Goddammit."

Akamai turned around slowly. Nate had the crossbow extended at arm's length. A streak of tears ran from the corners of his eyes down both sides of his nose. He was looking for a reason not to do what he was fully prepared to do.

"I don't want you to do it, either, Braddah. As far as tripping with you is concerned, if that's what you really want, I have no problem with that, as long as nobody in this room turns me in afterward."

"How about sitting down, douchebag? Do you have a problem with that?"

"No." The policeman resumed his seat. "You know, it used to be that when I got pissed off at you, I could say so without having to worry that you might shoot an arrow through my chest. It used to be that if you were pissed off at me, you would say so rather than threaten me and people I care about with deadly force. This is about a hell of a lot more than one night's magical mystery tour, Nate. You want to tell me about it, or not?"

Nate grinned. "Hell, yes, man. I do want to tell you. But I can't."

"Because I'm a cop?"

His friend gave a reluctant, affirmative shrug. Akamai caught his breath. His eyes became moist, too. "Whatever this thing is, you're thinking about killing me over it."

Another shrug, followed by silence.

Stella ran her fingers through her hair and clasped them together behind her head in a gesture of openness, of trust. She bent her head backwards and pulled her hands down against the back of her neck. It had been a long day. She was not sleepy; the circumstances prevented that. Her mental faculties, though, were not at their optimum, to say the least. "May I ask—?"

The half-Hawaiian stared at her, and she stopped. "At first," he said, "I was angry that you were here. You can see that the situation between George and me is—is not necessarily served by the presence of a stranger. But now, I'm not so sure, Stella. Your presence has been a restraining influence on the lieutenant. Without it, I expect he would have tried something foolhardy by now. And I'm pleased to have discovered our mutual interest in enlightenment."

"Are you and George going to take LSD? If you are, I'd be willing to serve as a guide."

"A *guide*?"

"I understand that in psychedelic sessions it's advisable to have a guide."

"Yes, it is, particularly for the uninitiated." Nate gave her a fierce look.

"Well, I know, of course, that you are an experienced user, but George isn't, and with you under—"

"Ah! That's your point, is it? You would remain above the fray and help this humble acid enthusiast and your straying copper through our drug-induced nightmares. Have you performed this kind of service before?"

"No, not really. But I'm the only other person here."

"True enough, but a bad guide can be worse than none at all." Nate paused. "Did you know, according to Leary, Metzner and Alpert—the father, the son and the holy ghost—the guide should not separate herself from the psychedelic experience?"

"No, I—" That was exactly what Stella was trying to head off. "The path I'm on right now wouldn't permit—"

"Oh, come now, Stella. The days when humans could—or should—take refuge in dogma are long gone. If your religion is a constraining rather than a liberating experience, you ought to kick its ass out of your life."

"Nate, why not leave her out of it?" Akamai interjected. "Christ, she could have stayed in Poipu tonight at the house her family rented, and I talked her into coming up here for safety's sake."

"If it'll make you feel any better, George, she wouldn't have been any better off at that house tonight."

Akamai started to ask what he meant, but Nate raised his hand and shook his head. "The hurricane is supposed to hit late this afternoon. Maybe we should get started. The effects of the salts will be completely over in half a day, which would leave us in good shape to cope with the storm when it hits."

"I can't believe you would force me to do this," Stella murmured. "I've done nothing to you, and yet, on a whim, you're content to destroy my whole inner life."

Nate watched the tears well and said, "Not destroy, Stella. Enhance. Many, many people use LSD or mescaline as aids in reaching a state of mind where they're receptive to enlightenment. There's a whole literature on the use of psychedelics in connection with the Buddhist religious experience, sistah. You could look it up. What difference is there—what *difference* is there between using drugs, as we're going to do tonight, and using pain, or fasting or chanting, as the ancients prescribed, to reach that mindset?"

"On my path, I won't be using any of those methods, Nate. I will learn and prepare, listen to the voice of God inside me, and if I'm enlightened, it will be because I'm ready. If you try to leap ahead of your preparedness, the transcendental experience is incomprehensible."

"Some guru who was charging you by the hour told you that. Not a very good one, either. Buddhists don't believe in God."

"What?"

"Buddha spoke against belief in a supreme spiritual authority. Right?"

Stella glared at the gaunt bowman, her mind suddenly numb. The Swami had claimed to speak to God and his minions, and to be able to teach her how to do the same. She turned to Akamai, not knowing what to say. If she challenged Nate's assertion and was wrong, her embarrassment would be so heavy that it would crush her.

"Tell her, George. Tell her!"

Akamai slid his hand over Stella's. "I'm no expert, Stella, but I think what Nate's talking about is that Buddhism teaches that there is no greater authority than the individual, and that you develop that authority by following the eightfold path."

"I've seen the ultimate unity, Stella," Nate interjected. "You haven't, so don't try to tell me about the transcendental experience."

Stella felt like a fool. Nate couldn't have wounded her more deeply if he had put a bolt through her heart. Of course he wasn't an authority, and neither was Akamai, but the accuracy of their understanding wasn't what bothered her. What bothered her was that she had never read the teachings of the Buddha. She had simply taken the pontifications of Swami Shivalinga as the revealed wisdom of Buddhist thought.

"Nate, for God's sake," Akamai boomed. Stella squeezed his hand. Her inner voice, whatever its source, had just told her that it would be best not to resist Nate's proposal.

"Don't, George. It's all right. We're all talking to one another, now, instead of at one another. If I have to take this trip with the two of you—" She took a breath, caught in a conflict of beliefs. "—then there's a reason for it. There are no accidents in life," she sighed.

"Hold on. This isn't just another event in your daily life," Akamai objected. "Some people die from this stuff. Some go crazy. And given Nate's frame of mind, it's not a good idea for you to be losing contact with reality."

Stella glanced at Nate. He slumped back in his seat, lifted the weapon and aimed it first at one of them and then at the other, then lowered it again. "George has a point," he conceded. "I've never done anything violent under the influence of acid, but I have seen demons, and if I were armed, I might have shot at them. Here's what we'll do, George. After we drop the acid, I'll give you the bow and the bolts and you can lock them away somewhere."

At Nate's request, Stella brought water for each of them. She shook as she handed Akamai his glass. He took her hand, still holding the glass, in both of his. His grasp was gentle, warm and steady, his palms and fingers reassuringly dry. She felt calmness and composure radiating up her arms and into her heart. She nodded at him and smiled.

When she gave Nate his glass, he pointed to the low table next to him. On it were twenty tiny tablets. "Five for each of you. Ten for me. Fifty micrograms per pill, George. A dose big enough to give you the full effect but not incapacitate you. If you don't mind, let me see you take them." Once they had all ingested the LSD, Nate disarmed the crossbow and handed it and his quiver to Akamai, who stashed them on the floor of the hall closet and locked the door. The disappearance of the weapon and the fact that the drug had no immediate effect relieved most of the tension in the living room. Nate suggested that the others might be more comfortable, once the drug began to work its magic, if they were lying down, and not too close to one another. "You'll find that this is a very personal journey and that sensing the presence of others is not conducive to a happy trip."

Akamai relinquished the sofa to Stella, and lay down on the floor with his head on a small pillow.

"This is juvenile, Nate," he remarked.

"Yeah, the run-up can be childish, but the experience itself is definitely for adults only." The core of it, see, is a dissolving of the boundaries between self and other, between illusion—which you would call the real world, George—and the ultimate reality—for which you probably have no name. Now, Stella, you will be able to relate to the trip better because of your experience with meditation, but even so, the loss of differentiation will scare you, Sugar, and probably cause some weird and disturbing visions. Let me read you something," he suggested, pulling from his rear pocket a dog-eared paperback copy of the Leary-Metzner-Alpert book, *The Psychedelic Experience*:

"You must be ready to accept the possibility that there is a limitless range of awareness for which we now have no words; that awareness can expand beyond the range of your ego, your self, your familiar identity, beyond everything you have learned, beyond your notions of space and time, beyond the differences which usually separate people from each other and from the world around them—You must remember, too, that the experience is safe (at the very worst, you will end up the same person who entered the experience), and that all of the dangers which you have feared are unnecessary productions of your mind. Whether you experience heaven or hell, remember that it is your mind which creates them. Avoid grasping the one or fleeing the other. Avoid imposing the ego game on the experience—"

Feeling nothing unusual, the threesome conversed for a while longer. Akamai was not interested in the metaphysical dimension of what he considered to be nothing more than drug-enhanced dreaming. Whatever it produced would overtake him soon enough, and soon enough be over. Then the hurricane would arrive and give him a more corporeal, more serious concern.

"Hey, Nate," he said, changing the subject, "I've been trying to figure out why you came back here without telling me. I mean, why you came back is no mystery; you're father's about to sell the Ranch out from under you, and you wanted to have some say in the matter. But why didn't you call me? At first, I thought, Well, maybe he's only here for a few days, and things are moving fast at the Ranch, bidders parading in and whatnot, but I put myself in your shoes, and that excuse doesn't cut it."

"You know damn well why I didn't phone you, Akamai." The edge that had gone out of Nate's voice was back. On the sofa, Stella, who was staring at the ceiling, thought she saw his face turn bright red and even enlarge a bit at the periphery of her vision, but when she turned to look, everything seemed normal.

"No, honestly," Akamai responded. "I was hurt. Barry Saga told me he thought he saw you at the house when he came out to visit Web, but I was so sure he was mistaken that I never followed it up."

"This is not the time to be upsetting one another, George. We should be calming ourselves, getting ready for the visions."

"Fine, then just answer my question, and I won't ask anything more. Why didn't you call?"

Nate fell back in his chair and put his hands over his eyes. He sat like that for some period of time, leading Stella to think that perhaps the drug had taken hold, that as a frequent user Nate might be more susceptible to it. Eventually, though, his fingers parted enough that he could see Akamai, and his palms separated over his mouth. As though he were announcing it through a bullhorn, he said simply, "The will."

Akamai frowned. "The will, did you say?"

"The will."

"What kind of an answer is that? What will?"

"You said you weren't going to ask any more questions. Anyway, you know exactly what I'm talking about. Now let's be quiet for a while, shall we?"

Stella turned back to the ceiling. *The will.* Could Nate be referring to anything other than his father's will? Was there something in it that would cause a rift between these lifelong friends? She could speculate, but she felt now that she must let go of earthly matters and open herself to the impending internal voyage. As she watched, the ceiling seemed to approach her. The sheet rock, which had been up to now an undifferentiated ivory plane, began to reveal itself as a terrain of little hillocks and depressions. At first, they seemed to be arranged at random, but after examining them for a while, she realized that they were arrayed in patterns, some abstract and some more recognizable. There were faint shadows between and among the subtle undulations of this landscape, not grey shadows but colored, and in various frequencies of the visible spectrum. Certain areas were cooler and darker, some warmer and brighter. The dispute between Nate and Akamai, whatever its nature, faded into triviality in the face of the mystical light show unfolding before her eyes—or was it behind her eyes? Two tiresome boy-men, burdened by a foolish lifelong love-hate relationship that held both of them back. She would have to lecture them about it, but later. A glass-like wall seemed to be bringing itself into being between them and her. So much the better.

She noticed an unusual clumsiness, a weightiness, in the musculature of her body, and with it both an embarrassment that the body was part of her and a relief that she had no need to make the massive thing operate for the moment. Gradually, the objects at the edges of her vision melted into streams of color that rose to the ceiling and merged into the landscape there, enriching its hues and engorging it. After a while, the swollen ceiling burst open, and shards of pure color and ethereal texture washed not over her but right through her, as if she had lost all substantiality. The space above the ceiling was a field of white light. She sensed that it went on forever, and longed to dive into it and swim away, not using her hateful arms and legs, not even taking them with her. Just her mind, navigating the infinite mind, the pure void. The infinite mind. *Are you there?*

Though she could not move, the light obliged her by coming toward her. She saw that it was a brilliant cloud, made up of tiny presences, like raindrops but much smaller and brighter, and each one of them had a *meaning*, but a meaning too abstruse for her to fathom. They drifted past her, changing direction now and again. She had no idea how long she spent suspended in the ethereal realm, but she did know that she had never experienced such joy. As she looked back on her life from this exalted perspective, it seemed so petty and insignificant that she could barely stand the thought of returning. Her family, her friends, her guru and co-workers, the government—everyone was on the wrong track, concerned about the wrong things, thinking the wrong thoughts. Her perspective was so much more encompassing now. *The pure void.*

A breeze blew in around the plywood sheets at the windows. Stella did not feel it so much as she heard it on her skin; a silvery symphony that played in harmonic tones. Outside, palm fronds scraped against one another as they swayed. She didn't hear the noise as much as she saw it—the approach of a figure wearing a robe of dried palm leaves. He emerged out of the light and they spoke, not in words but in thoughts.

"Who are you?" she asked.

"I am Akamai," the figure replied.

"George?"

"The ancestor, six generations removed, of that one on that lies nearby."

"Why are you here?"

"To free my land."

"Free it?"

"From those trying to shackle it, bind it by complex chains of words, wall it off with papers written and sealed, with fences and towers, as surely as if guards were posted at its boundaries to keep my family out."

"And I have a role in this?"

"To be strong. Evil is in pursuit of good. If you are strong, justice will be done."

The Hawaiian turned around, and vanished. The light grew dimmer and dimmer, until there was nothing but unremitting black all around her. Realizing that her eyes were shut, she opened them to relieve the darkness. The lamp on the side table loomed over her head, but now it was a dragon with white hot fiery breath about to pounce on her. The front door bulged inward with the force of an unseen demon attempting to force its way into the house. The coffee table was a vulture sitting at her side, its wings spread wide, pecking at her exposed entrails. In the plaid armchair, the devil himself sat naked, his skin covered with mold, his three penises erect. On the floor, George Akamai lay dying, the skin peeling from his face and arms, exposing raw flesh across which ants were swarming, pulling away little pieces with their mandibles.

She shut her eyes again, but the horrors didn't go away. They became abstract, swirling and changing around her, threatening her with extinction at every moment. *Be strong,* she told herself. But what did that mean now? All her strength was aimed at resisting the demons, but perhaps it would take more strength by far to cease resisting, to succumb to them. Could she let go?

She decided she had the strength, and just like that, she dropped her defenses. At once, the forces of evil swooped in on her, devouring her and becoming her at the same time. This sensation, too, continued for what seemed a very long time, until all the evils in the world were contained in her person, making her violently ill. With extreme difficulty, she roused herself from the sofa, went into the bathroom and retched into the toilet. Somehow, as they came out of her, all the malevolent forces were turned into a harmless jelly that swam on the surface of a crystalline lake until with a whoosh they simply disappeared. She returned to the living room and resumed her place on the sofa. There was a pounding in her ears as if the house were being struck repeatedly by a wrecking ball. Through a crack in the plywood, she could see daylight. On the floor, George Akamai seemed to have recovered quite remarkably and was trying to explain to her something about a colleague, Lieutenant Tong-Yi Han, who had knocked on the door—an annoyance because it caused Akamai to have to get up, open the door and convince his fellow officer that everything was fine in the house.

In the plaid armchair there was no longer a devil. Indeed, the chair looked unoccupied. Though inspecting it seemed an impossible chore, she felt she should undertake it nonetheless and roused herself once more. The chair was indeed empty. She closed her eyes, trying to recall why that fact was significant enough to warrant her attention, and all at once noticed another sound that had been a steady pressure on her ears for a while now. It was an insistent, moaning sound, as if all the residents of the island were gathered below the hill, all crying at once. She opened her eyes again and went over to where Akamai sat. She refrained from touching him, because she thought the sensation would be too intense for either of them. Instead, she sat beside him on the floor.

George, she thought. *Can you hear me?*

Akamai nodded.

Do you hear that sound, George? The sound of people wailing?

It sounds more like—sirens to me. Police sirens and fire sirens all at once.

Maybe. George?

There was no answer.

I think Nate is gone.

Akamai opened his eyes. "Are you sure?" He clambered rockily to his feet. "Oh, God, I'm thirsty. Aren't you thirsty?" He looked at his watch. "Five past eleven. What is that racket outside?"

He opened the front door, and a large palm frond being held across the door by the wind hurtled in at him. At first he fought with it as if with a lion, but his senses quickly returned. He shut the door again. "The storm's here already," he said. Recalibrated by the fresh air from outside, his sense of smell told him that something was wrong inside the house. At first it came to him as a vision, the walls of the house heaving outward as though they were going to burst. Then the reality of it registered. *Propane.* The burners were on. Lying on the floor where the fumes collected, he had been breathing the stuff. He could feel a poisonous cloud in his lungs, moving into his bloodstream, slowing his body and his already impaired mind, like an octopus whose tentacles were reaching into his limbs and skull.

Mechanically, he went over to Stella and grabbed her wrist. "We have to get out of here," he yelled. The house was quaking in the gusting winds. He could hear a loud rumbling sound, like a *mo'o* on the roof. It was the sound of tin panels rippling as Iniki pried them loose. There was a creaking noise as nails in the roof joists came free. Stella dragged herself woodenly after Akamai as he walked to the door. He opened it, and at the same time a section of roof rose up at its base, a giant wing flexing before taking flight. The motion pulled a length of electrical conduit, breaking a splice inside the kitchen wall, which sparked as it parted, igniting the propane miasma. In the explosion, the pair were blown off the porch. For a split second they were suspended in air, as the winds of Iniki contended for dominion over them with the force of the detonating gas. Then they fell to the ground, where they watched in detached fascination as the walls and roof of Akamai's house sailed away, followed by all its contents.

In a matter of seconds all that was left standing on the foundation slab was the bathroom plumbing. Rain riding the unstable winds that mounted the steep hillside thrashed their naked backs, their shirts torn away by the explosion. Stella turned to face the storm, and found herself in a cruel echo of her joyous dream. Raindrops as big as quarters sailed at her in a field of menacing grey, and dirt and debris flew over her head.

"Let's get to the car!" Akamai hollered.

Pressed on by the wind, the pair reached the jeep and jumped in. Instead of heading down the driveway, Akamai drove into the backyard and onto a cane road.

"George!" Stella cried, tugging at his sleeve, holding her naked breasts with her other arm to protect them against the wild motion of the jeep.

"Don't worry!" he shot back. "I'm not thinking entirely straight yet, but I know that driving down the road into the mouth of the hurricane isn't a great idea. This road comes out near the plantation house at the Makai Ranch. There's a basement there."

They drove through a field of mature cane. Normally, the spiky-leafed stalks would have towered over them, but Iniki had flattened the plants on both sides of the road into twisted hummocks as far as they could see. On the *makai* side, the hummocks, no taller than five feet high, provided some protection from the wind, but the dirt road itself was carpeted with razor-sharp leaves.

Akamai drove slowly because of the conditions and because his reaction time did not permit him to go faster. What was normally a twenty-minute ride would at their present rate of progress consume the better part of an hour. The sound of the hurricane through the cloth top of the jeep drowned their senses, and they could not speak. Iniki was so big and so powerful, and so loud that it was hallucinogenic in itself, a presence beyond simple physics. Pele's harsh will riding the storm.

The rhythm of the windshield wipers, the ceaseless fury of Iniki, the prostrating sugar cane all made it difficult for Akamai and Stella to avoid sliding back into a dream state. Stella began rubbing Akamai's neck to help keep him alert and a moment later couldn't recall, except with considerable thought, why she was doing it. She felt her breasts moving energetically, looked down and wondered how her shirt had come off. Without remembering her duffel bag, she turned around to look at the space behind the seats. After aimless rummaging, she found her clothes, pulled out a bikini top and put it on.

Half an hour later, the road ended in a "T" intersection. Akamai turned south toward Web Chamberlain's house, exposing the jeep to the full onslaught of the hurricane. The winds were now screaming up the hill at over a hundred miles an hour, and the jeep was not making any progress against them. With the rain and debris obscuring the view through the windshield and speeding past them on both sides and the cane whipping horizontally all around them, it took some time before the couple inside the jeep realized that the vehicle was not moving forward. By then, Akamai had dug the four wheels into the soggy track up to the axles. "This is very bad!" he shouted to Stella. "We can't get down the hill."

"What's in the other direction?" Stella called back.

Akamai couldn't visualize the upper road without retracing it from the intersection in his mind. When he came to the little reservoir, he saw, down a driveway near the water, the small brick pumping house.

"There's a place where we might be safe!" he bellowed. Putting the car in reverse, he took advantage of the pressure of the tempest on the front of the jeep and rolled out of the grooves that cradled the wheels. He turned around at the intersection and headed north, struggling to keep the vehicle on the road while Iniki tried to lift the rear end off the ground. A hundred yards on, an empty pickup truck sat nose down in a ditch. "Nate's," Akamai yelled.

After a few nerve-wracking minutes of fighting Iniki, the going got easier. The road turned to the west and went into a bowl-like depression, where the travellers were temporarily out of the wind and rain, though still bedeviled by the howling of the storm.

"There it is!" Akamai called, pointing past Stella across the reservoir inside the grassy crater in which they were riding. Out her window she saw what looked like a large brick outhouse with a flat roof. On the opposite side of the reservoir, Iniki was eating at the upper rim of the crater, stripping the grass away and washing the dirt up and over the edge. In the sky over the crater was a sight that made Stella gasp.

"George!" she shouted, "am I hallucinating or is that a—" By the time she had said that much, the incipient tornado was gone. A moment later a new one formed in the same place and shot off, still diaphanous, carrying its initially light charge of debris with it. "Tornado!" she yelled.

As the hurricane ran up the hillside, its airspeed near the ground slowed in comparison to the airspeed higher at higher altitudes. That differential, together with a source of lateral displacement, like the crater, provided the optimum conditions for the formation of tornadoes, which were rampant on Kauai that afternoon.

As they watched, another spout formed. Stella turned to Akamai to ask whether he thought the tiny building would protect them. She saw that he was staring at it, his brow knit. "What's the matter?"

"The door," he said. Reaching under his seat, he dragged out a sculpted black case from which he extracted a pair of binoculars. He looked through them at the pump house, then handed the binoculars to Stella. "Take a look at the lock." The door had been secured with a padlock, but the hinge holding the assemblage to the jamb had been torn off and was hanging loose from the door. Akamai took the car key out of the ignition and unlocked the glove box. Inside was a forty-five caliber semiautomatic pistol, a set of handcuffs and a flashlight. He took them out. "We're going to leave the jeep here, so he won't hear us coming." he said. "When we get to the building, I'll open the door. Nate may come out, and if he does, I'll arrest him. If he doesn't come out right away, I'll persuade him to in fairly short order. I want you to stay around the corner of the building until I call you."

They approached the pump house across rough-cut grass, the storm raging overhead. Akamai positioned himself next to the door, and Stella went around the corner behind him, and stood peeking out tentatively. Akamai lifted the door latch, pulled the handle, stepped backwards, took a two-handed grip on his weapon and waited. Nate did not emerge. After a moment, Akamai shouted, "Come on out, Nate!"

When nothing happened, he stepped in front of the opening, fired a shot into the wooden roof of the pump house and called again, but still there was no response. With the flashlight, he scanned the interior. It was empty. "Oh, Jesus," he said to himself. He put the pistol in his right pocket, and without looking around he bellowed, "Goddamn you, Nate!"

"I think he already has, Georgie." The voice came from his left. He turned his head. There, framed by the fulminating hurricane, Nate Chamberlain stood with one arm across Stella's chest and, in his other hand, a cane machete, its blade held against Stella's neck. "The place wasn't real well-stocked," he hooted, "but it had the essentials."

"So now you want the gun."

"And the car keys."

"And then you're going to shoot us."

"I don't know, Braddah. I came up to the house with the idea of killing you, then vacillated, then found courage with the help of the sacred salts, and now—I don't know."

Akamai shook his head. "Why, Nate?"

"The will, Georgie," Nate seethed. "It's driving me crazy."

"I don't know what you're talking about," Akamai retorted. "I'd like to help you, if it's not too late."

Nate snickered. "It's way too late, pal. The most you can do for me right now is drop the pistol onto the ground."

Akamai smiled a bitter smile. He fumbled in his pocket, brought the pistol into view and dropped it in the grass. Then he reached for the car keys, and dropped them next to the gun.

"Okay. Into the reservoir, Georgie, and swim out to the middle."

When the police lieutenant was in the middle of the reservoir, Nate took a long, quavering breath. "Okay, Stella. Here we go." He pushed her toward the gun. "One little slice with this knife—it would hardly even hurt you—one little slice right where I'm pressing it now, would slit your carotid artery, and you'd bleed to death out here like a slaughtered sow."

"My sense of anatomy is pretty good, Nate."

"Glad to hear it. Say! I know it's a—an awkward moment, but this may be my only chance to ask: how was your trip?"

"I—I felt, uh—Nate, it's hard to discuss this with that machete digging—"

"Humor me, Stella."

"I felt, you know, a vastly expanded consciousness. A union with the universe, I guess."

"What did I tell you?"

"Right, but I—Jeez, couldn't you just let me go? I mean, what the hell can I do to you?"

They were just a few feet away from the pistol. Nate stopped. Stella held her breath. She visualized the pulse at the side of her neck, blood streaming through her carotid artery just a quarter of an inch away from the blade of the rusty machete. Nate turned her around so that she could see George Akamai treading water in the lake, the air in turmoil above his head. "He's not what you think he is, Stella."

She started to ask what he meant, but something told her not to. "The question for the moment, Nate, is whether you are what I think you are."

"What do you think I am?"

"A killer."

"You think I killed your French friends?"

"Among others."

"Why would I do that?"

"Because of the Ranch."

"I'm not the only one with an interest in what happens to Web's Ranch, honey," Nate hissed into her ear.

"Is that what you meant by the will?"

"Don't you think Web would have provided for the golden boy there?"

The pressure on her breasts relaxed. Nate drew his hand heavily across them and then released her. He brought the machete down to his side. "But what?" he shouted. Stella turned to face him, confused at the *non sequitur*. His aspect was unsettled, but not manic.

"But what?" he repeated. "You never finished describing your trip."

Even at the slight distance, Stella felt safer, although she thought she could hear Akamai saying, *Run, run!* "Well, I felt this breathtaking stuff," she answered nervously, "but now here I am, back in my body, not sure what I saw and unable to get to it without these pills that might do to me what they did to you."

"Which is—?"

"Deprive you of your morality."

The last of the Hawaiian Chamberlains looked into Stella Chase's eyes. A tic played at the side of his mouth. "Pick up the gun, Stella," he said. "Pick it up!" He raised the machete again.

Glancing over her shoulder, she saw Akamai swimming to shore. She bent down, keeping her eyes on the arm with the machete. The weapon was a metallic affront in her hand, not a thing she would ever voluntarily touch. The voice in her head said, *If you are strong, justice will be done.*

"Now shoot me!" Nate commanded.

She stared at him, confounded. Strong enough to shoot or strong enough not to shoot, she wondered. The forty-five was shaking in her hands as though it were trying to free itself. "D-do you want to die, Nate?" she stuttered.

"I think so. I think maybe that's what's really been going on here, don't you?" He took the machete in a two-handed grip, and cocked it behind his head as if he were about to strike at her. He was going to give her no alternative.

If you are strong, justice will be done.

"Then do it yourself!" Stella cried and tossed the gun at Nate. He let loose of the machete and brought his hands down in front of him to catch it. By then Stella was running. She sped past Nate and headed for the reservoir, where Akamai was just emerging from the water. Her actions were based on trust alone. Common sense told her to expect a bullet between her shoulders at any moment.

Nate gripped his right wrist with his left hand, and looked down the barrel at the fleeing woman. He squeezed the trigger. There was an impotent clicking noise. He shot again. Nothing happened. Seconds later Stella was in Akamai's arms. The lieutenant reached into his pocket and retrieved the clip, which he held up for Nate to see.

The two of them watched Nate put the pistol to his head. He was laughing hysterically. He pulled the trigger and was overtaken by another fit of laughter. He doubled over, scooped up the car keys and laid Akamai's pistol back on the ground with a flourish. Then he blew them a kiss and ran off toward the jeep. Akamai sprinted after him, but by the time he reached his jeep, Nate was inside it and had started the engine.

Akamai leapt at the spare tire mounted on the rear of the vehicle. Mud thrown up by the back wheels coated his body, but he had a good grip as Nate started off. Once the jeep was moving at high speed over the ill-maintained road, though, the lieutenant couldn't hold on. Jarred loose, he spun into the grass across the road and jumped to his feet. Stella, running up the rise of the crater toward him, could see the jeep turning north on the cane road and rocking convulsively in the wind.

She reached Akamai and put her arms around his mud-stained body, feeling his chest heave, his heart pound, his arms hanging limp against his side. Iniki, resonating in the crater, shook them to their bones. Its tumultuous roaring was far louder now than when they had arrived. Akamai gestured at the debris flying over the crater. "That stuff is moving at close to a hundred and fifty miles an hour now. He's not going to get very far." The cane road traced the north rim of the reservoir, and they could just make out the top of the jeep swerving and zigzagging as the driver struggled to keep it upright.

"Hasn't he seen the tornadoes?" Stella cried.

Akamai nodded slowly, his lips compressed.

"Omigod, look, George!" A funnel had just formed, adding its own destructive dizziness to the northerly blasts of Iniki's eye-wall. Akamai turned away and shut his eyes. Stella raised her shaking fingers to her mouth. As the tornado raced away over the lip of the crater, Nate drove into it. The jeep was lifted into the air. It tipped inward as it was drawn into the vortex. The cloth top tore off. The contents of the interior whirled out and upward, away from the vehicle's carcass, which fell to earth.

Darkening as it sucked earth and vegetation into itself, the twister moved on. Just before it disappeared from view, Stella thought she sighted a tiny human figure, its arms and legs spread-eagled, whirling in the upper reaches of the funnel—or perhaps it was just a pair of crossed wooden beams. A wail broke from her lips followed by sobs that racked her body. She fell onto the grass beneath the tumultuous sky. She wasn't crying for Nate. If he had died in the twister, he had gotten what, in the end, he seemed to have wanted. She cried because there was nothing else she could do, no other action she or anyone could take, no human strength that could stand up to the power massed against the residents and visitors, the flora and fauna, the very earth of Kauai.

Could that much energy really be insensate, or did Iniki have a dark soul? Energies were central to Stella's now-uncertain spiritual philosophy—manifestations of God's movement across the void. But a grand malevolence tearing apart this beautiful island? Why would God create such a presence? Why? She beat at the ground in her helplessness, her insignificance, her ignorance, while Iniki roared above her.

A pair of hands reached underneath her body and lift her into the air. She put her arms around George Akamai's neck and buried her face against his chest. "I wish you could have known him before," he said into her ear. "He was a completely different person. A real man and a true friend." The policeman looked into the sky, his thoughts the same as Stella's. "The power in this storm is so overwhelming, it overshadows any drug hallucination; if I didn't know better—and I'm not sure I do—I'd think it was the vengeance of the Hawaiian gods on humankind for what we've done to their creation."

He carried her down the hill. "Let's get into the pump house. The worst hasn't hit yet, but before it does, the eye is going to pass over us, and at that point we may be able to make it down to the manor. If it's still there."

Stella nodded. She had questions, but now was not the time to explore them. Did Akamai have an interest in the Makai Ranch? Could he be the murderer they were after? Or were things more or less as they seemed to her? Had justice in fact been done? At the moment, she was willing to bet on George Akamai.

13

When the evacuation siren sounded in Koke'e, it roused Andrew Chase from a deep slumber. Just before he awoke, he and Janet, married again, had arrived at a big luau on one of the beaches owned by the Makai Ranch. Crowds of men in aloha shirts and women in muumuus strolled along the shore and through the groves of palm trees. The official greeters for the affair were Niki Makana and Barry Saga. Niki draped a flower lei over his neck, gave him a deep French kiss and moved quickly on to greet the next male arrival in the same fashion. When he looked for Janet, he saw that she was wearing a lei but nothing else and was quite involved with the naked police captain. This, of course, was adultery, and although in his dream Andrew was not terribly upset, the county police apparently were, for all at once a stream of police cars rolled onto the beach, their lights flashing and their sirens blaring. Oddly, even after the cars stopped and the police stepped out, the sirens continued to sound. They interfered with conversation, and it was this annoyance, rather than Janet's exceptionally brazen infidelity, that woke him.

He was alone in the cabin, and not far away an evacuation horn was blaring. He retrieved his shorts from the bathroom, where they had been hanging over the curtain rod in the shower. They were still damp, but they were all that he had. He put them on, and walked outside.

It was dark and foggy. The interior light cast a luminescent shaft on him and past him into the yard, so that his own shadow was a ghostly vacuity in front of him. Niki stood at the edge of the park road about thirty yards ahead, her long black hair flowing almost down to her buttocks, her arms canted out slightly at the elbows. Unclothed, the shape of her against the darkness across the street was one of the most perfect visual experiences Andrew could remember having, but its overall effect was marred by the unceasing cry of the siren. He walked to her across the glistening grass.

"Did you put in for this wakeup call?"

"Oh! Andy, you startled me," Niki said. She made no move to cover herself or withdraw from the light. She seemed so comfortable in her nakedness that Andrew Chase was embarrassed at his arousal.

"This is a hurricane warning, I guess," Andrew said, looking away.

"It's an evacuation signal. Something's happened to the hurricane overnight. We need to listen to a radio."

Andrew's sense of responsibility emerged from its state of suppression. He had planned to be down at the Poipu house by noon, or earlier if Robinson had not scheduled a meeting for him with Chamberlain, to collect his family and head straight to the airport. If the tocsin was summoning people to evacuation shelters before sunrise, his plan had probably grown obsolete while he was sleeping and would have to be replaced by a more urgent one. "Why don't you check out the radio?" he said. "I'm going to walk up to the lodge and call Janet."

He had to press the receiver tight against one ear and put a hand over the other ear to hear anything but a caterwauling siren. There was no answer at the house, but Andrew played back the messages and learned that all the members of the Chase family had spent the night elsewhere than in the rented house. There was also a message from Carter Robinson, saying that Web Chamberlain and Li-Ann Low would meet him at ten the next morning, but that he, Robinson, couldn't make it and he and his client would waive any ethical problems that his absence might create, which Andrew read as meaning nothing of any importance would happen at the meeting. Finally, Galen Khoo had called with the information, also reported in Liz's voice note from the Sunshine building, that Paracorp had failed to come to terms with Xerxes, but that Harry Wong's lowball bid for the Makai Ranch should stand while they scrambled to find another lessee.

When he got back to the cabin, Niki was making coffee and cooking toast on the stovetop burners. She was wearing a halter top and cutoff jeans. "My namesake is making a rush for Kauai," she reported. "Direct hit. Landfall around one this afternoon. They're evacuating the coastal neighborhoods."

"I don't know if I can handle two fast Inikis in one day," Andrew said, in an offhand attempt at gallows humor.

Iniki didn't laugh. "Yesterday, I was a kid, today I'm a fast woman? A convenient lay on your way back from Hong Kong?"

"Niki, please! It was just a casual comment." Andrew saw nothing to be gained from reminding her that having sex had been her idea—or at least that she had advanced it first.

"I'm sorry, Andy." Niki put a hand to her forehead. "I don't know why that phrase set me off. I am a pretty fast woman by your standards, I'm sure."

"I didn't mean 'fast' in the sense of 'loose.'"

"In what sense, then?"

"Well, in the sense of—decisive, taking charge. It was a poor choice of words, I guess." He attempted to kiss her on the neck, but she wriggled away.

"I know what the problem is," Andrew said, his own sense of guilt pressing in on him. "I'm too old to be attractive to you."

Niki looked at him in disbelief. "Let's talk about something else, like the plan for the morning," she suggested, taking the blackened toast off the burners.

"Well, for starters, my own plan is down the tubes. There's nobody home at my place. All the Chase women seem to have found other men to entertain them last night."

"Fast Kauaian men, no doubt."

"Touché." Andrew didn't laugh at Niki's joke, either. "It doesn't sound as though Janet and the girls will be going back to the Poipu house today. But if not, where would they be going? We're supposed to leave the island late this morning."

"Maybe they headed for the airport."

"At this hour, and without having talked to one another? It's conceivable, I guess, with the sirens. I should probably cancel my meeting with Chamberlain and drive over there, just in case."

"I don't want you to cancel your meeting with Chamberlain," Niki said.

"Why? What difference does my meeting with Chamberlain make to you? Based on Paracorp's current posture, I have next to nothing to say to the man anyway."

"I thought you might introduce me to him."

Andrew Chase sank down onto the back of the old sofa. He felt himself deflating like a punctured beach ball, his guilt replaced by chagrin. "So there's the truth. It wasn't my mature charm after all," he said as if waking from a dream, "or my sexy eyes or my irresistible banter. You were just buying a ticket to see the Sugar King."

The young Hawaiian woman sighed. "In some respects, men of all races are the same inside," she said. "Here." She walked over to him and kissed him passionately and repeatedly, until he was once again able to believe that she truly loved him as much as, if not more than, any man on earth. She felt him rising to the occasion and pushed him over the top of the sofa and onto the cushions.

Afterwards, she sat on folded legs on top of him, ruffling his hair idly with her index finger while he dozed. A nice man, she concluded, but trapped in that strange Euro-American idea of what is civilized. A world in which sex is not a form of expression but a prehistoric nuisance, like the appendix. A world in which doing the right thing violates the code of ethics. A world in which helping people ravage God's beauteous garden is not only permitted but rewarded. Nice men like Andrew Chase, and nice women like his wife and daughters, had stolen Hawaii from its people and transformed it into the bad old U.S. of A.

"It's the least you can do," she murmured.

"Hmmm?" Andrew Chase opened his eyes. A heavenly voice was speaking into his ear.

"I mean, after two centuries of rape and oppression, you can't even introduce me to Web Chamberlain?"

He pulled himself up on his elbows. "Sorry. Have I missed part of a conversation here?" What was it about this trip, he wondered, that kept him waking up with beautiful women straddling his torso? At least this time, the occasion was more pleasant. In fact, the sight of her took his breath away. The sight of him had no such effect on Niki, he was sure; his diminishing chest, his augmented belly, and match stick arms. A physiology begging for exercise.

"No, you've just missed an opportunity, that's all."

"Will the brass ring come around again?"

"Sure. Here it comes right now. Ready?"

"I guess."

"Repeat after me. 'Niki, darling—'" As she spoke, she began to move her arms and upper torso in a slow, fluid hula, her head following the motion of her hands gracefully from side to side.

"Niki, darling."

"'I'd be happy—'"

"I'd be happy—"

"'—to take you—'"

"—Didn't I just do that? Ouch! Okay, to take you—"

"'—to Chamberlain's house!'" The brief hula ended with arms raised to heaven, bent slightly at the elbows, palms upward and fingers curved out, the head thrown back. The lines of her body, held that way, were so elegant, so refined, so sophisticated that he wondered how the missionaries dared—how they dared!—try to suppress this glorious sign language, a language so much more angelic than theirs.

Hearing no response, Niki looked down through the arc of her arms.

"To Chamberlain's house," Andrew echoed. "You're right, it's the least I can do."

She leaned forward and kissed him on the forehead, her breasts tickling the graying hairs of his chest. "You're a good man, Andrew Chase."

After cleaning up and dressing again, they sat at the little table and had coffee, toast and passion fruit jam. "I think," Iniki said as they ate, "we should take everything in the refrigerator with us. The food in the cabinets, too."

"What? All your uncle's provisions? Won't he be a little upset?"

"Naw, he isn't coming. The first thing the hurricane will do is take down the power. Guaranteed. Our electrical system here is so delicate, if two guys sneeze on Rice Street at the same time, the power's out for an hour. You can just imagine what Sistah Iniki's effect will be. The streets are going to be blocked with branches and stuff, maybe the low parts of the coast road will be covered with sand. It'll be a mess." She shrugged and put on a distinctly local face. "Uncle no come in da kine sitchuashun."

"Okay," Andrew laughed, "but the perishables—?"

"I have a cooler in my trunk. Maybe all the beer won't fit, but the other stuff, no problem. I'll split it up with you after the hurricane passes."

"I'm leaving the island, Niki."

"That's what you think, Andy. Tourists all over Kauai are packing up right now and heading for the airport all along our fabulous two-lane superhighway. That means big traffic jams. Big! And long lines at our high-tech, one-story airport. Long!"

"Okay, so we don't wait till ten o'clock to visit Chamberlain. We go there now."

Niki shook her head. "Say we leave here now, don't pack any food—which could be a real bad idea, depending on how long the power's out—it's an hour and a quarter by the time we get down the mountain and to the gates of the Makai Ranch, if there's no traffic and no cops to stop you for speeding. But today, there'll be plenty of traffic. *Haoles* heading for the airport, locals buying whatever's left at the grocery store, *makai* folks going *mauka* for the day. Add another hour.

Say, eight a.m., you drop me at Chamberlain's, maybe say a few nice words about me, and leave for the airport. Minimum, an hour and a half in traffic, so you arrive at nine-thirty, turn in the car and get in line."

"That doesn't sound so bad," Andrew offered.

"No? Got a reservation?"

"We couldn't make reservations until I knew when I would be meeting—Uh-oh."

Niki drank the last of her coffee. "Uh-oh. There are probably fifty thousand tourists on this island, and starting an hour ago, a big proportion of them began motivating toward the airport. So several thousand, minimum, have a substantial head start on you, and are either in line at the airport or crawling along the road to get there. If the rest of your family made it there early enough, they may have got passage out, but you? By the time you get to the check-in desk, it'll probably be closed."

"Closed?"

"At some point before Iniki comes ashore, the planes will stop flying, don't you think?"

Andrew pushed his plate away from him, set the knife and spoon in it and stared at the table. Once again, he had not planned his family's movements adequately. "I hope Janet and the girls don't fly off on me again," he muttered. "That's what got us into trouble here in the first place."

Half an hour later they left the mountain retreat. As with other areas of the island, there was as yet nothing in the air, except the unusual warmth, to suggest the brutalization to which Kauai and its residents would be subjected by lunchtime. Niki's car was a 1958 Corvette, restored, she said, by a boyfriend who had died in a surfing accident earlier in the year. "We were going to be married in September," she told the lawyer with a sad smile, "but instead of him, I inherited the driver's seat."

The car was parked behind the cabin, and Andrew had not seen it the evening before. As he rounded the corner of the building, he was lugging a cooler containing a bag of buns, a jar of jam, a pound of butter, a dozen eggs, a pound of bacon, two pounds of hamburger meat—stocked by uncle in case the fishing was bad, Andrew assumed—and two six-packs of beer, with the contents of a five-pound bag of ice scattered over all. When he saw the rolling fifties icon for the first time, he smiled. Quadruple headlights bugged out of the curved front fender skins. The squared-off oval grill with an insert of chromed vertical spikes looked like bared teeth. The ersatz, aerodynamic side scoops were outlined in curving chrome strips. The 'Vette was painted in nontraditional colors—a pale yellow, which Niki had called "pineapple," and, in the side scoops, guava pink—using a technique that gave the surface an unusually reflective finish.

The low-slung cruiser had been fitted with a pale aquamarine tonneau cover, and perched on top of the windshield was what appeared to be a stuffed parrot. Andrew's smile broadened at this scrap of island whimsy, and vaguely wondered whether Niki removed the ornament before driving the car, and if not, how it stayed in place when the vehicle was in motion.

Andrew opened the trunk and set the cooler inside. When he shut the lid, he saw that the bird had turned his head, and was giving him a mistrustful one-eyed stare. It opened and closed its beak with little shudders. It was not tethered in any way, so the lawyer stepped back a few paces, giving it the respect due a live parrot.

"What's your name?" the parrot croaked.

Andrew started. "An—Andrew," he replied.

"Hello, An-Andrew. My name is Huhu."

Andrew was on the verge of expressing pleasure at making the parrot's acquaintance, when Niki appeared, carrying a paper bag with all the edible contents of the pantry in it. Her hair was tied up in a loose topknot. "Oh, good!" she exclaimed. "So you've discovered Huhu. I hope he introduced himself."

"He did. Clever trick." He took the bag from her and deposited it in the trunk.

"It's not a trick," Niki said as they got into the car. "Huhu has the intelligence of a four-year old human. Watch this." The parrot had turned around, as if to emphasize its interest in their conversation. "Pick a number, Huhu."

"Three," the parrot responded, bobbing up and down in a display of delight.

Niki held up four fingers. The parrot stopped bobbing, and started rocking from one foot to the other. "No. Three," it said. She folded one finger, and the parrot commenced bobbing again.

"Smart Niki."

"What are these?" the Hawaiian asked, wiggling her fingers.

"Fingers."

"What shape?"

"Long. Thin."

They got into the car. Niki started the engine and pulled away. The bird turned around to face the wind, lowered its body against its feet and stretched out horizontally. Andrew shook his head. "Amazing," he exclaimed.

"My neighbor is an avian psychologist at UH Manoa. Commutes to Oahu three days a week. He's adopted Huhu, and taught him many things. It's like having a kid around." Niki flashed a wan, involuntary smile as she stared through the windshield.

"You'd rather have a kid, though," Andrew ventured.

"I don't play 'I'd rather,'" Niki said, shaking her head. She accelerated as they left the improved portion of the park. The wind tossed her hair around, and she reached behind her seat, produced a white baseball cap and pulled it on with the visor in back. "I play, 'I'm going to.'"

"And you're 'going to' have kids?"

"Yeah, Andy. But don't worry—not yours."

Even though he had no desire to father any more children, particularly Niki's, her words cut him deeply. Why would she say such a thing? It dawned on him that he had not been listening to her. He had heard her well enough, and had understood the words she had been saying, but he was not listening with what Stella called inner wisdom. The same persistent failure to comprehend what people meant, as opposed to parsing the words they used, was at the core of Janet's unhappiness with him, and he had vowed to work on his sensitivity as a way of winning her back. In a book he would never admit to having read, he had encountered a corrective protocol, a mind set that was similar to a standard negotiating technique he used all the time. *Look at it from her point of view.* Mid-twenties. The great love of her life lost to a fractious wave. Just spent the night showering her affections on a complete stranger twice her age. And for what reason? Not because she loved him. The explanation he had given her already, that she seduced him to get to Web Chamberlain, seemed the most likely to Andrew. And in the face of that, he asks her if she wants to have kids! Where the hell did that come from, anyway? "I'm sorry," he said. "That question. It was stupid. It's just that we've been so—well, intimate. I guess I felt closer to you than I should have."

"It's okay, Andy. I feel close to you, too." She tapped her fingernails against the steering wheel, then blew her breath out through her mouth. "Don't worry. It'll pass."

The parrot had its wings outstretched now, using them both for balance and as spoilers to keep himself low. Niki yanked on its tail feathers and yelled, "Down, Huhu!" The bird squawked in protest, but let go of the windshield frame, folded its wings and dropped into the passenger compartment. In what was clearly an oft-rehearsed move, he landed on the emergency brake lever. There, he bobbed up and down, stabbing involuntarily at the lawyer's upper arm as he did so. Andrew pressed himself against the door.

"Would a little music bother you?" Niki asked as they emerged from a dizzying series of downhill switchbacks. She reached for the power knob, but before she could turn it, Andrew placed his hand on hers.

"I'd rather talk for a minute first," he said, stepping into the emotional ground rather than away from it as had been his lifelong habit. "I don't want the feeling between us to pass, Niki." In the instant before he said it, he thought the phrase poetic and emotionally open. In the instant after, he knew it was the wrong way of expressing what he felt, but couldn't see how to recover without making matters worse.

Niki gave him a sidelong glance. Her lips quivered briefly before she thought to press them together to stifle the effect. Her hand fell away from the radio and she waited, obviously reluctant to react to such an incompletely stated thought.

Andrew pressed on. "I—this is a burden you may not want, I appreciate that, but I'm afraid I now care about you; you and your island life, your deep feelings for your cultural heritage, your commitment to this cause of yours."

"Oh, Jesus," Niki sighed, her voice breaking. "Now I feel like the little dark-skinned *wahine* playing therapist while Captain Cook rationalizes away his guilt."

Andrew cursed his clumsiness, but he was committed now. "This isn't not coming from guilt, Niki. I don't regard the last half-day as a prostitute-john scenario." The Hawaiian was paying close attention to the road in front of her. "Yes, we made love—and I say it that way advisedly. It was the right thing to do at the time, but there probably won't be another right time. I accept that—embrace it, even. What might happen again, though, is that one of us wants to talk to the other, or—or needs advice or—"

"—What advice would you ever need from me?" Her voice was almost inaudible in the moving convertible.

"You and I are in the same leaky boat, Niki. We've each lost a life partner, and deeply wish we could have our partners back. For you, there's no chance. For me, almost no chance. We each know what it's like to have an unconditional confidante, someone to freely share life's questions, big and little, with—"

"—And you think," Niki interjected, at once agitated and distressed, "—that we developed that kind of relationship through one night of screwing?"

"No! Now, see—I know it's—the sexual angle is bothering you. It bothers me, too. I mean, we're both adults, but I'm almost twice your age, for Christ's sake. All I can say is what I said before. It was right, but it probably won't happen again. The important thing is, for every moment we spent making love, we probably spent ten or fifteen minutes talking. All I'm saying, I guess, is that we may have talked ourselves into a friendship."

Niki Makana down shifted two gears as they approached a tight turn. She didn't speak until she had negotiated the corner, by which time her composure had returned. Andrew wished for the power to divine what was eating at her.

"Maybe we did, Andy," she said quietly. "Maybe. It's—different for me than for you. I don't think you see that. Age has nothing to do with it. It's just different, being the Hawaiian woman. But—maybe." She turned on the radio.

They reached Kekaha at about quarter to eight. Under the brooding sky there was frantic activity as residents closed up their dust-coated houses, filled the trunks of their cars or the beds of their pick-ups with clothing, sleeping bags, provisions and valuables and headed off to the safety of whatever reinforced structure was shelter for the town. Traffic was light here, but the closer they got to Poipu, the less progress they made. Vehicles merging from side streets, particularly the slow-moving cane trucks and bulldozers seeking higher ground, forced a stop-start rhythm on the traffic flow. The resulting congestion pleased only the parrot, who was able to resume his place atop the windshield. "Move it, pal," he shouted whenever they braked to a halt, and, "Whoopie!" whenever they were in motion again.

At about half-past nine they saw the gates to the Makai Ranch ahead of them. The wind, Iniki's energetic harbinger had risen by then. It toyed with the sugar cane to either side of the road, setting the plants into frenetic motion and raising a din that sounded like television after a station has signed off for the night. Niki pulled left out of the snarl of traffic and made a run down the opposite lane for the gates. Once they passed under the sign she hit the brakes, bringing the car to an abrupt stop. Huhu flung his wings into the air and flapped madly to keep from losing his foothold, and Andrew pressed his hands against the dashboard. "What is it?"

"I'm nervous, dammit. On top of everything else, now I'm nervous," Niki shot back.

"About meeting Chamberlain?" She nodded. "He's only human, Niki. Puts on his pants one leg at a time, like the rest of us."

"That's the way you see it. You and he belong to the same fraternity, you've got the secret handshake. To me, he's this giant symbol of oppression, the living ghost of the white invaders."

Andrew leaned toward her. "I've met the guy once; that doesn't make me an expert on Web Chamberlain. But, believe me, he doesn't have fangs. My guess is that he will be the soul of politeness toward you, very careful not to give offense or concern. He's no invader. He was born here just like you. I think you'll end up liking him."

Niki bit her lip. "No, I don't want that, and I don't particularly care if he likes me, either. All I want is to be taken seriously."

Andrew patted her on the shoulder. He couldn't assure her of that, and they both knew it. As they sat there, the parrot turned around. With one small, round, polished blue pearl of an eye, he stared at his mistress, waiting for a sign. When none came, he leapt onto the steering wheel and gently pulled at her hair with his beak. "Move it, pal," he squawked. She laughed and put the car in gear.

When they drove into the entrance circle in front of the plantation house, Webster Chamberlain was standing on the lawn, supervising the collection of statuary and potted plants for storage and the covering of the smaller of the decorative trees in the yard with burlap to prevent wind damage. He broke off when he saw them, and walked laboriously down the brick walkway toward the car.

"Andrew!" he called out. "I'm surprised you're here. We thought that with Iniki's change of heart you and your family might have decided to leave Kauai for the day."

"No!" Andrew hollered back. "It looks as though we'll be sharing the hurricane experience with you." He strode up the path to meet the older man. Niki put the top up on the car, with the parrot inside, before joining them.

"Forgive the informality, Web," Andrew entreated, waving his hands along his torso. "I was camping out last night and didn't have time to get back home to change."

"No need to apologize. You're in Hawaii." Chamberlain said as the two men shook hands. "I see you've brought someone with you. She's not your wife, whom I've met, or your daughters, whom I assume are of pale complexion. A fellow camper, perhaps?" He turned to Niki and extended his hand. "Welcome to the Makai Ranch."

"Thank you," Niki replied, returning the handshake. "I'm Niki Makana, Mr. Chamberlain."

"Web, please; it'll make me feel so much younger. Makana, is it? There's a large family by that name up Anahola way."

"Yes, sir. I'm one of them."

Chamberlain's brow was knit, as though he were trying to recall something. "I believe a member of the younger generation of that family is active in the sovereignty movement on this island," he ventured.

Andrew glanced at his companion. Her jaw had gone slack and her eyes widened. He looked back at Chamberlain, and saw an impish grin starting to form at the corners of his eyes and mouth.

When Niki realized that she was being teased, she laughed despite herself. "Oh, Mr. Chamberlain—Web," she scolded. "You are a man to watch out for."

"I certainly used to be, my dear." He took her by the arm and led her toward the house. "I certainly used to be."

The front doors and the windows on both stories were boxed in with plywood sheeting. The window shutters and all the porch furniture had been removed to a warehouse, Chamberlain told them. The only access to the house now was through the back door or the cellar. They walked around the side of the building which, with all its lights sheathed, looked abandoned, a ruin already. About them as they walked, beds of flowers waited helplessly for the storm: birds-of-paradise, orange-beaked and blue-tongued; crimson torch ginger on slender stalks; proteas with flowers like scoops of pale ice cream seated atop rings of rose petals; and dozens of orchid plants, their voluptuous flowers vying for attention along delicate, curving stems.

"So tell me. What is your relation to this slick Eastern lawyer?" Web asked.

Niki turned her head in Andrew's direction, wearing a look that said, "What, indeed?" but to the sugar boss she replied, "I helped find his younger daughter, and I asked him to introduce me to you."

"To me? Well, well. 'Goddess, allow this aged man his right to be your beadsman now, that was your knight.' Here, let's go in." He took Niki's arm and led her and Andrew through the back door. Inside, it was nighttime. Lights were on in all the rooms off the hall. Niki caught a glimpse of the capacious kitchen with its twin iron ovens and suspended copper pots; the small dining room where a table for eight was overhung by an antique double-hulled canoe; and the conference/banquet room where Andrew had met with Chamberlain and his advisors earlier in the week.

They passed through the front hall with its assortment of Pacific Rim collectibles and entered a drawing room of moderate size, lit by translucent wall sconces that appeared to be fashioned from real shell. A wooden idol stood just to the right of the doorway, its boldly-carved surface feathered with age and exposure to the elements. The image was that of a fearsome deity, its mouth gaping angrily, all its teeth exposed, its eyes wide and menacing. Niki stood before it, moving her hand along the contours of the sculpture, her fingers not touching it, but feeling its ancient provenance. "Where did this come from?" she asked.

Chamberlain exhaled an embarrassed sigh. "One can't know for sure," he murmured apologetically, "but the folklore is that it was taken from the old Ka'awako heiau—"

Niki gasped and clutched her sides.

"It was supposedly taken from there by some of Cook's sailors. It—I'm so sorry, my dear."

Iniki Makana had fallen to her knees, pressed down by the force of a primeval religion. The Ka'awako altar, reputed to have sat atop fog-shrouded Mount Wai'ale'ale—if indeed it ever existed at all—was lost to modern Hawaii. Its memory—or its legend—lived on in the dreams of the Kamehamehas of Kauai. "Oh, my God," she whispered, sitting on her haunches, her head bowed. "Oh, my God."

"It—ah—fell into the hands of my forebears a few generations ago," Chamberlain said, kneeling with difficulty beside her. "I—ah—never knew quite what to do with it—you understand? The Kauai Museum didn't seem the right place for something so venerable. No one knows where the original site is, so I couldn't bring it back. Perhaps—" He waved his hands helplessly. "Perhaps you would have some thoughts as to a proper location for this deity."

On the other side of the room, Andrew shook hands with C. B. Freeman and—cautiously—with Li-Ann Low, who stared at him with icy poise. As they chatted about the impending storm, the realtor pointed a slender finger in the direction of the poignant tableau. "Look," she breathed in awe. "It took me years to get Chamberlain to sit and talk to me, let alone to kneel and pray."

Niki felt their eyes on her back. She stood up and helped the old man to his feet. As they crossed the room, her composure returned. She explained that the idol was a very special piece; that seeing it unexpectedly had moved her. Andrew introduced her to the publisher and the realtor. The latter, always attuned to matters of status, asked Niki if she lived on Kauai, and what she did.

"I'm a paramedic and a hostess at Duke's restaurant," the Hawaiian replied.

"She's too modest," Chamberlain put in. "She's a significant political figure on the island already, despite her youth." He waved his arm in the direction of a small sideboard on which plates of cut fruit, buns, muffins, juice, coffee and hot water for tea had been set. "I've given my household staff the day off, as Ms. Low—who stayed here overnight—has already discovered. I'm afraid we'll have to fend for ourselves. 'Hell is oneself,' Eliot said. 'Hell is alone.' I wonder if he meant to include the collective loneliness in which we find ourselves this morning."

"'Nothing to escape from and nothing to escape to,'" Li-Ann enunciated in a theatrical voice.

"Ms. Low, you surprise me," Chamberlain remarked, delight sparkling in his eyes.

The realtor waved him off. "It's serendipity, not erudition, Web. I wrote a thesis on Eliot's plays when I was in college."

"In any case," Chamberlain offered, "we will definitely have something to escape from today, and hopefully someplace—to wit, downstairs—to escape to, if necessary."

"I wasn't planning to stay—" Andrew interjected.

"But, my good man," his host objected, "you can't do anything but stay." He held up his hand as the lawyer began to explain. "I think you'd better listen to Mr. Freeman."

The publisher rubbed a finger alongside his nose. "I... stopped by your house early this morning, to... to see if I could help you and your family organize an evacuation. It appeared that the front door had been kicked open. The frame was torn and the lock mechanism was poking out the side of the door. I went in to see if anyone was—inside. Anyway, there was no one, and no other signs of violence. I called Web because I thought he might know where you were, and he invited me up to ride out the storm and report to you on what I had found, if and when you showed up this morning."

"And in the process, perhaps, get a scoop?" Andrew sighed. "Forgive me, C.B. I'm so suspicious of everyone these days. You're right, of course, it was important that I know about the break-in."

Freeman nodded. "Yes. It suggests that someone may have—"

"—intended to do harm to my family," said Andrew, finishing the thought. "The question is, who was it? Any idea, Li-Ann?" Andrew shot a stern-faced glance at the Chinese American, who recoiled in mock horror.

"For heaven's sake, Andrew, why her?" Chamberlain asked.

"Yes, why me, Andrew? Do I look like someone who could kick in a door?"

"You look like someone who could—and would—do whatever she wanted, Li-Ann."

Chamberlain cleared his throat. "Well, shall we take some sustenance before all hell breaks loose outdoors? I believe I hear rain already."

They helped themselves to food and drink, and, carrying their selections in fine china, silver and crystal on lacquered Chinese trays, followed Chamberlain across the foyer and into the conference room. "It's the only room with natural light today," Chamberlain noted as they walked into the cavernous space, "by virtue of those skylights, which we can't cover." The little party looked up at the inverted Plexiglas bubbles some twenty- five feet over their heads. Rainwater was sliding over them; and under the lowering clouds the meager light that came through them was more ominous than cheery.

Chamberlain bade them to be seated at one end of the big table in the configuration that Andrew concluded was the planter's favorite: Freeman and Li-Ann Low on one side, Niki and Andrew on the other, and Chamberlain at the head.

"It seems that at the same time the elements threaten to engulf the Makai Ranch from out on the ocean," the old man brooded, "a nasty mystery is threatening to do the same from right here on the island. Or is it just me who is in the dark?"

Andrew stared at C.B. Freeman, wondering how much he knew. He decided to grab the initiative. "We're all in the dark to one extent or another, Web. Let me take a shot." The lawyer shifted his chair to face Chamberlain more comfortably while still keeping an eye on Li-Ann Low. He felt Niki's gaze on him and wondered if what he was about to say would be of any help to her cause. It wouldn't, he concluded, unless Web Chamberlain was so sickened by the true nature of the commercial bids as to turn into a total ascetic right there at the table.

"There've been three murders this week of representatives of companies bidding on your property. As you know, two were connected with France-Orient, and one with ROC Overseas. Those bidders had something in common that you may not have known about, Web. You'll recall my mentioning a company called Xerxes Industries the other day, and you may also remember Li-Ann and Carter Robinson acting a little funny after I did so." Andrew looked over at the realtor, who was shrugging and shaking her head, wearing a look that said, "The man's crazy."

"Xerxes is a big, Iranian-owned project developer," he continued. "Petrochemical plants, nuclear reactors, refineries, that kind of thing. The company has a subsidiary here named Sunshine Resources. Sunshine is run by a man known as Ravi—Rafi—" Andrew gestured with his hand for Freeman to help him.

"Palahved," the publisher offered. "You know him, Web."

Chamberlain nodded. "He was here for a charity luau last year. I wasn't impressed. Well, you should know him, too, I think, Niki."

Niki blushed. "Yes," she murmured. "Yes, he was quite generous to the Kamehameha Society, the sovereignty organization I run here on Kauai." The way Chamberlain had described her earlier, as a "significant political figure," had made it easier for her to mention the movement, Andrew concluded.

"I'll get to him in a second," Andrew put in. "The important thing to know about Xerxes is that they've been attempting to tie up all the bidders for this property. Every one of them. Of the six bidders, they had three corralled into leasing the Makai Ranch to Sunshine. Two others could not come to terms with Xerxes. They were France-Orient and ROC Overseas."

"You're suggesting that Palahved had these companies' representatives killed? I mean, Muggeridge did say that life was only cheap melodrama, but really, Andrew!"

"Does the assault on your front door signal a falling out between Xerxes and your client as well, then?" Freeman asked.

Andrew looked at him closely, and then back at Chamberlain.

"I can't comment on attorney-client communications, Web, but I will say that I'm deeply concerned that my front door was forced some time during the night."

"But come now," Chamberlain objected. "This is not very convincing at all, my good man."

"There's more, Web. My daughter says she's found a document—I should have it tomorrow—demonstrating that Mr. Adibi, the fellow killed at the Pakala Inn, was double-dealing: working for Sunshine on the one hand, and passing information to one of the bidders for the Ranch on the other. It appears that Palahved discovered that fact, and Adibi was dead a few days later. Coincidence?"

Chamberlain rubbed his chin. Overhead, rain hurled by a gust of wind pelted the skylights so hard that the drops sounded like marbles. Everyone looked up. The Plexiglas was flexing and rattling. "The weak link," Chamberlain muttered. Then, to Andrew, he said, "Coincidence? Maybe not. Do you have anything else?"

Andrew nodded. He turned to Li-Ann Low, and raised an eyebrow. She returned the gesture, but said nothing. He raised his other eyebrow, and cocked his head in Chamberlain's direction.

The realtor took a deep breath. "Web," she said, her voice trembling, "there's something I should tell you. I should have told you some time ago. I—I was hired by Sunshine Resources before you called me in to help you sell the Ranch. They were looking for a very large site in the Hawaiian Islands. If you hadn't decided to put the Ranch on the market, I think they'd have ended up on the Big Island. After you engaged me, I really should have stopped dealing with Palahved, but—" Her lips trembled, and her eyes were blinking rapidly, but no more words came forth.

"Don't fret, Li-Ann," the old man said. "The Bible says no man can serve two masters, but it doesn't say anything about women. Bad joke. I apologize. But I don't really see any conflict between the two engagements. I wasn't negotiating with—" He stopped in mid-sentence, and thought a moment. "Why is that, Li-Ann," he said slowly. "Why wasn't I negotiating directly with Xerxes?"

In his time, Andrew Chase had been in a number of negotiations in Asia where the threat of shame or humiliation in a business setting had incapacitated someone on the other side of the table. He recognized the signs at once. Li-Ann Low's eyes glazed over, her head bowed slightly and her hands slid from the tabletop into her lap. "Shall I, Li-Ann?" he asked, and she jerked her head up and down stiffly. "Xerxes Industries has a major development project in mind for the Makai Ranch," Andrew explained. "It plans to dredge one of your beaches as a deep-water harbor for tankers carrying oil and chemicals, construct an oil refinery and petrochemical plants, and build a self-contained city for employees and managers—a fifty-billion dollar attempt to seize a major slice of the Pacific Rim market for petroleum processing."

Chamberlain stared at the lawyer stonily. A blast of wind shook the house, heralding an intensification of the storm. Rain began to hammer against the outside walls and the plywood window coverings, creating a din that echoed around the conference room. The cathedral-ceilinged room itself, not being hermetically sealed, signalled its permeability to rapidly-moving air by issuing a hollow, low-register howl that rose and fell morosely.

"I think what Ms. Low would say," Andrew continued, raising his voice, "is that Xerxes' management was working through intermediaries such as Paracorp on the theory that if you didn't know that the real party was a builder of large industrial facilities, you'd have less reason to be concerned about future uses of the Ranch."

"Well, my family have been stewards of this land for a century and a half. I have a very deep feeling for its welfare."

Andrew saw Niki Makana straighten in her chair. She murmured something to Chamberlain, who nodded at her soberly.

"What was that?" the lawyer asked.

"I said, *malama 'aina,*" she replied. "It means, Caring for the welfare of the land."

Chamberlain rose to his feet. "I'd like to check on the condition of the residence," he announced, scowling in the direction of his realtor, "to make sure that we're not shipping water. Perhaps you'd like to come on a tour with me, Niki." He held out his hand, and Niki placed hers gracefully in his.

The old planter and the young Hawaiian walked out of the room, leaving behind a state of tension. Li-Ann Low was sitting still as a statue, staring at Chamberlain's empty chair, her face bereft of expression. Andrew, having seen the woman in an unbalanced state once already, was pleased that Freeman was seated next to her, rather than he. When a person larger than life is crushed, not by external forces but by a flaw of character, he thought, one is in the presence of tragedy, and tragedy can make people unpredictable. Though his guard was up, his heart softened toward the elegant Oriental woman.

"I hope I spoke appropriately, Li-Ann," he said. At that moment, the lights went out, leaving them bathed momentarily in the gloomy cast from the skylights. From some distant quarter of the house, the whining sound of a generator was quickly heard, and the room was illuminated again. "I...was under no...obligation—" the realtor stammered.

"To disclose? Certainly not, unless there was something unusual in your letter agreement with Web. He accepts that, I'm sure. I've been where you are now." It was a lie, but a kindly lie, and also prudent. Having experienced Li-Ann Low in full- blown derangement once already, Andrew was not anxious for an encore. But there was another reason for his kindness, one that surprised and confused him. Though he didn't know why, he was beginning to feel a kinship with this woman. "It's not uncommon," he continued. "Two clients, neither one long-term; two deals that relate to the same subject matter but not to one another. There's not necessarily a conflict of interest. But you develop a personal relationship. The client thinks of you as a general guardian of his interests, rather than just a paid facilitator of a transaction. He's disappointed, and you feel guilty because he's disappointed. You shouldn't feel guilty, though. Sorry, perhaps, but not guilty."

"Thank you, Andrew," the woman breathed.

C. B. Freeman cleared his throat. "You left a significant piece out of the story you told Web, Andrew. Did you do that intentionally?"

"I didn't mean to leave out anything significant," Andrew said. "What did I miss?"

"The part about his son."

Andrew shrugged, not comprehending.

"Well... while I was at your house this morning, I noticed that the answering machine was flashing, and I thought that there might be... you know, a message with a clue as to the family's whereabouts." Freeman was clearly embarrassed at his inquisitiveness, which he knew would truly be understood only by other members of the journalistic community.

"So you pushed the button, listened to our private messages, and learned that I was coming here this morning," Andrew cut in, relieved that he had erased the earlier messages remotely when he called in from Koke'e.

"Yes, but there was also a message from your wife, calling from a bakery up in Hanalei around eight this morning." Freeman said, flashing a sheepish smile.

Andrew shook his head and, unseen, kicked the heel of his shoe against the carpet in frustration. *That was after I called in.*

"Apparently," Freeman continued, "Chamberlain's son was at George Akamai's house causing trouble or something. There was a possibility that the police were going to send a SWAT team over."

"What? Was my daughter there?"

It was Freeman's turn to shrug. "That's what I gathered from the message."

The lawyer looked back and forth between the two people across the table. "Where does Akamai live?" he demanded.

Li-Ann Low stared blankly back at him. Something was beginning to bother her again, Andrew could see, and it didn't have anything to do with Stella's welfare.

"About fifteen minutes up the highway and then left into the hill country," the publisher answered, "but you can't go there now. Driving is much too dangerous."

Just then they heard a call from the foyer. "C. B. Come up here. There's something you should see. The rest of you, too."

Web Chamberlain was standing at the top of the stairs when they entered the foyer. He waved them up and led them into a sitting room that normally opened out to the ocean through a long, diamond-paned window. The plywood sheet was not quite as wide as the window; it left a couple of inches of glass exposed at either end. There was a telescope in the room, and Chamberlain had aimed it through the left edge of the window.

"Isn't that your house, old boy?" he said.

Freeman bent down and looked through the eyepiece. The view was obstructed by rain spattering against the windowglass, but between rivulets, Freeman was able to see his waterfront home. "My

God!" he exclaimed. "Waves are breaking over the top of the roof! Take a look, Andy."

"Wh-what about your wife?" Andrew asked as he bent to the eyepiece.

"Oh, she's at the paper up in Lihue. She'll be fine."

"Storm surge," Chamberlain grunted. "It's just beginning, I fear." Leaving the newspaperman to ponder the fate of his homestead, he turned to Li-Ann Low. "My dear, I can't tell you how disappointed I am in you," he said, sighing.

The realtor was restored to a semblance of her usual assertiveness. "My job is to help you sell your land at a price that's comfortable for you, Web. That's what I was doing."

"But you knew of my concerns about how the land would be treated."

"Web, once you sell the land, what happens to it is out of your hands. The first buyer may want to let it revert to nature, but the next may want to turn it into a theme park."

"But I could have insisted on covenants—"

"Not and sell the place, you couldn't. The Makai Ranch is one huge white elephant. Buyers aren't clamoring for it. If it weren't for Xerxes, there wouldn't be any current interest at all."

"That's not true. Three of the six bidders aren't working with Xerxes any more."

"Only two of those three have made offers, and both offers are ridiculously low—"

"Excuse me." Andrew Chase stepped between the broker and her client. "Your son, Web. My wife apparently left a message on my machine to the effect that he was at George Akamai's house causing trouble for George and my youngest daughter. Do you have any idea what that would be about?"

The elder Chamberlain seemed genuinely surprised. "Why, no," he answered. "Causing trouble? No, George Akamai is like a brother to Nate."

"May I use your phone?"

"You want to call George? The phone's over in the corner there. Here, I'll dial the number for you."

Chamberlain shambled over to the phone, picked up the handset and listened. "No dial tone. Sorry, Andrew. Not surprising in wind like this. If it's any assurance to you, I know of no animosity between Nate and George. When they were kids they use to tussle some, but it was normal adolescent stuff."

"I'd like to go over to George's house."

"There's a road that goes up the hill through the cane fields. Fifteen, twenty minutes on a dry, sunny day. But look out the window, Andrew. The cane roads have turned to slurry already, and the wind is so high it's knocking the cane over. This is no time for a drive."

"Maybe the highway?"

Chamberlain shook his head. "Come with me. Let's have a look outside."

Except for Freeman, who could not tear his eyes away from the sea's stately demolition of his Poipu compound, the little band descended the staircase and traversed the hall to the back door. Chamberlain opened it and stepped out onto the low porch. The others followed him. The sound of the wind was deafening, even though it would be another hour before Iniki's eyewall came ashore.

Andrew leaned against the outside of the house. He could feel the effort the structure was making to stay upright as a mighty trembling through the back of his tee shirt. The wind was laden with rain, twigs, leaves, cane stalks and dust. "Look!" Chamberlain shouted as an unruly flock of asphalt roof tiles flew past. "There's no house between here and Highway 50. That means we just saw the roof from a house on the other side of the road go by. That's more than a mile downhill from here. Andrew, the wind is perilously strong now, and it's getting stronger by the minute."

"Could I please borrow a car?" Andrew implored.

"There's no car up here," Chamberlain replied. "I don't drive any more. All the cars are down below in a big garage. You couldn't even walk that far in this." He gestured out into the yard.

Andrew turned to Niki Makana, who just shook her head.

"Please, Niki."

"Andy, the 'Vette is high-torque and low chassis. You wouldn't get ten feet out into the cane road before it would be up to its doors in mud."

"Please. If it gets stuck, what's the difference? We can haul it out tomorrow."

"Hello, Niki!" C. B. Freeman came hollering down the hallway. "Was that your Corvette in the driveway?"

"Was?"

"It's not there anymore. It's lying on its top on the lawn. I saw it roll just a minute ago."

"Oh, shit!" Andrew cried in frustration.

"Huhu," Niki exclaimed. "Maybe as long as the body of the 'Vette wasn't crushed.... Let's have a look!" she said, to Chamberlain, not Andrew.

"I don't think it would be wise to go out front right now, but you can check from upstairs," Chamberlain suggested.

As Niki reached the hall, there were two loud popping noises from the front of the house, like champagne corks being extracted from two giant bottles. The sound of cascading water filled their ears. "It's the skylights," Chamberlain cried. "The weak link has broken." A small, messy waterfall dropped past the conference room door. Andrew bent down, peered upward through the cascade and saw that the Plexiglas domes had been sucked out of their stations on the roof. Rain was flying like automatic weapon fire into the upper part of the room, colliding with the inner wall and falling in a stream to the floor, accompanied by clusters of brush and an occasional roof tile.

"'Lo! thy dread empire, Chaos! is restored,'" Chamberlain wailed. "This could be the beginning of the end for the plantation house. Iniki will dump its torrents and its garbage in through those holes and chew at the inside walls upstairs. If it's able to penetrate those, it could flood the whole of the second floor."

Andrew followed Niki upstairs, and through the slit in the plywood covering at the right side of the window, saw her sports car resting against a palm tree on the sloping lawn. The side window had shattered outward, spewing out bits of glass that sat like glistening diamonds in the lee provided by the upended vehicle. Underneath the car a greenish-grey figure could be seen pacing to the edge of the broken window and then back into the interior.

Once Niki was satisfied that her parrot was safe, she, Freeman and Andrew returned to the front hall. When his party had reassembled, Chamberlain took them down a second staircase into the basement. At the bottom of the stairs there was a door straight ahead and an open hallway on the right, along which Chamberlain led his guests.

Through windows that lined the interior wall of the hallway, they saw a cavernous space, replete with workbenches, cork boards and shelving, on which were stored hand tools, power tools, paints, solvents, oils, pesticides and other domestic chemicals. On the floor were pieces of old lawn furniture waiting in vain to be refurbished, several bicycles in a rack, a motorcycle, and bins full of wood left over from forgotten building projects. In an unlit corner sat a large gasoline-powered generator with its exhaust pipe vented through a hole near the top of the wall. In the middle of the far wall was an open wooden door and a set of concrete steps that ended at the outer cellar doors.

The hallway led into a large, panelled playroom, with a regulation billiard table, a shuffleboard table, a bar, two sofas and several occasional chairs, one of which was placed at the end of a glass and lava rock coffee table that sat between the two sofas. Andrew deciphered the seating arrangement immediately, but as he was the last person into the room, C.B. Freeman was able to claim the seat next to Niki, leaving Andrew the place next to Li-Ann Low on the other sofa. Chamberlain's housekeeper Emma had mixed a large quantity of planter's punch and stored the elixir in half-gallon jars in the refrigerator. There were also several bottles of white wine well-chilled on the lower shelves, and bottles of Primo beer stuck in all the free space on the shelves and in the door.

"I'm not fond of hurricane parties," Andrew called to the host, who was busying himself at the bar. "There was that famous one in a seaside apartment building during Hurricane Camille, which was going fine until a two-story storm surge and two-hundred-mile-an-hour winds came ashore and turned the place into an acre of used building materials."

"This isn't a party!" Chamberlain shot back. "We are not celebrating Iniki, for God's sake. We are cowering here in the dark cellar of our trepidation, and I, for one am prepared to 'pawn my intelligence and buy a drink,'—cummings—rather than face the monster sober." He brought five frosted tumblers full of punch over to the coffee table in a wrought iron glass caddy. "We'll start with a glass of punch, and then you can each choose your own poison."

As he had two days earlier, Andrew found Emma's planter's punch seductive. The blended fresh tropical fruit juices submerged the bite of the rum in a sensuous bath of flavors, balanced slightly for sour over sweet, and left one just thirsty enough to take another sip.

In the subterranean playroom, the storm sounded oddly distant. When he mentioned the change in decibel level to Chamberlain, the planter explained that the playroom had been built when his son Nate was entering adolescence, with a view to allowing him and his friends to carouse freely and to give the boy a reason to spend time at home. Chamberlain had thought it wise to soundproof the room. Buffered by the insulation, the growing roar of the hurricane was muffled. It sounded, and felt, rather like a subway passing beneath a sidewalk.

To Andrew, the artificial muting of Iniki's roar made their circumstances even more tenuous. It gave them a false sense of security. If the integrity of the structure above them was seriously in jeopardy, as their host seemed to believe, then the integrity of the subterranean playroom was also in question. Not being able to hear the way the winds were blowing and the way the house was reacting to the assault might be a real threat to their safety.

Chamberlain's view was that the roof would hold. It had been reinforced several years earlier with hurricane clips that would keep it down against the storm's attempts to suck it off. The most serious problem was the invasion of the interior. They discussed what kind of damage the eruption in the conference room would cause to the interior of the house. Images of flooded rooms full of soggy carpets and armchairs, waterlogged plaster, warped floorboards, upended and ruined furniture and piles of organic debris were conjured up, and these speculations led the planter to recount the histories of some of the more interesting collectibles acquired by him or his forbears.

He was an accomplished raconteur, and his tales of cross-cultural marketplace negotiations in Indonesia, Fiji, the Austral Islands and Vietnam, of odd barter deals struck in the jungles of Burma and Thailand, of priceless antiques "lost" at sea and recovered by shrewd detective work, all entertained his audience and kept their minds off the natural rampage at their door. He was, Andrew realized, performing a service similar to that performed by the band on the Titanic; and at the same time exhorting them to drink themselves calm—to "take your vitamins, now,"—and making sure their glasses were never empty.

The noon hour arrived. At Chamberlain's direction, Andrew and Li-Ann retraced their steps down the hall to retrieve Emma's sandwiches from a refrigerator in the basement work space. Andrew once again found himself both alone with the realtor and not in complete command of his faculties. Neither of them spoke until, just before they reached the door to the open area, Li-Ann touched Andrew's arm. He turned to her warily.

"You know," she said in a confidential tone, "that was the worst moment of my life up there. I just want to thank you again for your kindness to me in my moment of shame, and for giving me the strength to do what is right." She slid her arms around his neck and kissed him, her lips warm against his, her teeth parted. She's either sincere, or drunk or both, Andrew thought. He responded with an intensity he thought appropriate to the occasion. Afterward, she clung to him tightly, her cheek against his chest, as if she were adrift on an ocean and he were a strong swimmer.

"You're destroying your image," Andrew said softly, holding her.

"I'm no different from any other woman," she sighed.

"Oh, yes you are. You have a range of emotion, a commanding presence and a powerful sensuality that I've never seen in another woman."

"You mean one day I'm choking you and the next I'm swallowing your tongue?"

"Something like that."

"I'm not crazy, Andrew. Just intense. Too intense, sometimes, I know, but I can't help myself. I wonder—Maybe after the hurricane, we can get together in Honolulu and talk about doing deals together after all."

"Sure," Andrew replied. "I'd like that." It was both a more flexible and a safer answer than the line that she had used the other night: *In your dreams*. "Li-Ann?"

"Mmmm?"

"You don't really care for Caucasian men, do you? I mean, on a personal level."

The broker leaned back against his arms and stared at him with that powerful gaze of hers. "In Hawaii, we cross the racial and ethnic lines all the time, Andrew. I've had deep romantic relationships with Euros before. The only thing about you guys that throws me off is your eyes. They say so much, it's like being with someone whose screaming out his darkest secrets all the time. Once you get used to it, it's sort of diverting, but at first—it's startling."

Andrew felt as though he were standing naked on the Star Ferry. The sensuality of the moment evaporated, and he looked away. "There's one thing I don't understand," he said.

The realtor tilted her head to one side, waiting.

"When you and Robinson went to visit Adibi on Monday, were you representing Chamberlain? Even though you yourself didn't have a conflict, as a lawyer, Robinson couldn't possibly be representing Web and Xerxes at the same time."

"You're right, Andrew," Li-Ann Low said. "There's more to the story than what came out upstairs; but the rest would give Web so much more pain than what he's already heard."

Andrew stood stock-still while her words sank in. What could hurt Chamberlain more than the sale of his land to Xerxes? He tried to assemble what he knew about the Makai Ranch situation into a framework that would point to the answer, but without success. After watching him for a moment, Li-Ann Low reached up and with her delicate fingers smoothed out the furrows in his brow.

"It's not what you know, Counsellor. It's what you don't know."

Her simple statement was like a key sliding into a lock. All the driver pins in Andrew Chase's mind moved clear of the hull, and when he turned the key, the mystery opened. He grabbed the realtor by the shoulders. "My God! Chamberlain's son."

"Yes! Until this morning, when I heard about the guy from ROC Overseas, I was sure that Harry Wong—I owe you and your wife one huge apology. God help me." Her eyes burned into him. She reached her hands up and gripped his wrists tightly. "I have to tell Web, don't I? No, don't answer. I know what I must do." A great sadness clouded her face, followed by a thin smile. "Well, to me, embarrassment is the same as death, and so, since I'm already dead, I may as well give Web the rest of it when we get back."

"Li-Ann, Chamberlain's son is with George Akamai and my daughter right now. You know that Paracorp has just rejected Xerxes lease deal."

"I know, Andrew. I'm just—I don't know what to say. There's something else you should know, too. Nate Chamberlain was concerned about his father's will. He thought there might be a problem with changing the use of the land. I couldn't get him to tell me why, so I asked Robinson to let me see the will—"

"—And he let you?"

"Let's say he made it possible for me to peek at it. There's a covenant that the land be used only for farming or hunting, or for residence by the owner, and Akamai is a contingent beneficiary. He inherits everything in the event of Nate's death. Nate was concerned that Akamai's rights would have to be taken into account in connection with the sale of the Ranch."

"Oh, Jesus." There was no question now that Stella had spent the night with the killer. The only hope was that she and Akamai—Akamai? An unwelcome realization stung Andrew. George Akamai had a potential interest in the Makai Ranch, a piece of land that had once belonged to his family. What if he were unhappy with Chamberlain's plan to sell? He released her and turned toward the door. "Um... we'd better get the sandwiches."

"Actually," Chamberlain was saying when they returned. "Nate never did spend much time at home after the age of sixteen, though he was still on the island. I saw as much or more of George Akamai after that than I did of my own son. My horseback psychoanalysis of the situation was that he was rebelling against our wealth and my influence on the island—factors that set him apart from his friends."

As a dozen wrapped sandwiches were being set down on the coffee table, he explained to Andrew and Li-Ann that he and the others had been trying to figure out what Janet's phone message about the younger Chamberlain had meant. "My son and I haven't got on well for several years now. To tell you the truth, I was surprised that he showed up here a few weeks ago."

"Not so surprising," Freeman said. "You were about to sell his inheritance out from under him."

"But I just told you, he's been running away from the Ranch since childhood. I'm sure he'd prefer the money."

"Are you? Maybe he was running away—not from the Ranch, but from you."

"Hah! Going to print that in your paper?" The sugar king was about to move on to a new thought but stopped himself, and squinted at Freeman. "You know," he intoned, "you could be onto something there."

Andrew glanced at Niki. "Have they had enough punch, do you think?"

"I think we all have," she said, wiping a finger repeatedly across the area above her upper lip until Andrew followed suit, felt his finger slide, looked at it and saw a streak of Li-Ann Low's lipstick on his fingertip.

"Perhaps you're right," he mumbled as he wiped his mouth sheepishly with a napkin. "We need to keep our wits—"

His thought was interrupted by a sharp ripping sound that pierced the soundproofing tiles of the playroom. It was accompanied by a several deep bumping noises. With each bump, the room's ceiling shook and dust settled on its inhabitants. The five looked at one another and waited. In their windowless cave, their helplessness was palpable.

Iniki's eyewall had come ashore. What was left of C. B. Freeman's seaside enclave after the storm surge had buried it was now spinning in small pieces through the air at over a hundred- fifty miles an hour, forming part of the storm's deadly arsenal that shredded trees and buildings further inland. The base of the seven-mile high toroid of energy was moving at more than twenty miles an hour across the coastal plain and up the hill, sweeping beaches clean of their sand, lifting chunks of asphalt out of the highway roadbed, uprooting trees and telephone poles, blasting windows, walls and furniture out of oceanfront hotels, snapping concrete cantilevers and bending steel supporting beams, lifting automobiles into the air and spinning them like twirlers' batons, rending resort condominiums asunder.

Advancing through the cane fields, the maelstrom tore sugar cane out of the ground as it went and carried it aloft as dark clouds of swordlike leaves. At its perimeter, phalanxes of tornadoes formed and marched forward, some as small as dust devils, others large enough to devour a house. What Andrew and his companions heard ripping above them was the sound of the plantation house surrendering its roof to the outer edge of the eyewall. The capitulation did not result from a failure of the hurricane clips. Those sturdy brackets clung to the joists as advertised, but the powerful suction created by the high-speed winds pulled upward on the roof with such force that the joists themselves were riven apart, severing and splitting until the roof lifted off the house in sections and flew up the hill.

The storm played with the mansion like an unruly child throwing a tantrum over her doll house. It reached into the upper rooms, flung the furniture around, smashing some pieces against the walls, lifting other pieces out and throwing them away, pouring water onto the floors and filling bed chambers with green sugar cane. As the fiercest regions of the eyewall reached the yard and drove debris against the structure at race-car velocities, the uncapped walls of the house began to shudder like flower petals in a summer breeze. The thudding and vibration reached the ears of Chamberlain and his guests as an ominous hum. Water stains began to spread across the ceiling.

Web Chamberlain glanced up. "This room is right under the conference room," he said. "Why don't you put the punch away now, Andrew?"

The lawyer nodded. He stood up, bent to pick up the jar, and felt the effects of the punch as a faltering of his equilibrium. As he opened the refrigerator door, he heard Li-Ann Low say, "I have another confession to make, Web." He turned to look at her, and saw that she was composed, even serene.

"My dear, save yourself the trouble," Chamberlain urged with a wave of his hand. "I hereby pardon you for all commercial transgressions. My palace is falling down around my ears. What venalities do you think could concern me now?"

"Web, about a month ago, Rafi Palahved asked me to put him in contact with your son."

Chamberlain, who had sunk glumly down in the cushioned chair, pulled himself upright.

"It wasn't easy to find Nate on the mainland, but I managed," Li-Ann continued. "We had a three-way phone conversation, in which Rafi invited Nate back to Kauai to review what he called Project Thermopylae, his plan for a 'city of industry' on the island. The plan appealed to Nate. I was quite surprised by that at first, but later found out from Adibi that Nate had been offered the possibility of wealth far beyond what the sale of the Makai Ranch would produce, as well as a position of prominence—at least public prominence—in the project."

Her host was now sitting ramrod straight in his seat. His mouth hung slightly open, and his fingers gripped the arms of the chair. The humming above their heads had turned into an uncomfortable growl, and the ceiling was shaking. Water droplets formed in the centers of the damp smears overhead, fattened, and fell to the floor. "But he's never cared for such things," Chamberlain protested after a long pause.

"What—for money? He's always had money, until you cut him off when he moved away from here. Position? You were in the position that he coveted. Palahved offered him a way to be you, Web, but on a grander scale and without really having to worry about running a business."

Andrew Chase glanced across the table. Opposite him, C. B. Freeman was also slack-jawed, staring at the broker as though she were the Oracle at Delphi. Niki Makana, on the other hand, sat rocking slowly back and forth, nodding her head in a sign that Li-Ann Low's testimony was something she fully expected to hear. He moved slightly to catch her eye. She glanced in his direction, thought for a moment, and then made a stealthy little pantomime. First, she tapped at her tee shirt; then made an upside-down "V" with the fingers of one hand and slid the first joint of the index finger of her other hand through the apex of the "V" from behind; then touched her temple with an index finger. It took the lawyer a while to decipher the sign language. The rumble of the storm, the dripping water, the punch and the realtor's revelations had taken over much of his information processing capacity.

"Shirt-penis-thinking" was his first construction. Then, "tee-penis-thinking". Next, "tee-man-thinking" and "tee-man-headache," followed by "tee-man-crazy" and finally, "white-man-crazy." When Niki saw the comprehension breaking, she turned away again, to watch the unfolding drama in mute fascination.

Chamberlain shrank back against his chair. His breathing became labored, as if a weight were sitting on his chest. "I assume," he said hoarsely, "that Palahved exacted some sort of exchange from my son for his promise of wealth and privilege."

"I think so," the Chinese woman whispered. She slipped off the sofa and onto her knees on the floor next to him. "I beg your forgiveness for what I have done, Web. I just didn't realize until the man from ROC was killed. If I had, I could have prevented...."

The old man stared at her for what seemed an endless moment, his face set. Li-Ann Low's breath came in little sobs as she waited. The other three sat still as gravestones. Finally, the old planter reached a limp hand out from the arm chair and laid it on the woman's shoulder. "I perceive that, as against the two principal members of this complot, my dear, you are relatively innocent."

Li-Ann Low caught her breath. "I gave Palahved the names of the six firms that had expressed interest in the Makai Ranch. He passed that information along to the top management at Xerxes, who then made high-level contacts with each company to begin leasing discussions. The thing that worried Xerxes most was that one or more of the bidders would find an alternative lessee, perhaps someone who would propose a more traditional use of the land. Such a bidder could comfortably make full disclosure of its lessee's proposed use, which would cause you to insist that all other bidders do the same. That would force Xerxes either to bring Project Thermopylae into the open or commit a fraud that would void the sale of the Ranch. My job...." She sighed, shut her eyes and drew a deep breath. "My job was to report which bidders, if any, were refusing to deal with Xerxes, or were also talking to other possible lessees."

"Report to Palahved?" Chamberlain asked.

"No, Web." Li-Ann Low sank back on her haunches, away from the planter's touch. "Report to Nate."

She bowed her head. Her shoulders heaved. In the armchair, the Sugar King closed his eyes. The air left his lungs as it does when someone dies. After a moment, tears forced themselves between his lids and ran down his flaccid cheeks. Andrew could think of nothing to say, nothing to do. Freeman appeared to be deciding about how to write the story. His eyes darted from side to side, wide but unfocused.

Niki Makana rose from the sofa and slid behind the armchair. She knelt between Chamberlain and Li-Ann Low, put a hand in each of theirs and began to chant in Hawaiian. Her voice was soft and barely audible over the many coarse voices of the hurricane, but it seemed to soothe the other two and cast a net of peace and reconciliation over them. Her words had no meaning to Andrew, but the Gregorian rhythm and tonality of her singing touched a place in him that had not stirred since childhood—the part of him that believed the mysterious Latin cantillations echoing from a raised altar could summon the presence of God into the cathedral.

Noe wiwo'ole i ke anu,
Anu i ke ala kipapa ola e,
Ala e kuhikuhi lima
kanaka 'o Mauna Hina e.

Behind the bar, the walls were dripping. Looking up, Andrew saw the ceiling sagging between the spots where it was nailed to the ceiling joists. The stains, now covering its surface, had turned the previously white expanse a dull gray.

E hina no paha 'o wau wale no.
E hina no paha e kaua, e ka 'aha nui e.
Alia lae!
He anu, he anu
wale no.

The skin of the sheetrock bubbled and bled rainwater from small apertures. "I think we should vacate the playroom," Andrew announced as soon as the chanting stopped, "before the ceiling falls in on us."

He and Freeman lifted the spiritless Chamberlain to his feet. Niki and Li-Ann walked ahead of them, still holding hands. Clumsily, the men worked themselves and their burden into the hallway. As they did so, the far end of the ceiling ripped through its nails and splattered over the bar. With every few steps, it seemed, they could hear another section of sheetrock give way. Andrew imagined that, with the sodden barrier fallen, torrents of water would descend into their erstwhile sanctuary; and indeed, when they entered the unfinished area of the basement proper and turned on the lights, they could see water seeping in from under the wooden skeleton of the playroom.

There was little to say, and little else that could be done in the uninsulated outer basement. The house sounded as though a herd of cattle were stampeding through it. The five of them settled into the damaged lawn furniture to wait out the storm. Water dripped through subflooring over their heads while joists rattled and screeched above them. The concrete floor of the basement was coated with a film of oily water, which slid from every direction into a drain in the middle of the room. Thinking was difficult because now they could hear every insult delivered to the plantation house by the storm, and with each one the fear that the entire house would collapse increased. Andrew looked for protection from a cave-in. The best he could see to do was to dive under one of the workbenches.

It took almost half an hour more for the eyewall to take down the Chamberlain mansion. The speed of the burst of wind that demolished the mutilated structure would have defied measurement by ordinary meteorological instruments. At about the same time, on a ridge open to the wind some miles distant, a similar wild rush of air savaged a remote weather station, destroying its sensing devices. As it was being sundered, the anemometer was posting a reading of two hundred twenty-seven miles per hour, the highest wind speed measured during Iniki's onslaught.

There was no anemometer at the Makai Ranch, just the five occupants of the basement of the plantation house, whose ears suddenly registered a mighty shriek as the gust rocketed across the lawn, followed by what sounded like dynamite exploding just overhead. The subflooring and supporting joists heaved, opening new leaks from which deluges sprang into the basement. The concussion blasted the front and easterly porches upward, torquing the outer walls on those sides of the house free of their footings. They flew off, allowing the screaming air to erupt into the first floor of the house and slam the ceilings and inner walls off their moorings.

Much of the elegant old structure blew in pieces into the forested hills. The rest toppled over, flat as a fallen house of cards. For Andrew and the others, the deafening cacophony was the sound of the end of the world. Their ears rang with the crashing at the same time their eyes were deprived of sight as the house's wiring system came apart. In the corner, the generator continued to run, but it had danced a few inches away from the wall, opening a small leak in the gasoline line where it attached to the generator housing. "Are we all here?" Andrew shouted over the din of the storm and the clattering of the tumbled remnants of the plantation house.

"Freeman here!" an unsteady voice called from the darkness.

"And Niki and Li-Ann!" Niki reported from close by.

"Web," Andrew cried. "Are you with us?"

Chamberlain answered in a rasping voice. "'Why shrinks the soul back on herself, and startles at destruction? 'Tis the divinity that stirs within us, 'tis heaven itself, that points out an hereafter, and intimates eternity to man. Eternity! thou pleasing, dreadful thought!' Yes, Andrew, I'm with you, for the moment!"

"We may all only be here for the moment," Niki warned. "I smell gasoline."

"Is there a flashlight down here?" Andrew asked.

"You passed one on the stairs coming down" Chamberlain called weakly. "There's a shelf. It would be on your left going up, if the staircase is still there."

"Niki, see if you can find it. But be careful. There may be rubble in the staircase. Web, I assume there's an 'off' switch on the generator?"

"I believe it's a button on the narrow end of the casing."

Andrew felt his way across the floor, bumping into Freeman, a chair and a workbench before finding the outer wall of the basement.

He inched toward the generator, the aroma of distilled petroleum growing in his nostrils, a vision of a fireball exploding his body into small shreds growing in his mind. Not wanting to scorch his hand on hot metal, he didn't reach ahead of himself as he went, but rather inched sideways along the stone and concrete wall.

Several lengths of iron rebar had been stored overhead and held up by cross-members nailed to the exposed joists. One of the cross-members had failed during the destruction of the mansion, and the rebar now hung precariously in his path and unseen in the darkness. He bumped into them with his shoulder, and as he reached up to feel the nature of the obstructions, they slid off their remaining support and came clanging down along his left side and leg. He was knocked to the floor, where he lay with his left foot caught under some of the iron rods. The stack of rods had also banged against the generator, moving it half an inch and opening the tear in the pipe a bit wider.

A spray of fuel shot over the top of the whirring generator. Droplets descended in a fine mist into venting slits in the machine's cover, and there they ignited. Andrew saw a glow coming from inside the machinery, then climbing out as an advancing sheet of flame to consume the spray and shoot quickly down the slender jet of gas toward the opening in the copper tube at the side of the generator. He closed his eyes, expecting a huge detonation.

There was no fireball. Instead, there was a sound like a dragon exhaling. When he opened his eyes again, Niki Makana was kneeling in the illumination of a flashlight she had set on an inverted pail, removing the rebar rods from his ankle. Next to her sat a fire extinguisher, the lip of its exhaust nozzle coated with foam.

"Where did that come from?"

"I found it while I was feeling around for the flashlight. How's your ankle?"

"I...I don't know yet." Up to that point, Andrew had no sensation of pain.

Niki removed Andrew's shoe and sock and began applying pressure.

"Ouch! That hurts."

"And this?"

"Jesus! Yes!"

"What about this?"

"Ow! Yeah, now you've got it hurting all over."

"Okay, there's serious contusion here. I can't tell whether this is just a sprain, or whether you've got broken bones. I'll splint this for you. Do you like lying here in the water?"

Andrew looked around and saw that there was about an inch of water on the floor—another fact he hadn't noticed until just that moment. The rain was coming in faster than the drain could take it away.

"Sure," he answered. "The skim of gasoline on top is particularly appealing. Is it still leaking?"

"No, there was a shutoff valve near the wall. Come on," Niki said. "We'll help you up."

She handed the flashlight to Li-Ann Low, who had come up behind her, and she and Freeman got Andrew to his feet, or rather onto his good foot.

When Niki was finished with him, Andrew's left ankle was wrapped in a splint made of rags, rope and dowels. She gave him a length of two-by-two to use as a crutch. Then she turned the flashlight off, and the party sat quietly in the dark, listening to the astounding ferocity of Iniki as the water slowly rose around them. An hour and a half passed, and then, more suddenly than the storm had come, all became quiet outside, as if an angel had worked heavenly magic to their favor. They were in the eye of the hurricane.

"I have to go outside," Niki declared.

"Why?" In his impaired condition, Andrew was not interested in perambulating the grounds during the lull.

"This hurricane is my namesake. We're in her peaceful heart now, but all around us the force of her rage is still manifesting itself. I feel have to... to see her." She took the flashlight and went to the outer doorway. Freeman went with her, sensing a pressworthy moment. Andrew heard them grunting and straining in the little stairwell.

"What's the matter?" he yelled.

"There's junk piled on top of the doors," Freeman returned. "We can crack them a little, but that's all. Looks like sugar cane, mostly."

Andrew struggled to his feet. "I'm not going to be of much use to them," he mumbled into the darkness, "but for whatever it's worth.... Shine that light over here," he called, "so I can get to you without any more broken bones."

Li-Ann Low helped Andrew to the cellar door, and Chamberlain followed. The additional strength, such as it was, did not help to lift the doors open.

"What about the interior stairway?" Li-Ann Low asked.

"We can look again," Niki responded, "but when I was over there, it appeared to me that a lot of the house had fallen over the top of the stairwell."

They made their way across the floor and stood in a semicircle around the other stairway as Niki shone the flashlight on the refuse that covered it. "Mostly," she said, "it seems to be the remains of the main staircase. You see the undersides of a couple of steps right there. But above them—you can see it better if I move the light this way—there's a pinkish wall, which I think was the color of the small dining room, wasn't it, Web?"

They stood talking about their prospects for escaping the basement once the storm was over. Freeman wondered whether they couldn't make a bomb or two with gasoline from the generator intake pipe. Andrew proposed that they just saw and hammer their way through the material at the top of the stairs. Chamberlain speculated that when the eye passed and the storm resumed, the wind would blow in an easterly or northeasterly direction, instead of toward the west or northwest. They might do well, he said, to wait and see if the overburden on the outer door would bee blown off by the storm itself. While they were talking, Andrew heard faint noises coming from the other side of the cellar. He quieted his companions, and they stood listening. There was definitely activity of some sort outside the outer door, and faint talking or shouting. The little group crossed the open area again, Andrew hobbling behind.

"Hello!" a muffled voice barked. "Is anyone down there?"

"George Akamai, is that you?" Andrew yelled back.

"Yes," the voice returned. "Stella, too."

"Hi, Dad!" Stella screeched. "Are you okay?"

"Stella! Thank God! There are five of us down here. Can you get us out?"

"I think so," Akamai answered. "Just hang tight."

Inside of five minutes, they were in the daylight. Where the graceful plantation house had stood, there was now only an exposed oak floor, badly scratched, torn open in places, waterlogged, and half-covered by a six-foot high stack of wood-framed sections. Sugar cane had accumulated against the rubble and the foundation of the house. After walking around the wreckage and speaking the platitudes of loss, the party stood at the edge of the scoured earth that used to be Chamberlain's lawn; except for Li-Ann Low, who sat alone on the basement steps.

Before them lay an incredible sight. Most of the trees on the property had been snapped off partway up their trunks; the rest had lost all their leaves. The south coast of Kauai looked as if it had just risen fresh from the sea. Much of the land was denuded, including the cane fields of the Makai Ranch. The crops had been torn up by the roots and carried off into the forests above the property. Red earth lay bare to the sky all over Chamberlain's plantation, and beyond. In the distance to the east, the storm surge was beginning to drain from the lowlands of Poipu, and the flooded areas glistened in the half-sunlight. A distinct line of debris, mostly building materials, lay several hundred feet inland where the water-dome had deposited it. The normally lush, well-watered hills and valleys now resembled a New England landscape in winter. The houses and shops they could see in the villages below them had lost all or parts of their roofs; there were many barren concrete slabs where buildings had once stood. Beyond the shoreline, the ocean was in turmoil. Inside the otherwise placid eye, a clash of surface currents coming from all directions had the water chopping and rolling as if in a gargantuan washing machine. Near the horizon, the eyewall rose up, a seething mass of fast-moving clouds that terminated in a bright area many miles overhead.

"Your business has been destroyed, Web," Freeman muttered.

"No, C. B. My life has been destroyed. The family homestead has been destroyed. But my business has probably improved. Between the insurers and the Feds, I'll probably be paid for my lost crops without having to undertake a harvest. However, this will put any sale of the Ranch off for quite some time, I'm afraid." He turned to Akamai. "Where is my son, George?"

"We're pretty sure he died out in the storm, Web," Akamai said, moving to the old man.

Chamberlain pulled an arm tight around his middle and slid his other hand over his eyes. Akamai held him until the tears subsided.

When Akamai let go, Chamberlain' expression was still pained. "They said he caused some trouble at your place. Did you have to—" Chamberlain said.

"No, no. He didn't cause any trouble, Web. We talked about old times, about growing up and women and all that. Stella got a real earful. When the storm started to blow hard this morning, he decided he should get back down here with you. A while later, we tried to do the same. We couldn't get down the hill, the storm was so bad, so we went up to the reservoir. Nate was there. We hunkered down with him for a while, you know, but then Nate wanted to try one more time to get home. He drove out of the crater, Web, and right into a twister. Right smack into it, and that was that."

Chamberlain stared at Akamai, trying to read beyond the look on his face. "Thank you, George," he said quietly. "Did he... mention my will in the course of your discussions?"

Akamai nodded. "He mentioned something about a will at some point. I didn't know what he was talking about, and we didn't really discuss it."

The planter sighed. "Well, this is not the time or place.... George, I want you to talk to Niki about—Where did she go?"

Niki Makana was searching the yard for her parrot. The palm tree against which her Corvette had been resting was lying on the ground, and the car was nowhere in sight. She called for Huhu repeatedly. There was a broad scrape across the yard where the car had apparently been pushed when the tree fell, and she followed it to the foundation of the house, where it disappeared, and then picked it up again some fifty yards in the distance.

Because the approaching eyewall consisted primarily of wind and raindrops, it was not easy to tell when the storm was close enough that taking shelter was advisable. When the rain began again in earnest, Chamberlain clapped his hands.

"We should prepare to return to our damp little purgatory," he said, with forced animation. "Are we all accounted for?"

Andrew glanced around. Niki was out of sight behind a rise, and Li-Ann Low was no longer visible at the cellar steps. Indeed, the doors were closed again.

"Stella," he said, "go after Niki, will you? Tell her it's time—"

"No, no. You take George and Stella into the dungeon," the planter insisted. "The playroom is a mess, George, but the tan fridge is full of food, and of course there is drink in the other. Oh, and with the generator out, you should look for the coolers, put the food in them, and the ice from the freezer compartments. I'll collect our young sovereignty advocate, with whom I need another word before I... ah, descend."

The lawyer hobbled over to the cellar door with his daughter, her lieutenant, and the newspaperman. Akamai pulled on the handle, but the door did not budge. He tried a few more times, without success. "I think it's locked," he said.

"Locked?" Andrew and Freeman exchanged glances.

"She seems to have had a change of heart," the publisher said bleakly.

Andrew put a hand to his forehead. Freeman had no idea of the madness that could overtake Li-Ann. He climbed onto the exposed floor, struck on it loudly with his crutch and then got clumsily down on his hands and knees. "Li-Ann," he bellowed. "Li-Ann, let us in. Can you hear me? Open the door!" He put his ear to the floorboards, but heard nothing. "The storm is back. We need to get in!" There was no response, no sound at all from below.

"Could she have killed herself?" Freeman wondered.

Akamai looked from one man to the other. "What's going on here?" he demanded.

Andrew gave him the gist of Li-Ann Low's confession, judiciously avoiding mention of Chamberlain's will.

"Is there any other way to get in?" Stella asked Akamai.

The policeman shook his head. "Not with that pile of junk on top of the stairway. There are some holes in the flooring. If we had a crowbar—" He shook his head again. It was already necessary for them to brace themselves to avoid being pushed around by the wind. "There's no time. We need to get up to the reservoir right now. The little pump house will hold all of us. Stella, you start out with your dad and Mr. Freeman. I'll run after Web and Niki."

A gust of wind pushed the little group apart. It lifted sugar plants off the pile near the cellar door and rolled them across the yard. "Too late!" Stella yelled. "We won't make it. We need to settle down here, George."

"Where, Stella? All the land here is exposed to the storm."

"Over there," Stella answered, pointing to the north side of what used to be the plantation house. "If we lie behind the foundation, we'll be protected from the wind."

Andrew frowned. The foundation on that side was about sixty feet long. Half of it was covered by the remains of the house. "What about that big pile of crap, Daughter? When the wind hits maximum speed, that stuff is going to start flying and sliding and bouncing all around us."

"Let's have a look, Dad!"

"All right. C. B., why don't you keep trying with our unbalanced friend down there. You have a way with women."

Stella helped Andrew walk around the foundation while Freeman pounded on the floor and yelled, and Akamai went off after Chamberlain. On the north side of the groundwork, there was a clearance of about two feet between the top of the foundation and the ground. The reflecting pond near which Andrew had first tasted Emma's planters punch, was now engorged by rain and runoff and lapped the earth not more than ten feet from the foundation. Amid the trash from house, forest and field that marred its surface, the ancient tiki from Chamberlain's sitting room bobbed indignantly.

Andrew leaned into the wind to remain upright. "There's barely enough height here to protect us from the hurricane, Stell. We don't know how much higher the pond will rise. And we run the risk of being crushed by these large sections of wall here. The only merit your idea has is that there doesn't seem to be a better one."

The storm was now bearing small objects aloft. The Chases and Freeman ducked behind the wall and peered out to look for the rest of their party. Andrew felt like a target in a video game, constantly on the lookout for clots of earth, twigs and branches, Styrofoam cups and other projectiles that came sailing toward his forehead. Niki and George came across the yard, supporting Chamberlain between them. With the wind more or less at their backs, they moved quickly to join the others. "The parrot is missing," Chamberlain announced wheezily as he settled on his side between Andrew and C. B. Freeman.

Looking down the line of sheltering bodies, Andrew felt he understood what it must have been like to be in a foxhole during an artillery barrage. The others seemed equally apprehensive, except for Niki who, lying between him and George Akamai, was gazing all around her in wonder at the escalating intensity of the tempest. He marvelled at the grace of her repose and the sense of transport rather than fear that she seemed to be experiencing. It occurred to him that while she may have shared her body with him for a night, her spirit was far beyond his reach.

Just then, the cellar door burst open, and Li-Ann Low ran out onto the lawn, flailing her arms over her head. A grey-green creature sat clinging to her hair. It flapped its wings, pecked vigorously at her scalp and whistled, "Whoopie!"

As soon as it felt the full force of the storm, though, the parrot folded its wings, dived to the ground and, flattening itself against the earth, struggled back to the ruined mansion, where it crawled across the floorboards using beak and claw before disappearing through a hole into the basement. Li-Ann Low, hysterical, staggered on, struck from behind by debris. Realizing the danger she was in, Andrew leapt up without his crutch, and ran at her, pain shooting up his left leg. The hurricane pulled the skin of his face back toward his ears, scoured it with grit and struck at his body with sticks and stones that definitely could break his bones. Stalks of cane shot through the air on every side. Was he acting out of courage, or foolhardiness? In the few seconds it took him to reach the realtor, he felt not courageous but terrified. What drove him on his protesting leg, in the teeth of the hurricane, against well-justified dread, to save the fallen Ice Queen was a sudden, overwhelming empathy. Loss of face had turned Li-Ann Low into a epically tragic figure. Andrew himself had been gripped for months by an unshakable panic that the impending collapse of

Fowler & Greide would work just such a transformation on him. He knew what was going on inside her.

He ran head-on into her and, in a bizarre reversal of their positions two nights earlier, knocked her down and held her struggling arms against the muddy ground until she subsided. As he lay on top of her, covering her with his body, breathing hard and wincing in pain, she stared at him with tormented eyes. "I think I need help, Andrew!" she said.

Her coiffure was an unstructured, tangled mat cluttered with bits of leaf and twigs. Streaks of blood, the evidence of Huhu's bravado, crisscrossed her forehead. The sides of her mouth were pulled back in a grimace that flattened her lips against her teeth. Andrew would never again see her as a forbidding empress of carnality.

"I'll help you, Li-Ann, if you'll let me," he heard himself say.

She searched his face, then gave a little nod and turned her head to one side.

"Let's get to shelter," Andrew urged. He slid to the ground beside her, gripped her hand, and crawled back toward what little was left of the house. Looking up, he saw that Stella and George Akamai were trying to herd the others toward the basement doorway. Freeman was already in motion on his hands and knees, but Niki Makana seemed to be resisting, while Web Chamberlain sat numbly against the foundation wall.

As the lawyer and his remorseful charge joined the group, Niki pulled away from Akamai's grasp, rose to her feet and stepped onto the floorboards. Andrew called to her, and Akamai reached for her again, but she waved him off, shouting, "She won't hurt me!" The young Hawaiian turned to face the storm. Reaching up, she unbound her hair. It flew out behind her, like a black flame on the wind. She held her arms out in front of her body, palms upward as if to receive a gift.

From his vantage point behind the foundation, Andrew couldn't believe that Niki was not being struck down by the tempest. Indeed, none of the growing amount of refuse riding the hurricane seemed to hit her at all as she stood there, nor was she having any great difficulty remaining on her feet against the force of the winds. *This isn't possible,* he said to himself. Just barely above the deafening clamor that engulfed them, he could hear the young Hawaiian chanting again. It was an ineffably powerful moment, beyond comprehension or account. Whatever stroke of luck allowed Niki to stand there unharmed made her appear to be of equal might to the roaring hurricane. Stella crept up beside him and watched in awe while Iniki

Makana communed with the measureless force that an hour ago had rendered Stella a helpless ball of tears. "I need to find out who her guru is!" his daughter shouted into Andrew's ear.

Webster Chamberlain, also transfixed by the sight, pulled on the lawyer's sleeve. "There are more things in heaven and earth, Andrew, than are dreamt of in our philosophy." With an alacrity irreconcilable with the Sugar King's halting motion around his manor earlier in the day, the old man scrambled onto the exposed floorboards and crawled up behind the chantress. Akamai lunged for him, but the old man kicked at the policeman and moved away. Niki Makana reached down a hand and assisted him to a standing position at her side. The despondent old man made his hands into fists and, leaning forward, shot arthritic jabs into the wind.

"'Blow, winds!'" he shouted, "'and crack your cheeks!
'Rage, blow,
'You cataracts and hurricanoes, spout
'Till you have drenched our steeples, drowned the cocks!'"

He staggered back in a gust, almost falling over, but Niki reached for him and pulled him forward again.

"'You... You sulph'rous and thought-executing ...unhf...fires,
'Vaunt-couriers of oak-cleaving thunderbolts,
'Singe my white head; oooh!'"

A frond from the fallen palm tree tore loose and struck him, shaft first, in the abdomen. He doubled over, but straightened up again.

"'A-and thou all-shaking thunder,
'Strike flat the thick rotundity o'th' world,
'Crack nature's moulds, all germens spill at once
'That makes ingrateful man.'"

Iniki Makana turned to the Sugar King, a strange fire glowing in her eyes. He put his arms on her shoulders; she put hers around his neck. He spoke into her ear for half a minute, words the others could not hear. She pulled back, and then kissed him, not romantically, but as if exchanging wordless thoughts.

When they parted, Niki was trembling. Her eyes closed and she fell to the floor in a swoon, just as a large cane plant came through the air, backwards like a giant squid. Chamberlain made no attempt to dodge it, and its leaves swiped hard against his face and neck, leaving deep lacerations. His blood sprayed into the wind, and he fell to his knees. Next to him, the young Hawaiian woman lay motionless. Beyond pain, he bent over her and ran his fingers through her hair.

"'We two alone will sing like birds i'th' cage,'" he intoned sadly. "'When thou dost ask me blessing...'"

Akamai reached him first, saw the blood spurting from his neck. "Jesus, Web," he cried, tears mixing with the rain that spattered his face. At the sound, Niki roused herself. Seeing Chamberlain's life force spurt into the air, she reached up to press a hand against his neck. Blood pumped out between her fingers.

"'When thou dost ask me blessing,'" Chamberlain pronounced, his eyes on Niki, "'I'll kneel down and ask of thee forgiveness...'"

Now the whole entourage was on the floorboards, grabbing the two of them.

"The Almighty has allowed me two wonderful things just now," the old man rasped. "To play Lear in such a magnificent storm and to such a magnificent Cordelia. 'Look there,'" he entreated the others, pointing a limp finger at Niki. "'her eyes, her lips.' And to vanquish the ghosts of the Chamberlains."

The Sugar King's eyes closed. They carried him to safety in the basement, and laid him on a workbench. In the anemic ray of the flashlight, his face shone waxen and white, and he was barely breathing. Niki Makana did her best to stanch the flow of blood, but to no avail. At the end, the old man reached a bony hand up and pulled George Akamai down by his shirt. He whispered something, private words again, inaudible to Andrew and the others. Akamai rocked back on his heels momentarily, a look of utter incredulity on his face, and then bent forward to hold his second father in a last embrace, while outside the world bent to the will of Hurricane Iniki.

Epilog

JANET: OK, we're all on-line. Let's chat! Stella, you first.

STELLA: OK. Well, it's the fifth anniversary of Iniki. There's no public celebration, but lots of private parties. Remember the week we spent here after the storm?

LIZ: Remember! I think it was the best week of my life. I never saw anything like it before, or since.

JANET: Well, the first day of the storm was rough, all of us being apart and not knowing—

LIZ: Until the police—

STELLA: Once George and Barry connected—

LIZ: Yeah.

ANDREW: I suggest you girls give each other time to express complete thoughts, or this isn't going to be very coherent. Stella?

STELLA: OK. Well, I'd have to say that after five years, Kauai is really beautiful again. There are still some barren spots on the ridges, but as you know from your trips since, the foliage has really come back strong. Even the Tunnel of Trees. Remember how stripped and broken it was? Now its a tunnel again. What I like most is that the aloha spirit has hung on ever since the storm. The way everybody helped everybody else, how we all gathered at neighborhood cookouts, ate the C rations the National Guard was handing out, and sang and laughed all night. Locals, stranded tourists, soldiers and imported construction workers, all working together. It hasn't disappeared, that feeling. The newcomers don't get it, but folks that went through Iniki still have it in their hearts.

JANET: I always will, too. Even though I was taped up and drugged against the pain in my ribs, I loved slinging a hammer alongside those women, trying to put that little church back together. All races, all ages. God, it chokes me up just to think about it.

LIZ: I remember walking back to Poipu from Kapa'a the day after, the roads full of downed utility poles, tin roofs, overturned cars, refrigerators, etc. In places, the road was impassable even on foot, and we had to trek through people's yards or blasted cane fields. Everybody outdoors, walking around, dazed, some of them with nothing left but the clothes on their backs, but cheerful, friendly as could be. As if to say, "Well, Kauai's still here, and we're still here, so what's to complain about."

ANDREW: It's amazing that there were only four deaths—not counting Nate, who wasn't officially there. Something like eight thousand utility poles blew down, if I remember correctly; several thousand homes destroyed or seriously damaged.

STELLA: Right. And then we had torrential rain a couple of days later. What a mess! It took months before the island was "civilized" again.

LIZ: In a funny way, it was a more enchanting place after Iniki decivilized it. No phones, no electricity, no tourist buses.

STELLA: Not everyone here would agree with you. Iniki hit just as Japanese investors were pulling their money out of Hawaii. The economy here went into a tailspin, and it still hasn't come out. So today, lots of Kauaians would view Palahved as a hero, not a villain.

LIZ: Maybe, but their grandchildren wouldn't.

ANDREW: How's the father of my grandchildren?

LIZ: I'm sure that wasn't addressed to me.

STELLA: George is fine. He said to me the other day that being a sugar planter is something like being *ali'i*; more responsibility than authority, more burden than pleasure. Really, it's a terrible business. We've figured out how to break even, which is a lot better than Web Chamberlain was doing, but as employees retire or quit, George is scaling back the operation. He and Niki are working on a plan for a kind of cooperative farm on the land we donated to the Kamehamehas, and if it works, we'd gradually expand the idea to the other half of the Ranch.

JANET: And the kids?

STELLA: They are still absolute wonders. Web is looking forward to seeing his *haole* family again at Christmas, and little Niki is finally sleeping through the night.

JANET: I'm looking forward to staying at the new Pakala Inn. It looks great from the brochure. Thatched huts on stilts and that long house.

STELLA: How about that picture of Artemis in an aloha shirt and a lei? He dresses like that (or should I say "li dat"?) all the time now. And he's so courtly. A changed man.

ANDREW: How goes the search for enlightenment?

STELLA: Well, I still haven't sorted it all out. I guess parenthood is enough enlightenment for now. I certainly have a much more mature view of metaphysics than I did five years ago. Still, after what I saw Niki do during the hurricane, I can't let go altogether. Probably get back on track when the kids are a little older. What about you, Dad? Is your spiritual side developing? You witnessed that miracle, too.

ANDREW: Well, I saw something I can't explain. But I can't explain why the Poipu house was basically untouched by the hurricane either, while the houses around it were flattened or damaged beyond repair.

JANET: Oh, come on, Andy, don't be defensive. You've told me many times that watching Niki stand up in that storm was the only truly mystical experience you've ever had.

ANDREW: Did I now? Okay, Stella, I guess I can admit to being a definite potential closet believer. Of course, to me the most important thing Iniki did was to bring us all closer together.

JANET: Which was your plan all along, but a fairly hair-raising way of doing it.

ANDREW: Not to change the subject, but how's work, Liz?

LIZ: Great. Stell. Tell big Niki that I've just been assigned to a case for the Mohawks. They're claiming that they own all the land under the city of Buffalo! Tell her if we win that one, Honolulu is next!

STELLA: My sister the lawyer. Who'd have thunk?

ANDREW: Sure has opened up new avenues of communication between Liz and me.

LIZ: It's nice to be noticed, Dad.

JANET: No need to jump out of planes any more, thank God.

STELLA: *Et bien, dans ce qui concern M. Kendall?*

ANDREW: Uh-uh. English only please. No secrets from your parents.

STELLA: I tried, Liz. How's Race?

LIZ: Fine. Booked solid with assignments for the next eight months.

STELLA: I saw him fully nude in one of those cologne advertisements the other day. What a hunk, Sis!

LIZ: It's mortifying to think that millions of other women all over the world are ogling his as—oops! Sorry, Dad. It's not as though he needs the money. But modeling's made him famous and opened a lot of doors for both of us, so I guess I can deal with it for now.

STELLA: Does he still hate the Big Apple?

LIZ: Yup. He'll be back in Hawaii in a couple of months for his surfing fix. One of these days, he and I have to decide where we're going to live.

ANDREW: Maybe the subject of marriage should be part of that discussion?

LIZ: We're in negotiation now, Dad. Stay tuned.

STELLA: Hey, Dad! You've given a lot of great stage direction here, but haven't shared much yet.

ANDREW: Just a slow typer, I guess. Let's see. I heard from Li-Ann Low the other day. She's done with her treatment and sounds fine over the phone.

LIZ: What is it with you and her, Dad?

JANET: Let's not get into that. Your father was very helpful in getting that poor woman a sound diagnosis—

LIZ: —I still can't believe she lived thirty-six years of her life with a soy allergy and didn't know it!

JANET: —and as far as I can tell, they've had a completely platonic relationship through it all.

ANDREW: Scout's honor. I just felt very sorry for her, and, in a way, sorry that I brought on her last attack by inducing her to 'fess up to Chamberlain on the day of the hurricane. The only reason I mentioned her is that until this last call, she and I had hardly discussed the Makai Ranch affair at all. I wasn't about to bring it up, for fear it would set her off, and I suppose she never felt strong enough to talk about it. The other day, she went on for over an hour.

LIZ: My, how chatty!

ANDREW: It turns out that she had done a lot of snooping on her own, got a lot of background on Palahved, Xerxes and all the bidders. And of course, she got to see that will.

STELLA: That's right. I knew we had a close call at George's house the morning of Iniki, but I had no idea how close until Mr. C's will came to light. Sounds as though Li-Ann would make a pretty good detective, Dad.

ANDREW: That's what I figured. So I put her—I mean, your mother and I put her on the payroll.

LIZ: What? You approve of this, Mom?

JANET: How could I not approve, with your father having approved letting Barry run our Honolulu office? She'll be working with Barry, but focusing on getting us more Pacific Rim business. I think they'll make a great couple, too. She needs someone like him—don't we all—and as long as she keeps her body chemistry in balance, she could be just what he and his kids are missing: a strong woman in the family.

LIZ: Generous of you, Mom, but I counsel you to watch out for a sexual harassment claim out there.

STELLA: Oh, Dad. Big Niki says to thank you for arranging the contribution from Paracorp. Even though it only took five years. She'll call you herself next week. Also, she's moving her wedding to Christmas time so you all can attend.

ANDREW: I still don't know what she sees in the guy. He was old when we were there.

LIZ: Let's see—In 1992, he was two and a half times her age, while you were only twice? She sees a newspaper, Dad. And access to the white community. Since his wife died, Freeman had been a lost soul, and the paper was suffering, too. He can't work too hard with his lungs the way they are, so she can give him a little help and happiness and get a soapbox for the Kamehamehas at the same time. She's already got the twins, thanks to one of her pureblood lovers, so why not?

STELLA: So, what's new with Chase & Chase?

JANET: Well! We continue to enjoy working together. And Dad slept in the big bedroom the other night. It wasn't too bad at all, was it, Andy?

ANDREW: Was that a compliment? From my viewpoint, it was a lot better than sleeping by myself in the guest suite.

LIZ: A few more lessons from Saga-sensei, and who knows?

ANDREW: I'm doing my best. I never thought that a substantial pay cut would be a blessing, but your Mom and I have actually benefited from the fact that Chase & Chase doesn't produce enough income to fund separate residences.

JANET: Or separate romances. But it's a lot more fun than that stuffy law firm of yours ever was. Oh, we just solved the little diamond theft that I told you about last month, girls. Very sad; it was one of her children. And we landed a new case. The infamous Henry Wong has disappeared from his yacht off the coast of Thailand, and, for some uknown reason, his wife wants him back.

STELLA: Love really is blind, I guess. Hey, Dad, what's happening with your novel?

ANDREW: Fatal Paradise? I've just now finished the third rewrite. It's as good as I can make it. Now, if I could only find an agent.

After the chat session ended, Andrew and Janet met in the kitchen of the house they were sharing once again. The afternoon sun flooded the space with late summer light. Through the open windows, a little breeze brought the sounds of chickadees reporting to one another on the quality of sunflower seeds in the porch feeder, and catbirds calling from the berry bushes in the back yard. One of the maple trees had already begun to turn colors in anticipation of New England's flamboyant season. The couple sat across from one another at the central butcher-block counter that served as both a cooking and dining surface, drinking tropical fruit smoothies.

Janet smiled. "The girls seem really happy."

"Yes, they do." Andrews smile was equivocal.

"Oh, come on, now. The mystery was solved long ago."

"There's absolutely no hard proof that Nate Chamberlain was the killer. All the evidence was circumstantial."

"He held Stella hostage. He tried to kidnap me. He was conspiring with Palahved. He was out of his head."

"Yes, that's all true. But he had what we might call business reasons for hiding his presence on the island and couldn't meet with us simply by coming up and knocking on the door of the Poipu house."

"To warn us about George, right."

"Well—"

"There's no proof there, either, Andy."

"That's true, too. But there's circumstantial evidence, just as in Nate's case. After the first murder, George attached himself to you, and then to Stella, instead of assigning a patrolman to drive you around. That made him privy to my schedule. When Stella disappeared, he knew exactly where to look, even though the site was highly improbable, and he also walked straight to that boy's body, even though—I'm telling you—it was invisible from the trail. He told Stella how disrupted and pained his family was after they lost that land. Nate Chamberlain warned Stella that George wasn't the man she thought he was. If he knew about the will—"

"—But he didn't."

"Do we really know that?"

Janet stood up and walked around the counter to Andrew. She spun him around on his stool. "Listen, mister, you're talking about your son-in-law, the father of your grandchildren. Fine, there are a couple of circumstances that are scientifically unexplainable, but even Barry, who is as levelheaded as they come, thinks that George has extrasensory abilities. Let go of your rationality, will you, and just feel the answer. He's an exemplary human being, Andy. Stella loves him and believes in him, and he's given us two beautiful grandchildren. I don't care what that creep Nate said. This case is closed."

Andrew pursed his lips. It was hard for him to embrace the intuitional, but Janet was right: when you stood back from it, there was no sense in trying to solve the Makai Ranch case by weighing one inferential scenario against another. If you could present the case to a jury of randomly-selected Kauaians, it was obvious which man they'd convict.

He reached for Janet's hands. "You're so much wiser than I am," he murmured.

Janet grinned and moved closer, her thighs pressing against the cushion, parting his knees. "It's about time you realized that."

"I'll tell you something else," Andrew said, letting go of Janet's hands and sliding his own hands to her waist. "When you've been as close to death as we were on that trip—I mean, for each of us there was at least one instant where our lives were truly at stake. Well, after that, you know what's important in life."

"And that is—"

"—Relationships.Weaving the living fabric, in which each of us is just a thread that unravels when we die. And doing good."

Janet Chase shut her eyes, raised her face toward heaven, and let out a tremulous sigh. A tear ran down her cheek.

fin